KEEP YOU CLOSE

Lucie Whitehouse

BLOOMSBURY

LONDON · OXFORD · NEW YORK · NEW DELHI · SYDNEY

Bloomsbury Paperbacks
An imprint of Bloomsbury Publishing Plc

50 Bedford Square   1385 Broadway
London   New York
WC1B 3DP   NY 10018
UK   USA

www.bloomsbury.com

BLOOMSBURY and the Diana logo are trademarks of Bloomsbury Publishing Plc

First published in Great Britain 2016
This paperback edition first published in 2016

British Library Cataloguing-in-Publication Data
A catalogue record for this book is available from the British Library.

ISBN: HB: 978-1-4088-6730-3
TPB: 978-1-4088-6729-7
PB: 978-1-4088-6732-7
ePub: 978-1-4088-6731-0

4 6 8 10 9 7 5 3

Typeset by Integra Software Services Pvt. Ltd
Printed and bound in Great Britain by CPI Group (UK) Ltd, Croydon CR0 4YY

To find out more about our authors and books visit www.bloomsbury.com.
Here you will find extracts, author interviews, details of forthcoming
events and the option to sign up for our newsletters.

In memory of Old Finger, my lovely dad,
James Paul Whitehouse, 1938–2014

Prologue

Before she opens the door – before she even sets foot on the drive – she is on her guard. She knows he's there, he'd told her he would be, and yet the house is dark. If he'd left for any reason, he would have texted – *Gone to buy wine. Back in ten* – but when she checks her phone, there's no message.

The moon slips between a gap in the clouds, sending a momentary gleam across the house's blind eyes. It is still early, not even seven, but with the emptiness of the street, the absence of any human-made sound, it feels like the small hours. The only movement comes from the wind shivering the leaves on the evergreens, rattling the thin branches of the willow that bows its head on the drive.

She glances over her shoulder then crunches across the gravel and up the steps to the front door. The carriage lamp is off so she locates her keys in her bag by touch.

A strange pressure on the door makes it harder than usual to open, as if someone is pushing against it from the other side. When she turns to close it behind her, a gust of wind seems to come from within the house and slams it shut. In the silence, the sound is violent.

She is not imagining it: the wind *is* coming from inside the house. There must be a window open but where? Not at the front, she would have noticed. But why would he open a window at all? It's below freezing outside.

1

Something's happened. As soon as she thinks it, she knows she's right.

'Hello?'

She puts on the light and the hallway materialises around her. The draught, she realises, is coming down the stairs. She stands at the bottom and calls up but again there's no answer. The sitting-room door is open and she slaps the light on, goes quickly to the fireplace and picks up the poker.

When she reaches the landing, fear forms a fist in her stomach. The cold air is coming from the very top floor. The studio. She climbs the final set of stairs with her pulse thrumming in her temples.

In the glow of the moon she sees the chaos of sketches strewn across the worktable and the floor. When she sees the open skylight, the stepladder underneath, the poker drops to the floor with a heavy clang. She is almost sick with fear but a break-in, even an intruder, is not what frightens her now.

As she starts to climb the ladder, her hands are shaking.

He is waiting for her at the top, perspective making him a colossus, his feet planted wide. The wind snatches at the sheet of paper in his hands but she doesn't need to see it to know what it is. She has lost him forever; that is clear – his face is closed. Hard. Vengeful.

The paper buckles and cracks, wind-whipped. There is nothing she wouldn't do, literally nothing, for it to be torn from his hands and erased from his memory. To go back even one day.

Behind him is the roof-edge. She can feel its power, the force field it exerts, the weird push-and-pull. It's so raw, unprotected – a four-storey fall, death almost guaranteed. He sees her looking and steps to one side.

'Do it,' he says.

One

The parcel of fish and chips was warm under Rowan's arm as she agitated the key in the lock. 'Come on.' She pulled the key out then jammed it in again just as the automatic light timed out and plunged the hallway into darkness. At the same moment, she heard the first shrill note of her ringtone.

'Christ's sake.' Leaving the key in the lock, she pulled the phone from her pocket. Its screen was a bright rectangle in the dark. A London number but she didn't recognise it. 'Yes?' Impatience made her brusque.

'Rowan?'

She hadn't heard it in years – a decade – but she knew the voice immediately. The sound of it was otherworldly, seeming to reach through time as well as space, light from a distant star. Her heart gave a beat like a punch in the sternum. It was a moment before she could speak.

'Jacqueline?'

'Yes. Yes, it is. Oh, I'm so glad I've got you – thank God. I didn't know if you'd still be on this number – you weren't on her phone. I've found an old address book but most of the stuff in here's useless – everyone's moved and changed number or . . .'

'I haven't.' Rowan's stomach clenched and, despite the cold, there was suddenly sweat on her forehead. Something had happened to Marianne. 'How are you? How—'

A low keening sound came wheezing down the line, a single corrosive note. It went on and on, only for five or six seconds in reality, but to Rowan it felt like forever. She knew that sound, how time stretched around it, became irrelevant, a joke. The aching, hollowed-out kind of loss that could never be made better.

'I'm . . . heart-broken,' Jacqueline said, as if she understood the true meaning of the word for the first time. Then, after a pause, 'Marianne's dead, Rowan.' The sound again, its eerie, awful note. 'She came off the roof into the garden. Her neck . . .'

A momentary flash, the floor giving way underfoot, and the horrifying image of a body in freefall.

Jacqueline was talking and crying at the same time. 'It was Sunday night, in the snow, but she wasn't found until Monday morning. She was out there all night in the dark. She was soaking – freezing cold. Her skin – Rowan, they told me her fingers were frozen. I can't stand thinking about it but I can't stop—' She broke off and started sobbing desperately.

Marianne's hands – the long fingers with the nails she'd kept short for her work, always stained with ink or paint. Her hands – frozen, white. Lifeless. Rowan closed her eyes as pain and horror swept through her.

In the dark hallway, the sound of Jacqueline's sobs was harrowing, too much to bear. Rowan put out a hand and ran it up and down the wall's cold flank. Where the hell was the light button? She was on the brink of tears herself now, grief threatening to bubble up and overwhelm her. She took a deep breath but her voice shook as she said, 'Came off – do you mean, she . . . slipped?'

A hard swallow at the other end, an audible attempt at control. 'The police said it was an accident. She used to go up there for cigarettes when she was working – you remember, don't you?'

I remember everything. 'She was still doing that?'

4

'In the snow, the roof would have been slippery and . . . she slipped,' said Jacqueline, and to her horror, Rowan understood that she was telling herself, too. 'But no one saw her. No one can tell us what actually happened. After Seb died . . . I used to worry – I banned her from going up there – you remember?'

'Yes. Yes, I do.' Rowan's skin was prickling, cold running down her back. 'Jacqueline, there's no chance she could have . . . ?' She couldn't say the words. 'She didn't . . . ? I mean, did it ever come back? The depression.'

'No. I don't think so. She'd have told me, wouldn't she? She wouldn't have tried to hide it? But I don't know – unless she thought it would hurt me.' A gulp. 'As if anything could hurt as much as this.'

'There wasn't anything going on that might have upset her? Brought it back?'

'No. Everything was going so well. Her work – she's got a show coming up in New York, a solo exhibition . . .' Jacqueline stopped talking and for a moment there was silence on the line.

Rowan heard footsteps outside and then the rattle of keys against the front door. Before she could compose herself, the door swung open and the fox-faced man from the ground-floor flat slapped the light on. Blinking, she raised a hand, as if it were completely to be expected that she would be standing here in the dark. She felt his eyes on her back as she gripped the key in the lock and forced it. At last, the door yawned open, revealing the steep flight of stairs immediately on the other side.

'Jacqueline,' she said, but the back of her throat was dry; she coughed, tried to swallow. 'I'm so, so sorry. What can I do? I'm still in London, just south of the river – if there's anything you need, anything at all, will you tell me?' She reached the top of the stairs and carried the fish and chips to the kitchen where she dropped them straight in the bin. 'I'm studying at the moment, I'm a student, so I'm around, I'm flexible.'

'Thank you.' There was another pause. When she spoke again, Jacqueline's voice had an edge that Rowan could only remember hearing once before, that dreadful night in the kitchen. 'I had a call this morning,' she said.

Rowan felt a cold hand come to rest on the back of her neck. 'A call?'

'From some poisonous little cretin at the *Mail*. He wanted my "reaction". *My reaction*. Can you imagine?' The horrible keening wheeze again, twisted with laughter. 'What did he *think* my reaction was going to be?'

'My God, that's . . . monstrous.'

'It's not just the *Mail* – they're all here. I'm surrounded.'

'What?'

'Men with cameras – just like old times, sitting across the street in their cars. Waiting. I hate them,' she said savagely. 'I want to fetch Ad's old cricket bat from under the stairs and get out there and batter them, crack their heads open. I would – if it weren't for him, I'd do it. Can't you see it? A picture of me on the front page of the *Mail*, all pig-eyed and wild. *Bereaved Mother of Sex-scandal Artist Hits Out*.' The laughter became bleak sobbing.

'Jacqueline . . .' But what could she say? What would make the slightest difference?

'It's all right.' With an effort, she brought the crying under control. 'It'll die down when they realise there's no fresh meat. They'll just rehash the old stories and move on. But if they *do* track you down, could you . . . ?'

'I wouldn't dream of speaking to them.'

'Thank you.' Real relief in her voice. 'Rowan, look, I know you and Marianne had lost touch with each other but you were such an important part of her life – and not just hers, all our lives.'

'I loved her – all of you.'

'Please come to the funeral. It feels right for you to be there. It'll be next week, Thursday, at the crematorium in Oxford. We'd all like it if you were there. We . . .' She stopped talking as she realised. 'Adam and I would, I mean. Both of us. We've missed you. I told Marianne that she should get in touch with you again, that with proper friends, it doesn't matter if you have a stupid row and lose touch, however long it goes on.'

'It was my fault, too. I should have . . .' But what? What could she have done that she didn't?

Rowan stood phone in hand as the news reverberated through her body. *Dead.* She felt the grief coming closer and closer, gathering, and then it broke over her, a wave of despair. She took the few steps to the sofa, swept the books onto the floor and lay down, curling in on herself as if she were being beaten, blows raining on her head and back. Marianne was dead. Gone beyond contact forever. She would never see her or speak to her again.

She cried silently, as if the sadness were too powerful for sound. It was a physical, muscular thing: her back ached, her mouth stretched open until her cheeks hurt. She was shocked by the depth of it: she'd lost Marianne as a friend years ago; surely, after all this time, she couldn't really have thought they would make things up, be close again. Now she knew that part of her *had* still hoped, had nursed the idea that one year, perhaps, there would be a Christmas card with a tentative note. But now the possibility was gone forever. This was it, the full stop. The decree absolute. And to announce it – the irony – her first contact with the Glass family for ten years.

When the tears stopped, she sat up. She felt raw, hollowed out, and when she stood, she caught sight of her swollen eyes in the cheap sixties mirror above the fireplace. Her skin looked sallow and her hair was dark at the roots, its winter colour. It had reached the length, a couple of inches below her shoulders, at which its weight killed any volume; she would have to have it cut before the funeral. She wondered if Jacqueline and Adam would think she'd changed. She doubted it: she hadn't really. Her face was still round and unlined, never arresting and elegant as Marianne's had been even at sixteen, but pretty in a safe, old-fashioned way she'd never particularly liked, like a girl in a Victorian soap advert.

She went to the window and raised the blind, releasing a wall of cold air that had worked its way in around the rotten sash the landlord was too mean to replace. The wind was harrying light-stained clouds across the rooftops, rattling the topmost branches of the cherry tree that had been the reason she'd taken the flat. It had been a riot of flirty blossom when the agent had shown her round. 'Like frilly pink knickers at the *Folies Bergères*,' she'd said and the woman had looked at her as if she were mad.

Across the road, blue light flickered behind the curtains of the old woman who stood at her door each morning and berated her luckless Jack Russell in a language that Rowan had never been able to identify. The street was deserted.

The snow that had fallen here on Sunday had been gone by Monday morning, ploughed up and ruined even as it was coming down, leaving everything sodden and muddy, litter and dead leaves plastered to the pavement. She pictured the garden at Fyfield Road: the lawn white over; the wide stone steps to the patio padded and pillowy; the branches of the silver birch like lace against a creamy sky. The image was crisp and clean as winter light, and Rowan felt a burst of pure longing that she quickly suppressed. The snow at Fyfield Road hadn't been perfect. It had been lethal.

Now she made herself examine the thing that had struck her the moment she heard it: the story didn't make sense, not, at least, the version that Jacqueline wanted to believe. Marianne couldn't have slipped. She had vertigo, paralysing vertigo: she never went near the edge of the roof, not within twenty feet of it. Not once in all the countless times they'd been up there had she ever moved – inched – more than three feet away from the safety of the hatch. Not once.

With a crack, Rowan yanked the blind shut. Her heart beat against her ribs as she left the front room and went down the narrow landing, feeling the usual rush of cold as she opened her bedroom door. Stooping, she moved her hand gently through the darkness until she touched the hessian shade of the bedside lamp. Down on her knees on the old rag rug, she cast around beneath the bed until her fingertips found the glossy cardboard box. She paused then pulled it out into the light.

For a minute she looked but didn't touch. Originally it had held printing paper, the expensive ivory stuff she'd bought at Ryman's in her final year at university when she started thinking about job applications. In August last year, when she'd split up with Anders and packed the car, she'd chocked it carefully next to her on the passenger seat, within arm's reach, but she couldn't remember how long it had been since she'd opened it. Over the years, it seemed to have become heavier, and it had power now, a presence. Hearing the pulse of blood in her ears, she had the idea that it wasn't her heart that was beating but the box's: *open, open, open.*

'Marianne's dead, Rowan.'

Quickly she picked up the box and turned it over. The Sellotape was yellowing, and when she tried to peel it off, little dry shards of it stabbed the tender flesh under her thumbnail. There was a small *whoomph* of suction as she lifted the lid.

On top was a wad of tissue to hold the contents in place. Immediately underneath, fingers curling towards its palm, was a hand – her hand: the short round nails, the pronounced vein over the knuckle of her index finger, the teardrop scar on her thumb that she'd had since the age of five when, Mrs Roberts' attention focused on one of her afternoon chat shows, no doubt, Rowan had put her fist through the glass in the kitchen door. The drawing was black and white, just ink on a page torn from a spiral-bound sketchbook, but it had energy, reality: it brought the hand to life. Even someone who'd never seen an artist's work before would have known this was good. No, not good – exceptional.

Her hand rested, palm up, on a single line that ended in a whorl like the top of a fiddlehead fern: the arm of that button-back chair. Into Rowan's head came a vivid snatch of memory. A Saturday morning in late May or the first week in June, the air already warm at nine o'clock. Marianne wore a red-and-white striped Breton T-shirt and her denim dungarees; her hair was in a knot on the top of her head. Green Flash tennis shoes grungy with age; no socks. The chair had been standing on the pavement outside a house in Observatory Street. It was antique, with lovely arms and ball-and-claw feet, but it had been reupholstered in tarty cherry-red velvet and overstuffed to the point where it looked positively buxom. Marianne had stopped; she'd always had an appreciation of the dissonant.

'How would you describe it?' she asked. It was a game they played all the time, challenging each other: describe that colour; that sky, that man.

'Strikingly incongruous – a lady of the night dragged blinking from the knocking shop into the light of a Christian morning,' Rowan said.

Marianne laughed. 'Exactly.' She put her hand out and stroked the velvet. 'I love it. I want to paint it.'

'Take it,' said a disembodied voice, and they'd turned round to see a man in jeans and a baseball cap standing in the doorway. 'Seriously. It was my aunt's. I've never liked it – that's why I put it out. If you want it, it's yours.'

They'd lugged it back to Fyfield Road, one arm each. The size and heft of it. 'Like trying to carry an old drunk,' Marianne said. It had taken them an hour and a half to go less than a mile and the episode had assumed an epic quality: *Marianne and Rowan versus The Chair.* There was blood when Marianne cut her finger on a rough piece of wood under the seat, sweat, and tears of hysterical laughter when they'd finally reached the house and Adam, opening the door, said, 'Why didn't you ring? I would have come with the car.'

Suddenly the drawing blurred and Rowan swiped her hand across her eyes. The pain in her chest was intensifying. How could Marianne be dead?

She lifted the drawing out of the box by its edges and laid it in the circle of lamplight on the rug. Underneath was another drawing of her hand, this time holding a Victorian glass etched with swallows in flight, their tails tiny tapering Vs. In the next, her palms were pressed together as if she were praying; in the one underneath that, she was holding an old paperback *Heart of Darkness*.

Altogether, she had seven sketches of her hands but, over the years, Marianne must have drawn forty or fifty in pencil and charcoal, pen and ink, some done quickly, impromptu, on the back of an envelope; some carefully posed and laboured over. That was how she worked: she drew things again and again and again until she was satisfied, until what was on the paper reflected her mental conception in every detail. Also in the box were several drawings each of an intricate silver vinaigrette that had come down through Seb's side of the family; of a plate of blemished windfalls; and then of the grey-striped cat that used to climb over the wall from the Dawsons' place. Jacqueline was allergic but Marianne had let it into the kitchen one afternoon and it made a beeline for the sofa where her mother liked to read.

'*Read?*' Marianne's voice all of a sudden, deep, dust-dry and as immediate as if she were sitting on the bed, released from the box along with the pictures. '*Nap, you mean. Let's have some honesty here.*'

Rowan felt herself smile and her eyes filled with tears. She caught them quickly with her cuff before they could fall and damage the sketch. For the first time, it occurred to her that, quite apart from their personal significance, the drawings might be valuable. Even the paintings in Marianne's first exhibition had gone for several thousand pounds each and she was almost unknown then. And now, of course, there was a finite amount of her work: that would have a huge effect on prices.

So far all the drawings had been A4-sized or smaller – here was a holly-leaf skeleton on pale blue Basildon Bond note-paper, its tracery of veins cobweb-fine – but towards the bottom of the box was a thick piece of paper folded several times. Rowan opened it gently and laid it out on the bed; at its full extent, it was perhaps five feet long.

There she was, drawn in charcoal, her nineteen-year-old self, naked. She was sitting on a kitchen stool, facing away, bare heels hooked over the upper rung, head bowed so that her face was hidden from view, her hair tied up, because Marianne wanted to study the 'machinery', as she'd called it, of her neck and back: the muscle, the round ball of bone at the top of her spine, the twin tendons where her neck met her shoulders. Her scapulae were sharply delineated, their edges shadowed with hatching. Had she weighed less then? She looked at her neck and thought how narrow it was, how vulnerable.

Her neck.

The drawing had been made late in the year, maybe already December, and just before they'd started, while they'd been eating lunch at the kitchen table, a cloudburst had strafed the garden with hail. The house was cold; the space heater had to be on for half an hour before Marianne's room was warm enough for Rowan to undress.

The drawing had taken the whole afternoon and, eyes fixed on the floor, Rowan had watched her tripod shadow deepen and stretch like a spill of viscous ink in the fading winter light. Marianne worked without talking, the silence broken only by the low whirr of the heater and the scuff of her feet as she shifted position at the easel. Whenever the heater cut out, which was often, Rowan could hear the scratch of charcoal on paper and Marianne's breathing. She'd synchronised her own so they breathed together, in and out, in and out, and it had become a meditation. Her mind had emptied but she'd become hyper-aware of her body: the tiny hairs on her arms that stood up just before the heater clicked back in, the straightness of her spine, the tendons in her feet tensed against the curve of the rung. Time became fluid, she imagined it eddying around the legs of the stool, and then she'd had the idea that what they were doing was creating someone else, a third person in the space between them: the image that Marianne was making on the paper using her own brain and eyes, and Rowan's body.

Kneeling on the rug now, Rowan bent her head until her forehead touched the sketch. The pain in her chest had spread to her stomach. She sat up and traced a finger down the charcoal line of her back, over the curve of her haunch, the rounded square of a shoulder. Marianne's hand had been here, brushing the paper as she drew the lines to make this other person, the shadow Rowan who would be nineteen and her friend forever.

She sat back on her heels. However valuable they were, she wouldn't sell the sketches unless it was literally a case of starving otherwise.

And even if she were starving, there was one she would never let go. It was still in the box, the last one, wrapped in several layers of tissue of its own and carefully Sellotaped. She lifted it out gently. Like the others, it was featherweight, just a single sheet of paper torn from a sketchbook, but resting it between her hands, Rowan could feel how solid it was, how heavy. She turned it over and examined the old tape but there was no need to undo it and look at the drawing inside. It was enough just to know it was there.

Two

The drift of post in the hallway testified to the frequency with which people came and went here. It was eighteen inches high and stretched further and further along the wall as the weeks passed. Every time she arrived home before the people downstairs and picked the day's mail off the doormat, Rowan found things for three or four former residents, the now-familiar names of those who'd moved on recently but often ones she'd never seen before, too. It wasn't just flyers and catalogues but meaningful things: voter registration cards, bank letters, birthday cards. The paper-chase evidence of disorganised lives.

This evening she wasn't first back – she'd heard the thump of bass from a hundred yards down the street – and the day's post had already been tossed on to the pile. She wasn't expecting anything and might not even have looked if she hadn't seen a statement from Barclays lying on the top. She checked – yes, hers – picked it up, and stopped.

Underneath was a cream envelope the size and shape of a postcard, her name and address written on it in black ink. The handwriting – she recognised it straight away.

The shock was like a camera flash going off. The narrow hallway vanished, replaced by white light, silence, and then it rushed back in: the thumping bass behind the thin door, the hectic pattern of the cracked mosaic floor-tiles, suddenly

14

dizzying. Like the box of sketches, the envelope pulsed with energy. Once, as a small child, she'd stood at the feet of a pylon and heard the electricity humming overhead. Alive. Deadly.

Now, a decade later, the day after Jacqueline's phone call – it couldn't be a coincidence.

Rowan hesitated a second longer then snatched up the envelope as if someone from the other flat might lunge out from their doorway and grab it. She held it pressed against her chest as she unlocked her door then, turning awkwardly on the bottom step, locked it again from the inside and flicked the catch on the deadbolt.

If she'd had cigarettes in the house, she would have smoked them. Instead, she poured a glass of wine and drank it like medicine as she paced the short distance between the kitchen sink and the sitting-room window. The bass coming up through the floor felt like a heartbeat now. Either Placebo or Muse: pounding, anxious music.

The envelope was on the table, a magnet whose poles reversed constantly, pulling then repelling her. She wanted to open it but the idea made her nauseous.

Marianne's handwriting – broadly spaced letters; risers and descenders that spiked and plunged like the trace on a heart monitor. Extraordinary to see it again after so long, like getting mail from a different life. At university, they'd written; the letters had shuttled back and forth between them, Oxford to London, every few days. They'd texted and emailed, too, of course, but the letters were different, long and discursive, written late at night, as if, without ever saying so, they'd been continuing the conversations they used to have up in Marianne's room when the lights went out and they lay in their beds in the dark. Rowan had looked for this writing for ten years, every day at first, and then, protecting herself from disappointment, less and less often until she'd let herself hope only around certain key dates: Christmas, New Year, their birthdays. The anniversary.

And that it was *this* address; that told her something, too. That Marianne had known to write to her here could mean only one thing, realistically: that she'd got Rowan's Christmas card and opened it. Saved it. Despite everything, the thought made her heart swell.

The envelope was postmarked five days ago – Marianne had posted it the day before she died. Five days. Had it taken that long to make it the sixty miles from Oxford or had it been downstairs before today? She'd been back late every evening this week; she hadn't once collected the post directly from the mat. Perhaps it had been in the pile and she just hadn't seen it. Perhaps the people downstairs had picked it up with their mail by mistake. Marianne had died in the evening – it might have been sitting on a kitchen worktop in the flat downstairs as she fell from the roof at Fyfield Road.

Rowan took a swig of wine and picked it up. Hands trembling, she tore it open and pulled out a matching cream postcard with the same black writing.

I need to talk to you.

Nothing else, no signature, not even an *M*, but there didn't need to be. Blindly, Rowan pulled out a chair and sat down. She stared and the words started to pulse on the paper, their edges blurring then straightening, blurring again.

Why? What had happened? Because something had – this eliminated any doubt.

She stood up quickly, nearly knocking over the chair, and ran the few feet to the sink where she threw up the wine and what little remained of her lunch. As she straightened up, the film of sweat on her forehead turned cold.

After all this time, she'd begun to believe that it could stay buried. With each year that went by, she'd imagined it sinking deeper and deeper, new earth settling on top, making it harder and harder to uncover. Now she could see that she had been naïve. What Marianne had done was only buried, not gone. It had been there all the time, lying dormant, waiting for the moment when it would stir, stretch and break out into the light.

Three

Rowan had lived in Oxford for twenty years but she'd never been to the crematorium. She'd been too young to go to her mother's funeral. Looking online for directions, she'd discovered it on the very eastern fringes of the city, out among the fields beyond Headington. It made sense, of course, you wouldn't build a crematorium in the centre of town, but at the same time, the location felt cruel, as if the idea were to remind the dead that they were out of it now, on their way to oblivion.

Turning off, she followed the driveway between an avenue of trees and out across a sodden but immaculate swathe of grass dotted with rosebushes and weedy saplings. Restfulness and order were the intended effect, no doubt, but instead it felt soulless. Crematorium was a word that sounded right: ceremonious, foreboding, heavy with finality.

The building itself was single-storey, made of bricks that the rain had turned the colour of turmeric. It was strikingly plain, its walls blank apart from a row of narrow windows high up under a roof of ugly clay tiles. It looked like a public lavatory.

But there was the chimney, frank and unapologetic. Ready. Rowan was hit by sheer horror: they were going to burn her. They were all going to sit and watch as Marianne was trundled off into the fire.

She parked the car and drank some water to moisten her mouth. A stream of people passed the window, some barely a foot away, but they were hunched under umbrellas, intent on keeping their feet dry, and it was impossible to tell if she knew any of them. In the rear-view mirror she watched them congregate in the porch. It was almost twelve-thirty. She took a moment to steady herself then opened the door and put up her umbrella. The cold air felt bracing as she made the dash across the car park.

There were so many people waiting that she barely found space to stand under cover. The lobby area inside the large glass doors was packed, too. How many were here? A hundred and fifty? Two hundred? Nonetheless, it was quiet, the few murmured conversations almost drowned by the hiss of rain on tarmac.

The air smelled of perfume and wet wool. She buttoned her umbrella and looked around. Next to her on one side stood an elegant couple in their late sixties, she guessed, both impeccably groomed. When Rowan's hand brushed against it, the woman's coat was soft as down, obviously cashmere. On her other side, by contrast, a woman with a biker jacket and an earful of studs rested her cheek on the shoulder of a shaven-headed man in a fringed cotton scarf. The crowd seemed to divide along these lines: those in their twenties and thirties belonging to the art world, she guessed, and older, affluent-looking people, Marianne's patrons perhaps, the people who collected her work. Rowan scanned around for Charles Saatchi; she'd read a rumour that he was a fan. There was no sign of him but, of course, he wouldn't be standing outside, would he? By the pillars, she recognised a man who'd come to lunch at the house years ago – he'd been a colleague of Seb's at St John's, another don – and then, with a jolt, she spotted Marianne's aunt Susannah and her husband. Susannah was Jacqueline's sister; they'd always looked alike.

A ripple ran through the crowd, a collective straightening, and the murmured conversations died. A man in a morning suit pinned back the glass doors and Rowan heard the melancholy opening notes of Elgar's *Cello Concerto in E Minor*. It would be Jacqueline du Pré's recording, Marianne's favourite. A flash of memory: lying on the sitting-room floor at Fyfield Road as twilight threw petrol colours across the sky outside the bay window, Marianne standing to set the arm of the record player back at the start of the first movement again and again. Neither of them had spoken and they'd let the music flow over them like water, revelling in the drama of it.

Beyond the silhouetted heads and shoulders in the lobby was a large doorway through which came a pall of weak light. Into it now, shoulder-high, was lifted the dark shape of the casket. Stomach turning, Rowan joined the edge of the crowd as it began to shuffle its way forward.

The chapel was much bigger than it seemed from the outside. The dais accommodated an organ, a substantial wooden lectern and a standing arrangement of Stargazer lilies six feet tall, but the space looked bare nonetheless. There was very little ornamentation; the thin January light fell on white walls and the twelve or fourteen long pews were modern and utterly plain. By the time she had filed in, the coffin with its spray of evergreens and white roses had been set down on a long covered trestle. She looked at it in disbelief: she was in there, Marianne was in that box.

Rowan edged along the penultimate pew, moving up close to the woman next to her so as many as possible could squeeze on. She looked to the front, searching for Jacqueline and finding her almost immediately. She was in the middle of the first pew, sitting very upright, shoulders back, her chin lifted so that her profile and the outline of her famous brunette mane were picked out by the light from the narrow clerestory windows. Jacqueline the Lionheart. To her right, head bowed, was Adam, Marianne's brother. His hair was cut shorter now, the waves gone, at least at the back, but it was as dark as ever, almost black. Like his father's hair. At the sight of him Rowan felt an odd twist of emotion, pity mixed with a painful nostalgia.

To Jacqueline's left was a man Rowan had never seen in the flesh before, Jacqueline's new partner, the Irish writer and commentator Fintan Dempsey. Partner or boyfriend: what had she called him? In an interview Rowan'd read, Jacqueline had said she hoped to be with him for the rest of her days but she didn't want to marry again. After what had happened with Seb? the journalist had pressed, wanting blood, but Jacqueline had just said no, she'd had her children and that part of her life was over; she was in a different phase now. Middle age, said the journalist, late middle age, really; did she feel that her power as a woman – a woman who'd always been physically attractive – was diminishing? *Light the touch paper*, Rowan had thought, *and retire*.

Next to Dempsey but encircled by the arm of the man on her other side was a woman – no, a girl – with long dark-blonde hair. Rowan watched as she brought a tissue to her face. She'd never seen her before, either, but she could guess who she was because the arm around her shoulders belonged to James Greenwood, Marianne's boyfriend.

An amplified cough and the room pulled itself to attention. Elgar stopped awkwardly, the stereo turned off mid-phrase. At the lectern a chubby man in church vestments and heavy square-framed glasses smoothed his notes and cleared his throat again before looking up.

'Welcome, friends,' he said in a Welsh accent. 'We are here today to celebrate the life of Marianne Simone Glass. The fact that there are so many of you – apologies to those who are standing – is a tribute in itself.' The room shifted, those in the pews turning to look at the twenty or thirty people packed in at the back.

'As we all know,' said the vicar, if that was what he was, 'though it was cut tragically short, Marianne's life was one lived to the full and made remarkable by great talent and achievement. We'll hear a tribute from Marianne's mother, Jacqueline,' he made a sort of half-bow in her direction, 'but let us start with a prayer and then the first of our hymns, *Lord of All Hopefulness*.'

He spoke the prayer quietly, as if he were murmuring its promises of resurrection and renewal to Marianne in her casket rather than the mourners. The raw sound of crying could be heard from the front of the room, rising over it the single sustained note that Rowan had heard on the telephone. The sound brought tears to her eyes, too, and she fumbled in her pocket for tissues only to discover she'd left them in the car.

It was a relief when a slight blond man slipped onto the stool at the organ and without any preamble started to play. Caught out, the congregation got quickly to its feet but they were several lines into the verse before the singing assumed any kind of conviction.

'Jacqueline,' she heard the vicar say as the last notes faded and they took their seats again. Leaning to see around the man in front, Rowan watched her stand. Adam was still holding her hand. Jacqueline turned to whisper something to him and for a few seconds, Rowan had a view of her face. A movement in the room, an intake of breath quickly suppressed, told her that everyone else was watching, too. Jacqueline looked as if she'd been beaten. Her eyes were so swollen, the lids and the skin underneath so pink, that from a distance, she appeared to have been punched. The rest of her face, by contrast, was gaunt, the blood and flesh leeched away, leaving her pallid and eerily aged. She was sixty or sixty-one but usually looked ten years younger. Today a stranger wouldn't question it if she'd said she was seventy.

They watched as she squared her shoulders and walked to the microphone. She took a few seconds then gripped the sides of the lectern and looked out over the room.

'My daughter,' she began and then stopped. She'd brought nothing with her, no notes, but her eyes were down and she held on to the stand as if a rip tide were running round her feet. Rowan felt the tension in the room, the sudden collective alarm that they were about to see Jacqueline Glass fall apart. *Come on*, she willed her. *Come on*.

Inhaling sharply, as if drawing strength from the air, Jacqueline pulled herself upright. 'My daughter. How proud I am to be able to stand here and say those words, my darling.' She looked at the coffin and gave a small nod: *yes*. 'No one could be prouder of a daughter than I am – and always will be – of you.'

She dipped her head momentarily but then raised it again and looked squarely ahead: *See my face. I am not ashamed*.

'What can I say about Marianne? She was wonderful – absolutely wonderful. I know you're not supposed to say these things about your own children, not if you're English, but I'm going to: she was wonderful. Which is not to say she was perfect . . . of course not, far from it . . . but she was full of *spirit*.' Jacqueline's voice cracked and she cleared her throat once and then again. 'She was a creature of contradictions: fiery sometimes but kind, very kind, spiky sometimes and bloody stubborn but tremendously loyal. If she loved you, she loved you – she'd forgive you anything, walk on hot coals to help you. She could be a loner at times – she needed to be alone to think and work, that was essential to her – but she was also very funny and she had many, many friends and people who loved her in return.' She looked around the packed room and smiled.

'If Marianne is remembered, though – and I think you will be, darling – it won't be as a daughter or a sister or a friend or a partner,' Jacqueline's eyes lighted on James Greenwood for a moment, full of pity, 'but as an artist. That she achieved so much in so short a time – thirty-two years – is incredible. Talent, yes, she had that in spades, but talent is nothing without work. Marianne was a worker. Even as a child she worked at her painting with a fury. It was all she ever wanted to do, and she did it.

'As most of you will know, she did her degree at the Slade, finishing with a show that earned her a top first, and she sold two paintings from that show to Dorotea Perling. For those people not in the art world – there are three or four of you here,' a painful attempt at a laugh, 'Dorotea is considered to be building one of the finest collections of contemporary painting in the world. She bought a work from Marianne's first solo exhibition, too, and so did Tate Modern and the Museo d'Arte Contemporanea di Roma. Her work's been shown in France, Italy, Germany, Spain and Israel. One of her life's ambitions . . .' Here Jacqueline seemed to lose focus. There were several seconds' silence and the room held its breath but then the microphone picked up the sound of a hard swallow. 'One of her life's ambitions was to have a solo exhibition of her work in America. That's about to happen, at the Saul Hander gallery in New York.'

Jacqueline turned to look at the casket again as if she, too, had to keep reminding herself that it was real. She was shaking, it was visible even to Rowan in the penultimate row, but when she resumed speaking her voice was strong. 'I have a thousand memories of Marianne as a child, of course,' she said, 'some of my favourite memories of all, but one in particular captures her for me. When she was seven, she fell in love with a huge book of paintings that we – her father, Seb, and I – had bought at the Louvre. For months and months Marianne was inseparable from it. She carried it everywhere – she could barely lift it – she wouldn't go to sleep unless it was open by her bed, refused to eat unless she could have it at the table. So for her birthday, as a surprise, we decided to take her there. When we told her – God, forget Christmas or presents, I've never seen excitement like it.

'To cut a long story short, we lost her. The Louvre – it's so huge, of course, and so busy, and the moment we turned our back for a split second, she was gone. It was one of the worst half-hours of my life – Seb and I running through the museum trying to find our newly eight-year-old daughter, imagining all the horrors that might have befallen her. I found her in the end. She was sitting cross-legged on the floor – completely hidden, of course, by the people standing behind her – in front of Rembrandt's *Saint Matthew and the Angel*. Eight years old – you'd have thought she'd like Degas' ballet dancers or Dürer's animals – but no, there she was in front of a Rembrandt, and a religious one at that. I shouted at her, I'm sorry to say, I'd been so terrified I couldn't help it, but it didn't matter because she was in another world. "But look, Mummy," she said, as if I were missing the whole point. "Look at the book. Look how he painted the book."'

Another long pause. 'That was one of the worst half-hours of my life until I heard, my darling. Since then, it's been one worst half-hour after another. Goodbye, Marianne, and thank you for all the passion and brilliance and love and light you brought into our lives. Sleep well.'

Four

As a teenager, Rowan had spent an hour or so every Saturday browsing in Waterstones or Blackwell's. She'd never told anyone but she harboured the idea of one day writing a novel of her own, and standing surrounded by shelves and shelves of books, breathing their fresh sawdust smell, had given her a feeling of expansion, possibility, a waiting world. Her allowance had covered a new paperback every week and two cappuccinos over which she lingered as long as she decently could.

One afternoon the autumn she was fifteen, it had been raining almost as hard as it was today and, leaving Blackwell's, she'd made a run for the Covered Market. Georgina's, the tiny café up in the eaves, was usually packed, but that day, a couple at the corner table had been putting their coats on just as she arrived.

She'd been reading for ten minutes when Marianne appeared at the top of the stairs. It was early October and she'd only started at St Helena's at the beginning of term; Rowan had never seen her out of school before. She was wearing a man's tweed coat that hung from her shoulders like a cape, so huge that the pockets were beyond reach of her hands. A couple of pencils held her hair in a bun and there was a bag from Blackwell's Art and Poster Shop tucked under her elbow. She looked like an undergraduate.

By chance, another table was coming free but, after ordering at the counter, Marianne had walked straight over. 'Can I?' When Rowan nodded, she'd shaken off the giant coat and slung it over the back of the chair. Underneath, she'd been wearing a thin cotton shirt of the sort Rowan's father wore with his business suits and a pair of denim dungarees smeared with cygnet-feather patches of grey and white paint.

She had a hot chocolate and one of the soft flapjacks with a seam of raspberry jam through the centre that Rowan still thought of as peculiar to Oxford cafés. As she came to discover, Marianne lived largely on biscuits and pastries; she wasn't bothered about meals. Left to her own devices, Seb had said, she'd live like a honeybee, existing on nips of sugar taken at random points through the day. That afternoon, she'd broken off a corner of the flapjack, eaten it and nodded at Rowan's book. 'What are you reading?'

Rowan held it up: *Love in the Time of Cholera*.

'I loved that.'

'You've read it? Well, obviously, if you loved it – stupid question.'

'Over the summer, on holiday. *One Hundred Years of Solitude* as well.'

'I've read that this year, too. Do you like South American stuff, then? I'm going through a phase. Have you read *Aunt Julia and the Scriptwriter*? Or any Borges?'

Marianne shook her head. 'Bit intimidated, to be honest.'

'Don't be.'

'You read a lot.' It was a statement rather than a question. Marianne swallowed her mouthful of flapjack and clarified. 'I've seen you at lunch at school – you've always got your nose in something.'

Rowan made a non-committal noise but she was surprised. She was definitely visible at school and being one of the most academic girls there drew attention, too, but she wasn't part of the cool gang. To be fair, though, Marianne hadn't shown much interest in the cool gang, either. 'What have you got in the bag?' she asked.

Opening it, Marianne handed her a brand-new coffee-table-sized hardback. Rowan raised her eyebrows, surprised.

'What?'

'Nothing. It's just, I like him, too, Andrew Wyeth.'

'You know about him?' Marianne looked almost suspicious. 'How?'

'I saw a postcard of *Christina's World* in the art shop and I liked it so I got a book out of the library. I like his portraits best. Do you mind if I . . . ?'

Marianne shook her head and Rowan opened the book and leafed carefully through the glossy pages. 'Like this one – Karl Kuerner.' She showed Marianne the plate of a ruddy-cheeked man whose head seemed to float disembodied beneath a cracked ceiling studded with vicious black hooks. 'Wyeth painted him a lot, didn't he? Kuerner in the winter in Pennsylvania, Christina in the summer in Maine.'

A crease had appeared between Marianne's eyebrows. 'Yes.'

'That's your thing, isn't it? Art?' That was a stupid question, too, though. Marianne had established herself as the best artist in the school within days of arriving, and for the past three weeks, Mrs Orvis, the head of the art department, had put her charcoal sketches on the big easel at the front of the class and analysed them, explaining what made them so good, how each effect had been achieved. Marianne had sat on the edge of a table swinging her legs but watching carefully. 'Embarrassing,' she'd said afterwards to deflect bad feeling but there wasn't much bitchiness about it. Most people liked Mrs Orvis, which helped, but from the beginning Marianne herself had – in her low-key way – commanded respect. She hadn't tried to insinuate herself into one of the established groups as the other new girls had done. In the canteen at lunchtime she joined in the conversation, often dryly funny but always un-showy. She gave an impression of self-containment, as if she knew what she was doing and was getting on with it regardless of what anyone thought.

That first afternoon at Georgina's, she'd crossed her legs, extending a flaky-looking snakeskin boot from under the table, and, without any hint of self-consciousness, said, 'I'm going to be a painter.'

On a Saturday evening when she hadn't arranged to meet Niamh and Emma at the cinema, especially after the clocks went back and it was dark, Rowan had often felt depressed as she let herself into the house. She'd started teaching herself to cook from a copy of Delia Smith's *Complete Cookery Course*, partly because she was bored of omelettes and soup but mostly because moving around making a noise made her feel less isolated than reading or watching TV. Since the spring, when her father had been promoted to handle Stern Rizer's pharmaceutical business in South America, he had been away more and more often at weekends. He'd dispensed with Mrs Roberts, thank God, eighteen months earlier, the week Rowan had turned fourteen and he'd deemed he could reasonably leave her alone without legal repercussions.

That evening, however, instead of feeling lonely, outside the circle to which everyone else belonged at weekends, Rowan had felt restless, excited. She had friends – Niamh and Emma, and also Rachel, who liked to read – but no one she talked to like she'd just talked to Marianne. Even with Rachel, she sometimes had to be careful not to look like she was showing off, but that afternoon, if anything, she'd needed to be on her mettle. She'd read more South American novels but Marianne, it transpired, had read Flaubert and Zola and a lot of Dickens.

The following week they'd eaten lunch together in the common room three times, and on Friday, when the Upper Fifth was allowed into Summertown at lunchtime, Marianne had waited to walk with her. The week after that, when they were talking about the drawings she was working on, she'd asked Rowan to come over on Saturday and look at them.

Parked across from the house now, rain drumming on the roof of the car, Rowan remembered she'd been nervous that afternoon, and she'd stood a little way down the street and scoped the place out for a minute before going to the door. Her father's house, an Edwardian terrace in Grandpont, had three bedrooms and a back garden big enough for the mouldy summer house she'd used as a hideout when she was younger, but this was something else.

Park Town was the most beautiful area of the city. In summer, its huge trees cast a dappled shade over the streets and even now, at the tail end of January, the laurels and camellias in the walled front gardens gave the place a dripping evergreen lushness. The houses here were redbrick Victorian mansions for the most part, detached or semi-detached but either way large enough to contain six or seven bedrooms each. For that reason, many had been used by the colleges to house graduate students and some still were, those easily identifiable by the bicycles chained to their railings and the thin curtains. Mostly, however, they'd been sold off and the drives were filled instead with Mercedes and Range Rovers.

Fyfield Road was one of the furthest back from the Banbury Road, nearest the river and Lady Margaret Hall. It was accessed by a network of other streets of similar grandeur but got no through-traffic itself. The Glasses' house was the left-hand side of a handful of four-storey semi-detacheds that looked substantial from the kerb but revealed their true size only once you were inside. How much was it worth now? Two million? Three? Even in 1999, Seb and Jacqueline must have paid a million. But Seb had had no shortage of money: *The Lioness Who Loved the Silverback* had been a bestseller around the world.

'They're not *famous* famous,' Marianne had said that first week. 'It's book fame, which doesn't count – I mean, no one's going to recognise them walking down the street.'

Which hadn't been true, in fact. They weren't Mick Jagger and Jerry Hall, obviously, but both Jacqueline and Seb were memorable-looking and, in a town with a high concentration of *Guardian* readers, Marianne's mother in particular drew attention. It irritated Seb, Rowan had understood even at sixteen, that though he earned far more and his writing was the result of cutting-edge psychological research, his commercial appeal lowered his stock among the academic community. He had the cash but Jacqueline had the intellectual kudos.

From the outside, the house hadn't changed in seventeen years. The old willow tree still overhung the pale gravel at the front and helped shield the bay window from any passing gawpers, and Virginia creeper still covered the façade. In autumn, its leaves turned flame-red, setting the house on fire, but it was in its winter avatar now, a great network of veins that spidered up from roots outside the kitchen windows. The carriage lamp by the door was on and light shone from the bay, though upstairs the windows were dark and blankly reflected the scudding clouds, as if the house were trying to put on a brave face but couldn't sustain the effort where no one was looking.

Rowan had taken the long way around to make sure she wasn't one of the first to arrive but there had been heavy traffic through town and now she imagined she'd be one of the last. As she quickly ran a brush through her hair, the rear-view mirror showed her a man in a waxed jacket getting into the old silver Audi parked behind. It was a second or two before she realised who he was.

At the crematorium there had been a nasty scene. As the service had ended, the rain had stopped for a few minutes and, grateful for fresh air, the congregation had followed Jacqueline and Adam outside. Rowan had been coming through the door when a man's voice shouted, 'Jacqueline!' and, seconds later, there was a scuffle on the far edge of the crowd. She hadn't been able to see, there were too many people, but she'd heard sharp intakes of breath from those at the front.

Quickly she'd made her way forward and seen Adam pulling Fintan Dempsey off a man with blood streaming from his nose. Ten feet away, and partially screened by a laurel bush, another man, the one now getting into the Audi, had been taking shot after shot: Fintan straining, Adam holding him back, Jacqueline being gathered away into the safety of the group like a wounded animal. A large camera lay in a puddle on the tarmac.

'Leave her the fuck alone!' Fintan shouted, trying to shake himself free.

James Greenwood's voice was low and calm. 'Let it go, Fint. You'll just make it worse.'

'She's lost her *child*. Do they understand that? Her daughter is *dead*.'

'Yes,' Greenwood said, flat, and Fintan realised his mistake.

'I'm sorry,' he said. 'Oh, Jesus, James, I'm so sorry.'

The photograpgrapher lunged forward suddenly and snatched his equipment from the ground, triggering a new rush of blood. He swiped his nose with the back of his hand, wincing at the contact. 'This is assault – I'll sue.'

'Do it.' Fintan's breath made clouds in the air as Adam and Greenwood led him away towards the car park. 'Do it,' he'd shouted back over his shoulder.

Rowan got out of the car now, raised her umbrella and walked over to the Audi. The photographer was biting into a baguette and looked up, startled, as she rapped on the glass. He pressed the button and the window came down.

'How much do you want for the pictures?' she said.

'What?'

'I want to buy your pictures from the funeral. How much are they?'

'They're not for sale.'

'Oh, come on. Why would you take them otherwise?'

'They're not for sale because they're already sold – sold and emailed. They'll be in the *Mail* tomorrow if you want to see them.'

The camera was on the passenger seat together with a laptop. Rowan imagined reaching in and grabbing it. 'Aren't you ashamed of yourself?' she said. 'Papping a funeral.'

'Never look at that sort of stuff yourself then?' he said. 'Turn the page, do you? Do me a favour.'

'You're like a carrion crow.'

He shrugged. 'We've all got to eat.'

She nodded at his sandwich. 'Well, enjoy your lunch.' She turned and walked away.

A few seconds later, he called after her, 'Hey!' and as she spun around, the flash went off in her face.

The china button was still cracked and when the doorbell rang inside, the sound was so familiar she might have heard it yesterday. From the top of the steps, she could see through the bay window into the sitting room where a girl in a black body-con dress and biker boots was perched on the arm of the old tapestry chair talking to a man in torn jeans. Through the glass came the muffled conversational buzz of a large group of people.

The door swung open and there was Jacqueline. Before Rowan had a chance even to drop her umbrella, she was pulled into a hug so tight it made her ribs buckle. Under Rowan's hands, Jacqueline's vertebrae felt like stones through her silk shirt, shocking. She must have been thinner anyway; she couldn't have lost so much weight so quickly. She was warm, though – Jacqueline had always seemed warmer than other people, as if her natural thermostat ran hotter – and with another pang of nostalgia, Rowan smelled her smoky bergamot scent. '*Goes round smelling like a pot of Earl Grey,*' said Marianne's voice in her ear.

'I'm so sorry,' Rowan said.

The hug tightened for a second and then Jacqueline let her go and stepped back. The shock of seeing her face up close – a network of capillaries marbled her cheeks and her eyelids were so swollen that they didn't fully open. She scanned Rowan's face as if she were looking for something. 'You haven't changed.'

'God, I hope I have.'

A glimmer of a smile. 'Well, maybe a bit. Come in – come and have a drink.'

'Jacqueline?' A woman in a long white apron appeared at her shoulder. 'Sorry to interrupt: could I just ask you quickly . . . ?'

'Go on in, Rowan, I'll catch up with you in a moment. You'll know lots of people. If I see Adam, I'll tell him you're here.' Jacqueline turned to the woman in the apron as another indicated to Rowan that she'd take her coat.

The hallway had the same dust-and-paint smell it had always had, though today the scent of warm pastry was also in the air. There was the same wallpaper with the same green trellis pattern, the same telephone table with its lamp with the bronze elephant base. Rowan had a momentary mental image of Marianne sitting on the bottom step of the stairs, twisting the phone cord around her finger and rolling her eyes. It had probably been Peter Turk on the other end, telling one of his shaggy-dog stories.

At the entrance to the sitting room Rowan took a glass of wine from a man with a tray – disorientating to see waiting staff here – and began to edge her way around the crowd. Though the double doors were open and the dining room was full of people, too, the room felt claustrophobically packed. It was large, running almost the whole width of the house, and the furniture had been pushed back but the only pocket of space she could see was by the fireplace. She made her way towards it, holding her glass aloft and trying not to knock

34

anyone else's, catching snippets here and there above the quiet roar of conversation.

She soon understood why there was a space. A fire had been lit to make the room look welcoming but with so many people crammed together, the extra heat was stifling and she felt light-headed within a minute. She undid her collar button, taking the opportunity to scan the crowd. Among the sea of faces and backs of heads, was there someone who knew something? Who knew what had compelled Marianne to get in touch with her after all this time? That, one way or another, had taken her to the roof-edge? Despite the heat, the idea sent a shiver down Rowan's arms.

On the mantelpiece, the Glass family photographs occupied their ranks of frames. The largest, unchanged since the last time Rowan had been here, was a simple silver one with rounded corners that held a picture of the family in the Mediterranean somewhere – Corsica, was it? The picture was twenty years old now, more even: Marianne looked to be nine or ten, Adam twelve, although he'd been so skinny in those days he could have passed for ten, too, with his narrow chest and xylophone ribs. They were having lunch at a beach restaurant, plates of calamari in front of them, glasses of wine and Coca-Cola making condensation rings on the white paper tablecloth. In the background, the sea was visible as a blue stripe beyond a handful of parasols. Marianne was grinning and her front teeth looked enormous, adult-sized in a face that was still a child's. She was wearing a stripy bathing costume with a halter-neck similar to the one that her mother had on, though Jacqueline's, Rowan thought, was working significantly harder, containing those boobs.

And there was Seb. He was laughing, leaning back in the canvas chair, a glass of white wine in his hand. He looked like a French film star taking a break from the Cannes Festival, his eyes and teeth bright against his tan, his chest covered with thick black hair. It wasn't the physique of your typical academic at all but he'd always run and played squash, and he'd swum at the health club on the Woodstock Road, too. He had taken care of himself.

'Rowan.'

Turning quickly, she saw that the hand on her elbow belonged to a tiny woman in a navy bouclé jacket. It was a second or two before her brain made sense of that face beneath white hair. Of course, she must be in her seventies now: she'd retired the summer they left St Helena's.

'How are you?' the woman was saying. 'It's good to see you again though I wish, I *wish*, it weren't like this. What a terrible thing – what a *waste*. All that talent – just . . . gone.' She made a starfish gesture with her fingers, *pouf*, a magician's disappearing trick.

'I know. And poor Jacqueline.'

Mrs Orvis glanced at the photograph, too. 'A husband *and* a daughter – very cruel. But you'll miss her as well. I remember the pair of you, your friendship – you always used to interest me. In many ways you were different – with respect, my dear, you were one of the worst draftswomen I ever had to teach.'

Rowan smiled.

'But you were similar, too – I could see why you were close. Marianne had her talent and you had your brain and you were both . . . driven. You sparked off each other.' She took a sip of her sherry. 'I had a friend like that but she's been gone for many years now. Breast cancer.'

'I'm sorry.'

Mrs Orvis tipped her head a little. 'Some people in life change us. Not many – two or three, maybe, over the course of a lifetime. Speaking as one of great age.'

A woman inched past with a tray of canapés. Mrs Orvis – 'Please, call me Rosemary' – took a miniature quiche. 'But tell me, what are you doing now? I hoped I'd bump into you at one of Marianne's shows – she always invited me – but we never seemed to cross paths.'

'I'm a student.'

'Still?' She looked shocked.

Rowan smiled again. 'No, I've gone back. I was in TV production – documentaries, history mostly – for a long time, straight from college, but it wasn't really . . . I didn't feel . . . satisfied. I'm doing a PhD now.'

'Interesting. What are you writing on?'

Out of the corner of her eye, Rowan saw James Greenwood come into the room. 'Sorry?' She pulled her attention back.

'Your thesis.'

'Oh. Catholic rebellion in the seventeenth century.'

'Guy Fawkes and friends?'

'Exactly, yes. Among others.'

'Here? You did your first degree here, didn't you?'

'Wow, you remember everything.'

'Contrary to popular belief, we teachers do care about our students, you know.'

'As a teenager, you can't imagine that. But no, I'm not here. I'm in London, at Queen Mary.'

'Well, good for you.' Mrs Orvis – Rowan really couldn't call her Rosemary – drained the last sticky drops from her glass and edged it onto the mantelpiece among the frames. 'God, that fire's hot. Do you think Mrs Glass was expecting so many people?' She lowered her voice. 'You can see how highly Marianne was rated – it's a *Who's Who* of British art. Pennie Muir is over there,' she tipped her head like a grass giving the nod to the police, 'and there's Jenny Higgins. Charlie Gilpin took my arm on the steps on the way in. Now, I hope you'll excuse me but I have to go. My husband's not very steady on his pins these days and I told him I wouldn't be gone too long. Good to see you, my dear.' She squeezed Rowan's forearm. 'Best of luck with the thesis and look after yourself – it's hard, losing someone important, especially like this.'

When she was gone, Rowan angled herself for a better view of the room. Charlie Gilpin was easy to spot, with his height and auburn hair. Together with a shaven-headed man who was almost as tall, he was looking at a large framed sketch that Marianne had made of Adam asleep in the garden the summer before he started Cambridge. Beyond them, talking to a woman with a sharp hennaed bob and hands knuckled with turquoise rings, was another man Rowan knew was an artist. After a moment she remembered his name: Simon Freemantle, the sculptor. He and Marianne had had a show together, Marianne's first professional exhibition, at the gallery in Westbourne Grove that had taken her on while she was still at the Slade. Freemantle made angry, sexually explicit bronzes of figures from mythology; Rowan still sometimes thought about his liberally endowed Minotaur, five feet tall, who'd stood in a corner thrusting his groin at browsers like a vertically challenged pervert at a bus stop. Freemantle commanded huge money these days, apparently; he'd been profiled in the *Sunday Times* Culture section not long ago.

Over by the window stood the Dawsons, the Glasses' next-door neighbours. They had to be in their late sixties now: Mrs Dawson's blonde hair had faded to silver and her husband had developed a vulture-like hunch in the shoulders. It was strange to see them again after so long; Rowan felt as if she were watching time-lapse photography, life fast-forwarding to the grave.

With a small start of recognition, she spotted Martin Harriman and Josh Leavis. They were with two women she'd never seen before, their girlfriends maybe – both were good-looking, one very. Martin and Josh had never had any trouble on that front, though: back then, girls stuck to the band like flypaper, and all four of them had cleaned up, or could have. Turk only ever had eyes for Marianne, of course. Josh, Rowan thought, looked better now than he had at nineteen; he'd filled out. She remembered his stomach, the seam of light brown hair that had tapered down from his breastbone to his navel. Sometimes, before he'd had breakfast, his stomach had felt hollow when she ran her hand over it. She looked away before he could feel the pressure of her eyes on him.

But where *was* Turk? She hadn't seen him at the crematorium, either, but he had to be here. She turned to check the crowd in the dining room but as she moved, she locked eyes in the mirror over the fireplace with the shaven-headed man who'd been talking to Charlie Gilpin. For a moment they both held the stare. Even reflected, his expression was searching – almost confrontational. The natural thing would be to smile, nod, break the tension, but neither of them did.

After what seemed like several seconds, he took a sip of his water and Rowan reached after a passing tray of canapés, largely as an excuse to move. She was embarrassed, as if she'd been caught eyeing him up, and maybe that was what he thought: he gave an impression of physical confidence even though that wide, full face and heavy brow weren't what most people would call attractive. Hazarding another glance – he'd turned and was heading into the dining room – she saw that though he was in his early forties at most, he was nearly bald, his remaining hair shaved as a pre-emptive measure. He was one of those men who suited it, though: his head was well shaped, and his neck and shoulders strong-looking, so that rather than prematurely aged, he looked sophisticated. Urbane. Who was he?

Turk would know. Putting her glass down, she sidled back towards to the door. He wasn't in the dining room so she took the stairs to the lower-ground floor, passing three waitresses who seemed in a particular hurry to come up. When she reached the kitchen, she saw why. Jacqueline was standing at the door to the garden, her back to the room, and she was crying.

Rowan hesitated a moment but then, remembering the hug at the door, she crossed the room and put her arms around her. Jacqueline gave a sob that she seemed to heave up from deep inside; Rowan felt it rise and break, shudder out. She tried to think what to say but nothing would make the slightest difference so she just held on to her and hoped that in the tightness of her arms, Jacqueline would read solidarity and support.

It was a minute or so before she lifted her head and wiped the heel of her hand under her eyes. She pulled a piece of kitchen roll from her sleeve and blew her nose. 'What did I do wrong, Rowan? What did I do – or not do – to make this happen? Marianne – all of it.'

There was the sound of footsteps on the stairs and Fintan Dempsey appeared in the doorway. When he saw Jacqueline's face, his creased in distress. 'Oh, sweetheart.'

Coming back up, Rowan glanced out of the small window at the turn of the stairs. Peter Turk was standing under the dripping eaves of the garden shed, his collar pulled close around his throat with one hand, cigarette smoke curling from the other. She let herself quietly out of the front door and made a dash along the side of the house and through the gate.

'There you are,' he said as she stepped under cover next to him, as if it were he who'd been looking for her. 'I saw you at the crem.'

'Why are you out here?'

'I've been inside – briefly. I can't face it.' He took a long drag on his cigarette and a column of ash joined the small pile of sodden dog-ends at his feet.

'Can I have one of those?' She'd regret it later but what the hell; she needed it now. Turk came closer and stooped to light it for her, his face inches from hers. He *was* what most people would call attractive – for a few months in 2005, he'd been the heart-throb of thousands – but Rowan found him faintly unsettling, she always had. Nothing about him made sense. He was tall and strongly built, for example – burly – but the way he dressed bordered on effete. Even today he'd pushed the concept of a black suit to its limits with his drainpipe trousers and Nehru jacket, the eighties-style skinny tie. The last time she'd seen a picture of him – in the *Evening Standard*, out with Marianne at some hip event in East London – he'd been wearing a velvet jacket with a cluster of Victorian cameos pinned to the lapel. It was just the latest variation on a theme, though: he'd been like it at seventeen when they'd first met him. He'd gone through a nail-varnish phase long before he'd had any professional justification.

'What are you doing here?' he said.

Rowan looked at him but his expression was curious rather than hostile. 'Jacqueline rang to tell me, and I said I would come.' She exhaled a lungful of smoke, watched it feather in the damp air and disappear. 'It wasn't just that – I wanted to. I needed to, even though Marianne and I hadn't seen each other for so long, even though we'd fallen out. She was such an important part of my life.'

He shook his head as if he'd despaired of them both a long time ago.

Rowan thought of the letter on her kitchen table, Marianne's heart-monitor handwriting. 'Pete, had she mentioned me to you recently?'

He shrugged, shook his head again. 'Should she have?'

'No, I just wondered. Now's she's gone, I . . .'

'The whole thing was such bullshit. You should have sorted it out then, the two of you.' He took another deep drag on his cigarette. 'Anyway, you've missed your chance now.' His eyes kept returning to a spot in front of him and, following his gaze, Rowan saw a patch of lawn by the patio steps that was completely ruined. The grass was worn away, the earth underneath turned to mud, and with a shock she realised it was where Marianne had landed: the grass had been rubbed away by all the feet that had come and gone since, the paramedics and police. Crime-scene investigators.

'What do you know about it?' she said.

'What?'

'The accident.'

'She fell, didn't she? The roof was slippery and she fell off it.'

'Do you remember when we used to go up there?'

'Of course.' He sounded insulted by the implication that he might have forgotten anything so sacred. 'We still did it occasionally, she and I, when we had something to talk about.'

'Was she the same?'

Turk turned and gave Rowan a long look. 'If you're talking about the vertigo, yes.'

Her heart thumped. 'When did you last see her? How did she . . . ?'

With a dull thud from inside, the kitchen door opened. It had always stuck in wet weather; you had to kick it. Holding an old Fair Isle sweater over her head, Jacqueline ran up the steps and across the lawn, the heels of her shoes sticking in the mud. 'Have you got one of those for me, Peter?'

They stood in a line behind the bead curtain of rain coming off the shed roof. Jacqueline cupped shaking hands around the flame that Turk gave her and her swollen face lit up in the gloom. It was three o'clock at the latest but the day was already shutting down around them, the darkness gathering.

'I'm sorry, Rowan, about just now.'

'Please. Don't even . . .'

'I had a bit of a moment,' she said to Turk. 'It all just . . . over-whelmed me.'

'You've been incredibly brave,' he said.

'I'm lost,' she said. 'Shipwrecked.'

'You're strong.'

'I don't know.' Jacqueline pulled the sweater around her shoulders. It was pilled and a little shrunken-looking and Rowan recognised it as one that Marianne used to wear sometimes when she was painting. Had it been one of Seb's originally, a relic from the seventies?

'It's strange, seeing you both again,' Jacqueline said. 'Together like this, I mean. The three of you then . . . I keep expecting Marianne to come through the gate.' Her eyes filled with tears that she brushed quickly away.

For a few seconds, only the crackle of burning tobacco interrupted the low hiss of the rain but then she asked, 'What are you studying, Rowan? You said on the phone you were a student.'

'Seventeenth-century history – I'm doing a PhD.'

'I thought you were in TV,' said Turk.

'I was but I realised it was the research I enjoyed, and the more senior I got, the further away I was from it so . . .'

'*Brava*,' Jacqueline said. 'It's hard, giving up a salary.' She reached over and rubbed Rowan's arm in a way she'd seen her do to other people a hundred times before, part encouragement, part, Rowan had always suspected, consolation. Then she finished her cigarette and ground the butt underfoot. Her shoes were covered in mud. 'I just want to stay out here all day but I'd better go back in. I haven't even spoken to James since the service, or Bryony. Come inside, Peter, have a drink – you look like you need one. I know I bloody do.'

They followed her back in via the kitchen, carefully skirting the area of ruined grass. As she walked by, Rowan felt it pull at her, tugging at her sleeve as if Marianne herself were trying to get her attention: *Look, Rowan, look*. She'd died there, just there, on that patch of muddied, flattened ground. *Died* – the enormity, the utter finality of it. In a matter of seconds, Marianne's personality – the very stuff of being a person: Rowan had never understood the word literally before – was extinguished and her body turned into a *thing*, a collection of cells that almost at once started the process of breaking back down into the water and minerals of which they were made.

But had it been seconds? In the days since Jacqueline's call, she'd tried hard not to think about the details. Confronted with the blunt fact of the muddy ground, however, there was no choice. Marianne had broken her neck. What did that mean? Immediate death or had it taken time? Some people who hanged died slowly of suffocation. Had Marianne been conscious? Rowan imagined her lying in the snow, paralysed, knowing she was going to die, and she wanted to lift her own face into the rain and shout with the horror.

As they came into the kitchen, the smell of food and the ravaged trays of canapés on the work-surfaces made her feel sick. Upstairs, the crowd had thinned out and, though she'd never wanted a drink more in her life, she turned down the wine Jacqueline offered. 'Driving,' she said, and could have kicked herself.

Jacqueline seemed not to notice. 'Do you have to go?' she asked. 'Or have you got time to say hello to Adam? He'd be disappointed not to see you.' She started to make her way across the hall then stopped to say goodbye to a man in his sixties with hair so thick and straight it seemed to stand perpendicular to his scalp. Rowan waited by the table at the foot of the stairs. Hearing someone coming down, she looked up and locked eyes with Josh Leavis. 'Hello,' she said as he neared the bottom but he passed her without a word. She frowned, puzzled: hadn't he recognised her?

Jacqueline turned. 'That was Brian,' she said, as they started walking. 'Marianne's framer. They used to drink tea and talk art for hours on – oh!'

As she'd rounded the sitting-room door, she'd been talking back over her shoulder and almost collided with James Greenwood coming the other way, his eyes trained on the carpet. He put his hands up, shocked out of his reverie.

'Sorry, James, I didn't mean to startle you.' Jacqueline rubbed his arm. 'Have you two met?'

His hand, when Rowan took it, was surprisingly cool to the touch. She had the odd sensation that she was seeing not the man himself but a poor copy. She knew him from the news-papers – his silver hair, side-parted fifties-style, was almost a brand in itself – but there was a blurred, out-of-focus quality to him today, as if he were both here and not. Perhaps it was because he himself seemed to be struggling to focus: his eyes were wide open and barely appeared to blink. If he was in shock, she thought, it wasn't doing much to cushion him. Interviews always mentioned a glint in his eye, the irreverent sense of humour that prevented his intelligence being intimidating, but looking at him now, it was hard to believe he'd ever laughed in his life.

'Rowan was one of Marianne's best friends from school – well, for years,' Jacqueline said. 'Not just Marianne's – a family friend.'

'Yes, she talked about you,' Greenwood said.

'Did she?'

'They were thick as thieves,' said Jacqueline, 'when they were Bryony's age. Where *is* . . . ? Ah.' She put out her arm and drew the blonde girl Rowan had identified as his daughter into the circle. She was tall and slender, fine-featured, sixteen or seventeen, Rowan guessed, with the same high forehead and deep brown eyes as her father. Her hair was the colour of golden syrup, shining and heavy.

'Okay?' Greenwood asked her and she nodded.

'Rowan.'

Adam's voice. It came from behind her, and, turning sharply, she saw his face for the first time. He looked tired out, sadness had sapped the energy she remembered, but in her chest she felt an echo of the old buzz nonetheless. He stooped to kiss her cheek. 'I saw you earlier but then you disappeared.'

'We've been out by the shed,' Jacqueline said. 'Smoking.'

'You rebels.' A smile that failed to reach his eyes.

'You've changed,' Rowan said, without thinking.

'I've aged.'

'No, not that. It's . . .' She stopped, embarrassed. Adam looked at her, expectant.

'It's probably the suit, Ad.' Jacqueline took pity on her. 'I doubt Rowan's ever seen you in one.'

She smiled slightly. Maybe that was part of it. Adam had barely seemed to notice what he wore back then. The last summer she'd been here, he'd arrived home after a research trip to Cuba in jeans so grimy that Jacqueline, only half joking, had lifted them out of the laundry basket with a pair of barbecue tongs. But even given the circumstances, the suit seemed to signify a deeper change.

'How would *you* describe Adam?' Marianne had asked her once, their old game. She'd been working on an oil portrait and couldn't get it right. 'It's him but it's not *him*.'

Rowan had thought carefully. 'Like Ariel,' she'd said at last. 'A sprite.' It had been his energy – he'd seemed to vibrate even when he was sitting down, his knee bouncing under the table, fingers drumming – and his brain, of course. Also, very basically, it had been his eyebrows, dark circumflexes that gave him a permanently quizzical look.

They hadn't changed but the rest of his face had. Like Josh Leavis, he'd filled out and with the new solidity had come gravitas. Whenever she'd thought of him over the years, she'd pictured the old Adam, twenty or twenty-two, wearing jeans and Adidas sneakers, hollow-chested under a Joy Division T-shirt or his threadbare grey flannel workshirt. That man – that *boy* – was gone.

'The suit,' she said, 'and the tan.'

'I've been in California, at Berkeley. I was there for a couple of years, got back just before Christmas.'

'Are you here now? At Oxford, I mean?'

He shook his head. 'Back at Cambridge. Mum said you're in London?'

'Yes, and I'm at university, too, but I'm just a student. I saw your *Observer* piece about the economics of extremism – it was very interesting.' She'd read so many of his pieces over the years, the sight of his byline causing her the same odd twist in the stomach every time.

'Thanks,' he said. 'I'm doing a book on it – trying. I'm supposed to be done at the end of February – it's due to be published in September so I was up against it anyway and now . . .'

'Will you be able to concentrate enough to write?'

'Work first; fall apart later. And there's so much to sort out, too. I don't want you to have to do it all, Mum, just because I've got a deadline. It's too hard.'

'It'd be hard for you, too. The thing I'm most worried about at the moment,' she said to Rowan, 'is the house. There's so much of Marianne's work here and the story's been all over the papers. Her work sells for quite a bit of money these days' – she looked slightly embarrassed – 'so an enterprising thief could do very well.'

'*Would* someone break in and steal her work, do you think? I mean, to sell art at value, you'd need specialist knowledge, wouldn't you? Contacts?'

'To get the right sort of money, yes. It wouldn't be like knocking off a TV.' Jacqueline glanced at James Greenwood, who gave a slight nod. 'The thing is, Rowan,' she lowered her voice, 'Marianne had been saying for a while that she thought someone was taking her work.'

'What?'

'She said things were going missing. Not big things, paintings, but smaller pieces – sketches, preparatory drawings. They wouldn't sell for the same sort of money, obviously, but given the kind of prices she was beginning to fetch, they still would have been valuable.'

'And harder to trace and a lot more portable,' said Adam.

'She thought someone was getting in here?' Cold fingers on the back of Rowan's neck.

Jacqueline nodded. 'But I don't know. You know what she was like – she never got the hang of filing. And you remember how many sketches she made before starting anything – could she really keep track of them all? The police came a couple of times but there was never any sign of a break-in.' She ran her fingertips through the roots of her hair, leaving the shorter strands at the front standing up like antennae. Rowan had seen her do it a hundred times. 'I don't know. Probably it was disorganisation but I want to move the work somewhere secure just in case. James is going to keep it at the gallery's storage space until we figure out what we want to do. The work for the New York show's still upstairs. She'd only just finished it.'

'Saul Hander's people are going to come and pack it up,' said Greenwood. 'She was going to fly over there, of course, to help hang it.'

There was silence for several seconds and Rowan guessed they were all thinking the same thing: that Marianne would never fly anywhere now or hang a show again. Before she'd even thought it through, Rowan opened her mouth and started talking.

'If it would help – just until the work can be moved – I could come and house-sit. Keep an eye on everything, put the lights on at night so the place didn't look empty.'

Jacqueline looked at Adam.

'I'm sorry,' Rowan said quickly. 'It would be too odd, wouldn't it? We haven't seen each other for so long and I didn't mean to put you on the spot like that. It was just a stupid, spur-of-the-moment idea. I . . .'

'No – no,' Jacqueline said. 'That's not it at all. It's just – it might be brilliant, if you mean it? We'd even thought about hiring someone – Adam's term's just started and I . . .' She looked down while she wrestled herself under control. 'I can't be here, Rowan. I can just about cope with it today, with the place full of people, but without that, knowing what happened out there . . . I just can't.'

'No,' she said. 'I understand. To be completely honest, it would help me, too. There's a couple of archives in the Bodleian I really need to look at and I've been putting it off because I haven't got anywhere to stay. The hassle of driving back and forth, especially in the winter . . .'

'Your father's not here any more?'

'No, he moved years ago – ten or eleven years. He remarried and his new wife – not so new – is from Kent. Just outside Canterbury.'

'Oh, of course, that's right – I remember now. But, Rowan, yes. If you're absolutely sure and it really would help you, too, then we'd be very grateful if you'd come and be here for a while. Incredibly grateful.'

Five

It was dark when she let herself out of the flat, sunrise still more than an hour away. She'd been awake since four, her humming brain making it futile even to attempt getting back to sleep. In the end, she'd got dressed and made some coffee.

The grilles were still down at the corner shop so she walked on, hoping the newsagent on Replingham Road would open at six. Only a handful of houses showed lights in their upstairs windows and the streets were quiet. The Tube clattered by behind the little blocks of flats across the road, overground here.

In the spill of light from the window, the newsagent's son, a boy of sixteen or seventeen already dressed in his school uniform, was loading the papers into the stand on the pavement. She waited while he cut the binding on a bale of *Independent*s and stacked them in the last empty cube, weighting them against the breeze with a grubby block of wood. He nodded as he bounced back inside, the automatic door releasing a gust of warm air.

Fintan was on the front page of the *Mail*. The photographer had caught him mid-lunge, eyes ablaze with righteous fury. *Leave My Woman Alone: Fintan lashes out at funeral of lover's daughter. New agony for Jacqueline as art world gathers to pay tribute to Marianne. Full story, pages 4 and 5.* The *Express* had a picture of Jacqueline holding Adam's arm, her face gaunt, eyes staring as if she'd just witnessed the end of the world: *The Lioness Who Lost Her Daughter*.

Inside, the newsagent put the papers in two bags. 'A lot of reading here.'

'Work,' Rowan said.

Back at the flat, she microwaved the last of the coffee then laid the papers out next to Marianne's card and the copy of the *Mail* she'd bought at the Tube station the morning after Jacqueline's call. She'd said on the phone there were photographers at the house, but Rowan hadn't expected the story to make the front page. With her shining hair and full mouth, though, her soft eyes, the editors had known Marianne would sell papers. Oblivious to the commuters elbowing past, Rowan had stood at the kiosk and stared at her. Marianne had stared back, demanding engagement: *Look, Rowan. Look at me*. Her card had arrived that evening.

Today the *Mail* gave the story a whole double-page spread, a long report and several pictures. One close-up showed the photographer with a bloody nose; another Jacqueline and Adam, her head bowed with grief, his usually gentle face grim. The three photos of 'celebrity mourners' included Peter Turk.

The largest picture was captioned *Happier times: Marianne and James Greenwood at last year's Venice Biennale*. Taken at a party, it showed them standing together, Greenwood in a dinner suit, Marianne wearing a yellow cocktail dress and tuxedo jacket that by rights should have looked awful. They were pressed together and smiling, her head tipped towards his shoulder, his arm round her waist. It was an odd way to describe a man but as she looked at James Greenwood, the word 'radiant' came into Rowan's mind. His eyes were shining, every nuance of his body language expressing pride and love.

The article was broken into several sections, each with its own lurid subheading: *Fintan Attacks*, *Art World Grieves*, *Tragic Family* and, inevitably, *Broken Marriage*. Four years ago, when it happened, *that* story had run for days. It was tabloid catnip: Greenwood had been married to Sophie Lawrence, the Channel 4 arts journalist and daughter of Derry Lawrence, the former cabinet minister, who, famously hot-tempered, had seen Greenwood and Marianne having lunch together near the gallery in Mayfair and barged into the restaurant to confront them, eventually sweeping a carafe of water to the floor in dumb fury. It had all been regurgitated last week with the first reports of Marianne's death but here it was yet again, no detail omitted: the beautiful, intelligent wife – *blonde!* – traded in for the beautiful, intelligent artist – *younger!* Bryony, the bewildered daughter; thunderous Old Harrovian Derry. The tone of the piece was one of lip-biting reproof, as if Marianne could only have expected this after luring poor vulnerable James away from his wife of twenty years. There was something almost comforting, Rowan thought, about the *Mail*'s confidence in cosmic justice being served. Steal a husband and plunge to your death, scarlet woman.

Deadly Fall was the final subheading. There was no question that anyone else was involved, the piece reluctantly admitted: Marianne was alone and the death had been pronounced accidental. Nonetheless – and no doubt the wording had been carefully vetted by the paper's lawyers – they couldn't resist including the fact that Marianne had taken antidepressants after Seb's death. Yes, it was ten years ago, but still, wasn't this evidence enough of instability, the kind that might lead someone to jump?

But if no one else had been involved, then Marianne *had* jumped, she must have. Before speaking to Turk, Rowan had permitted herself a cotton-thread of hope that in the years since they'd last seen each other, Marianne had somehow conquered her fear of heights. Vertigo: the terror not of falling but of being compelled to jump. She never went near the edge, she'd told Rowan once, because she was afraid of how it made her feel. It was like a fight within herself, she said: the conscious part of her mind screamed at her to come away while another, darker part held her there, woozily infatuated, reeling, out of control.

Rowan remembered Turk huddling against the shed in the rain, lighting one cigarette after another. He thought she'd jumped, too.

She reached for the *Express*. The tiny credit printed up the side of the photo was the same. When Fintan had smashed the other paparazzo's camera, he'd handed this one a pay-cheque. *The Lioness Who Lost Her Daughter*. She looked at Jacqueline's desolate face and burst into tears.

On the mantelpiece at Fyfield Road yesterday she'd looked for one photo in particular. It was the smallest, six inches by four, and unlike many of the later ones, its frame was wooden. From a distance, the wood looked like mahogany but when you picked it up, it was too light. Its border of raised beads, though pretty, was clumsily carved.

Many of the silver-framed pictures showed the Glasses on special occasions or foreign holidays: in the Piazza Navona in Rome or on board a ferry in Puget Sound. In one, Seb wore black tie to give a speech at his Goddaughter Emily's wedding, Jacqueline next to him snorting with laughter, her hair a full-blown dandelion clock. In the wood-framed picture, the major background detail was a revolving washing line.

But in the foreground, Jacqueline held a baby Marianne tight in her arms. She was in profile, her eyes half-closed against a low sun, her nose pressed into the fin of velvety hair on the top of her daughter's head. Marianne was eight or nine months old; her birthday was in February, and the leaves on the beech hedge just visible were turning golden brown. She was looking at the camera and smiling with her whole face, her mouth a joyous O, her little eyes sparkling. Her hands were pressed against the front of Jacqueline's plaid shirt. *Me and my mummy*.

Rowan didn't have a picture like it taken with her own mother – her father wasn't very interested in cameras at the time, he'd said. The closest thing was a professional shot taken at her grandmother's insistence, apparently, at a photographer's studio in Abingdon, Rowan buried inside a frothy christening frock, her mother – who by all accounts had been near-crippled with shyness – wearing a startled expression and a suit that would have done for a job interview. Six months after it was taken, she'd been dead.

As a child, Rowan had had a collection of scenes that she'd imagined in such detail they felt like memories. In her favourite, she stood on a chair while she and her mother made cakes together. Her mum wore the turquoise ribbed sweater she had on in her honeymoon pictures; the paper cases were red with white polka dots; sun streamed through the kitchen window. Rowan had almost been able to feel the stickiness of the spoon.

In another, it was her mother, not Mrs Roberts, who picked her up from school, chatted to her friend Alison's mother at the railings, pocketed a letter about swimming lessons. She was wearing a trench coat and had just come from the hairdresser's; that one was accompanied by the scent of Alison's mother's Elnett hairspray. There were scenes for all the major annual events: Rowan's birthday, Easter, Bonfire Night. At Christmas, they decorated the tree together, unwrapping baubles from the tissue paper in which her mother kept them carefully packed. The scenes had been talismanic, comfort and protection. Whenever she'd felt aggrieved or sad or unfairly accused, Rowan had summoned one up and pulled it around her like a blanket. *Mum would have looked after me.*

It was only when she started spending time at Fyfield Road that she'd understood how alone she'd really been. Letting herself into the house in Vicarage Road one weekend when her father was in Mexico City, she'd had the idea that their front door was a portal and every time she went through it,

54

she disappeared. If no one saw her or spoke to her or even heard her moving around, maybe she ceased to exist.

The front door at Fyfield Road was a portal, too, but behind it, life had been *more* real, and loud: the phone rang every five minutes, Seb ground coffee beans, *Bizarre Love Triangle* played on repeat in Adam's room, the postman needed signatures for boxes of books. Unless Jacqueline was writing, Radio 4 babbled constantly in the kitchen. The doorbell rang with deliveries of pizza in the evening or curry from Saffron in Summertown and there was the noisy unpacking of cartons, the clatter of plates, rattling ice. Unless Rowan put the TV on, the silence at Vicarage Road was absolute.

Within weeks of meeting Jacqueline and starting an intensive self-prescribed course of feminist reading, Rowan became aware of how hackneyed her scenes were and how 1950s: Betty Friedan might never have written a word. Jacqueline had no interest at all in things domestic – when they moved in, it was Seb who hired someone to organise curtains, Marianne told her. But the picture in the wooden frame, the tightness with which Jacqueline held Marianne, the look on her face as she smelled her baby head, captured for Rowan the essence of her imagined scenes, the feeling she needed when she conjured them up: warmth and love. Protection. And while she'd been Marianne's friend, part of the family, almost, at Fyfield Road, that protection, that warmth, had surrounded her, too, like a circle of light.

How much had the papers paid for the photographs? Many thousands, surely, if they'd put them on the front page. She could never have bought them, she didn't have that sort of money – any money, actually – but if she had, she would have spent every penny of it to spare the Glasses pain, offer them some protection in return.

Picking up the card, she ran her fingertip over the letters that Marianne had written, as if by doing so she would hear her voice.

I need to talk to you.

I'm sorry, Mazz, she said silently, *I'm so sorry I wasn't there.*

The last time Rowan had seen her, that afternoon on the pavement in Fyfield Road, she'd made a promise. 'If you ever need to talk,' she'd said, 'if you ever need me, I'm here.'

Marianne had stared at her, that look on her face, and then she'd grabbed Turk's hand and pulled him after her. 'Come on, Pete. Let's go.'

'Mazz, hold on,' he'd said. 'Just wait a moment. At least listen to what she . . .'

'No.' The loudness of Marianne's voice had startled them both. 'I said no.'

They'd fallen silent as the Dawsons' front door came open. The air between them shimmering with Marianne's hostility, they'd waited until a car door slammed and Angela Dawson's throaty diesel Volvo started up.

'Are you coming or not, Peter?' Mazz said quietly. 'Your choice.' He'd looked between them, bewildered, and then, shooting Rowan a look of mute apology, he'd followed Marianne through the gate.

But she *had* listened. She'd heard. Ten years later, she'd known that she could send those six words and Rowan would know exactly who they were from.

With every hour that passed yesterday, she'd become more and more certain that Marianne's death was connected to what she'd done. Many people had loved her – Jacqueline and Adam; James Greenwood; Turk; new friends, no doubt, among the throngs at the crematorium and the house – and yet finally, after all these years, Rowan was the one to whom Mazz had reached out. It was her help she'd needed because she, Rowan, was the only person who knew. Or had been.

She'd kept Marianne's secret for ten years, a decade in which they hadn't spoken a word to one another. She'd proved she was trustworthy: there could have been no doubt in Mazz's mind that she could rely on her.

That it had been too late, that the card hadn't reached her in time, was too painful to think about. When it came to it, though by no fault of her own, Rowan had broken her promise. She hadn't been there.

Could she have prevented her death, if she had got the message in time? She'd never know. Marianne was gone, and Rowan would have to live with the question for the rest of her life.

There was only one thing that she could do for her now: she could keep Marianne's secret – go on keeping it. She could make sure that what Marianne did stayed buried. That Jacqueline and Adam never found out.

But had someone *else* found out? The question had kept Rowan up past midnight and woken her again at four. If Marianne's death was connected to what had happened back then, why, after ten years, had she needed to talk *now*? Why had she jumped now? Something must have changed. Something had frightened her. Threatened her. What? Or who? If she was going to keep the secret, preserve Marianne's memory, Rowan needed to find out.

To spare the remaining Glasses some pain, to repay, albeit silently, some of the care and support they'd given her when she'd needed it, she would do everything she could. With a final look at their pictures, Rowan closed the *Mail* and turned it face down. Marianne's death was front-page news but if what she'd done ever came to light, the media storm would rage for weeks. And the effect on Jacqueline and Adam would be devastating.

Six

A key had been left with the Dawsons but, as she rang their bell, Rowan saw an envelope with her name on it propped against the porch window. The door was unlocked and when she reached in and picked it up, she felt the weight of a Chubb inside. A note from Angela Dawson said they'd gone to help their daughter for a few days at short notice; she had a new baby.

The street was quiet, and Rowan's boots crunched conspicuously on the gravel in the front garden. She scratched up the wide stone steps to the door and glanced over her shoulder, feeling like a burglar. The house loomed, all its windows dark. No need for the public face today.

When she shut the door, silence closed over her head like water. Here, where there had always been noise, it was jarring. Bags still in her hands, she stood and listened. Nothing at first but as her ears grew used to it, the silence came alive. She heard Adam's voice – *'Maz-zer, Rowan's here!'* – then, *b-bump, b-bump, b-bump*, the sideways gallop at which she'd always come down. '*Marianne, for the love of God, stop running on the bloody stairs!*' – Jacqueline's voice from the kitchen. The phone, and then the click of Seb's door as he took the handset into his office. Rowan felt a longing so intense it was physical. *I'm here*, she wanted to say. *I'm back. Let's do it again. Let's not fuck it up this time.*

She let the emotion wash over her. After ten years, she'd thought she'd never come back. Three days ago, filled with mourners, the house had felt different but now it was as if she'd opened the door and stepped back in time. On the motorway this morning, she'd thought about homecoming. To Oxford, yes; she'd been born and brought up here, she'd done her degree at the university; but really it was to this house. When she'd left, she'd mourned for it. If her primary motivation for house-sitting was unselfish, she acknowledged now the less altruistic part of her that had jumped at the opportunity to spend time here again.

She dropped the key in the china dish and the chime echoed up the stairs like a warning. The air had a heavy, ashy smell but when she went into the sitting room, the fireplace was swept and the furniture had been moved back into position. The room looked almost exactly as it always had; Marianne hadn't changed it. The pale light through the bay window fell on the two low sofas and the chest that served as a coffee table, and Rowan had the idea that she was looking at a stage lit for a play in which two of the main actors were dead.

Briskly, she walked back to the hall and switched on the elephant lamp. Apart from what looked like a bill from Thames Water and something from HSBC, the mail tray held only flyers. A car passed on the street outside but, within seconds, the silence settled back in after it.

She carried her bag of groceries down to the kitchen. The epicentre of life here – Jacqueline had called it the engine room – it took up the entire lower-ground floor. At the front of the house were two sash windows, the reading sofa between them, but at the back were folding glass doors to the garden that made the room bright even on a sunless day like this. The zinc-topped table was long enough to seat ten. Rowan saw Marianne in her paint-covered dungarees wriggled down low in a chair with her feet up, Seb pushing them off as he walked past to get a bottle of wine. His office upstairs was large and expensively equipped but Jacqueline said working in the kitchen kept her in the real world. On her hard wooden captain's chair at the far end, she'd been the ship's navigator, plotting their course.

Opening the fridge, Rowan found butter, eggs and a pint of milk. *R: a few things to get you started*, said a Post-it on the bread-bin in Jacqueline's distinctive square writing. Inside, a crusty white loaf nestled in a sheaf of tissue. Everything perishable had been thrown away but the cupboards were stocked with bags of beans and rice, cans of tomatoes. Marianne's food, bought but never eaten.

Putting the kettle on felt like a gentle first step in establishing herself here, legitimate occupation. Burglars didn't make tea, generally speaking. While she waited for it to boil, she went to the door and looked out. Winter had the garden in a stranglehold. Frost covered the patio and the roses that climbed the wall by the shed. Against the colourless sky, the silver birch trees looked wraithlike.

The back door key was where it had always been, in the clay ladybird made by Adam at primary school. On the back of a chair hung the Fair Isle sweater that Jacqueline had used to keep her head dry on the day of the funeral. Rowan put it on, catching a trace of bergamot scent.

Her lungs tightened with the cold as she climbed the steps to the lawn. Underfoot, the ground was adamantine. The temperature hadn't risen above freezing since Friday and it had been sodden then. There would be flooding when it thawed.

As she neared the ruined grass, she experienced the same strange pull she'd felt before, as if what had happened here had created an energy field. The area was four feet wide by eight long – about the size of a cemetery plot. Stepping carefully, she examined the ground. Rain had flattened the earth but at the far end, frost glittered on ridges of mud raised by shoes or boots with heavy treads.

To her relief, there was nothing more to see. What had she expected, though? Whoever dealt with these things would have cleaned up when they finished; they wouldn't have left anything significant or distressing.

What did surprise Rowan now she was thinking more clearly was how far the area was from the house: twelve or fourteen feet, the width of the patio and the little flowerbed. She looked at the roof and tried to visualise a trajectory. Granted, she didn't know much about the physics of falling but she'd have guessed that someone slipping off the roof would have landed much nearer the house. Clearly, there was nothing remarkable about it, however: if there had been, the police would have been on to it.

Back then, the top floor had belonged to Marianne and Adam. To give her the space she needed to paint, Adam had let Mazz have the bigger room at the back of the house, which also got the best natural light. Even at fifteen, she'd treated it more like a studio than a bedroom.

When the three doors to the upper landing – their two rooms and the skinny bathroom they shared – were closed, the top of the house had been dark but now, even though the day was beginning to fade, it was filled with light. The doors weren't open, however: they were gone.

On the middle landing Rowan hesitated, apprehensive. There was a growing tension in the air, as if all the time that she had been down in the kitchen, drinking her tea, Marianne had been up in the studio, waiting. *Come on, Rowan, what are you doing? Hurry*.

When she reached the top floor, she saw that it wasn't just the doors that were gone, but the rooms themselves. Instead, there was one huge white space interrupted only by a short surviving section of what must have the bathroom wall, presumably load-bearing. The carpet was gone, too; her boots made a hollow, stranger-at-the-saloon sound on bare boards. The change was disorientating, violent, as if a bomb had gone off. Apart from the bit of wall, all that remained of the bathroom was the plumbing. The bath and old washbasin had been torn out and replaced with a deep china trough underneath which huddled a stash of dirty glass jars full of brushes, the source, she guessed, of the boat-yard smell of oil paint and turps.

She was standing now where Marianne's easel had been the day she had posed naked on the stool, the old heater panting like a lecher in the cold. What would she have thought that afternoon, if she'd known that fewer than fifteen years later, Marianne would be dead? That she wouldn't have spoken to her for a decade? It was ridiculous, Marianne was a professional artist, of course she'd needed a proper studio, but nonetheless, Rowan was hurt. Her old room had been the locus of their friendship, too, their op centre, and its transformation felt personal, as if Marianne had chosen to rip up that time and start again with this big blank canvas. When had she done it? Had Rowan spent years imagining her in a room that no longer existed?

Footsteps ringing, she walked further in. There were windows to the east and west now as well as the two large north-facing sashes that gave the pure light Marianne used to talk about. The sun would slowly rotate around the studio as the day went on, eventually setting beyond Adam's dormer.

Rowan ran her eyes over a pine table covered with plastic bottles and aerosols, wrinkled aluminium paint tubes, a Mason jar full of pens and pencils, a pile of sketchpads, a folded cloth stiff with paint. On the wall next to it, a huge corkboard bristled with sketches and postcards, handwritten notes, newspaper pages, a swatch of Art Deco Liberty lawn. Marianne had always had a board, a repository for anything that triggered an idea, a spark of inspiration. She'd called it her external brain.

Rowan walked into Adam's part of the space and immediately stopped.

Ranged along its three sides was a series of paintings of girls – young girls. There were ten or twelve, variously posed, all of them naked or very nearly. She found the switch and hit it, replacing the gentle natural light with the searching glare of artificial.

The canvases were the same size, all stretched on frames about six feet high by four wide, all leaning against the wall at the same gentle angle. At a fleeting glance, the first couple looked like traditional nudes but it was quickly obvious that Marianne's purpose was both more complicated and more disturbing.

They were arranged in sequence, starting by Adam's window. The first one showed a girl who looked a little too slim, perhaps, but otherwise healthy. She was sitting on an old wooden school chair, her legs crossed, arms folded across small breasts. In a pale hand with nails painted glittery blue, she clutched an apple so shiny and red Eve might have offered it to Adam. The off-note was her smile, which, though pretty at first, gradually revealed itself as sly and withholding.

By the third picture, it was clear that Marianne's real subject was anorexia. The girls got thinner and thinner as the series progressed. The fifth was a redhead with an unravelling bun who stood directly in front of a mirror so that her reflection was hidden from the viewer. She wore the sort of plain white cotton knickers sold in packs of five at Marks & Spencer, and their sheer ordinariness gave the painting poignancy. Her hips were barely wide enough to hold them up; her spine was a string of pearls beneath her skin.

The last girl lay on her side on a beautiful varnished floor, her knees pulled up to her chest, her wasted arms wrapped around them. Down covered her cheeks and forearms, her body's attempt to keep itself warm. As the series went on, the palette changed, the yellows and pinks of the first paintings giving way to an increasingly bleak range of blues and greys and whites. Where her hair had fallen out, this girl's scalp was a morbid ivory, but for her slack mouth with its missing teeth, Marianne had used black and furious shades of red.

The girls shrank not only in weight but in their painted dimensions. The first couple were life-sized, five foot five or so, but the girl in the third painting was smaller, both in height and general proportion. The sixth girl was perhaps three-quarters the size of an actual adult or adolescent, and she'd noticed the floor in the final picture, Rowan realised, because there was so much of it: standing up, the woman curled in foetal position would have been two and a half feet at most.

Marianne's work had often been political but these paintings vibrated with a new anger. What is happening to these girls? they demanded to know. What for? Why are they starving themselves?

Killing themselves, because death was in every picture. The first one hinted at it, the end of Eden, but it loomed larger and larger as the sequence progressed, so that by the end, it was impossible not to think of famine, concentration camps. The woman in the last picture was near death, no doubt, but she seemed also, Rowan thought, to personify it, to *be* it, with that raw, hideous mouth – that maw. Here is suffering, said the painting, here is pain. Here is the end of hope.

Going up on the roof had been Rowan's idea. The summer they left school, there had been a heat wave that lasted three weeks, the temperature in the high eighties day after day, the sky deep and cloudless. They'd spent most of their time sprawled on blankets on the lawn but at four o'clock every afternoon, the sun had disappeared behind the gable and thrown the garden into shade. After a week, Rowan had started looking at the flat roof above Marianne's bedroom and wondering if the sun stayed longer up there. Eventually she'd persuaded her they should find out.

The first time, they'd moved a chest of drawers under the skylight and pulled themselves up; but when they saw the view, they'd made a trip to Homebase to buy the stepladder now propped against the wall by the sink.

Arms above her head, Rowan shoved the hatch open. The ladder wobbled under her as she climbed gingerly on to the top step and put her hands either side of the opening. As she clambered out, she felt a physical echo: Marianne must have done exactly this the night she died.

The daylight was fading quickly now, the sun almost set. She moved away from the hatch and waited for her eyes to adjust. Along the backs of the houses, the gardens were dark, the branches of the trees like black coral in silhouette against the sky. In the three-storey block of flats in Benson Close, the little dead-end street behind, the windows glowed yolk-yellow.

Fyfield Road was the last full street before the River Cherwell, and on a summer's day, the view from this flat expanse at the rear of the house reached in a dazzle of blue and green across the grounds of Lady Margaret Hall and the playing fields of the Dragon School to the meadows on the other side of the river and all the way to Marston. Now, in the thickening twilight, Rowan could see the John Radcliffe Hospital glistening at the top of Headington Hill.

The band had been around a lot the summer they finished school. On the first day the temperature touched ninety, Turk had turned up at lunchtime with an inflatable paddling pool. They'd taken turns in it, cooling off, and then, when the sun left the garden, they'd come up to the roof. While the rest of them had stretched out on their blankets, Marianne had stayed on the low wall by the hatch, her back pressed hard against the chimneystack as she sketched a view of the rooftops.

'Come on, Mazz,' Turk had called, 'don't be antisocial.' He'd rolled gingerly on to his side, keeping a careful eye on the opening of his boxer shorts. He'd had the brainwave about the pool on his way over and couldn't be bothered going all the way home for his trunks. 'There's room on my blanket for you.'

'And mine.' The new guy gave her a twinkling smile. He'd been one of five potential bass guitarists who'd answered the band's ad on *Daily Information* and, according to Josh, he'd been promising, which was why he was with them that afternoon. With his big brown eyes and blond hair, he was good-looking, though, and Rowan knew from the death-stare Turk gave him that he'd just signed his own marching orders.

'I dare you, Marianne,' Turk had said, less flippant. 'There's nothing to be scared of – we're nowhere near the edge. Come on, what have you done with your balls?'

She'd carried on sketching without looking up. 'I don't need to air mine to the four winds for everyone to be sure I've got them.'

Rowan walked towards the back of the house now until she had a view of the patio. She was eighteen inches from the edge. Her eyes saw the muddy patch of lawn directly below and her heart started to pump faster. She was standing where Marianne must have gone off.

All of a sudden, the roof-edge came alive. Like the ruined grass, it seemed to develop a force field – it tugged at her, pulling her forward. The drop was dizzying, sickening, almost irresistible. No – *no*. With an effort of will, she took a heavy step back and then, as if someone had let go of her hands without warning, several stumbling short ones.

She walked quickly back towards the hatch, shaken. It would have been so easy – a second, not even that. A split second's decision – *Yes!* – and it would all have been over. She'd never had a problem with heights; she'd never felt anything like that in her life. That – it was what Marianne had been talking about.

—

Rowan's hands shook as she grappled with the corkscrew. The cooker said 5.47 but it felt like midnight, and the darker it got, the larger and stranger the house became. Walking downstairs, she'd thought about all the empty rooms behind the closed doors, all the places someone – a thief, an intruder – could hide. With the Dawsons away, the other side of the house was empty, too.

But if she was going to do this, she couldn't cower in the kitchen. Filling a glass, she carried it back upstairs to the first-floor landing where she stopped outside one of the closed doors. She took a long swig, cranked the handle and went in.

When she turned on the light, she was startled. She'd guessed that Marianne would have kept it as it was, so little else having changed in the main part of the house, but this was something else. It was a tableau, like a room in one of those museums that preserved things as they'd been at a precise moment in time, *Mary Celeste*-style. Should Seb ever come back from the dead with work to do, his study was ready, the scorpion-esque ergonomic chair pulled up to the desk, his iMac G4 with its bubble base – cutting-edge then, geriatric now – still plugged in. To the right of the mouse pad, a week-to-view diary lay open, a pen laid ready across the pages. The gold letters in the top right-hand corner read 2004.

On the other wall, reaching from floor to ceiling, were the fitted shelves packed with *The Lioness Who Loved the Silverback* and its two sequels. Standing here, Seb had been photographed countless times for the newspapers and magazines, British and foreign, in which he'd expounded his theories of mate selection in the animal world and what humans might learn from it, more often than not, as Jacqueline pointed out, to good-looking female journalists.

'It's been translated into forty languages,' Marianne had said as they tried to decipher his name in the different alphabets of the translated editions. 'That one's Hebrew. It's sold nine million copies so far, world-wide. Weird, isn't it?

Somewhere in South Korea right now, someone might be reading Dad's book.'

Also on the shelf was a photograph Rowan remembered, the lack of tarnish on the frame suggesting it had been recently polished. Picking it up, she looked at Seb and Jacqueline at the party celebrating the sale of the millionth UK copy of *Lioness*. It was like a wedding photo, the pair of them standing next to a giant cake iced to resemble the book's cover, Seb brandishing a knife, about to cleave it in twain. They both looked so young, but then, they were. Seb had been in his early thirties when he'd written the first book, Rowan's age now. She looked at him more closely. It was the late eighties when the photograph was taken but apart from the hair, which had a little too much volume at the front for current tastes, the picture was ageing well. Seb was wearing a classic black blazer – no risible boxy shoulders for him – and, underneath, a simple pale blue chambray shirt, the top button undone. Perhaps he'd chosen his clothes with posterity in mind; she wouldn't have put it past him. He was laughing, shining with youth and success and acclaim, confident of all his powers, the hand without the knife resting on Jacqueline's hip. Rowan put the frame quickly back on the shelf, the image striking her all of a sudden as prophetic. Cleaving things in twain had turned out to be a talent of Seb's.

Seven

Compared to Jacqueline and Seb's en suite, the bathroom shared by the other three bedrooms on the first floor was dated, even shabby, but it appeared that Marianne had been using it. A dressing gown with an embroidered hibiscus hung on the back of the door, and next to the basin were a toothbrush and paste. There were male things, too. Here on the shower shelf, a bottle of Molton Brown men's shower gel nestled among the shampoos and conditioners, and in the cabinet Rowan had seen an electric razor. She wondered how often James Greenwood had stayed here. Marianne had lived alone; he hadn't moved in. It seemed unusual for a couple who'd been together four years but, as Jacqueline said, Marianne had needed to be alone to work, and he had his daughter. How much time had they spent together, then, and where? The person to ask was Peter Turk. He was masochist enough to want to hear as much as Marianne would tell him about her love life, and he would have made it his business to find out about Greenwood.

Rowan turned up the temperature again and stepped closer to the showerhead. The cubicle was full of steam but she couldn't get the chill out of her bones. Overnight, the temperature had dropped sharply; the frost on the lawn was so heavy that when she'd opened the curtains just now, she'd mistaken it for a fine layer of snow.

When it came down to it, she thought, how much did she really know about Marianne's life in the past ten years? Beyond the little she'd gleaned at the funeral and the handful of facts in the papers, close to nothing. It was extraordinary, to know someone so well, intimately, and then not at all. She was starting almost from scratch.

Drying off, she wrapped herself in a towel and scurried down the arctic corridor to the guest room she'd chosen. It was minimally furnished, just a double bed with a patchwork cover and a small bedside table with a lamp and a pile of books – Katherine Mansfield, John Le Carré, Ted Hughes' *Birthday Letters* and a broken-backed copy of Gibbon's *The Decline and Fall of the Roman Empire*. There was a low chair and a framed Edward Lear print above the bed in which a man in a tailcoat danced with a giant fly, but the only furniture otherwise was the wardrobe, a huge beast with a yellowing, age-spotted mirror. When she'd opened it yesterday, its cavernous insides had jangled with empty hangers but last night she had unpacked, hung up her clothes and put the few precious things she hadn't wanted to leave in London on the deep top shelf.

She dressed in jeans and a thick sweater then went down to the kitchen where she had toast and coffee at the table, surrounded by memories of other breakfasts. In those days, though, she would never have spent the night in a guest room; she'd slept on an airbed in Marianne's room so they could talk in the dark. On clear nights, they'd left the blinds open so that the moon shone in and picked out the shapes of the furniture, their hands and faces, with its ethereal white light. Marianne's idea, of course: she'd had a gift for that kind of alchemy, for transforming the everyday into something memorable, otherworldly.

Reaching for her laptop, Rowan Googled a number then tapped it into her phone. When the call was answered, she gave her name and asked for Theo Marsh.

His direct line only rang twice before he picked up. 'Rowan?' he said. 'This is a blast from the past. How are you?'

'Okay. I'm back in Oxford for a few days and I wondered if I could buy you a drink.'

When she'd turned off the light last night, Rowan had lain awake for a long time. In the dark, the task of working out what had happened grew until it felt monumental, impossible. Her chest started to tighten but then, as she'd trained herself to do if ever she felt overwhelmed, she remembered the advice Seb gave them when they'd had a revision panic the week before A-levels. '*Gradatim*,' he'd said. 'Remember your Latin? Step by step.'

The call to Theo, she'd decided, would be her first step; the second was going through the two large lidded baskets she'd noticed yesterday under the worktable in Marianne's studio. Kneeling now, she pulled the first one out into the open. It was about eighteen inches square and, when she took the lid off, she saw that it was three-quarters filled with loose paper. Looking at a couple of random points in the pile confirmed that this was where Marianne had kept her sketches, or where someone else – Jacqueline or Adam, Greenwood perhaps – had collected them since.

Marianne's voice piped up suddenly, half amused, half incredulous. *'You're really going to do this? You're going to go through my stuff?'*

'Sorry, Mazz. I have to.'

At the top, over several pieces of high-quality paper, was a study of a horse chestnut tree in its various parts: a leaf; bark; a number of conkers in different stages of growth, and then mottled, wrinkling decay. Rowan lingered on one that hadn't been fully mature. Somehow, with lines of black ink, Marianne had captured the spiky greenness of the shell, its foamy lining and then, like a rolled eye, the blind white orb of the conker inside.

71

There were other studies – a dead sparrow with stiff scaled legs; a fox-fur with beads for eyes; a pair of knitted gloves – but informal sketches, too, things she seemed to have done on the hoof but liked enough to save. The back of an old window envelope had a little pencil acorn on it, and Rowan imagined Marianne standing at the hall table, the phone jammed under her ear while she drew it. Perhaps she'd picked it up on a walk and dropped it there when she came in. She'd used to do that a lot, collect small things and put them in her pockets to study later.

Most of the sketches, maybe four out of five, were preparatory work for the anorexia portraits. In charcoal, chalk and red pencil, Marianne had drawn body after body: hands, feet, shoulders and collarbones, backs, tiny breasts, forearms whose radius and ulna were like bow and string. Girls faced forward, faced away, stood or lay on their fronts and backs and sides, stretching, curled. Some of the drawings were lovely, those that still had some softness, but the ones that studied the emaciation were powerful. In a disembodied knee or forearm, she'd managed to convey both suffering and pity for it, both particularity – *this* knee, with its mole and fine white scar – and something universal.

'Incredible, Mazz,' Rowan said out loud.

When she'd seen them all, she put the sketches back in the exact same order then reached for the second basket. This one held admin paperwork and correspondence and would take a lot longer to deal with. The thatch of paper was about a foot deep and, if the top half-inch was anything to go by, without any order at all. Apparently, Marianne had simply tossed things in as she'd dealt with them or, maybe, as they'd arrived.

On top was a letter from Yale University Press requesting permission to reproduce *Blood Sport II*, one of the paintings from her graduation show. Underneath it, a letter from an art school in Glasgow invited Marianne to address its students.

Both were dated mid-December. Had she replied? There was no way of knowing.

Two phonebook-size exhibition catalogues – one from the Met in New York, the other from Tate Britain – accounted for a good deal of the box's weight and there were glossy brochures from numerous private views and openings as well as twenty or thirty invitations.

Four letters came from galleries hoping to lure Marianne away from James Greenwood. Painstakingly worded – Rowan imagined their writers labouring over every phrase – they boasted about the careers they had made and let her know that should she *ever* think of changing representation, 'for whatever reason' as one of them said, they would be delighted to talk to her. Two went so far as to suggest meetings. Were they just fishing or had there been rumours that Marianne might move? If so, what did that say about her relationship with Greenwood?

Another request for a university visit; an invitation to contribute to a literary journal discussing the body in contemporary art; a batch of printed emails about an interview for a German magazine; and then an *eau de nil* envelope embossed with the linked Gs of the Greenwood Gallery. It had been opened but the paperwork was still inside. Easing it out, Rowan saw a remittance advice form dated November for a work referred to as *Eldritch*. The amount at the bottom, transferred by BACS to Marianne's account, it said, was £227,500 plus VAT. The payment was net of the gallery's commission of thirty-five per cent: the sale price of the picture had been £350,000. For a few seconds, Rowan stared at the numbers. She'd known, of course, that Marianne's work sold for a lot of money, she'd even guessed at these sorts of prices, but it was something else to see it. A third of a million for one picture.

It took two hours to work through the box but there was nothing that hinted at any discord in Marianne's life, nothing suspicious. The only thing Rowan noted mentally was how much money James Greenwood was making from her work. His cut on *Eldritch* alone had been £122,500 and by the time she reached the end of the papers, Rowan had counted another five remittances with sums similar and, in one case, bigger. If Marianne had been earning a lot of money, so had he.

Eight

The Gloc wasn't an obvious place for a senior policeman to drink but Rowan had known Theo would suggest it. Where else would he have chosen? As soon as she pushed open the door, familiarity wrapped itself around her along with the smell of warm beer. The walls of the tiny vestibule were crusted with flyers for metal gigs and motorbike-repair ads, just as they always had been, and AC/DC were on the juke-box, 'Back in Black'. The barman had a head of hair to rival a young Ozzy Osbourne.

It was darker inside than out. When her eyes adapted, she ordered a pint of the IPA and took it to one of the dim alcoves that contained the seating.

She'd been here a few times with Marianne back in the days when they'd relied on the fail-proof ID Turk had had made for them, but The Gloc – The Gloucester Arms – really belonged to her time at university, when she'd come once a week or so with a group from Brasenose that also included Theo. Hidden down an alleyway off towny Gloucester Green, this old pub with its low ceiling, wooden floor and exclusively metal playlist had been their way of checking back in with the real world. From her current vantage point, she could see a pair of bearded dudes in their fifties wearing T-shirts and leather waistcoats, and a couple in his-and-hers biker jackets who looked as if they'd been sitting there since the last time she'd been in. The only real change was the absence of smoke: back then, before the ban, it had swirled overhead a foot thick by the end of an evening.

Metallica took over on the jukebox. Ten to seven. She was early but having been alone in the house all day, it was a relief to get out. This afternoon, she'd been in Marianne's new bedroom on the first floor but it hadn't told her much. She didn't seem to have spent much time there: there was no radio or television, and the only book on her bedside table was a well-thumbed copy of *Bodies* by Susie Orbach. The one photograph showed her with Adam and Jacqueline at the dining table, a recent Christmas, judging by the ivy woven around the candlesticks. Who'd taken it? Fintan or James Greenwood? She hadn't seen or heard of one at the funeral but perhaps Adam had a girlfriend.

'Rowan.'

She looked up sharply to see Theo standing beside the little table.

'Sorry.' He smiled. 'I didn't mean to startle you.'

She shook her head. 'You didn't.' She edged round to give him a kiss on the cheek. 'Lovely to see you.'

'And you, though I almost didn't. Was it always this dark in here?' It was still there, she thought, the faint stamp that growing up in the Black Country had put on his accent.

'I think so, but we were always too wasted to notice.'

He grinned. 'On which note, to the bar.' He nodded at her glass, eyebrows up.

'No, fine for now. Thanks.'

She watched as he gave his order to Ozzy, stooping slightly to be seen under the rack of hanging glasses. He'd come straight from the office – the station – and under the long black coat, he wore a dark jacket and white shirt that made her think of school uniform. Theo had always been boyish. Possibly it was his amiable expression – he'd had smile lines around his eyes at twenty – or perhaps it was the hair, which

76

was dirty-blond, thick and cut in a sort of thatchy non-style. Like a tow-headed toddler's, post rough-and-tumble, she thought, describing it for Marianne.

He pocketed his change and returned, sliding onto the bench and taking a pint pot of pistachios from the deep hip pocket of his coat. 'Here. Dive in.' He touched the rim of his beer glass to hers. 'So what are you doing back?'

She told him about the doctorate and the Bodleian archives. 'But you're obviously doing really well,' she said. 'I saw you on TV just before Christmas with the Marley Farm thing. Chief Inspector Theo Marsh at Oxford Crown Court – I nearly fell off the sofa.'

'You saw that? God, how embarrassing.'

'No, you looked good – television suits you. Nasty case, though.' It had been a murder trial, a pair of broke, semi-literate brothers who'd been siphoning diesel from a tractor when they'd been caught by the farmer and shot in the back. It had become a national news story that led to much debate in the papers and on *Question Time* about rural poverty and inadequate policing.

'It was a mess,' Theo said. 'Glad it's over.'

'You like it, though, generally – the police?'

He nodded. 'Love it, sometimes. Even though everyone else seems to wish I were a corporate lawyer.'

'Everyone?'

'Well, my parents. Police pay? Goodbye, retirement villa in Spain.' He pulled a face. 'Poor Mum – I'm an ungrateful sod. But I've wanted to be a detective since I saw *The Pink Panther*. The cartoon version.'

He sipped his beer. 'I've thought about you lately, too,' he said. 'Which was why I was so startled when you rang. It was like I'd summoned you.'

'Really?' She looked at him. 'Why were you thinking about me?' She reached for the nuts.

'Marianne Glass – your friend.'

Rowan put the pistachios down. 'I wondered if you would remember.'

'Of course I did.'

Theo, she'd thought earlier, must have met Marianne two or three times when she'd come back from London to visit Rowan at college. She'd always made an impression on the men she met; every time she came, Rowan spent a couple of galling days afterwards fielding unsubtle enquiries from people who would never have been interested in *her*. Theo had never been one of the enquirers, though, and, anyway, they'd all been out of luck because Marianne had started seeing someone almost as soon as she'd arrived at the Slade.

'That's partly why I'm back, too,' said Rowan. 'The timing, anyway. I'm house-sitting, to help her mother out.'

'The house in Park Town?'

'Hmm.'

'Big place. Are you there on your own?'

'You know it, then?'

'I was advising the Investigating Officer on the case – for as long as it lasted.'

She raised an eyebrow.

'Well, there was no one else involved, it was obvious, so . . .'

'How did you know?' Rowan looked at him over the rim of her glass.

'She was on her own when it happened. It's frustrating not to be able to say for sure why or how she fell—' He broke off. 'Sorry. Are you sure you want to talk about this?'

'Yes, it's okay. Had she been drinking?'

'No more than a glass. Why do you ask?'

'No particular reason. About the booze, I mean – it's not like she had a problem. Generally, about the accident, if that's what it was . . . It's just, I've got so many questions – I hadn't spoken to Mazz for ages – but the people who might know are the ones I can't ask. I can't talk to her family about whether she might have jumped.'

He frowned. 'Why? Do you think she did?'

'Like I said, I hadn't spoken to her. But . . . well, she'd been depressed in the past, after her father died, so I suppose it's possible she might have been again. Jacqueline says not, though – the little she's told me.'

'Strictly,' said Theo, 'I shouldn't talk about it, confidentiality, et cetera, but we – the police – are sure it was an accident. There was no evidence she was depressed and there were a lot of reasons why she wouldn't have been: she was in a good relationship, she had an exhibition coming up . . .'

'In New York. It was one of her dreams.' Rowan drained her glass. 'I don't know. The thing is, I keep thinking about how scared she was of heights. We used to go up on the roof a lot and she never went anywhere near the edge.'

'When were you last up there with her?'

'Years ago,' she admitted. 'Before her dad died.'

'People change, you know.'

'Yes, but . . .'

'It's hard, I know it is, and it's still really fresh but I don't think you need to torment yourself by thinking about suicide. Honestly.'

She took a deep breath. 'Okay. Thanks.'

He picked up their glasses and stood. 'Let's have another drink.'

'Did you hear about Clare Donaghue?' he asked, cracking a pistachio with his thumbnail. 'She and her husband – Simon, he's a good bloke – they'd been trying for ages to have a baby, nothing going on, then she had IVF and had triplets.' He grinned. 'Three girls.'

'Oh my God.' Rowan laughed. 'Were they happy?'

'Overwhelmed, I think. And then, a month after they were born, Si was seconded to Kuala Lumpur so he had to pack up and ship out leaving her with these three tiny creatures. They didn't get medical permission to fly for months because they were so small. She used to send me these emails at three a.m., poor girl.'

'Didn't you go out with her for a while?'

'That was Claire With An I.'

'Oh, yes.'

'How about you? Who are you in touch with?'

Rowan put down her glass, realising as she did that it was nearly empty again. 'I saw Alex Busby quite a bit when I was at the BBC – not a surprise that he's doing so well.'

'I wondered if he'd be interviewing me about Marley Farm – that would have been really odd.'

'And actually, a couple of weeks ago, I bumped into Sarah Gingell on Tottenham Court Road. I was on my way to Foyles and she was getting off a bus.'

Theo frowned. 'How did she look?'

'Frankly? Terrible.'

'Was she off her face? What time was it?'

'Three, maybe half-past. Wasted. Neither of us was saying anything funny but she kept laughing – it was weird. Depressing.'

'You go along thinking you're immune, that things like that aren't going to affect you and your friends, but . . .' Theo shook his head. 'You just have to be grateful it's not you and make sure you take your opportunities when they come.' He reached round the corner of the table and rubbed the top of her arm. 'It's good to see you.'

Out on the empty pavement, Iron Maiden muzzled by the heavy pub door, their voices were suddenly loud. The wind had picked up, driving away the cloud that had smothered the sun during the day and revealing two or three stars bright enough to compete with the light pollution.

'So.' He smiled and his breath made a cloud.

'So.'

He moved towards her and backed her gently up against the wall. His hands were warm around the sides of her face. 'I've wanted to do this since I walked in.' Rowan smelled the sweetness of beer on his breath as he leaned in another inch and let his lips touch hers. A shiver travelled over her shoulders and down her arms.

'Are you seeing anyone?'

She shook her head. 'Not really. Not at the moment.' She tipped her face up, expecting him to kiss her, but instead he pulled away.

'Let's get out of here.' He tucked her arm under his and they walked down towards Gloucester Green, past the student theatre onto Beaumont Street. The façade of the museum was lit up like an ancient Greek temple. By the entrance to the car park at the Randolph, he led her into the shadows and kissed her properly, sliding his hands inside her jacket, touching the small of her back with cool fingertips. 'So now just one question remains,' he said.

'Which is?'

'Your place or mine?'

'Yours,' Rowan said. 'It wouldn't feel right, going back to Fyfield Road.'

'Yeah, I know what you mean. The thing is, I live out in Wytham these days.'

'Do you?' She was surprised.

'We can't drive, we've both had too much to drink and, frankly,' he pulled her against him, 'I can't wait that long.'

'It's funny,' he said, smoothing a strand of Rowan's hair over the pillowcase. 'I have a really distinct memory of looking at your hair. It was the morning after Worcester Ball – do you remember?'

81

'I remember going in the lake in a dress that was dry-clean only. It was ruined – I had to throw it away.'

'Your hair was still wet when we got back. I remember looking at it on the pillow like this and trying to work out what colour it was. It's not blonde, is it, but it's not really brown, either. There're bits of copper but you don't see them unless you look quite closely. Perhaps tawny's the word.'

'Tawny? I like that.'

Repositioning his elbow, he leaned over and kissed her slowly. 'Why did we never go out?'

'We were young and stupid?'

He pulled her closer and she turned onto her side. Cheek resting on his shoulder, she gently stroked the fine hair on his chest. They lay in silence for a minute or two, enjoying the warmth of the bed in the cold room.

'You know what you said about Marianne being alone?' she said.

'Hmm.' He'd closed his eyes.

'What made you so sure?'

He shifted a little, not falling asleep, Rowan realised, but concentrating on the sensation of her hand on his skin. 'The snow,' he said. 'There was one set of footprints going into and out of the house and she made them both.'

'Oh.'

'She had wellies on – navy blue Hunters. She was wearing them when she died and we've got CCTV footage of her in them buying cigarettes in North Parade a few hours before, after the snow fell, so ...'

'Were there prints on the roof?'

He made a noise in the back of his throat: no. 'By the time the folks next door saw her, the sun was up. The garden's shaded, luckily.'

'If there had been, you might have been able to tell exactly what happened.'

'Maybe.' He turned so that he faced her again and shifted closer, putting his hand on her hip.

'No one could have been in the house – hiding – and then left after you'd gone?'

He broke away and looked at her. 'No. The house was searched from top to bottom, Miss Marple. No one was here and no one had gone before we got here.'

'I'm sorry, I'll shut up.'

'Do you know something, Rowan?' He was watching her intently now. 'Do you think someone wanted to hurt her?'

'No. Well, I mean, I don't know – as I said, we hadn't been in touch – but I really doubt it. She wasn't like that.'

'Then accept it for what it was: an accident. Awful, a bloody waste of life and talent, but an accident.'

She was falling asleep when the mattress dented under her. Opening her eyes, she saw Theo sitting on the edge of the bed. A moment later, he stood and picked his boxer shorts off the floor. She watched as he put on his shirt and trousers.

'You're not staying?'

He spun around, caught in the act of zipping his fly.

'I can't. I have to be in early tomorrow. Meeting.'

'Stay in town, then. Quicker from here.'

'I need to change, have a shower. I . . .' Seeing her face, he sat down again and reached across the bed to touch her cheek. 'Ro, I wish I could but Emily would go crazy. Being very late's one thing – I can find an excuse, something came up at work – but staying out all night . . .'

'Who's Emily?'

He shook his head. 'Come on, let's not play that game.'

'What . . . ? Christ.' Rowan pulled the patchwork quilt off the bed and wrapped it around herself. She stood up quickly, feeling suddenly at a disadvantage. 'I don't believe this.'

'Oh, you knew – I don't *believe* you didn't know. I've been married three years, for God's sake – I've got a son. You're telling me no one from college mentioned it to you?'

'Believe what you want. Do you think I would have done this,' she waved her hand at the bed, 'if I'd known?'

He bent and picked up his coat. 'Well, you'll have to forgive me,' he said, throwing it on, 'if I'd forgotten how morally upstanding you are.'

The slam of the front door reverberated through the house. Thank God the Dawsons were away. Furious and disgusted with herself, she leaned against the wall and listened as he stamped away across the gravel. She was still wrapped in the quilt: she hadn't even had time to get her jeans on. Bloody, *bloody* Theo. She took her coat down from the peg and put it on, the silk lining cold against her bare skin.

Tomorrow's hangover was already starting and her mouth was dry. She threw the quilt over the banisters and went down to the kitchen to get a glass of water.

The slate floor was icy underfoot. As she stood at the sink, the overhead lights made a mirror of the window, reflecting her image. The garden was invisible, the spot where Marianne died lost in the dark. Rowan thought about how her body must have looked as the sun came up, the snow around her head dyed scarlet. *They told me her fingers were frozen.* What had she been wearing? Jeans? A coat? Yes, surely, if she was wearing wellies. Wellies – in her mind's eye, the scene of Marianne's death was elevated, heroic even, but—

Something moved on the other side of the glass. Startled, she dropped the glass into the sink. She'd only seen it from the corner of her eye but it wasn't leaves on the wind or a bird or animal. It was larger than that, like someone moving, disturbing the light.

She turned off the tap and moved away. As calmly as possible, she crossed the kitchen and went upstairs, ducking past the window at the turn. Hidden from view from the garden, she ran all the way up to the studio and positioned herself by the window.

The lights were off and when her eyes adjusted, the garden was quite visible in the moonlight. There was no one by the shed or over by the wall. With the shadows, it was hard to be sure but there didn't seem to be anyone down at the end by the birch trees, either. Nothing moved.

Gently she lifted the latch and opened the window. She waited a moment then leaned out until she had a clear view of the lit area outside the kitchen window, the narrow patio and the steps to the lawn. No one. The only sound was the breeze.

She walked into Adam's space and looked out of the dormer. No one on the drive, and the pavement was deserted. Both the cars parked at the kerb were empty.

She pressed her forehead against the glass and waited for the pounding in her chest to subside. The anorexics were to her left, half-lost in darkness. Would anyone really break in to steal them, though? An opportunist hoping for some decent electronics seemed more likely.

Anyway, no one was in the garden. It had been the wind or she'd imagined it in her jittery, half-drunk state. And no one had been hanging round the house the night Marianne died, she knew that for certain now.

As she closed the window at the back of the house, she glanced over at the flats in Benson Place and her heart thumped again. On the top floor, almost on a level with her, a man was standing in the window, silhouetted by the light. He was looking her way. For a moment she was transfixed but then, nerves frayed, she thought 'What the hell?' and gave him a jaunty wave. Why shouldn't he look out of his window? She was looking out of hers.

Nine

'I get them online,' he said. 'From Square Mile. They only sell whole beans, you have to grind them yourself, but you want to anyway, don't you, for the freshness? This one's Brazilian, Capao. Wait 'til you taste it.' Turk took a Brita jug out of the fridge, filled the bottom of the espresso-maker then smoothed the grounds in the filter. 'They're the best in London, Square Mile. All the top coffee places use them.'

Rowan watched as he adjusted the gas so the flames didn't lick up the sides of the pot. He'd known she was coming so skinny black silk trousers with a paisley pattern were obviously what he thought the occasion demanded. He'd answered the door barefoot but, coming into the kitchen, he'd scuffed on a pair of beaded Indian slippers. He looked like a wrestler playing Aladdin in panto.

The kitchen was clean and ordered but beyond the back door, chaos reigned. Even now, at the end of January, a billowing mass of green engulfed the small paved area, and the sprawling laurel bush reached as high as the first-floor windows of the house behind. Dead nettles filled the narrow alley that ran alongside the kitchen.

'You're not tempted to do an extension?' she said.

'What?'

'Extend into the side return, like that.' She pointed to the house next door, whose outer wall now ran right up against the boundary of the property, making room for what – over Turk's mouldering fence – looked like a huge and very stylish kitchen.

'Oh, yeah. One day. It's just so disruptive, isn't it, building work?'

He filled the espresso cups and brought them over to the table. Rowan sat on a bench made from an old railway sleeper and he rummaged in a basket on the worktop. 'You're in luck,' he said. 'I went to Borough Market this morning. I get these biscotti from an Italian guy there – he makes them with lemon oil that his grandmother sends over from Sicily.' He glanced at the coffee, disappointed. 'I can never get a *crema* on top.'

'It's delicious, Peter. Probably the best coffee I've ever had.'

Gratified, he shook some biscuits on to a plate and came to sit down. 'So,' he took a tooth-endangering bite, 'nothing for years and then suddenly, twice in a week, here you are. You want to talk about Mazz, obviously.'

She'd decided just to say it. 'I can't believe she slipped.'

When Turk looked at her, she saw his face properly for the first time. Grey channels were scored out from the inner corners of his eyes, which were pink and visibly under-slept. 'I don't know,' he said. 'No, that's not true. She must have, if that's what the police think. If there was any doubt, they'd be investigating, there'd be an inquest, all that. This isn't bad TV – they're not idiots.'

Rowan thought of Theo and suppressed a shudder of disgust. 'I know.'

'But yes, it's weird – it doesn't make much sense to me, either.'

'You said she definitely still had vertigo.'

'The last time we were up there, it was the same as ever – she wouldn't get off that little wall. Got panicky every time I even walked about a bit.'

'When was that?'

'A month ago? Six weeks?'

'Was she all right? Not – down? Depressed.'

'No. She was *knackered* – she'd been working like a navvy for her new show, I hadn't even spoken to her for a couple of weeks – but she was high as a kite. You remember what it was like when she was doing good work – that excitement, like she was bubbling?'

Rowan nodded. Marianne had tried to explain it once. She'd said that when her work was going well, it felt like the world had organised itself specifically to help her: everything was poignant, relevant, brighter than usual. '"A brilliant kind of mania."'

'That's what she said?'

'Once. Do you think it was?'

'What, mania literally?' Turk ran a fingertip round the lip of his tiny cup. 'No. No, I don't. But she was definitely high, wasn't she? It was definitely an altered state.'

'But not drugs?'

'Mazz?' He half-laughed. 'She didn't even smoke weed any more. She wouldn't even get drunk. God, you're out of touch.'

Rowan took a moment to absorb that. Marianne had never been into drugs, neither of them had. They'd shared the band's weed if there was any going round and, twice, more out of curiosity than any great desire, they'd tried coke. It hadn't done much for either of them.

'And if she'd taken anything, the police would know, wouldn't they? I mean, there was an autopsy – any sudden death has to be . . .'

'I know.' She cut him off. She couldn't bear the parade of images the word triggered: a mortuary table, Marianne's body naked and cold, the tray of implements.

For a few seconds neither of them said anything. A cat emerged from the laurel and, to dislodge the pictures in her head, she watched it pick its way along the top of the fence. It was too thin; she could see the bones moving under its fur. A stray or else it was old, ill.

'Marianne changed,' Turk said suddenly. 'After it all happened. She wasn't the same. She was … muted. Serious. She didn't drink any more – I mean, she *drank*, she'd have a couple of glasses of wine, but she would never throw caution to the wind and get plastered like we used to. And the work – my God, if you thought she was a workaholic before? There were a couple of times when Jacqueline and I had to pretty much kidnap her from the studio.'

'Kidnap?'

'We were worried. She was living on biscuits, not sleeping, smoking *way* too much. I took her to a friend's place in Cornwall for a week and she basically slept straight through the first two days. At one point I went in to check she hadn't *died*.' He looked down, realising what he'd said, then picked up his cup and examined it as if he'd never seen it before.

'My theory,' he said, 'is that she felt guilty about what happened.'

Rowan's heart beat hard. 'Guilty?'

'About the woman who was killed.'

She stared at him.

'Yeah, it sounds crazy but you know how … conscientious she was. She felt responsible. Did you know she paid to put the son through university? Fees, living expenses – the whole thing.'

'What son?'

Turk looked at her as if she was mentally impaired. 'The woman Seb killed when he crashed – you remember? Who was in the other car. She had a son who was fifteen at the time. Mazz put him through college.'

Rowan brought her hands to her mouth. 'Sorry, yes. Of course. No, I didn't know she'd done that.'

'I think she was trying to *expiate* – you know what I mean? Not just by paying for his education but the whole mad work thing. It was self-flagellation – I think she thought that if she pushed herself to breaking point, denied herself everything, even her health, she could pay. Atone.'

'That's . . . insane.'

'I know. But you remember how mad she was about Seb, how much she loved him. I've even thought that maybe she deliberately took on the guilt – consciously – because it kept her feeling close to him. Connected.'

He stood and fetched the coffee pot. Still standing, he eyeballed Rowan. 'And of course that was when you disappeared.'

'Oh, come on, Pete. You know it wasn't my choice. You remember that afternoon – I was . . .'

'I'm not *accusing* you – don't get defensive. I'm just saying that maybe, if you'd still been around, it would've helped. That she needed you.'

'She could have had me. I tried – you know I did. I was *still* trying – every year I sent a card with my number. Every year – I sent one six weeks ago.' And Marianne had opened it, saved it, sent her card in return.

When he sat back down, Turk seemed heavier, resigned. 'I know. It was just odd, that's all. One day you were in our lives and then, abracadabra, you were gone. *We* didn't fall out, you and I, but you dropped me as well.'

'I didn't drop you.'

'You certainly didn't stay in touch.'

'You chose Marianne that afternoon.'

'That *afternoon*. For God's sake, I didn't know I was choosing forever.'

'I thought you hung around with me because I was Mazz's friend. That I was part of the package.'

'Well, *I* thought we were a gang.'

Rowan felt a pang of nostalgia so powerful it brought tears to her eyes. Turk saw.

'It hurts,' he said. 'Doesn't it? It hurts like hell.'

'At least you didn't waste the time you had.'

'Oh, I've wasted plenty. Other things. Relationships . . .' He shook his head. 'I've never had one that most people would dignify with the name. How could I commit to anyone else when I was in love with her? I've been dumped more times than you've had hot dinners, love.'

Rowan had another unpleasant memory of Theo Marsh, his face looming over her as he pressed her into the mattress.

'You know,' Turk said, 'I thought you'd get in touch when the record came out.'

'That was exactly when I *wouldn't* have got in touch. We don't speak for a year then you have a hit and, lo, here I am again? How much of a star-fucker would I have looked?'

'God, you're weird. How about a friend congratulating another friend on their success? Can't you see it that way?'

'I'm sorry, Pete.'

He rolled his eyes. 'It was a long time ago now – just ask my agent.'

'What a mess. The whole thing.'

They sat in silence until Turk picked up the plate. 'Have another biscuit,' he said, and the sheer absurdity of it made her laugh. He started, too, and then it was as if a lid had come off and they laughed until they were weeping, far beyond the point of knowing why they were even laughing at all.

Rowan got a grip first. 'I'd forgotten how ridiculous you are,' she said, running the pad of her thumb under her eyes.

'Speak for yourself.' He handed her a tissue.

'How well do you know James Greenwood, Pete?' she asked.

'A bit. Quite well now, I suppose, but only through Mazz.'

'What do you think of him?'

'Much as it pains me to say it, I think he's all right. Solid. Surprisingly bullshit-free for that world, too.'

'Jacqueline seems to like him.'

'Yeah, she does. And for all the tabloid furore about the break-up, he'd been with Sophie – his wife – for years; they might even have been at college together. He isn't some Lothario sleaze-bag who dangles big promises to get into impressionable young artists' knickers. And you saw Bryony, his daughter. He's a really good dad, Mazz said; he fought tooth and nail to get joint custody. Sophie – or Derry, probably – hired those people who did the Mills-McCartney divorce and it sounds like he had to hand over a kidney on a golden platter.'

'How old is she?'

'Seventeen. No, eighteen – her birthday was just before Christmas. She's leaving school this year.'

'Is she?' She'd looked younger. 'Did they get on, she and Mazz? She seemed pretty upset at the funeral.'

'They were best buds.'

'Even though Marianne split her parents up?'

'I met them for lunch in town a couple of months ago when they were shopping together. They'd been to a gig at the Roundhouse the night before. Marianne used to take Bryony to events, private views, all that; they used to share clothes and shoes. It was more a sister thing than Mazz being the evil stepmother.'

'Well, she was nearer Bryony's age than Greenwood's.'

'Meow.'

'It's true, isn't it – just? If he's forty-eight – is that right? – and his daughter's eighteen?'

He shrugged. 'Bryony loved Marianne because she treated her like an equal. That was Mazz's thing, wasn't it? She made you feel like when she looked at you, she really saw you. The real you, not the . . .' A rasp of stubble as he scratched his cheek, embarrassed. 'You know, even though I knew she wasn't like that at all, I wanted to believe Greenwood was a career move for her.'

'Oh, Pete.'

'But she was happy with him. Whatever she needed, he had it. I never did.'

She reached across the table and put her hand on his arm.

'Poor sod,' said Turk. 'Can you imagine how he's feeling?'

Down the hallway came the sound of a key in the front door. Rowan looked at him. Was he living with someone? A woman? Turk had turned away, though; she couldn't catch his eye.

The ticking of a bicycle being wheeled into the hallway then, 'Hello?'

'In here, Martin.'

Rowan raised her eyebrows.

'Friend of a friend. He's staying for a few days, that's all.'

Footsteps down the corridor and then in the doorway there appeared an ectomorph in an electric-blue Lycra all-in-one. He had a neat round skull with neat light-brown hair and a face that was strangely innocent for a man of thirty or thirty-five, an impression reinforced by the two pink patches in his cheeks. A naïve but friendly accountant, she thought, describing him for Mazz.

'Martin, this is Rowan, an old friend of mine from Oxford.'

'Lovely to meet you, Rowan. Are you staying for dinner? Thought I'd make the time-honoured chickpea curry, Pete, if you fancy it. I like to cook on Saturday nights,' he explained. 'Don't get much opportunity in the week, alas, by the time I get back from the office.'

Turk, Rowan noticed, was mortified. 'That's very kind,' she said. 'But I've got to get back. Flying visit.'

'Oh, that's a shame. Next time.'

Turk was still standing on the pavement as she turned the corner. She wound down the window and waved, and in the rear-view mirror he raised his arm in a kind of salute.

She'd told him she was heading straight back to Oxford but since then she'd had a better idea. Instead of joining the traffic crawling towards the North Circular, she pulled over and got the A–Z out of the glove box. A couple of minutes later, she swung the car round and headed east.

In her final year at the Slade, Marianne had rented studio space in Bethnal Green with a woman called Emma Hammond. Rowan had never been entirely sure whether Emma was at the Slade, too, or if she was just part of the artistic network that Marianne had plugged into when she came to London. She was a couple of years older, anyway, and made what she called 'cloth sculptures', bizarrely shaped fabric-covered frames that looked like tents erected in high winds by particularly dyspraxic people.

The studio had been just off Hackney Road. By the time Rowan got there, it was dark but the huge gas storage cylinders lit up against the sky told her she was getting close. She slowed down and the car behind overtook in an angry roar of acceleration.

After a couple of false starts, she found the street, recognising the 24-hour corner shop and the curry-house next door where they'd eaten together two or three times. There was a parking space outside.

The studio was a single-storey cube originally built as a garage, and its car-sized mechanised door was layered with graffiti. Emma had once made a joke about local Basquiats. On the street side, a filthy metal grille covered the single window but at the back, large glass doors opened onto a south-facing yard.

Next to the garage door was a standard-size steel one. The handwritten names in the display panel were bleached beyond legibility but Rowan pressed the buzzer and waited. A passing bus sent a tremor through a petrol-streaked puddle at the kerb. It was ten years since Marianne left – no, eleven – so Emma was highly unlikely still to be here. Could she really sell enough to pay for studio space anywhere, let alone Bethnal Green these days?

It was still worth a try. Turk had always been protective of Marianne but if there were any rumours doing the rounds, Emma would be delighted to share them. They had been friends in the beginning but the longer Emma had been around Marianne, the harder she'd found it. While she'd been stapling cloth to her wonky frames, Mazz had painted the still lifes that made up *Blood Sports*. The final straw came when *Artforum* mentioned her in the same breath as Sam Taylor-Wood. That night, fuelled by half a bottle of peach schnapps, of all things, Emma had let rip, telling Marianne she was a spoiled bitch who only got attention because her parents were famous and men wanted to fuck her.

Rowan pressed the buzzer again. It was working, at least; she could hear it. A car went by and when the blast of hip-hop faded, she heard a bolt being drawn. The door opened four inches to reveal a vertical slice of an Indian woman in pink dungarees.

'I'm sorry to interrupt,' Rowan said. 'I'm trying to track down Emma Hammond.'

'She's not here any more, sorry.' Her accent was pure Birmingham.

'That's okay; it was a long shot. I'm a friend of Marianne Glass – she and Emma used to share . . .'

The door opened several more inches. 'I know,' the woman said. 'I love it that Marianne used to work here. She left some really good vibes – this is such a productive place. Look, I don't know where Emma's studio is these days – she had somewhere in Stepney, the last I heard – but she still works at the Speakeasy at weekends. Saturday night – you should catch her.'

'Where is that?'

'Just round the corner, three streets that way.' She pointed to the main road and hooked her thumb left. 'About halfway down. It's not marked – hence the name – but you'll see it. There's a skinny window at eye height – if you look in, you'll see the bar.'

'Thank you.'

'No problem. I'm so sorry about Marianne, by the way. I never met her but I really loved her work.'

The entrance to the Speakeasy was down a pungent alleyway at the side of the building. Going in, Rowan found a room lit entirely by candles with a long bar backed by glinting bottles. The tables were half barrels, the chairs all old and wooden with the chipped paint of which hipsters seemed so fond. At the nearest barrel, two men with beards and plaid shirts were drinking beer out of Mason jars.

It was still early, barely half-past six, but four tables were taken and there was a small group at the end of the bar. Rowan looked but couldn't see Emma. The barman was wearing a beanie and a faded red T-shirt with a transfer that proclaimed the Flying Burrito Brothers. 'Yeah, hold on,' he said. While she waited, Rowan perused the drinks board, recognising none of the beers nor any of the extensive list of gins, all of whose names suggested they'd been made in someone's bathtub.

She'd doubted Emma would remember her but as she emerged from the kitchen, it was clear that she did. Emma looked quite amazing, Rowan thought. She was wearing a red fifties-style halter-neck dress covered in polka dots and a pair of studded biker boots. Since Rowan had last seen her, she'd acquired large tattoos of a bannered heart, a topless woman and several feathers. A matching polka-dot ribbon tied her black hair into a high ponytail.

'How are you?' she said, leaning her hip against the bar. 'I heard the news, obviously. Sorry.'

'Thanks. We weren't in touch any more, though.'

'Really?' Emma gestured to the barman who handed her a glass of what looked like lemonade. She took a sip through the straw, careful of her cherry lipstick. 'What did she do to *you*?'

Rowan shrugged. 'Nothing. Just one of those things.'

'Well, you know you didn't miss much.' Emma took another sip. 'But if it's nothing to do with Marianne, then why – with respect – are you here?' She raised plucked and pencilled eyebrows.

There was nothing to be gained from beating about the bush. 'I wanted to ask you if there was any gossip doing the rounds,' Rowan said.

'Like what?'

'Anything. You know everyone in the art world, I remembered, you're so well connected. I thought that if anyone knew anything, it'd be you.' Emma gave a cat-like tilt of the head, pleased. 'Look,' Rowan said, 'Marianne was with James Greenwood, obviously, but I wondered if there was anyone else. If she was messing around.'

Another coquettish sip, Betty-Boop mouth closing on the straw. 'If there *was* someone, I'd tell you, lovely, I promise, but as far as I've heard, there wasn't.' She reached across the bar and gave the glass back. 'I wouldn't have put anything past Marianne, though, would you? She just wound men round her little finger – personally, professionally, whatever. I used to watch her flirting with critics – no wonder she got such great reviews. Everyone's saying she only got that show at Saul Hander because she sucked up to Michael Cory.'

'Michael Cory? Really? I hadn't heard that.'

'Oh, yeah. He showed some photographs with Greenwood a year or so ago; that's how she met him. Useful, having a top dealer as your boyfriend, isn't it? Nice career move, Marianne.

Alfie – that's my boyfriend – he's a photographer and he went to the private view and saw her batting her eyelashes, fawning all over him.'

'He was there? Cory, I mean? In person?'

'I know – I guess that's Greenwood for you. Anyway, Cory's repped by Hander in the States and she clearly wanted him to put in a good word. Lo and behold: one exhibition for Marianne Glass in New York City, baby. Makes you sick, doesn't it?'

Ten

Rowan drove back from London with the sense of a day wasted. Even Emma's bitchy remarks about the New York show were toothless: the Greenwood Gallery's homepage mentioned an affiliation with Saul Hander, and Marianne had never needed to flirt to get ahead.

When she reached Fyfield Road, the house looked forbiddingly dark. She'd expected to be back from London before nightfall so she hadn't left any lights on, and anyone could see the place was empty. On the motorway, she'd been trying to contain her anxiety: what if someone had broken in, turned the house upside down, stolen Marianne's work? What would she say to Jacqueline? Now she swallowed the anxiety as best she could, unbuckled her seatbelt and got out of the car.

As she unlocked the front door, her heart beat faster, and she reached round the jamb and turned on the ceiling light before stepping in. Everything in the hallway was just as she'd left it, however, and when – turning on lights as she went, ears primed – she took the stairs to the kitchen, the back door was still locked and secure, all in order.

Nevertheless, the thought of an intruder had set her on edge, and after checking the whole house and making sure lights showed at both the back and front, she took her laptop, locked up again and got back in the car.

In those days, they'd spent a lot of time in Jericho. The area was only five or six minutes' drive away but where Park Town was serene and almost entirely residential, Jericho had pubs and restaurants and a distinct Bohemian vibe. The slope down to the canal was a maze of Victorian terraces built for workers at the old Eagle Ironworks, which had still been hammering away at the top of Walton Well Road when they were teenagers. It was gone now, converted into apartments, and the lovely yew-lined cemetery of St Sepulchre's was overlooked by modern blocks with names like Foundry House. Some of the old landmarks stood their ground, however: the Phoenix Picture House, Freud's, the Jericho Tavern, where Turk and the band had played several times, and this place, the Jericho Café, where they'd met on Sundays to read the papers.

Very little had changed here, even the red velvet curtain round the door looked familiar, and they still had Marianne's favourite carrot cake by the slice. Rowan ordered then took their old preferred table near the window.

In the car, she'd been thinking about Michael Cory. She'd encountered enough celebrities in her time at the BBC not to be star-struck but she was impressed – even a little jealous – that Marianne had met him. Despite keeping a Salinger-style low profile, he was still one of the handful of contemporary artists whose name was public currency. While Damien Hirst and Tracey Emin had been front-page news since the start of their careers, however, Cory's fame had been triggered by a particular incident.

Taking out her laptop, she entered the café's Internet password – the WiFi *was* new – and typed his name into Google. Even now, years later, Hanna Ferrara's name appeared in every one of the top hits.

Cory was a painter. His work wasn't sensational in the pickled-shark sense: he worked alone with paint on canvas; there were no piles of elephant dung or giant cartoon figures cast by teams of assistants. If he was unknown to the general public before Ferrara, in art circles he'd been acknowledged as a big talent, both for his technical ability and psychological depth.

Somewhere, Hanna Ferrara had heard him described as America's Lucian Freud and she'd decided he would paint her portrait. Rowan remembered reading at the time that Cory had always been adamant about turning down commissions, insisting he chose his own subjects, but Ferrara wouldn't have it. She was the star of *The Woman Who Had Everything*, one of the first comedies with a female lead to gross more than $300 million at the box-office, and people didn't say no to her: every time Cory turned her down, she became more determined, as if he were merely testing her commitment. She'd hassled and hassled, apparently, both in person and via her representatives, until, losing patience, Cory said he would paint her for three million dollars, a fee he'd never thought she'd pay. She'd agreed.

As the papers reported, he'd also insisted she agree to his usual terms: they'd work in his studio, and he would have total control over the picture, which no one, not even she, would be allowed to see until it was finished. Also as usual, he would show the work publicly before it became part of her private collection. Ferrara had agreed and blocked out time in her schedule for the sittings.

Eight months later, when she'd flown to New York to see it, she'd had a panic attack in the gallery. People who knew her said Cory had got her in a way none of her photographs did. He hadn't shown her as a vampy sex object or the approachable if stunning girl-next-door she occasionally impersonated, or even as an ordinary person stripped of Hollywood glamour. Instead, in her face, he had captured a mix of hunger, drive and desperate need. But that wasn't why she'd been taken to hospital. She'd been dressed for the sittings but Cory had painted her naked. Full-length, the portrait showed her standing in front of a mirror. Between her painfully skinny thighs dangled a long penis. He'd called the painting *The Woman Who Has Everything*.

Ferrara's nervous breakdown had stopped her working until two years later when she'd had a supporting role in a film panned in every review Rowan had seen.

Cory's behaviour had been discussed ad infinitum. Most people thought it was a cruel publicity stunt but many in the art world supported him. He was a serious artist, they said, too serious to jeopardise his reputation like that, and the picture was an outstanding depiction of a woman in acute psychological pain, dealing with body image, female ambition and the struggle of women to succeed in a sexist world. Months later, the *Daily Mail* discovered he'd secretly donated three million dollars to a foundation for young women with mental illness.

Cory himself said nothing. He'd been there when Ferrara first saw the painting – she'd lunged at him and scratched his face so badly he'd needed stitches – but a minute later, he'd slipped away through the gallery's back door. By the time journalists had got to his apartment, he'd gone from there, too. He hadn't answered his phone or been seen in public for a long time afterwards and he still refused to give interviews or attend events, even his own private views. If he really had been at the Greenwood, it was remarkable.

Rowan opened Google Images and typed his name again. The first twenty or thirty thumbnails showed either Ferrara or the portrait, and she had to scroll beyond the bottom of the screen before she saw a picture of Cory himself.

She double-clicked.

It was a pap shot. He'd been coming out of what looked like a New York deli, the collar of a long dark coat up around his ears, a dusty black fedora pulled down on his forehead. Between his fingers was a packet of cigarettes. As he'd turned to look at the photographer – hearing his name called, she guessed – his expression was both startled and furious, his eyes wide, mouth half-open.

Rowan experienced a jolt of realization: she'd seen him herself, in the flesh. The man at the funeral who'd caught her eye in the mirror and looked at her so frankly had been Michael Cory.

Immediately her mind flooded with questions: how well had he and Marianne known each other? Were they friends? Why hadn't she, Rowan, recognised him?

Movement at the corner of her eye: the waitress with her omelette. Distracted, Rowan thanked her and shifted the laptop to make room.

'Can I bring you anything else? Ketchup?'

'Sorry? Oh – no. Thanks.'

To have come to the funeral, Cory must surely have been more than an acquaintance. Opening another window, she searched for the show of his photographs at the gallery when, if Emma's testimony was reliable, Marianne had talked to him. October 2013: fifteen months ago.

It was understandable, at least, Rowan thought if she hadn't recognised him at the funeral: in every one of the scant recent photos, his face was partially hidden. He wore a hat in most, and in the few older ones where he didn't, he'd had a lot more hair. She went back to the deli picture. Under the coat he wore a wrinkled denim shirt with a conspicuous coffee stain, and one leg of his jeans was caught in the top of his boot, but even dishevelled and caught off guard, he projected the physical confidence she'd felt, the aura of someone with no doubt about his value and position in the world.

Clicking back to the gallery's website, she read the short bio. Forty-six, born and brought up in Chicago, he'd done his degree at the California Institute of the Arts and then moved to New York. A list of prestigious museums and awards, and then finally: *Cory has lived in London since last year.*

Wikipedia told her that his father owned a company importing Turkish carpets and his mother had been a good amateur water colourist. He had twin sons, now nine or ten, from a brief marriage to a folk singer called Jessa McKenzie but there were no details of his current personal life.

What if he and Marianne had been having an affair? What if she loved him and he'd ended it? Or maybe Greenwood had found out. Elbows on the table, Rowan pressed her fingers to her lips.

At a light touch on her shoulder, she jumped. 'Sorry.' The waitress again, smiling. 'I just wanted to say: we close at ten so . . .' She looked at the untouched omelette.

'Okay. Thanks.' The clock at the top of the screen said 21.44. Rowan picked up her fork then opened a new window and searched for 'Michael Cory profile'. *218,000 results.*

Into the silence of the kitchen at Fyfield Road, the bells of St Giles struck midnight, every note coming crisp through the freezing air. *Eight, nine, ten.* Marianne loved bells, they gave her a sense of continuity and order, she said, history, but Rowan could never hear the tolling of the hour without thinking about mortality, the counting off of time. Another hour gone, another day. *Eleven, twelve.* The stroke lingered then died. She pressed her fingers against her eyelids and resisted the urge to rub.

The next link took her to a *New York Times* piece from 2009, when Cory had had a new show at Saul Hander. The article was long, likely a full page in the paper, but in contrast with the ten or twelve she'd already read, it handled the Hanna Ferrara business only briefly. It focused instead on the new work, a series of portraits of his mother that Cory had made in the five years before her death of cancer in 2008.

The journalist, Jonathan Schwarz, wrote about the visible evolution and deepening of the artist's relationship with his subject, the delicate picking-apart and examination of a tangle of love and bitterness, gratitude and anger, resentment and painful tenderness. Cory did not flinch, he said, from showing his horror and disgust at his mother's failing body even while he acknowledged his debt to it. He referenced a painting in which he had depicted his mother covered by a white sheet that had barely covered her greying pubic hair, the twin focal points of the work a livid scar on her stomach from the removal of a large portion of her bowel and the faded white line of the C-section by which Cory himself had been born. In another painting, this one shown, he'd represented her cancer as an incubus crouching on her skeletal chest like the hideous figure in Henry Fuseli's *The Nightmare*.

No one, of course, could ask Rebecca Cory how she felt about her son's work but then it was nearly impossible, Schwarz said, to find *anyone* he'd painted who was prepared to talk. Whether this was another of his conditions or their own choice was unclear. Despite weeks of research, Schwarz wrote, he'd been on the point of conceding defeat when, almost by chance, he'd managed to make contact with Margaret Robinson, the pianist who had been Cory's upstairs neighbour in the East Village when he first moved to New York at twenty-four. She'd been in her late-forties at the time, almost fifty, but they'd become lovers the night they met and Cory had painted her over and over again during the three years they'd been together.

Despite his relative youth, she said, it had been one of the most intense experiences of her life. 'He wanted to know me,' she said, 'really *know* me, as if there was something inside me – an essence, a truth – that he could pull out, wind out of my chest like a silk thread. Or maybe it was the other way about and what he wanted was to go deeper and deeper, follow the thread into my psyche like Theseus in the labyrinth. I'm a New Yorker, I saw a shrink for years, but being analysed was nothing compared to sitting for Michael. I've never felt like that before – laid bare, exposed, but *seen*. *Witnessed.*'

Schwarz had also tried to contact Greta Mulraine, an old girlfriend and the subject of the six nudes Cory had painted at CalArts that attracted his first gallerist. In trying to track her down, however, he'd hit one brick wall after another: barring references to the portraits, she was invisible online and when he tried to contact her parents, he found they'd left Oregon for their native Australia. His efforts to locate them there had come to nothing. It was only when he left a Facebook message for one of Cory's old CalArts classmates that he'd discovered what happened. Six months after he'd painted her for the final time, Greta Mulraine had committed suicide.

Eleven

Outside the window, a winter landscape raced past. The fields resembled muddy corduroy, and horses stood disconsolate in paddocks drab with thistles. On the river at Reading, the little pleasure boats huddled under tarpaulin.

Despite the frost glittering at the track edge, the train was hot. It was mid-morning, she'd waited until after the rush, and the seat next to her had been empty all the way from Oxford. Rowan closed her eyes and let her head drop back against the bristly plush upholstery, the heat hitting her like a sleeping pill.

On Saturday night, she'd shut her laptop shortly after one but had lain awake again, brain humming. When St Giles struck three, she'd thrown off the covers, taken Marianne's dressing gown from the bathroom and gone upstairs. Marianne was everywhere in the house – every room, every picture and piece of furniture triggered a memory – but the studio was where she felt closest.

Rowan had looked at the anorexics, the last tiny woman so close to death, and thought about Cory's portraits of his mother. Had Marianne talked to him about her work? Might he even have inspired her to track the progress of a disease like this? Maybe he had nothing to do with it: *Mirror, Mirror*, Jacqueline's most successful book, discussed eating disorders, and Marianne was a feminist before she could spell the word.

On the other hand, both she and Cory seemed to have been drawn to women in extremis.

Had they been drawn to each other, too? She shouldn't rule out that possibility.

Turning to go, she'd switched off the lights but then, changing her mind, she'd walked over to the window. The moon was almost full and, when her eyes adapted, its milky glow showed her the garden quite clearly. Stillness, complete silence, as if she were the only person awake in the city. The flats in Benson Place were dark.

She'd leaned forward until she could see the ruined grass. *What happened, Mazz?*

Seconds later, she reared back. In the top flat opposite, the light had snapped on and she saw the same man silhouetted in the window. After a moment, she'd realised he couldn't see her, the studio was dark, but how long had he been there? She hadn't long turned the light off; had he seen it and come to the window? It was three o'clock in the morning.

Downstairs, she'd sat on the edge of the bed. Who was he? What was he doing? And how had he done that, turned on the light and yet been standing there motionless?

When the shock began to fade, she'd been a little ashamed of herself. This was a city – a city full of all kinds of highly intelligent, unconventional people. '*Nutters, to be plain,*' said Marianne's dry voice. Maybe the guy was an insomniac; maybe he just liked to work at night, when it was quiet.

But if he was up at night, she'd thought suddenly, standing at his window like that, perhaps he'd seen Marianne go off the roof. Perhaps he'd seen what happened. But the surge of excitement fell away as quickly as it had mounted. No, he couldn't have: as Turk said, the police weren't idiots. They could see as clearly as she could that the flats looked on to the back of the house and they would have interviewed everyone who lived there.

She needed to sleep, she'd told herself, but she'd still been awake when the first crack-throated birdsong started up outside. Again and again, she came back to Michael Cory and the longer her mind whirred, the more convinced she was that somehow he was involved. A girlfriend dead by suicide; Hanna Ferrara's nervous breakdown. The words of the pianist repeated themselves: *He wanted to know me, really know me, as if there was something inside me – an essence, a truth – that he could pull out.*

What if he had done that to Marianne? What if he'd got to her? What if he knew what she did?

Rowan fell asleep properly as the train reached the outskirts of London, and the heavy drugged feeling lingered as she walked down the platform to the ticket barrier. Marianne described Paddington as a whale, its elaborate ironwork a giant ribcage, but to Rowan, the station was a great ravening Dickensian engine fuelled by people. Today, only the prospect of trying to park in Mayfair had persuaded her to take a train but in the Sixth Form, they'd loved it, coming to London to see exhibitions and bands or just to wander about. There hadn't been any barriers then so they'd rarely bothered with tickets.

She bought an espresso then made her way towards the mouth of the Underground. At the top of the steps, she felt her mobile vibrate in her pocket. A number she didn't know. Stepping out of the stream of people, she answered it.

'Rowan?'

With the background noise, it was a second or two before she recognised his voice. 'Adam.'

'How are you? How's everything at the house?'

'Good. Yes, fine. I . . .' She was drowned out by an announcement that the eleven o'clock for Bristol Temple Meads would depart from platform six.

'You're not in Oxford now?'

'What?'

'Platform six. Oxford Station only has two.'

'Oh – of course. No, I'm in London. Paddington. I've had to come down for a meeting with my supervisor.'

'Ah. That's why I was ringing. I need to get some paperwork from Dad's desk and I wanted to let you know rather than barge in unannounced and give you a coronary.'

'Today?'

'This evening. I'm at a thing in Birmingham, a conference, and I can drop in on my way back to Cambridge tonight.'

'Of course – well, I mean, obviously, it's your house.' As she said it, she wondered if that was actually true. Who did own it? 'Sorry, that sounded rude, didn't it? What I meant was, I'll be back by then and thanks for ringing to let me know. It'll be nice to see you.'

She thought she heard him laugh. 'I'll see you this evening,' he said. 'Probably about seven.'

Queensway, Lancaster Gate – the Central Line clipped rapidly through its stations and she tried to concentrate. Adam had distracted her. She regretted having to tell him she was seeing her supervisor but the truth wouldn't have done any good, either.

Once, years ago, they'd kissed. The summer she left school, he'd come home from Cambridge for the long vacation. Seb had taken Jacqueline to Barcelona one weekend and they'd had a house party, Adam's friends and theirs, standing room only in the sitting room and kitchen, the garden full of people messing about in the paddling pool or sitting round the fire basket Turk borrowed from his parents. Yesterday, in fact, she'd seen the wine stain she'd made on the dining-room carpet, faint but still there nearly fifteen years later.

When she'd bumped into Adam on the landing, it had been after midnight. She'd spent most of the day getting the house ready but he said hello as if he hadn't seen her for months. He was carrying a stack of CDs. They looked at each other and then he reached for her hand and they threaded a path through the people sitting on the stairs and went to his room. Blondie's *Atomic*, playing on Jacqueline's stereo downstairs, faded only a little when he closed the door. A warm breeze riffled the papers on the desk.

Without saying anything, he'd pulled her towards him. Everyone smoked then, the house had been like a working-men's club the next morning, but she'd smelled sunscreen and washing powder on his shirt. A gentle kiss first, barely a touch of the lips, but then he'd put his hands around her waist and kissed her as if he meant it.

Sliding his hands to her hips, he lifted her backwards on to his desk. She'd pulled him closer and, at that moment, the door had burst open. Marianne.

He'd stepped quickly away.

'Shit.' She looked at them both. 'I'm so sorry, I had no idea you were . . . I just came to get some more music.' She glanced at the CDs he'd dropped on the bed.

'Mazz?' Heavy footsteps on the stairs and Turk appeared in the doorway, too.

Adam held out his hand and helped Rowan down. He gestured at his music collection. 'Have a look, Pete. Take whatever you want.'

She'd assumed they'd find each other again but somehow, they hadn't. She couldn't locate Adam and then he'd come looking for her just as the police arrived to shut them down. At five she'd fallen asleep on Jacqueline's reading sofa and the next day, he'd given her just a single embarrassed smile. They'd never talked about it and it never happened again, though she'd thought about it for years afterwards.

By then, she'd started to see Seb with adult eyes. The differences between them intrigued her, especially since, in some respects, Adam seemed more mature. He was quiet and calm where his father was extrovert, voluble. It made sense that Adam had become an academic but Seb must have struggled with the mandatory silence of libraries. She pictured him at the Bodleian, words building up inside, levels rising and rising until, sensing he couldn't hold them much longer, he'd come spilling out onto the pavement to pour them into his mobile in a great bubbling stream. He was constantly on his phone, it was never out of his sight, and the fluency with which he talked made him a natural for his radio and TV work, interviews and commentary and the documentaries he made from time to time.

When she was at college, he was interviewed on *Parkinson*. He was the first guest, just the opener for the musical act and the big Hollywood star, but from the TV room at Brasenose she'd watched him work his charm as she'd seen him do a hundred times at Fyfield Road. When he listened, he leaned forward as if he were paying attention with his entire body; his responses started out measured and carefully honest, respectful of the questions, but then lightened into self-deprecation and glinting humour. He wove back and forth, picking up themes, riffing on ideas, a conversational jazz musician.

The Tube rattled into Marble Arch and a gang of jostling Italian teenagers filled the carriage. When had Rowan realised he wasn't faithful to Jacqueline? Not long after she'd kissed Adam: she'd still been pretty young. 'Naïve,' Marianne's voice corrected, and it was true she'd struggled to understand. She dealt in absolutes then: you either did something or you didn't, loved someone or not. It was later that the greys began to shade in.

She'd overheard Seb on the phone. They were lying out on the lawn with books but Marianne had fallen asleep, her cheek crushing the pages of her paperback. Maybe he'd thought they were both sleeping or maybe he'd just forgotten his study window was open but she'd heard the phone and then, unmistakable, the low, teasing, confidential tones of a man – a flirt – talking to someone he'd either slept with or was planning to, soon. At first she'd thought it was Jacqueline – she'd heard him talking to her like that as they'd come out of their bedroom one afternoon – but then he'd suggested supper that night in Faringford. Jacqueline was at a seminar in New York.

Despite the sun flooding the garden, Rowan had gone cold. Her first impulse was to thank God Marianne was asleep but, sitting up, she'd looked at her friend's exposed neck, the fine hairs escaping her ponytail, and had felt a wave of incredulous anger: how could he? He was gambling all their happiness, jeopardising everything. She was furious with him, as furious as if he were her own father. She had to tell Marianne, she decided. They had to stop him before Jacqueline found out.

Hours later, when, freshly showered and shaved, Seb had left, her efforts to find a sensitive way to say it had failed and Rowan blurted: 'I heard your dad on the phone. I think he's having an affair.' Her mouth went dry; she'd expected Marianne to cry or scream at her, kill the messenger, but instead she'd walked to the fridge and taken out a Coke.

'I know.'

Rowan had been momentarily lost for words.

'It's hard not to – I live with him.' Marianne cracked the can open and took a sip. 'He's not subtle. I mean, he goes round with that look on his face, all smug and self-satisfied and *conspiratorial*, as if there's something exciting going on and he wishes he could tell us about it but unfortunately . . .'

Rowan had been engulfed by pain, a sense of pure betrayal: why hadn't Marianne told her? If *her* father were being unfaithful, she'd have confided in her friend straight away.

Marianne saw her expression. 'Here.' She pulled out a chair for Rowan then sat down next to her. 'He does this,' she said. 'It's not the first time.'

'You've never told me.' As if that were the issue.

'I didn't want you to know. I'm ashamed.'

'In front of me?' Another burst of pain. 'You *never* have to feel ashamed in front of me.'

Marianne covered her face with her hands. 'I know. I'm sorry.'

The fridge hummed into the silence.

'How long's it been going on?'

'This one? Not long – a few weeks. In general, years. Not continuously but . . .'

'We have to stop him, Mazz, before your mum finds out.'

Marianne raised her head. 'She knows.'

'*What?*'

'She always does. She knows him better than anyone else.'

'But . . .'

'She says it's about vanity – he needs it, *them*, for his ego.'

Rowan hadn't been able to contain a cry of disbelief. 'Your mum's not enough? She's *amazing*. He should be counting his lucky stars she even deigns to . . .'

'He is – he does. It's . . . different.'

'How?' She'd sounded hostile now, as if it were Marianne's fault.

'Ro, come on, you know my parents. Can you imagine them apart? They need each other. They *love* each other.'

'Then why would he . . . ?'

'Like I said, ego. It's the biggest cliché going: middle-aged man chases younger women to make sure he's still got it, he can still get the *ladies*.' Marianne gave a snort. 'Why do you think he's spent his whole professional life studying sex? Of course he's an expert, he's done enough research. But they burn out. A few weeks, a few months, and he gets bored. It never burns out with Mum. He never gets bored with her.'

'And she puts up with it.' Rowan's voice was flat with betrayal but this time the betrayer was Jacqueline. She, with everything she wrote and argued and *believed*, let her husband cheat.

Marianne went to the drawer where her mother, who'd been trying to give up since Rowan met her, kept her cigarettes. She got a saucer from the cupboard then lit two and handed one of them over.

'It took me years to understand,' she said, 'but I think I get it now. Most of the time, she turns her back on it, waits for him to get bored, but – you really don't want to think about this stuff when it comes to your parents but, hey, it's not like I had a choice.' She shrugged and took a puff. 'I think there's a bit of her that doesn't mind. Maybe there's something she even likes about it.'

Rowan stared at her again.

'Every time he ends one of these . . . flings, it's an endorsement of their relationship, isn't it? He chooses her over the other woman. He chooses her over and over again.'

Twelve

At the end of the room, a woman dressed in black sat at a long table. She looked up, said a curt hello then turned back to her laptop. Assessed and dismissed in a second, thought Rowan.

She hadn't recognised the name of the artist stencilled on the window but the paintings on show were still lifes, apparently traditional: a bowl of lemons and a pomegranate spilling blood-red seeds were the focal point of the first. From a distance, the surrounding canvas looked blank but as she got closer, she saw that a network of fine grey lines like map contours delineated a wine glass, the limp body of a rabbit and, next to it, a mobile phone and a set of keys with an electronic fob, as if it wasn't a carefully composed still life but an oil-paint snapshot of someone's hall table. What was the rabbit? Road-kill from the BMW? At closer range still, she noticed that each tiny area of canvas was numbered and at the bottom right, there was a guide. *2: Jaune Brillant; 3: Raw Umber Light*. Fine art colour-by-numbers.

The gallery was one long room with white walls and a dark polished-wood floor. The plate-glass frontage provided almost all the natural light; the only other window, high on the rear wall, was covered with vertical bars. Nonetheless, the space was bright, dozens of recessed bulbs in the high ceiling creating a shadowless light.

She looked at the paintings one by one, working her way towards the desk. After a while, she felt the woman's eyes on her, as if the length of time she'd lingered had marked her out as someone who was worthy of attention after all or – more likely – suspicion.

'May I help you?' The cool voice again.

Rowan approached. 'I hope so. I wondered if James Greenwood was in?'

The woman stood, revealing a pair of black trousers as spotless and well tailored as her pin-tucked blouse. 'Is he expecting you?'

'No.'

'Are you an artist? I'm afraid we don't meet people on an ad hoc basis. We get a huge number of enquiries and . . .'

'No, I'm not an artist. I'm an old friend of Marianne Glass.'

The woman looked at her. 'Let me call him,' she said after a moment. 'He's here today – at work – but he's popped out. Can I tell him your name?'

Rowan moved away while the woman rang Greenwood's mobile and spoke to him in a low voice. 'Rowan Winter. Yes.' It was impossible to gauge what he was saying.

'Rowan? He's just walking back now. He'll be here in five minutes.'

'Thank you.'

She dawdled, feigning absorption in the paintings. The first one had been mildly amusing but after three or four, it was hard to see them as more than a gimmick. The door opened and a couple came in, the man about sixty, the woman perhaps thirty and dressed in tight indigo jeans, a long camel coat and heels that gave her a bird's-eye view of her companion's shiny pink cranium. She reached repeatedly for an iPhone in a diamanté case into which she spoke rapid-fire Russian. *Niet, niet.*

When the street door opened again, it was Greenwood. He looked better than he had at the funeral but not much. His eyes were still hollow and grey-shadowed, and he seemed thinner, his coat at least a size too big.

He recognised her and came directly over. 'Rowan.'

'Mr Greenwood, I'm so . . .'

'James, please.'

'I'm sorry just to turn up like this without ringing.'

He shook his head, reflexive good manners.

'I wondered if I could talk to you?'

He glanced back at the desk and seemed to think. 'Would you like some coffee?' he asked. 'There's a place just around the corner.'

He gave the woman – Cara – a message then ushered Rowan towards the door. He was someone brought up to know how to make any social situation comfortable, she thought, but this was testing even his limits. He was stiff with tension, straight-backed as a meerkat. They walked side by side, both trying to find something to say that wasn't ludicrously trite. The weather, the cold – how British.

He held the café door open and she went up a worn stone step into a muggy room permeated with the smell of cooking bacon. Clustered around small tables were about thirty other people.

Greenwood went to the counter but within a minute he was back, unloading a milk jug from the tray, asking if she took sugar. He picked up a sachet for himself but then had second thoughts and put it on the table.

'Thank you for doing this. And for the coffee.'

He shook his head again: of course.

'I feel very insensitive. Selfish. I'm really sorry – I should have thought more before coming. The last thing I want is to make things harder for you.'

He gave a grim smile. 'It's difficult to imagine how things could be harder.'

She looked down and straightened her spoon in the saucer. 'I wasn't sure if you'd be at work.'

'I have to, for the sake of my sanity. I'm just going through the motions but the idea of sitting at home . . .'

'It was nothing like this, of course, but when Marianne and I fell out, I was – well, it doesn't feel right to say devastated now, in the circumstances,' Rowan inclined her head, deferring to his pain, 'but at the time, that's what it felt like. It'll sound stupid but when you said she used to talk about me, it made me happy.'

'It doesn't sound stupid.' Despite the heat, he'd kept his coat on and his cuff buttons rattled against the table as he put his cup down. He seemed to square his shoulders. 'What did you want to talk about?'

'Exactly that. I wanted to ask what she said.' A flicker crossed his face. What was that? Surprise? Rowan felt a stab of alarm: what had Marianne told him?

Greenwood picked up the sugar and tore it open. His spoon jittered against the vitreous china saucer. 'I'm a bit shot,' he said, looking at his hands, 'so you'll have to excuse me if I can't remember exactly.'

'Of course.'

'But also, she didn't talk about you often, I'm afraid. I had the impression – no, I knew – that it was painful for her to think about you. What happened?'

'She didn't tell you?' Rowan looked at the cup between her hands.

'No.'

'It was a mess. The whole thing.'

'I know it was about the time her father died.'

Her heart gave an exaggerated beat. 'Yes. *Because* he died.'

'What do you mean?'

Rowan made herself meet his eyes. 'I'm so ashamed of how I behaved. I understand why she didn't want to be friends afterwards.' He was waiting, watching her. Hadn't she come to ask *him* the questions? 'When Seb died,' she said, 'Marianne disappeared. I don't mean she ran away – just, she vanished.

She locked herself away. I wanted to support her but she wouldn't see me. At first I understood – she wanted to be alone with her family – but after a couple of weeks, I started to feel rejected. I know,' she glanced quickly at his face and then away again. 'Even saying it now, I'm mortified. The self-centredness.'

'It's not th—'

'Anyway, one day I went there when she'd told me not to and Jacqueline let me in. I went storming up to Mazz's room and told her that I wanted to help her, I was her friend, but it came out sounding . . . aggressive. She yelled at me – rightly – saying that I shouldn't have forced my way into the house, that Jacqueline shouldn't have let me in.' Rowan shook her head. 'I was so hurt, I flew off the handle.' She stopped for a moment and looked at her hands. In the past few days, she'd started biting her nails again and the tip of her index finger was red and swollen, throbbing. 'I don't know if Marianne told you but my mother had a heart attack at twenty-eight.'

He frowned. 'No, I didn't know that.'

'It was a congenital problem but no one knew until it was too late.'

'She died? How old were you?'

'Eighteen months. My dad brought me up but he was away a lot with work and there were a lot of babysitters and "aunties". The Glasses became a sort of surrogate family so when Seb died, I grieved, too, but all of a sudden I was on the outside. It was like being bereaved twice: Seb first, and then all of them.'

Greenwood looked pained.

'But I don't want to make excuses. I said some unforgivable things and she . . . didn't forgive me.'

'Her father's death obviously affected her very deeply. More deeply even than you would expect.'

'Peter told me. Turk.'

'Yes, he worried about Marianne. How hard she pushed herself.' His attention was caught by a movement under the next table: a pug curled at its owner's feet, concealed from view from the counter by a tartan shopper. 'Marianne used to say that about you,' he said, focusing again. 'You pushed her – challenged her. She said you made her think.'

Rowan was sceptical. 'She was surrounded by thinkers.'

'Of a different kind. Her parents, her brother, were into politics, current affairs, but she said the two of you talked about novels and films. And art – she said you knew a lot, especially for a teenager.'

'No. I'm interested but I don't know much. She was fooled by first impressions. The day we first met properly, out of school, we talked about Andrew Wyeth and I'd just read a book on him. Pure chance. After that, I'll admit, I used to mug up a bit.'

'She said she worked in images and you worked in words.'

'Total flattery.'

'Do you write?'

'No. Well, I start things, short stories, but then . . . I'm channelling my energy into my PhD. It feels more realistic.'

Greenwood's hands fluttered on the tabletop, a movement by which he managed to convey, *Maybe but is that everything?* Now the pug hauled itself to its feet and staggered arthritically in their direction. It went straight for Greenwood, bumping its head against his shin, and he put down his hand and made a surreptitious fuss of it. 'At some point,' he said to Rowan, 'I need to pick up my things but I can't face it just yet.'

'No, I understand.'

'But I do have to come round to the studio soon, I've been meaning to ring you. Saul – the gallerist in New York – he's going ahead with the show and I told him I'd draft some catalogue copy. I always wrote her copy so . . .' He looked down suddenly and she realised he was crying. To avoid embarrassing him, she put her hand down to the pug but it shied away.

In her peripheral vision, Greenwood blotted his eyes with a paper napkin.

'I've got a key but I'll call ahead. I live in Oxford so it's not a . . .'

'Do you?'

'Yes.' He was surprised by her surprise.

'With the gallery being in London, I assumed you lived here.' His media profile had led her to that conclusion, too, the pictures in Londoner's Diary and *Metro*.

'I moved when I split up with my wife. Marianne was in Oxford, obviously, but, quite independently, my daughter was about to start at St Helena's. The plan had always been that she would board but, after the divorce, we thought she'd have more stability if she lived with one of us.'

Interesting that he, not her mother, had made the move. But Sophie Lawrence's job was in London, too, at Channel 4, and perhaps she'd preferred not to live in the same city as her husband's new squeeze.

He drained his coffee and looked at the clock over the counter, not realising that she could see him in the mirror. Rowan felt a burst of panic: he was going to leave and she hadn't asked him anything yet.

'Had Marianne mentioned me recently?'

Greenwood frowned. 'No, I don't think so. Would she have? Why do you ask?' He looked at her with new interest and she shook her head as if to dismiss the query, irritated with herself.

'I suppose I'm just painfully aware that we won't have the chance to make things up now.'

'If it's any comfort, I know Jacqueline's pleased to be back in touch with you,' he said. 'She said she was sad when you parted ways.' Shrugging back his cuff, he rather hammily acted surprise. 'I'm afraid I have to go. I've got a meeting at twelve-thirty.'

'Apologies again for having ambushed you.'

'If it helped at all, I'm glad.'

Scrambling to think, she put on her jacket. Greenwood stepped aside to let her go first then reached forward to open the door. As casually as possible, she said, 'Do you represent Michael Cory?'

'Me? No. I wish I did but he's with Saul Hander. Saul and I have a relationship – hence Marianne showing with him – and I had a small show of Cory's photographs about eighteen months ago, but no, I don't represent him.'

'Marianne knew him.' Blood boomed in her ears. *So blunt, so unsubtle.* 'He was at the funeral.'

'Yes.' The door closed behind them, scooping the warmth and comforting hubbub back inside. A gust of wind ruffled Greenwood's hair and his voice sounded colder as he asked, 'Why?'

'We talked about him a lot at the time of the Hanna Ferrara portrait,' she said. 'It intrigued us, the idea that a picture could have an effect like that in the real world – make things happen. Her nervous breakdown – the end of her career, essentially.'

'That was never Michael's intention.'

'No, I'm sure.'

'So . . . ?'

'I just found it interesting that Marianne met – knew – someone we'd talked about as complete outsiders. I wonder whether she ever told him about it.'

Greenwood looked at her. 'It's possible,' he said. 'They were spending time together, talking a lot. Michael was painting her portrait.'

Thirteen

Last night, preparing for the London trip, she'd gone looking for Cory online. She'd been met with near-silence. Despite the hundreds of articles about him, there was almost nothing he had written himself or even said. She'd found three quotes in total, two of those about Picasso's use of colour in the portraits of Dora Maar.

The third was included in archived copy about his second exhibition, portraits of young actors whom he'd met by going to auditions himself. The exhibition had been called *Ambition*. 'What interests me about these people,' he'd said, 'is their confidence, hope, the will to do good work and succeed, but also, beneath the surface – not far beneath – their vanity, hubris, the fear of exposing themselves, failing publicly. Acting is intriguing because it's an egotistical profession – at least it has that reputation – but to do it well is to erase oneself and become a human canvas for a portrait of someone else.'

He'd been twenty-six at the time, and after that, he'd apparently gone off the idea of explaining himself. Just before midnight, however, she'd come across a reference to a book called *Stranger in the Mirror: Artists and the Art of Portraiture*, published last September. To her amazement, Cory was a contributor.

She'd rung from the train to find out if Blackwell's had a copy in stock and came directly from the station. As she walked through the door, she took a deep breath, filling herself up with the chemical smell of photographic paper as if it were the aroma of baking bread. Over the years, she and Marianne must have spent weeks here, looking at the posters and post-cards on the lower level or up among the bookshelves on the narrow mezzanine.

For the price, she'd expected a beautifully produced hard-back but when she located the book, it looked like a periodical, even a student anthology, with its flimsy paper cover and grainy image of a gilt-framed mirror. The interviews inside, printed verbatim in Courier and laid out as simple Q&As, were like transcripts of police interrogations. Nonetheless, the project clearly had cachet: the list of contents featured two other very well-known names.

The author, Elizabeth Rees-Hamilton, gave each artist a brief biographical introduction then interviewed him or her in depth about their process, how they selected subjects and conducted sittings, whether or not they worked from photo-graphs, their influences and preoccupations. Most of the interviews covered twenty pages but a couple extended over thirty.

Cory's entry was seven pages, and the introduction took up most of the first. Clearly, he'd been a difficult subject. Other artists were keen to talk about their craft; their answers often ran for a page or more, taking the question as a starting point for broader discussion. Cory, by contrast, gave direct answers but nothing more. None of his responses exceeded a paragraph, and his brevity created an impression of impenetrability. Control. Asked if he would describe how it was different to paint a woman with whom he was in a relationship, his answer was 'No'.

At other times, impatience shimmered off the page. 'I work exclusively from life,' he said. 'I never use photo-graphs. They're dangerous, they fix a person in a split second, and emphasise one aspect – the aspect of that second, which may not even be honest – above all others. People shift, change – they're Protean. When I paint, that is what I want to capture.'

'Lightning in a bottle?' Rees-Hamilton suggested.

'If you want,' he'd said, and Rowan imagined a dismissive shrug. 'For me,' he'd countered, 'a successful portrait is multi-layered, it reveals its secrets over time, like a person does. As a viewer, you get to know a good painting – you build a relationship with it. The layers of knowing are thin, fine – like paint itself. They are subtle. When I'm painting a portrait, my job is to take that knowledge, my understanding of the person, and express it. I get to know my subject intimately, understand him or her in a way that perhaps he hasn't been understood, even known, since childhood.'

'What do you say,' Rees-Hamilton had asked, 'to people who accuse you, quite literally, I think, of psychologically deconstructing your subjects, peeling back the "layers" you talk about until they are uncovered, unmasked? Naked.'

'I say, yes, I have achieved what I set out to do. I have been successful.'

St Mary's was chiming six as Rowan left Blackwell's, and the pavement was busy with students returning from their day's work at the library or the labs on Long Wall Street. As she crossed the road, eyes down, she was almost hit by a man on a mountain bike. 'Fuck's sake – watch where you're going!' he yelled after her.

Once she'd passed Wadham, the street grew quieter. Through the ornate wrought-iron gates at Trinity, the long lawn stretched away, empty and dark, towards windows whose yellow warmth seemed impossibly remote. Without the sun, the temperature had dropped sharply.

Nevertheless, she was sweating. Greenwood must have known about Cory's methods, his forensic psychological investigations – hadn't he been worried? Why had he let her do it?

'*Let?*' Marianne's voice suddenly, laughing in disbelief. '*Let? You think I would let my boyfriend – anyone – decide what I could and couldn't do? Come on.*'

'Yes, why did he *let* you? He knows about Hanna Ferrara, everyone does. Did he know about Greta Mulraine, too? A breakdown and a suicide, and he still let you do it? With your history?'

'*Maybe he knew it was what I wanted. Have you considered that? That you can love someone enough to let them make their own decisions?*'

'Did he know what you wanted? Really? I spoke to him today, Marianne, and I don't think he knew you at all. Not the things that mattered.'

When Rowan opened the door, Adam stood spot-lit on the step. He wore jeans and a dark jacket, no overcoat, but as he leaned in to kiss her cheek, he was warm, as if he'd worked up a cosy fug in the car on the way from Birmingham and it still surrounded him. She felt the old buzz again, still there.

'You didn't need to ring the bell,' she said, letting him in. 'How was the conference?'

'Windowless room, terrible coffee – pretty standard. How was London?'

'Oh, fine. Would you like a drink? Beer?'

'Love one but I'd better not.'

'Coffee? It's not Peter Turk-class but it's good.'

'No, thanks. It's terrible, the road to Cambridge, all cross-country, no motorway. I should get going; it'll probably freeze later on.' He looked at the table. 'Any post?'

'A few bits. They're in the box.'

'Great.' Flicking through, he pocketed the bank letter and bill from Thames Water. 'I'll pay this before we get cut off.' He glanced upstairs. 'Right, I'll run up to Dad's desk then I'll get going. I've got a supervision first thing with a student who actually does the work.' He glanced at the book in her hand. '*Catholic Gentry in English Society*?'

'It's a page-turner.'

He smiled. 'Well, I won't keep you from it.'

Squashing herself into a corner of the sofa, she listened as he moved around the study, playing the old floorboards like piano keys in dire need of tuning. Seb used to pace while he talked on the phone, and she'd pictured him as a lion, compact and muscular, measuring that area of carpet as if it were the footprint of a cage from which he might suddenly spring.

After a couple of minutes, the study door shut and there were footsteps on the stairs. Adam appeared in the doorway holding a thick A4-sized manila envelope.

'You found what you needed?'

He held it up. 'Deeds. When the dust settles, we're going to sell the house.'

'Sell it?' She spoke without thinking; the words jumped out of her mouth.

'I know. But after what happened . . .' The light seemed to fade from his eyes, as if he'd just remembered. 'Neither of us can imagine living here again, Mum and I. Every time we looked at the garden, we'd just . . .'

'No, of course.' She shook her head. 'Sorry, it was just the shock – I hadn't thought. And I couldn't imagine this place without you all here.' As soon as she'd said it, she wanted to kick herself again but Adam nodded.

'Exactly.'

—

His presence, brief as it was, made the house feel less alien, and when he'd gone, she stayed in the sitting room and watched TV. She was too unsettled to read. She considered going for a walk to try to burn off some of the nervous energy but she didn't want to come back into the empty house. Even at six, she'd spun around twice on Norham Road thinking someone was behind her.

She was starting to develop a siege mentality about the house, she recognised, as if as soon as the sun went down, a ring of darkness pulled around it, filled with threats. She'd never liked being alone at night. As a teenager, she used to sit up until the small hours when her father was travelling, her body tensing at every sound outside. Several times over the years she'd stood at the back door, knuckles white on the carving knife as she waited for the handle to turn from the other side. She'd gone to school exhausted. She'd be able to cope with that house now but Fyfield Road was different.

There was no blind at the window over the sink and at the end of the evening, she kept her eyes down as she washed up the dinner things. Reaching to turn off the tap, however, she caught her own eye in the reflection and thought about Cory at the wake.

I see you, his stare had seemed to say. *I see you and I am not afraid to look.*

She turned quickly, hair lifting off her shoulders, and as she did, she saw a movement on the other side of the glass. She went cold.

Giving herself no time to hesitate, she grabbed the key from the ladybird dish and rammed it into the hole. In a single fluid move, she unlocked the door, kicked it open and sprung out on to the patio.

Nothing. The patio was empty. She scanned the rest of the garden as far as it was visible – surely as far as anyone could have moved in the time – but no one was there. The bare branches of the birch trees rattled in the breeze, an ironic round of applause. She'd seen something blown on the wind, that was all, perhaps just the dead leaves that even now were whirling around her feet.

Fourteen

Summertown was the northernmost part of Oxford, the last airy streets before the bypass and then fields and villages, Woodstock, the Cotswolds. Beyond a certain point on the Banbury Road, there were few, if any, faculty buildings or university offices. The city's professionals lived here, doctors and lawyers, the more financially successful of the dons, sending their children to its clutch of over-achieving schools – Oxford High, Cherwell, St Edward's and St Helena's.

Resolutely middle-class, then, always, but since she'd last been back, the flavour of the place had changed. The Oxfam shop still held out, along with the Blue Cross and the independent bookshop, but Farrow & Ball had muscled in, and JoJo Maman Bébé. Bang & Olufsen was round the corner on South Parade. The video shop, the family-run Italian and the bakery where they used to buy sandwiches were gone and instead there were estate agents. How many, for God's sake? Hamptons, John D Wood, Savills, Chancellors, Knight Frank – by the end of the little parade she wanted to laugh.

She stopped to look in the window of Strutt & Parker. The prices were dizzying: two and a half million, three and a quarter. Her eyes found a house very like the Glasses' on Bradmore Road, the street that ran parallel to Fyfield. Like theirs, it had six bedrooms but the garden was smaller and a note said it needed updating, agent-speak for a total gut-job. The price was still four million pounds.

We're going to sell. Did Adam and Jacqueline own it together, then? Had Marianne owned a third? What if she'd been in the way, living there, while Adam had needed the money? The madness of the idea: Adam – hey, why not her mother? – bumping Mazz off to realise some cash.

She'd brought Jacqueline's African basket with her, planning to go to the Co-op, but in a what-the-hell frame of mind all of a sudden, she went to Marks & Spencer instead. She wanted that version of life today, easy and comfortable, no cutting corners, getting by. Under the bright lights, in front of fridges stocked with expensive pre-prepared meals, the phantoms of the small hours disappeared, vampires turned to ashes by the sun.

Shopping done, she headed back towards the centre of town but instead of going directly to the house, she turned left on Belbroughton Road and then left again.

St Helena's occupied a redbrick building with the same Neo-Gothic architecture as Keble College. A long grey-stone wall ran the length of the site, enclosing the playground and the netball courts, and blocking any view of the ground-floor classrooms. 'A castle's curtain wall,' Marianne said once.

Rowan had laughed. 'Keeping the succulent damsels of north Oxford safe from marauding gallants.'

Some of the current damsels were playing netball; the scuff of plimsolls on asphalt and urgent calls of '*Here!*' reached her over the top. Until she met Marianne, Rowan had spent a significant amount of time devising ways to get out of games. At thirteen and fourteen, she'd relied on the old standards – chilblains, twisted ankles – but then the fact that her father wasn't around to write notes became an advantage. The times she'd got him to do it – she only had to say the word 'period' – he'd written the letters on his computer, printed them off and signed at the bottom with an indecipherable tangle of blue biro. For her fifteenth birth-day, he'd given her his old laptop.

Friendship with Marianne changed her attitude. On paper Mazz had looked like the classic games-dodger but though she'd drawn the line at the human misery of hockey, she'd been enthusiastic about swimming and netball. She did it for herself, she explained, not because she was obliged to. 'Apart from swimming, I actually don't like sports – and I much prefer swimming in the sea. But you think better when you exercise. I sleep better and think better so I paint better, and I get it done on school time. Where's the negative?'

The idea that your attitude could repurpose a necessary thing, turn it into something you did for yourself, was one of several subtle but key shifts that Marianne caused in Rowan's thinking and, with each one, she felt less like a pinball batted between the twin flippers of school and her father, and more self-determining, in control.

But her relationship with the Glasses had opened her eyes in so many ways. Successful as her father was by that point, and despite the travelling, his focus somehow remained narrow, his engagement with the world confined to the sector of it in which he operated; he read the business pages, and the news for its effect on business. Jacqueline and Seb, on the other hand, were hungry for all the knowledge they could lay hands on, whether it related to their expertise or not. At Fyfield Road, newspapers and periodicals were filleted, every flake picked off the bone. They offered their opinions easily, in public forums as well as private. At an instance of gender inequality in any field, Jacqueline considered it her duty to engage. In those years, there had been several protracted scraps across the pages of the *Guardian*.

Rowan still detected an 'us and them' attitude in her father, lingering doubts about his right to be seen and heard in the world. He seemed to operate with the question, 'Why would it be me?' whereas, drafting an op-ed piece for the *New York*

Times at the kitchen table one afternoon, working herself into a righteous stew, Jacqueline said, 'If not us, girls, then who?'

He'd only met Jacqueline and Seb on two occasions: once when he'd come to a Sixth-Form parents' evening and the second time when, to Rowan's amazement, he'd picked her up on his way home from the airport. Seb had said a brief hello before disappearing to his study but Jacqueline had cajoled him into having a glass of wine with her and Rowan had had to endure the spectacle of her father trying to appear undaunted by Jacqueline's intelligence and confidence, her untamed hair and bangles.

She remembered her own anxiety that he would embarrass her by saying something that highlighted the gulf between them and the Glasses, or else by morphing into Uriah Heep in the face of Jacqueline's glory. At the same time, she'd felt proud: she, Rowan, was part of the furniture at Fyfield Road by then, accepted and liked by the whole family. The people who intimidated her father were her friends.

Until Marianne began at St Helena's, Rowan had been waging a campaign to start boarding. At the end of Lower Fifth, three teachers wrote in her report that she seemed tired and less able than usual to concentrate. In April, just as the term had begun, someone actually *had* tried the front door in the middle of the night. From an upstairs window, she'd watched as the old drunk who shambled up and down their road after closing time staggered away, but she'd had weeks of insomnia afterwards. Her father dismissed it, saying Jimmy Pagnell was harmless. 'And the only reason you go to St Helena's is because you got a scholarship – we definitely can't afford for you to board.'

'Aren't you head of South America now?' she'd yelled at him from halfway up the stairs. 'And you still earn nothing?'

'How dare you?' he'd growled and she'd watched him master the urge to come charging after her. 'Everything I do is for you – all the travel, all the hours.'

She'd looked him in the eye. 'Bullshit.'

By October, however, she'd been glad he'd said no. Strict rules determined when boarders could leave the school grounds; living at home, alone, she governed herself and could spend as much time at Fyfield Road as she wanted.

When James Greenwood told her he'd moved to Oxford so his daughter could live at home, she'd been jealous. It was ludicrous, she was thirty-two, but the contrast still hurt. What was it like to have a father who would uproot himself from London and commute for hours every day to give you a stable home life?

Inside the school the bell rang, the sound unchanged since their day. Lunchtime: 12.35. The scuffing stopped, and a minute later the girls filed off to the locker rooms, voices fading.

Bryony was eighteen, Turk said, she would leave school in the summer so, unless the rules were different now, she'd be allowed out for an hour at lunchtime. Sixth-formers would start coming through the side gate any minute.

Could Rowan really talk to her? Going to see Greenwood was one thing but waiting for his daughter outside school was a huge risk. Bryony was bound to tell him and if his antennae weren't up already, they surely would be then. She had to be so careful that, in trying to keep Marianne's secret, she didn't alert people to its existence. On the other hand, if they had been as close as Turk said, Bryony might know something valuable.

She crossed the road and hovered near the laurel bush where the Cherwell boys used to wait for them. Jacqueline's bag was heavy so Rowan took it off her shoulder and propped it carefully on top of the wall. Over the road, the heavy bolt was drawn and the side gate opened, emitting three girls in the Sixth Form's version of uniform: pleated navy skirts that took a liberal interpretation of 'on the knee', oversized navy jumpers and the grey school blazer.

135

Patent loafers and scarves so huge they were better suited for the gulag than a trip to Starbucks. All three clutched mobiles between fingers that barely protruded beyond their cuffs. Rowan felt a burst of nostalgia. Things had been so much simpler then, pure potential, nothing screwed up. Nobody dead.

Another pair came out, deep in conversation, one with a messy blonde topknot, the other with a dark one. The blonde girl took a pair of sunglasses out of her blazer pocket and put them on. Would she recognise Bryony? Rowan wondered. She called up a mental picture of her at the funeral and remembered her fine features and high forehead. Her hair was a honey shade of blonde, golden, not pale like that.

The gate opened again and again, barely closing between the little groups now, and she remembered the urgency of making the most of the hour outside school walls. Pairs and trios, a couple of fours. No one came out alone, it wasn't allowed. She used to think it was funny, the school's excessive caution regarding her safety for that one hour of broad daylight when, at night, she'd been home alone for years. A few girls glanced over, trained to be suspicious of anyone hanging round, but they saw a woman and looked away.

Her phone began to ring and she took it out of her pocket. Another unknown number. Casting a brief smile at a pair of girls who were looking over, she answered.

'Is this Rowan Winter?'

She barely had time to register the voice – male, an American accent – before he said, 'This is Michael Cory. I'm sorry to call out of the blue. James Greenwood gave me your number – I'm a friend of Marianne's.'

She spun around, turning her back on the school. 'Yes, this is Rowan.' She'd given Greenwood her number yesterday; Cory must have spoken to him since then.

'I'm a painter,' he said, as if she wouldn't know. False modesty? Yes: if they'd talked about her, Greenwood must

136

have mentioned she'd asked about Cory. 'I was painting Marianne's portrait.'

'James told me. I saw him yesterday.' On the other side of the wall, a spider negotiated the frosty spokes of a web constructed between the branches of a rosebush.

'He said. I wondered, could I come talk to you? I want to finish the portrait – more than ever now – and James said you knew Marianne very well.'

'As teenagers, a long time ago. We met when she moved here from London.'

'Right. I'd love to talk to you about her. It's very important to me, for my work, to understand the person I'm painting. Now she's gone, I'm having to find other ways. Would it be possible?'

'Yes,' she said, mind whirling. 'I think so.'

'Tomorrow?'

'Tomorrow?' It seemed very soon.

'In the afternoon, about three o'clock. You're not busy?' It was a question but only just.

'I can make time,' she said. 'We could meet for coffee at Chez Gaston on North Parade – do you know it? It's a few minutes' walk from Fyfie—'

'I'll come to the house,' he said, and before she could reply, 'I'll see you then – three tomorrow.' He hung up without saying goodbye.

Fifteen

As Rowan reached for the box inside the wardrobe, the spring in the chair seat gave way under her back foot. Without thinking, she grabbed at the shelf but the whole wardrobe came with it, empty hangers ringing in alarm. It loomed over her, poised at tipping point; time stopped. By some miracle, she regained her balance and shoved her shoulder against it as hard as she could. It smacked the wall, tottered, then rocked heavily back into position, hangers jangling. Looking down, she saw that the floor was visibly higher at the wall than at the wardrobe's front feet. It was a great lump of Victorian hardwood, a thug of a piece of furniture: it could have killed her. It certainly would have broken bones. Pulse beating in her head, she stepped gingerly down from the chair. The hangers chimed – *next time, next time* – as she transferred her weight back to the floor.

On top of the box was the velvet pouch with the silver locket she'd inherited from her grandmother and her mother's single string of pearls. She never wore them so they were visible, a girl in pearls she was not, but occasionally, if she was wearing a high-necked jumper, she put them on just to have them next to her skin. They'd been too precious to risk leaving in London.

Setting the bag aside, she put the box on the bed and lifted the lid off, feeling the little *whoomph* of suction. She'd thrown away the postmarked envelope but she'd kept Marianne's card and put it in here with the sketches; it had seemed the best place.

I need to talk to you.

Holding the card with both hands, she stared at the words as if they would tell her something new. Just as when she first saw them, they seemed to pulse with energy.

Why, Marianne? she asked. *Was it Cory? What does he know?*

As she put on her make-up, she rehearsed her answers again as if she were getting ready for an interview. '*Girding your loins?*' said a dry voice, and Rowan smiled at the mirror. They'd come across the expression in an old translation of the *Aeneid*.

She looked better today, at least. Nights of broken sleep had made her feel sick with tiredness, and needing a clear head, she'd come looking in the bathroom cabinet last night for antihistamines or Nytol to help knock her out. Instead, among a clutch of pill pots, she'd discovered a tub of Ambien with Marianne's name on it. The bottle had contained twenty-eight pills, the label said, *one per night as needed for sleep*, but when Rowan tipped the contents on to her palm, there were only five tablets left. It was dated last month. She'd put four pills back in and swallowed the other. When she'd turned off the light twenty minutes later, sleep came almost immediately, heavy hands pressing her body down into the darkness.

Ten to three. In the kitchen, she made sure that nothing telling would come up if she had to open her computer and then, to be safe, she cleared her search history.

Coming back upstairs to the first floor, she opened the door to Seb and Jacqueline's old bedroom. She'd been in when she'd searched the house but only briefly; that Marianne didn't use it had been obvious at once. Time seemed to have stopped here, too. Nothing was new or perishable, there were no magazines or house plants, but it didn't have the same museum feel as the study, the reverence implied by the order and cleanliness there. This room was clean, dusted regularly, but the air felt old, trapped unstirring, and though the curtains in the big bay window were open, the light was oddly muted, as if it came filtered through gauze.

The right-hand side of the dresser was empty but the left, she'd discovered, was still filled with Seb's things: socks, cotton boxers, white T-shirts, jumpers that she remembered. The short top drawer held his reading glasses and a dark leather wallet with some old credit cards, a paper driving licence, and a creased white-bordered photograph. Opening the wallet, Rowan eased the picture out again.

Twenty-five at the most, Jacqueline stood on a beach in winter, boots planted firmly on shingle, the backdrop a mass of leafless trees and a turbid sky rendered hyper-real by the film and the print's high-gloss finish. She wore a woollen greatcoat, her hands thrust deep in the pockets, and her hair streamed sideways in the wind as she looked at the photographer, her face soft with love. Twenty-five – before Adam and Marianne, before she was married. Rowan looked at her with a skein of emotion: nostalgia, love of her own, pride – here was her Jacqueline, a woman of substance even then – and yet, knowing what the future held, Rowan felt pain, a protective urge so strong she wanted to reach into the picture and grab her, King Kong-like, pull her out of the narrative that was already being written for her. Rowan felt her determination strengthen: she would do what she could. She would protect her now.

Putting the picture back in the wallet, she closed the drawer and went to the window where she positioned herself out of sight behind the curtain.

The street was empty, people at work, children still at school. There were five or six cars parked at the kerb, her elderly silver Golf among them, but none moving. The heavy glazed-cotton curtains smelled dusty. When she held her breath, the only thing she could hear was a single bird in the tangled branches of the willow.

As St Giles rang the hour, however, a sleek silver car, a Mercedes, came down Crick Road, paused at the junction then pulled sharply round the corner and parked. A few seconds later, the driver's door opened and she saw jeans, a dark coat, a shaved head. He locked the car with the fob, the lights flashed, then he turned and strode across the street. On the pavement, he stopped to look up at the house just as she'd done on the day of the funeral. What was he thinking? His face, upturned, gave nothing away.

Staying out of sight, she moved away from the window and made her way quietly downstairs.

Through the coloured glass panels, his silhouette was round-headed, square-shouldered. The tips of his ears stuck out slightly, as if primed for listening. She had the advantage of the step but he was still taller than her by several inches. Taking a breath to compose herself, she opened the door. A momentary impression: grey needle-cord shirt, black coat. Grey eyes.

'Michael? Hello, I'm Rowan.'

The hand he extended was dry and callused but of course, she realised, he worked with his hands, pencils and paints, brushes. Knives.

He made an infinitesimal movement forward into her body space. The natural thing was to stand aside, let him in, but she stood her ground, obliging him to shift back, wait.

'We've seen each other before, haven't we?' he said, looking her in the eye. 'At the wake.'

'Yes.' Now she opened the door wider and stepped back. 'Come in.'

'Thanks.' A twitch in his eyebrow said he'd registered the exchange, made a note.

In the hallway, he took off his coat. Rowan waited to see whether he would give it to her or, without thinking, turn to the pegs himself. How familiar was he with the house? Thwarting her, however, he did neither, and instead put it over his arm. He glanced into the sitting room and then up the stairs as if he expected Marianne to appear.

'Would you like some coffee?'

'Sure.'

On the way down to the kitchen, she felt his eyes on the back of her neck as plainly as if his gaze had physical weight. While she made the coffee, he moved around the room, and from the corner of her eye, she saw him tip his head to look at the books stacked by the sofa. Her computer and papers were at the end of the table and he stopped and picked up *Catholic Gentry*, turned it over to read the back. His self-assurance was striking: other people would hover, make awkward conversation, but he seemed to feel no need for that sort of social nicety.

'You're studying?'

'For a doctorate. History.'

'Where are you doing it? Not here.'

Was that last part a question or not? Rowan wasn't sure. 'No, not here,' she said. 'London.'

'Which college?'

'You're well informed. People don't necessarily think of London as being collegiate.'

He gave a half-shrug. 'I have a friend who's a professor at Imperial. She's American, an old friend from California, but she lives here now.'

On the point of saying something about it being good to have old friends around, living overseas, she stopped herself. Confident as he was, he'd no doubt be baffled by the idea of needing familiar faces. The kettle whistled and she filled the pot. Cory pulled out a chair at the table and dropped his coat over the back.

When she brought the coffee over, he gave her a crooked sort of smile, one side of his mouth lifting but not the other. His eyes were on her face again. 'Thanks for doing this,' he said. 'I appreciate it.'

'I hope I can help. How far along are you with the portrait?'

'I'll be painting soon.' He pulled his mug closer and looked at the raised pattern in the china. 'I've done a lot of the preparatory work, the drawing. Marianne was working hard herself, for her show, so she didn't have as much time as I would have liked but, you know, that was fine. If you want to paint interesting people, you have to expect them to be busy.'

How reasonable of you, Rowan was tempted to say.

'My method, what I try to do, is build up as complete a picture of a subject as possible. The intersection of personality, personal history and appearance, how the former influence the latter – that's what interests me.' He took a sip of coffee then set the mug deliberately back down. The nail on his right thumb was longer than the others, purposefully so, she guessed; by the look of the moon of gunmetal-grey paint trapped underneath, he used it as a tool.

'Marianne intrigued me,' he said, 'more than anyone I've painted before.'

'Really?'

'She was so . . . complex. We talked a lot, hours and hours, but the better I got to know her, the more convinced I was there was something else there, another layer, something that was key to *getting* her, you know?'

Rowan's stomach turned over. 'What sort of thing?'

'That's what I'm trying to figure out.'

She put her coffee down. 'Excuse me if this sounds rude but are you sure you *should* be painting her portrait? Now, I mean.'

'Absolutely.'

'I'm far from an expert but it's hard not to know your reputation.'

'Hanna Ferrara.'

'Yes, but, from what I've heard, some of your other work, too. Marianne's family are grieving; they . . .'

'Marianne wanted me to do it.'

'Have you talked to her mother about this?'

'We met at the funeral – James introduced us. She knows.'

'Are you going to talk to *her* about Marianne?'

'I hope so. I want to talk to everyone who knew her well.' Cory looked Rowan straight in the eye and at this range, across the narrow table, she saw that his pupils were ringed with a blue so dark it was almost navy. Tiny tendrils snaked out into his irises. The day of the funeral she'd thought he wasn't attractive but she could see now why some people might go for him. There was something purely masculine about the width of his face and the size of his nose, which was slightly longer at the tip, giving it an arrowhead shape when seen straight on. If anything, it was hooked rather than Roman but in combination with the shaved head and broad shoulders, it made her think of Romans – ancient ones. He looked gladiatorial. And beneath that nose, his soft, full mouth seemed particularly sensual. Strength and sensitivity – potent combination. Would Marianne have thought so? Yes, Rowan knew she would.

'Why did you two fall out?' he said abruptly.

'Because I was a moron.'

'Frank.'

'There's no point being anything else now. Did she tell you about it?'

He shook his head.

'It was just after her father died. She needed space and I didn't give it to her. It was stupid, she was so raw and I was too selfish to leave her alone.' Rowan felt her cheeks go red.

'It's a shame. James said Jacqueline told him you'd been pretty much part of the family. Hence your being here now, presumably?'

She held the eye contact. 'If I can help her feel easier about the house, Marianne's work being safe here, it's one thing she doesn't have to worry about. And I can work anywhere.' She gestured towards the pile of papers. 'Should I ever feel motivated to work again at any point. I'm supposed to be researching a couple of archives at the Bodleian but I haven't got there yet.'

She'd barely touched her coffee but Cory's mug was empty. 'You've seen her new work,' he said, and again she wasn't sure if he was asking or merely stating a fact. 'What do you think?'

Self-conscious about offering her half-baked amateur opinion, Rowan paused. 'I think they're incredibly powerful,' she said. 'The first time I saw them, especially the later ones, I felt . . . unsettled. Unnerved. They're angry, they're political. As I said, I'm no expert but I think they're brilliant.'

She waited for him to respond, to agree or disagree, but instead he pushed back his chair and stood. 'Let's go look at them. They're still in the studio, right?'

She hung back to see if he would take the lead but at the foot of the stairs, he gestured for her to go first. Manners or had he second-guessed her? It was impossible to tell; he was so difficult to read. She felt his eyes on her again as she reached the first-floor landing but when she turned, he smiled, unembarrassed.

'Where did you do your work with her?' she asked.

'Here, for the most part, to maximise the time. We worked around her schedule – she'd work and then when she needed a break, we'd talk and I'd sketch.'

Famous as she was, Rowan remembered, Hanna Ferrara had blocked out time in her schedule so that she could sit for him. Considering how much she was paid per film before he destroyed her career, it must have cost her millions. By contrast, Marianne had made Cory, so much more established than she was, fit around her. Rowan suppressed a smile, *that's my girl*, but then had another, more disturbing thought: if he was prepared to do that, he must have thought he was on to something good.

'Did you work up here?' She turned and saw his face washed in the cold January light spilling from the studio.

'Yes. It was where she was most herself.'

She made a noise meant to communicate 'Interesting' but he was right, of course. And it told her something else: Marianne had let him spend time up here. She'd always been protective of her studios, the one in Bethnal Green, too; she'd let people see them, she wasn't precious or superstitious, but in the years Rowan had known her, she and Turk were the only people Mazz had ever let spend longer than a few minutes in her work-space.

Two sets of feet echoing on the boards today. The pictures were behind the old bathroom wall, hidden from view, but Cory headed straight for them. She followed then stood back and watched him. Again, the apparent lack of social awareness: as soon as he saw the paintings, it was as if she ceased to exist.

His way of looking was physical. He moved frequently, standing away from the pictures and then swooping again to home in on a detail. At one point, his face was so close to the girl in the fourth picture Rowan thought he was going to kiss her. He tipped his head this way and that, pulled back, narrowed his eyes, brought his fingertips to within half an inch of the canvas and followed the movement in the paint as if he were stroking it.

For a couple of minutes, neither of them spoke. The silence in the room became a bubble that held them both inside, part of the world but separate from it, too. Rowan thought of the afternoon Marianne had drawn her naked, the way time had seemed to ebb and flow like water.

'You're right.' He spun on his heel.

The bubble burst and the world rushed back in. 'What?'

'They are brilliant.'

Rowan smiled, proud for Marianne and relieved not to have embarrassed herself.

'They're a self-portrait, obviously – you know that.'

'What do you mean?'

Was it her imagination or did Cory look as if she'd disappointed him?

'Did she tell you that?' she asked.

'She didn't need to.'

'What are you saying? That she had an eating disorder?'

Now he looked at her as if she were the village idiot. 'Plainly not. How well did you know her?'

Stung, Rowan bit down the sharp response that jumped to the tip of her tongue.

'She's expressing how she feels,' he said. 'Consumed, destroyed from the inside out. It's not about eating or not eating – it's about *being eaten.*'

Rowan's face was still burning as she followed him back downstairs. She was furious with herself: the idea hadn't even occurred to her. He might not be right, necessarily, but she should at least have considered it. And now he thought she was stupid. Of course Marianne hadn't been anorexic – Rowan had never thought that for a second. She'd only said it because he'd put her on the back foot.

'Was she popular at school?' he asked over his shoulder.

'Popular?' Embarrassed and angry, she had to shut down the acid voice that said his real question was whether Marianne couldn't have done better for herself, friends-wise. 'Well, not in a cool-gang sort of way,' she said. 'Knowing her as well as you did' – she couldn't resist – 'you'll know she didn't have a group mentality, but, yes. She was funny and interesting – people liked having her around. She was always invited to parties.'

'Makes sense,' he said. It had seemed like the start of a line of questioning but when they reached the hall, he stopped abruptly and turned around. 'My coat's in the kitchen. I'll get it then I'm going to go.'

Rowan bristled. No doubt it was a cultural difference, just a way of talking, but the announcement irritated her, the implication that he was the one who decided how things were going to work. She listened as he took the stairs to the kitchen and tried to picture his movements, estimating how long it would take him to round the end of the table and fetch his coat from the chair. The seconds stretched. Maybe she should have gone down with him. What was he doing? She was on the point of going after him when there were footsteps on the tiles and a series of quick creaks as he jogged up.

He went straight to the telephone table where he casually took a pen from the pot and scribbled something on the pad. He tore off the top sheet and handed it to her like a doctor with a prescription. 'That's my cell. I've got yours, obviously. I'm going to be in Oxford for a few days so . . .'

'Are you?'

'I've booked a hotel. I've just driven up from London now, I came straight here, so I'm going to go and check in but I'll come by again tomorrow. We've got a lot to talk about.'

Sixteen

She listened as he crunched away across the gravel. She'd been standing in exactly the same spot, naked bar the patchwork quilt, when Theo stamped off home to his wife. She shuddered at the memory, and as she did, the telephone started ringing. There had only been two calls since she'd been here, one a gas supplier scouting for new business, the other Miriam Jacobs, Jacqueline's old roommate from her undergraduate days at Sussex, who'd just returned from a kibbutz, heard the news and phoned in a panic, having failed to get Jacqueline on her mobile. When she picked up this time, Rowan was surprised to hear Adam's voice.

'You're in,' he said. 'I thought you'd probably be at the library.'

'I haven't actually got there yet.'

'One of those days?' Before she could clarify, he said, 'I wanted to give you a call: I've been in touch with Savills to ask if they'll value the house and they've suggested Friday morning. I don't know what time you usually leave but I wondered if you'd mind letting them in? It won't take long, apparently. I'm sorry, it's a pain and . . .'

'No, it's absolutely fine. No problem.'

'You're sure?'

'Of course. And if there's anything else, will you let me know? I'm watering the plants.'

'Oh, yes – thank you. I totally forgot about that. Actually, though, I had another reason for calling. I've got to be in Oxford again on Friday, I'm coming to see Marianne's solicitor, but not until later, the afternoon – I won't be able to get there any earlier. Anyway, I wondered whether you were doing anything.'

For a moment, she was confused. Did he want her to go with him?

'In the evening, I mean,' he said, 'afterwards. Can I take you out to dinner?'

Rowan saw him on the stairs ahead of her, the moon through the landing window casting him in silhouette, Blondie's *Atomic* booming up from the ground floor. Of course he wasn't thinking about that, though. Even if he was single, he was grieving. He'd just lost his only sister.

'As a thank you,' he said, as if he'd read her mind, 'from us both, Mum and me.'

'You don't need to thank me. But yes, I'd love to.'

A blanket of heavy white cloud had covered the sky since the morning but while Cory had been at the house, the wind had picked up and driven it away. When she reached the studio again, the setting sun was a ball of brilliant orange. It poured through Adam's old window, filling the room with a peachy light that looked balmy and inviting but in fact offered no warmth at all.

One by one, she examined the paintings again. The girl on the chair with her unsettling smile and that luscious red apple: a low-calorie food but temptation, too, of course. Into Rowan's head came the lines of a poem she'd learned at school. *If you should meet a crocodile / Don't take a stick and poke him; / Ignore the welcome in his smile . . .* The second girl was sitting on the floor, her body tucked tightly into a corner. A book balanced on her bony knees, but she stared into middle-distance with a look in her eyes that was either dreamy or glazed. The third, incrementally smaller, hunched over a desk, her little head clamped between a pair of bright red Beats headphones. Hollow cheeks and, etched either side of her mouth, the faint beginnings of the lines Rowan thought of as anorexic parentheses. *For as he sleeps upon the Nile, / He thinner gets and thinner.*

The final picture was propped directly opposite the window, and it glowed as if the light were coming not from outside but from within it. She approached slowly, as if the tiny wasted figure curled on the floor might find a final desperate burst of energy and lunge out, snarling. That mouth – maw, she'd thought, the first time she'd seen it – all black and angry red, the missing teeth. She'd interpreted it as slack, open because its owner had no energy to close it, to suggest hunger, but now it was a scream, *The Scream*, a stretched O of fear and anguish turned towards the lovely varnished floor because there was no point in crying out any more: no one could help.

Cory was right. Of course he was right.

She remembered what Turk said about Marianne taking on her father's guilt as a way of staying close to him. Self-flagellation, he'd called it. 'She thought that if she pushed herself to breaking point, denied herself everything, even her health, she could pay. Atone.'

Consumed, destroyed from the inside out.

Light-headed suddenly, Rowan kneeled on the floor and leaned forward until her forehead touched the boards. With a rush, the room seemed to pull away, taking with it the twilight, the sound of a car on the road outside, the solidity of the floor beneath her. She was suspended, floating.

She was back in that afternoon again. Walking along Fyfield Road, Echo and the Bunnymen playing on the iPod that the Glasses had given her for her twenty-first, the sky deep blue and wide, the leaves on the trees still green, not yet turned brown by the drought that came later. The distant sound of children on one of the Dragon School's summer programmes shouting and laughing in the outdoor swimming pool. Then, through the bushes inside the front wall, she'd caught sight of something white, large. When she reached the end of the wall, she saw what it was.

She yanked the buds from her ears, feeling the blood drop from her face in a single sheet. The nausea was instant, too – intense sickness, as if the ball of fear suddenly thrust into her stomach was something she could vomit up, rid herself of that way. If only.

Oh, shit, Marianne. Oh shit, oh *shit*.

A police car squatted on the drive again, incongruous as a spaceship and just as terrifying.

Her heart thumped the back of her ribs like a fist and sweat made beads on her forehead. The days had begun to slip past, one after another, and she'd allowed herself to hope. Now she saw how naïve she'd been. What Marianne had done could never have stayed hidden.

The front door was open. The Glasses weren't good at security, they came home all the time to find they'd left the garden door unlocked, a ground-floor window ajar, but even they never left the front door open.

She took a series of steadying breaths and started walking but her mind seemed to have disconnected from her body. Her movements felt unnatural, as if she were operating her limbs with controls, a new driver in the cab of a bulldozer. Jerking, ungainly. Across the drive to the steps, skirting the car as if it were a dangerous animal. She stopped to listen. Silence in the house, not a sound apart from the beating of her heart. The world had gone quiet.

The door creaked as she pushed it further open. 'Hello?'

A moment passed and then she heard movement in the sitting room on her left. 'Rowan,' said a low voice. 'A family friend.'

Jacqueline's voice but cracked, barely recognisable.

Soft footsteps across the carpet and a uniformed police-woman appeared in the doorway, her face arranged in professional compassion. 'Rowan.'

'What is it? What's going on?'

'Come and sit down.' The woman reached out and put a hand under her elbow.

On unsteady legs, she traversed the carpet. At the sitting-room door, her eyes went straight to Jacqueline's face. Shock and disbelief. Desolation.

'What is it?' she heard herself say.

'Ro, Seb's had an accident.' Jacqueline's voice rose and fell, reaching her ears in waves.

An accident? Seb? For a moment she didn't understand. Then she realised – she'd misheard. Or Jacqueline had got it wrong – she was disorientated by what she'd just learned about her daughter; she was ... But no, a man was talking now. Rowan swung around. In the car, she caught. Dead at the scene; severity of the accident; a second fatality – a woman.

Dead, dead, dead – the word replaced the beat of her heart.

'The A34,' said the policeman, and she had the sudden dizzying urge to laugh. *The A34!* As if he were giving directions. As if they needed to know. As if it mattered what *fucking road* it was.

That was when she'd made herself look at Marianne. Rowan had known where she was sitting from the moment she came round the door, her stare had burned, but when their eyes met now, the look Marianne gave her branded Rowan like an iron. Shock and loss and a warning, fierce and unmistakable: *Don't you DARE.*

She'd had to get out of there. She'd turned and run, the door banging against the wall as she pushed it out of the way. The steps were a blur, she'd missed one, landed on her knees in the gravel. Torn denim, dirt. Up on her feet again and away down the street, not thinking, not stopping even when she heard the crack of the iPod on the pavement. To Norham Gardens then the University Parks, the lawns covered with people, picnics, newspapers, a game of boules. Pelting down the path, breath jagged, people turning to stare, but she reached the footbridge, took the steps at full tilt and down the other side, falling again then wading off into the undergrowth.

Long grass, cow parsley, nettles. She staggered, tripping on roots and brambles as she worked her way further and further in, away from the world and the people until their voices faded and she slumped against a tree, chest heaving, lungs and legs burning with acid. She slid down, bark rough through the fabric of her T-shirt. The rich smell of earth that never saw direct sun, dappling light, not lovely now but flickering and uncertain. She pulled up her knees, wrapping her arms around them so tightly that the ligaments in her back and shoulders hurt for days afterwards.

Seb was dead. Seb was dead, and she'd lost Marianne forever.

The wall was cold against her back, and the moonlight streaming through the window over her head picked out the shapes of the canvases, areas of white and cream paint, flesh tones. She saw the last woman again, her skin pale in the half-light like something dug up from the earth: a tuber, a worm. Repulsed, Rowan stood up to go.

At the top of the stairs, however, she stopped, switched on the lights and went to the back window. She looked over to the flats in Benson Place. The first two floors were dark but light shone from the third, deep and yellow, and sure enough, as she watched, a large figure moved into view.

Her heart thumped but then she had an idea: Jacqueline used to have a pair of binoculars – where were they? She moved casually away from the window then ran down through the house. In the cupboard under the stairs, she searched the tangle of shopping bags and gardening jackets

154

on the back of the door. They'd usually been here, hanging by their leather strap. She looked on the shelves among the cache of spare light bulbs, an old hand-vacuum, a dusty wicker basket of hats and gloves, and then among the coats on the pegs by the front door. She also drew a blank down in the kitchen, in the deep drawer where the odds and ends accumulated, old sunglasses and instruction manuals, a ball of rubber bands. Maybe Jacqueline took the binoculars with her when she moved out. They'd had sentimental value, Rowan remembered; they'd belonged to her father.

She'd have another look tomorrow, in the daylight. For now, she poured a glass of wine and carried it upstairs. She couldn't sit on display in the kitchen, like a mouse in a laboratory cage for the man in Benson Place to observe. Who was he? How could she find out? Maybe she just had to swallow her pride – her disgust – and ring Theo: he'd know. But then she remembered how close she'd sailed to the wind with him that night. 'Do you know something, Rowan?' he'd asked directly. No, she couldn't risk letting him know she was still digging, not unless she had to.

In the sitting room, she turned on the lamps, drew the curtains then called Peter Turk. The phone rang for a while and she was formulating a message when he picked up.

'You sound echoey,' she said. 'Where are you?' There was a splash, the sound of a large amount of water being displaced. 'Oh, God, you're in the bath. And I thought the day couldn't get any weirder.'

'There was a time when this would have made you the envy of thousands.'

Despite everything, she laughed. 'What did that feel like? Knowing girls – and boys – you'd never met were fantasizing about you. I can't imagine it.'

'Bizarre,' he said, and she heard water again, pictured him sliding lower, his torso filling the width of the tub. 'I hated all that; it was really . . . unsavoury. It made me feel sleazy.'

She believed it. Even in the early days, when he and the band had played the pub circuit in Oxford and Reading, the occasional small London gig, he'd never, as far as she knew, got off with any of the girls who'd sidled up to him when he came off-stage.

'In the nicest possible way,' he said, 'what do you want? My arm's getting cold.'

'I wanted to ask you about Michael Cory.'

'Cory? Why?'

'Did you know he was painting Marianne?'

'What? No.' A slap of water. He'd sat up again.

'James Greenwood told me, and then he – Cory – came here this afternoon.'

'She never told me.'

'I don't know how long it had been going on,' said Rowan, hearing the hurt in his voice. 'And the whole thing seems to have been on the down-low, as far as I can tell.' She paused. 'Cory's an odd fish.'

'No kidding.'

'You've met him?'

'Twice. Once at his show at the Greenwood, the photographs, and then there was a dinner last year, end of September, October, maybe. And he was at the funeral, obviously, but I didn't talk to him. Hold on, I can't have this conversation in the bath.' There was a tapping sound as he put the phone down, a surge of water, then footsteps on tiles. A few seconds later, he picked up again. 'Hi.'

'Did you talk to him at the dinner?'

'A bit, yeah, afterwards.'

'What about?'

'Mazz,' he said, realisation dawning. 'Fuck.'

'What did you say to him?'

'Nothing.' He tried to remember. 'No, nothing important – nothing personal. Just that we'd been friends for a long time – teenage misadventures, all that. Christ, and he was painting her? The sly fucker.'

'How much do you know about him?'

'A bit. Well, quite a bit. I read up, before the show – and the dinner, actually. I wanted to look like I knew what I was talking about.'

In front of Marianne, thought Rowan. 'When you were doing your homework,' she said carefully, 'did you come across the name Greta Mulraine?'

His silence answered for him. She could almost hear him following the ramifications through. 'You think,' he said slowly, 'that Mazz jumped – committed suicide – because of Michael Cory?'

'No, I'm not saying I . . . I mean, who knows what happened with Greta. Clearly Cory's interested in people who aren't simple, isn't he? Or stable. Maybe he knew Greta had suicidal tendencies and that was why he was drawn to her in the first . . .'

'She killed herself in his studio,' Turk cut her off. 'Did you know that? She bled to death on the floor. Kind of *eloquent*, don't you think?'

Rowan took the few steps to the nearest sofa, sat down and bent her head towards her knees.

'Are you okay?' said a small voice from the phone.

When she was more or less confident she wasn't going to throw up, she asked him, 'Pete, did Mazz ever mention being watched?'

'What? What the hell, Rowan?'

'Look, it might be nothing, it might just be that I'm here on my own and she's dead and I'm freaking out, I don't know.'

'What's going on?'

'I don't know. There's this guy who stands at his window all the time in the building behind here – you know that little block of flats? Even at three in the morning.'

'How do you know that?'

'I'm not sleeping brilliantly,' she admitted. 'And I keep thinking there's someone in the garden but if I open the door or look out of the window, there's no one there.'

'Then . . .'

'Jacqueline told me Mazz thought her work was going missing. She thought someone was getting in here, taking sketches. She even went to the police.'

'They investigated that, though.' He sounded a little calmer. 'They didn't find anything – no evidence of a break-in. They thought she'd probably just got confused, mislaid the things she was looking for.'

'Confused? Marianne?'

'Well, either way, it can't have anything to do with what happened, can it? She was on her own then.'

'What about the guy in the flat opposite?'

'She never mentioned him to me.'

'You think she would have?'

'Until about three minutes ago,' he said, 'I would have said yes.'

'This is going to sound a bit mad but do you think it might be Michael Cory?'

'Cory? In one of those poky flats?' Turk gave a bark – *Ha*. 'What do you think he'd be doing?'

'What if that's part of his process – you know, watching people secretly?' Peeping: call a spade a spade, Rowan.

'You think he was hoping to catch sight of her in her underwear? If he was painting her, she was probably stripping off for him anyway.' Again the barely concealed hurt.

'They're selling the house, Pete,' she said. 'Adam told me.'

The out-breath was gentle, barely a sigh, but she heard it. 'I knew they would,' he said. 'They couldn't live there again, could they? Not now.'

Seventeen

On the radio last night, the forecast had talked animatedly of snow but she'd opened the curtains this morning to sheer blue and a rush of light that made her eyes water. Cory had called a few minutes later – while she was putting her clothes on – to announce that he'd come to the house at ten. Irritated, she'd told him that she was working and she'd meet him at half-one in the Covered Market.

There were a couple of things she wanted to do before then, the first being to come here to Benson Place and take a look around.

She could see at once that her mental image of it was out of date. She'd been picturing the flats as tired sixties construc-tions on a shabby cul-de-sac hidden away behind Fyfield and Norham Roads like a poor relation, but the tide of money that had swept through North Oxford had reached this little inlet, too, and the strip of grass that separated the flats from the pavement was manicured, as were the privet bushes and the japonica trained around the freshly painted windows. The first cars she saw were an Audi and a BMW.

She'd borrowed a baseball cap and as she walked the length of the little road, she kept it pulled down over her forehead. No silver Mercedes but that didn't mean anything. If Cory were living here in secret, he'd likely have the wit not to park outside. He could also be out.

She glanced around then went up the short path to the second door along. There were three buttons on the intercom box, and through the glass panel, she saw a brass '1' on the door of the ground-floor flat. The strip of card next to the buzzer for number 3 said 'Johnson' but again, she thought, that needn't be definitive. Maybe Cory put it in to deflect attention or maybe he was sub-letting the place. *Ha*, said Turk in her ear again.

In broad daylight, noon on a weekday afternoon, it was true the idea seemed ridiculous – how likely was it, honestly, that Michael Cory was lurking here, amusing himself by spying on her across the back gardens? But maybe he wasn't lurking, at least to his own way of thinking. What if he'd taken the flat to be close to Marianne and now couldn't bring himself to leave? She purposely hadn't said anything to Turk but she couldn't yet rule out the possibility that Marianne and Cory had been in a relationship.

Rowan reached up to press the button – she could lay the whole thing to rest right now – but then she stopped. If it wasn't Cory in the flat, it would be hard to explain herself, and if by some remote chance it was, she didn't want to show her hand until she had at least some idea of what he was doing.

When she emerged from the pedestrian shortcut on to Charlbury Road and took off the cap, she saw a line of cloud advancing across the sky. By the time she reached St Helena's, it was halfway over, a curdled grey cover on an azure pool, its edge bruised yellow.

She took the same spot by the laurel bush and waited. Three minutes after the bell rang for lunch, girls started coming through the gate, some in groups that Rowan recognised from last time. They looked up at the sky and rearranged their enormous scarves, shoved hands into blazer pockets. She rehearsed her approach. With luck, Bryony would come out in a group; it would be easier to get her to talk for a few minutes if she didn't have to keep a lone friend waiting. Rowan stamped her feet surreptitiously as the body heat she'd generated on the walk began to dissipate. *Come on, Bryony*.

For five minutes, the gate seemed to open every few seconds but then the gaps lengthened, became a minute, then two. Just before one o'clock, a handful of those who'd been first out returned with M&S carrier bags and vats from Starbucks. She waited until ten minutes past then put her phone back in her pocket and turned to go. Those who were coming out this lunchtime were out; she'd missed Bryony somehow or she'd decided to keep warm and eat at school. Either way, Rowan couldn't wait any longer.

A number of bus routes ran down the Banbury Road, a straight shot to the city centre, but she kept walking. She felt jumpy, over-caffeinated even though she wasn't, and walking helped, the beat of her feet along the pavement regulating the rhythm of her heart. The air was static, expectant.

The first tentative flakes of snow started to fall as she passed the Lamb and Flag, and as she rounded the corner onto Broad Street, she experienced a flash of déjà vu: the afternoon she'd bumped into Seb just here, it had been snowing, too. She'd been coming from a lecture at the Taylorian, heading back to college for lunch, when she'd collided with him coming out of the porter's lodge at Balliol. He'd been on the phone, of course, not looking where he was going, and he'd put his spare hand out and said a distracted sorry before doing a double-take. Then he'd smiled broadly and mouthed, *Hold on a moment*.

'Richard? I'll call you back. I've just bumped into a friend.'

A friend, not 'my daughter's friend' or even 'a family friend' – it was a casual phrase but she'd been charmed.

'How are you?' He'd dropped the phone into his pocket and leaned in to kiss her cheek. A momentary impression of stubble, warm skin, coffee. 'We haven't seen you in weeks. Here—' He stepped back under the cover of the archway, out of the snow.

'Finals next year,' she said, following. 'The work's starting to ratchet up.'

'Of course, yes. I haven't seen Marianne since October, either. She's been holed up in that garage in Bethnal Green painting all the hours that God sends, apparently.'

Rowan smiled: *that garage.* 'I went down to see her a couple of weekends ago.'

'Did you? So she's still alive? That's good.' He buttoned his coat and she'd thought he was about to say that it was nice to run into her and no doubt they'd see her at Christmas when Mazz was back, but instead he'd checked his watch and asked what she was doing.

'Now?' she'd asked, surprised.

'Yes. I was on my way to the White Horse. Have you had lunch?'

'I was just heading back to college to do that.'

'Come and keep me company instead.'

As they walked the few hundred yards along Broad Street, the snow was still light, a grey whirl in the air overhead, barely a dusting on the lawn at Trinity. Seb held the door open and she stepped down off the street into the semi-subterranean cave of the pub with its wood floor and enveloping scent of warm beer. Tinsel twinkled among the bottles on the bar-back, and though it was only the first week in December, the atmosphere was anticipatory, expansive. There were office Christmas lunches going on at two of the tables. Seb insisted on paying and carried their drinks to the large table in the window. Across the street, the great stone heads on the columns around the Sheldonian glared balefully down through the thickening snow.

Rowan had been out to dinner with the Glasses numerous times over the years but she'd never eaten alone with Seb before. Away from the house and his role there, he seemed different, younger. He was forty-nine – he and Jacqueline had both been twenty-eight when Marianne was born – but he could have passed for forty. His hair was still very dark, and his jeans and navy coat were classic, the kind he might have worn at twenty and could still wear at sixty. While they were eating their steak and ale pies, a couple of women in their mid-twenties walked in and, seeing him, came to say hello. 'Alison and Katya, two of my Experimental Psychology grads. This is Rowan.' They'd found a table at the other end of the room but she felt eyes trained on her several times and when they left, waving a flirty goodbye, she looked up in time to catch Katya, the prettier one, giving her an assessing stare through the window. Seb hadn't given the girl a second glance.

'I can't believe you two are graduating next year,' he said, recalling Rowan's attention. 'Do you know what you're going to do?'

'Actually, I've got an interview in London next week with Robin Poretta.'

'Have you? The *Time Capsule* guy?'

She nodded. 'My tutor put me in touch with him. One of his researchers is leaving in the summer and he asked Derek to recommend someone. He taught Poretta, too, years ago.'

'Is that what you want to do, then? TV?'

'Maybe. I thought about post-grad but I feel like I need to earn some money.'

'I was the same.'

'But you've got a PhD.'

'Got it later. I went to work on a research project for a couple of years first, found myself in an intense relationship with a rhesus macaque called Peggy Sue.' Seb smiled. 'Occupational hazard.'

He launched into a fond anecdote and Rowan drank her wine, watched the snow coming down and listened. She'd never had Seb to herself for so long and it was different – *he* was different from the versions of him she knew from Fyfield Road: husband and father; distracted academic trying to work in a house filled with noise; host at one of the regular kitchen suppers he and Jacqueline had for friends and colleagues. He wasn't the Seb she hated, either, the philanderer who couldn't help himself; instead, cocooned in the pub, she had the sense that they'd fallen back through time to when he was her own age and all the other stuff – marriage, Adam and Marianne, the books, the money, the girls – had yet to come.

'I should let you go,' he'd said abruptly, finishing his beer. 'I don't want to be responsible for you not getting your first.'

'A first?' She'd waved it away, self-deprecatory, but she was flattered and there *had* been talk of her getting one, Derek had mentioned it last week, though he'd made plain how hard she would have to work.

'My God,' said Seb as they climbed the steps back to the pavement. He seemed not to have realised how much snow had fallen in the hour they'd been inside. Where it was undisturbed, it lay an inch thick, and the giant stone heads looked down from under white caps like the negatives of judges passing a death sentence. She'd shivered and he'd reached out to rub her upper arms. 'Back to college. Go and warm up.'

'I will. Thanks for the lunch.'

'Thank *you*. It was fun – we'll have to do it again in the New Year.'

She'd said yes but without any expectation, and when she'd seen him over Christmas at Fyfield Road, they hadn't mentioned it. Her impression of the afternoon as a self-contained bubble of time outside the usual stream crystallised but then, two weeks after the new term started, she'd gone to the lodge to check her mail and found a hand-delivered note in her pigeonhole: *Lunch, redux – Lamb & Flag, Tuesday at one?*

She'd accepted the invitation – he hadn't flirted with her at the White Horse, there had been nothing inappropriate – and then spent two days beforehand questioning her decision: hurting or offending Jacqueline or Marianne was the very last thing she'd wanted. As soon as she'd walked into the Lamb and Flag, however, she'd seen that she had nothing to worry about. Seb had brought Steven, the new protégé he'd been talking about in hyperbole for the past year. 'I thought you two should meet,' he said, taking their orders for a first round. 'You'll get on like a house on fire.'

Entering the Covered Market from the High Street, one saw its fragrant side, the gift shop and the jeweller, the florist and the special-occasion cake-maker. Ben's Cookies filled the narrow alleys with the scent of melting chocolate. Coming in from Market Street at the back, though, you encountered a different, grubbier face, one closer, Rowan always thought, to how it must have looked in the seventeen hundreds when it first opened. The usual scurf of sprouts and onionskins lined the gutter by the entrance, and inside, the air had a rich animal-vegetable smell of ripe cheese, damp greens, cooking pasties, the fishmonger's and, underneath it all, the iron tang of the butcher's where deer carcasses hung on hooks outside, their flanks furry as children's toys as you brushed past, their necks circles of bloodied bone and cartilage.

She'd told Cory to meet her at Morton's, one of the cafés at the heart of the market. She'd lived in Oxford for more than twenty years but it seemed she could still be confused by the aisles that ran the length of the place. Thinking of other things, she took the wrong one and had to double-back past the barber-shop and the place with all the tie-dye that reeked of incense.

Late as she was, she was the first to arrive so she took a table facing the door and ordered some coffee. As she picked up her phone to check the time, it buzzed in her hand.

A text from Peter Turk: *Lent M cufflinks for party & want to retrieve them b4 her things sorted. Can I come & collect?*

Can find and put in post, she typed. *What do they look like?*

A few seconds later: *Not to worry, coming up to Ox anyway.*

She was surprised; he hadn't mentioned it on the phone. *When?*

Sat – coming to visit my mum. Rock 'n' roll!

The waitress brought the coffee. Cory was ten minutes late now and, remembering how punctual he'd been yesterday afternoon, Rowan couldn't help enjoying the idea that he might be lost somewhere in the maze of alleyways, cursing her for not choosing somewhere easier. As she had the thought, though, the bell chimed above the door and she saw him come in.

The waitress approached but he pointed to Rowan and made his way over, pulling the chair out and sitting down almost before he'd said hello. 'I like this place,' he said. 'The market.'

'You've been here before?'

'No.'

'Really? I thought Marianne would have brought you. She liked it, too.'

'We didn't go out too much.' An upward flick of the eyebrows.

Touché? she wondered.

'Coffee, please,' he said without turning to look at the waitress who'd come up behind him.

'Which hotel are you staying at?' Rowan asked.

'The Old Parsonage.'

'That's lovely.'

'As an American, of course,' he said, eyebrow lifting again, 'I get a kick out of old places, the idea that parsons were in there doing their thing before George Washington was a twinkle in his daddy's eye.'

'How long have you been in the UK?'

'Since two thousand twelve.' His coffee arrived and he turned to say thank you.

'What brought you?'

166

'Curiosity.'

She smiled to encourage him but he said nothing more. 'About what?' she prompted.

'Everything. Living overseas – I'd never done it. London, which I love. Your history, the culture. I like National Trust houses – what an amazing organisation that is.'

'You live in London?'

'I do.'

'But you worked with Marianne here for the most part, you said.'

'Yes.' He looked at her and Rowan thought she saw amusement in his eyes: *I know where this is heading.*

'Did you stay at the Old Parsonage then?' she said anyway.

The amusement vanished and he looked down, breaking eye contact. Again, she thought, his face was carefully composed to give nothing away. The silence stretched but she resisted the instinct to speak into the void. His move.

The women at the next table were leaving, taking their time to put on coats and gather their shopping, and it dawned on Rowan that he was waiting for them to go. She felt a burst of alarm that she quickly fought down. Whatever he was about to say or do, she had to stay calm. She sipped her coffee and tried to look as if it were natural for them to sit in silence.

Eventually the women moved out of earshot and Cory raised his head. He glanced around and then leaned forward. 'Look,' he said, barely audible. 'I think we should level with one another.'

'What do you mean?'

'Clearly you're suspicious about Marianne's death and so am I.' He looked around again. The café was busy, though, the table next to them the only one vacant now, and with the stone floor and plate-glass window, the acoustics were awful: it would be hard for anyone to hear him over the ambient roar of conversation, the coffee machine, the clatter of plates and cutlery.

'It wasn't an accident,' he said.

167

'What?'

'I went up on the roof with her three times, Rowan. I thought she was joking about the vertigo until I saw it. She was fucking terrified – *terrified*. There's no way that she went near the edge and slipped. That's bullshit.'

Rowan looked at him. 'Yes,' she said. 'I know.'

'So something else happened.'

'But she was on her own – no one else was there.'

'They're sure?'

Sparing him the details of how she'd come by the information, she told him what Theo had said about the footprints.

'And there's no way someone could have been hiding in the house before it started snowing and then left afterwards?'

'He said not. They searched the place top to bottom.'

Cory sat back heavily in his chair, as if he'd been listening to a long story and had finally heard the ending he'd been dreading. 'You looked at the pictures again?'

'Yes.'

He nodded. 'When we talked, she kept coming back to dying – death. Almost every time. The idea of it, the absolute finality.'

Rowan stared at him. 'Did you know she'd had a breakdown? Did you talk to you about that?'

'When her father died? Yes, she did.'

'And you didn't think to *tell* anyone she was obsessed with dying? Or suggest it might be a good idea to get some *help*?' Her voice drew the attention of the couple sitting two tables over, who looked up, startled, then quickly looked away.

Saying nothing, Cory turned around, motioned for the bill and stood up. 'Let's get out of here.'

He walked fast, striding through the market as if he were the only real thing in it, the tables outside the café, the shop-fronts and other people all just stage-setting for a drama in which he was the lead. Angry, she followed him, weaving around window shoppers and a double buggy, struggling to keep him in sight. He headed towards the High Street, barely looking over his shoulder. The snow was falling faster, starting to settle now where it wasn't disturbed, and as he came out onto the pavement, he pulled a blue knitted hat from his pocket. She saw him look at the road, assessing his chances, but the lights had just turned green and a line of city buses revved at the crossing, engines emitting clouds of oily breath. As they waited, not speaking, Cory lifted his chin and offered his broad face to the sky.

Across the road, he headed towards Carfax then turned the corner on to St Aldate's. 'Where are we going?' she called to his back.

'Somewhere we can talk.'

Past the entrance to Christ Church and on towards the river. Her heart was beating quickly, half in alarm, half because of the sheer speed at which he was forcing her to move. The pavement was slick, and twice she slipped and nearly fell.

When they reached the gate to the meadow, he made an abrupt left. Untrodden, the lawns of the formal college gardens were white over. The cathedral loomed, a dark hulk against the marbled sky. A group of tourists was taking pictures from the flagged path but for the first time she could remember, the wide unpaved avenue that bordered the meadow itself was deserted, not a soul in sight. Nonetheless, Cory went halfway to the river before he started to slow down.

'What are you doing?' she demanded. 'What the hell is this?'

'The reason I didn't try and get help for her,' he said, spinning round, 'is that I didn't think she was talking about suicide. Okay? You think I would have stood by and let that happen? You think I'm a monster? For fuck's sake!'

'What am I supposed to think? You tell me her pictures of dying girls are self-portraits, you tell me she couldn't stop talking about death . . .'

'Yes! I said she couldn't stop talking about death. *Death*. Not suicide.'

Rowan felt rage billow through her, hot and red. 'You . . .'

'They're a self-portrait because they describe how she *felt*. Eaten – consumed, you remember?'

She opened her mouth but anger made her temporarily speechless. She took a breath. 'Everyone says she was happy – or content. She had so much good stuff going on, things to look forward to. She was . . .'

Cory nodded, as if she was finally getting it. 'That's what I'm trying to tell you. Marianne wasn't suicidal.'

'Then what?'

He looked around, checking again that they were alone. When he spoke, his voice was barely a murmur. 'I think she might have killed someone.'

The world went silent. The snow on the field, the avenue, the expanse of white sky over her head – everything was still. Inside Rowan's head, though, the blood started to roar.

Cory was staring at her, she understood; his face loomed and receded, loomed again.

'That's . . . insane,' she said.

'It sounds it. Yes, I know. But I think it's what happened.'

'Why? Why would that even cross your . . . ?'

'In my early twenties,' he cut her off, 'I had a girlfriend who committed suicide. Greta. I know what it's like, despair, because I've seen it. Marianne, when she was talking, it was different.'

'How?'

'It was like she was exploring the idea. Sometimes it felt intellectual, philosophical, but other times it didn't – there was a point to it, in the real world. I told you she talked about

170

finality? She talked about "crossing the line", doing something that can never be undone. Black and white, dead and alive.'

The ground pitched under Rowan's feet, and the snow, coming down obliquely, added to the impression of a world that was tilting, shifting on its axis.

'Marianne was painting – spending a lot of time with – women who were very ill,' she said. 'Mortally ill, I think, some of them – the last one, almost definitely.'

'No, it wasn't that.' Snow was starting to settle on the shoulders of Cory's coat, frosting the wool. 'Listen to me. She talked about guilt.'

'Guilt?'

'How it crushed you – how you could never get away from it. She was eaten up with it – that's what I meant by consumed. I felt like she was fighting with her conscience – fighting to the death, as it happened. She couldn't talk about whatever it was so she was talking *around* it, as if that would help take even a little of the pressure off.'

'Peter Turk – you've met him – he was a mutual friend, mine and Marianne's.'

Cory looked at her: *And?*

'You know her father killed someone else when he crashed, a woman in another car? Turk says Mazz took on that guilt – felt it like it was hers – as a way of staying close to him. Emotionally. She paid for the woman's son to go to university; he said she . . .'

'I know, I know. She told me – we talked about that. That wasn't it.'

The frustration was almost overwhelming. 'Who, then? Who did she kill?' The words echoed among the trees, too loud.

'Be quiet,' Cory hissed, glancing back up the avenue. 'I don't know,' he said. 'I don't know yet.'

Eighteen

Rowan walked until he was out of sight then broke into a run. Down the avenue towards the river, the wet snow hitting her face, her feet scratching the muddy gravel. Gloom gathered under the trees, and lights came on in a houseboat against the opposite bank as the low cloud brought the evening in much too early. The wide river path was deserted.

At the end, where it turned away from the Thames, a steep wooden bridge led to the university boathouses. The bank was deserted here, too, the boathouses locked and dark between the strip of grey river and the fringe of leafless trees behind. When she reached one with tiered balconies, she took the concrete stairs on the outside wall and found a sheltered spot on the first floor. Huddled into the corner, she hugged her knees so hard she felt her pulse in her arms. Cory knew. While she'd been running, it was all she could think, the magnitude of it drowning out any other thought or interpretation. He knew – he *knew*.

And Marianne had *told* him, more or less. Into Rowan's head came a picture of Jacqueline's face at the crematorium and rage surged through her again. Typical Marianne – so preoccupied with how *she* felt, her apparently unbearable guilt, that she hadn't thought about how it might affect anyone else.

Is that why you needed to talk to me, Marianne? To tell me you couldn't hack it any more? You couldn't live with it? For Christ's sake! Did you even think about what it would do to your mother?

But what exactly had Marianne told him? How much did Cory have to go on? Rowan took a breath and tried to think clearly. If he still only *thought* she'd done it, it couldn't be much. The small comfort of that idea was erased at once, however, by a memory of his older woman in New York, the relentlessness with which she said he'd gone after the secrets of her psyche. Deeper and deeper, like Theseus in the labyrinth.

Was that why Marianne had jumped? Perhaps she hadn't *meant* to say anything – why would she, suddenly, after so many years? – but he'd got to her. Was that why she'd sent the card? Was that why she'd been frightened, needed Rowan's help? With a sick feeling, she thought of the five days it had taken to reach her.

A pattering sound pulled her out of her thoughts. The snow had turned to slush, and the clumps falling beyond the shelter of the upper balcony, inches from her feet, were so wet they melted on contact. The cold of the concrete reached through her jeans and woollen coat into her bones.

Why was Cory doing this, really? His portrait, some spurious rubbish about the 'truth' of a person? Rowan felt another surge of anger. What crap. It was about publicity, fame – *his* fame. The Hanna Ferrara story wasn't an unfortunate turn of events – you didn't need many operational brain cells to know that painting one of the world's most famous women complete with an eight-inch penis would get you media attention. No, what would take brainwork was devising a way to top that, up the stakes, keep yourself newsworthy. Unveiling a high-profile young artist as a killer, though – that might do it.

—

She stayed too long by the river and when she reached the gate out of the meadow, it was locked for the night. Nine in summer, said the sign, dusk in winter. The railings by Christ Church and the gate between Corpus Christi and Merton were both too high to climb so she had no choice but to stumble all the way back to the river in the dark to see if she could still get out behind the Head of the River pub. As students, she and three or four others from Brasenose – Theo was there – had found a way through when they'd crashed Corpus Ball but the sky had been lighter then, a summer's night, and the back of the pub had been much better lit. They'd been laughing, already slightly drunk, on an adventure, but now she was on her own, wet and shaking with cold. In the intervening decade, the thicket of elder and bramble in which the railings were embedded had grown very nearly impenetrable, and she cut her hands and left cheek as she fought her way through.

The slush had become rain and, finally, drizzle, and hazy orange clouds hung below the streetlights on Folly Bridge. The pavement was black. As she trudged back up St Aldate's past the police station, she was overtaken by exhaustion. Walking to Fyfield Road would take at least half an hour.

She turned to look over her shoulder and as if she had willed it into existence, a cab with its light on came around the corner. Her hips ached as she lowered herself into the back seat and gave the address.

Head against the rain-speckled window, she watched the city pass, shops closing, the pubs coming to life. Her worst fear had been realised but at least, she tried to console herself, the situation had come into clearer focus. At least she had an idea of what she was facing now.

She lit a fire as soon as she arrived back but even after a bath and a large glass of wine, she couldn't warm up. Her hands shook so badly as she buttered a slice of toast that she dropped

174

the knife and sent it skittering across the kitchen floor.

Finally, just after ten, she filled both the hot-water bottles in the airing cupboard, put an extra blanket on the bed and got in. She turned the light off but, almost immediately, her head filled with the kind of thoughts that morphed into horrifying nightmares so she switched the lamp back on and reached for her book.

She was still reading two hours later when, outside the window, there was a scraping sound – a scratch. At once, her body went rigid. Seconds passed, pressure building in her ears from the intensity of the listening. A tick from the floorboards as the house cooled, a clank from the radiator but, otherwise, silence. She'd imagined it or misheard – the day had been so extreme, she was so tired. She listened a few seconds longer then forced herself to relax her shoulders.

Not a scratch this time but a squeak – rubber on wet stone. A shoe. A trainer.

The hairs on her arms stood up. What should she do? The light was on, she couldn't look out of the window without risking being seen, but turning it off might draw attention, too.

As quietly as possible, she pushed off the blankets. Marianne's dressing gown was on the back of the door; she put it on and slipped her phone into the pocket. The door handle screeched. On the landing, she took one of the heavy brass candlesticks from the table outside Seb's office and crept downstairs.

Hand flat against the wall, she made her way to the kitchen. When she reached the bottom of the stairs, a faint glow came in from outside, making it easier to see. Keeping close to the shadow around the cabinets, she edged to the back of the room and leaned forward until she had a view through the window over the sink.

Nothing. The lawn was empty and so – she craned, looking right – was the patio. She peered into the shadows around the shed and down at the far end by the wall beyond the birches. Nothing. In the time it had taken her to get down, had he gone?

She let go of the breath she'd been holding then almost immediately froze again. There *was* something. There, behind the rhododendron at the end of the bed above the patio, just visible, a – shape, a black absence of light. As she stared, it began to take on form: an elbow, a knee. A hood.

She gripped the candlestick. The police – she reached for her phone then stopped. Cory knew.

The shape took on greater definition. He was facing *away* from the house, she realised, not towards it: she was looking at the tip of a shoulder, a back. He wasn't crouched but *sitting* on the stones at the edge of the flowerbed, just a few feet from where Marianne had fallen.

For a few seconds, neither of them moved. Did he know she was watching? Did he think he was hidden there, behind the bush? Then she realised something else. Cory was big – tall and broad. The darkness, the palimpsest of shadow around the bush, made it hard to be sure, but the figure looked slighter than he was.

Silently, she stepped away from the window and crept back to the stairs. At the little window at the turn, she paused and looked out. He was still there.

On the first floor she opened the door to Seb's study and slipped inside, tensing at every creak of the old boards. The spines of his books gleamed in the half-light. She moved towards the window.

Still there. Reaching up, she felt the catch on top of the sash. She expected a shriek, brass on brass, but the movement was smooth, as if the window had been opened recently. Bending, she got hold of the handles then shoved the window as hard as she could. Without resistance, it slipped up the runners and slammed against the top.

She saw him start and scramble sideways, almost falling as he got to his feet. A flash of white inside the hood, white hands, but he dipped his head, hiding his face, and darted into the shadow of the garden shed.

'Hey!' she shouted, leaning out, but all she heard was the soft sound of trainers on flagstones and then the crunch of the gravel path. She ran across the landing to Seb and Jacqueline's bedroom but their window was stiff and it took three attempts and all her upper-body strength to force the lower pane. *There* – it screeched upwards just as the hooded figure rounded the end of the front wall and was lost from sight. She listened to the footfalls on the pavement until they faded from hearing, sure she was right: Cory was too big – too heavy – to be so light on his feet.

Nineteen

'What happened to your face?'

And good morning to you. Still half-asleep, Rowan put up a hand and felt the raised line across her cheek. 'It's just a scratch.' He waited but she declined to elaborate. Why should she?

But perhaps she should be grateful. He'd woken her from a dream in which smoke had been filling a small low-ceilinged room with wooden walls, the air rapidly growing acrid, more and more difficult to breathe. A fire alarm had started ringing and she'd woken, breathing hard, only understanding when it rang again that it was the doorbell. A moment later, she remembered that Savills were coming to do the valuation, and she got up quickly and threw on some clothes. Instead of the agent, though, here was Cory, take-away coffees and a white paper bag in hand. The light in the sky behind him was weak, the sun still low.

'What time is it?' She suppressed a yawn.

'A few minutes before nine. I woke you.'

'No, I was up.'

He nodded, *Sure*, and handed her one of the paper cups. 'Can I come in?'

On the stairs to the kitchen, Rowan remembered the same spot at midnight, looking out of the little window. She'd lain awake until after three, despite having taken more of

Marianne's Ambien. Her mind had been spinning, a whirl of progressively more alarming possibilities.

'Plain croissant or chocolate?' He pulled out a chair at the table and opened the bag. He seemed somehow to have concluded that they were in this together, she realised; this was morning conference.

She weighed her options before deciding on the element of surprise. 'Was that you in the garden last night?'

'What?'

'Were you in the garden last night? About midnight – just after.' She was watching him carefully but if his puzzled expression was put on, it was very good.

'Someone was here?'

'Someone working for you – a researcher? An assistant?'

Cory looked at her as if she were gibbering. 'Researcher? What are you talking about?'

'You really don't know? You're telling me the truth?'

'You think I'm sneaking into the garden at night? Or sending someone. Seriously? To do what?'

'Watch the house.'

For a moment Cory looked as if he were going to laugh but as fast as the humour lit up his face, it died absolutely. 'No,' he said. 'No, it wasn't me – nothing to do with me. Here – sit down.'

Reluctantly she took the seat opposite and he put a *pain au chocolat* on a napkin and slid it across. 'Tell me,' he said.

She did, watching his face. His eyes narrowed as he concentrated, shutting out distraction, and he leaned forward, elbows on the table, fingertips pressed against his lips. When she finished, he was silent for several seconds and she imagined his brain flushing with colour, electrical impulses humming as he processed it all.

'What if someone else knows?' he said.

Nausea washed over her. It was her own thought, one of the three a.m. horrors, but spoken aloud, it had an authority, a reality, that she had managed to deny until now. 'Knows what?'

Cory gave her a look: *Come on.*

'No,' she said. 'No. What you said yesterday – it's . . . ludicrous.'

He shook his head. 'No. And you don't think so, either.'

'Don't tell me what I think.' A surge of anger. 'It's crazy talk – dangerous. What evidence have you got? I mean, for Christ's sake – you can't go around making those kinds of allegations. People loved Marianne – they still love her. Her family – James Greenwood. Do you have any idea how much hurt you could cause them? Or do you just not care?'

'I don't have any evidence,' he said, apparently unfazed. 'Apart from the fact that she's dead in circumstances that make no sense to either of us,' he waved his hand across the table between them, 'she was talking cross-wise about something that was evidently troubling her on a deep level, and now you're telling me that someone is hanging round her house at night.'

'There are any number of reasons someone might hang round.' Cory raised an eyebrow.

'Burglars – she thought someone was getting in here anyway. And everyone knows she's dead, it's been splashed across the front page of all the papers. The *Mail* even had a picture of the house so it would hardly be difficult to find it. It could be ghoulish teenagers, thrill-seekers, freaking themselves out by coming to sit where she died. A dare. He was right there,' she jabbed a finger towards the window, 'feet from where she fell.' In the small hours, the idea had afforded her a brief match-flare of hope but now, in the frank light of day, it burned and died in a second.

Cory wasn't buying it.

'It might also be a nutty fan,' Rowan said. 'Someone who saw her in the papers when the story about her relationship with Greenwood came out, got obsessed. That happened to Seb once. Or a hanger-on.' She eyeballed him. 'Marianne had a lot of hangers-on.'

If he heard the insult, he ignored it. 'You know, I've been wondering if someone was threatening her,' he said. 'Maybe they came here to try and scare her.' He frowned. 'But as you say, unless they've been hiding under a rock, they must know she's dead. So why would they still be coming?'

Before they could get any further, they were interrupted by the doorbell and the arrival of the man from Savills. Rowan saw the flicker of interest in Cory's eyes when she told him the Glasses were going to put the house on the market but he stayed in the kitchen while she let the estate agent in and took him upstairs.

As she showed Cory out a few minutes later, he stepped close to her and murmured, 'Look, you have doubts: that's fine.' He stopped, hearing the man moving around in Seb and Jacqueline's bedroom overhead. 'She was your friend, it makes sense you don't want to believe it. But the fact is, something happened and I need to find out what.'

'Why?' she challenged, her voice as low as his.

Again he looked at her as if she were completely alien. 'Because she was my friend, too,' he said. 'Because it seems wrong that no one knows the truth about how she died.'

'Have you considered that they might not want to know? That Jacqueline might prefer to believe it was an accident?'

He shook his head. 'Whatever Marianne did, the truth deserves to be known. And if she did kill someone, clearly it was an accident. Maybe she hit someone in the car. Perhaps it was self-defence – maybe someone broke in here. Something like that – an accident, plain bad luck or one bad decision. For God's sake, I'm not saying she was a *murderer*.'

When the estate agent had gone, too, Rowan lay down on Jacqueline's reading sofa and covered herself with the old tartan blanket. Pulling it close around her shoulders, she allowed herself to imagine for a moment that it was Jacqueline's arms, a tight hug, supportive, protective. She felt destabilised, unsure of her judgement. Was Cory genuine or was he playing with her? He'd seemed to be telling the truth about the garden but perhaps she'd got that wrong. Did he really think Marianne had killed someone in self-defence or was he backtracking, sensing that he'd gone too far and risked alienating her? When he'd said 'killed' yesterday, she'd been sure he meant deliberately, but today he'd seemed to suggest that was preposterous. She'd even heard a silent question, *What kind of a person are you, to entertain the idea?* when, in fact, she'd never given him any sign that she had. Everything he did felt like that, designed subtly to unsettle her, put her on the back foot.

But what if he'd been telling the truth about the garden? If it really wasn't him or someone sent by him, then who the hell was it? No one obvious: if the figure had been too small to be Cory, he was also too small to be Peter Turk come to grieve where Marianne had fallen, running away to avoid embarrassment. She didn't think it was Greenwood, either. Granted, he was slighter than the other two, especially now, but she couldn't imagine he was so fast on his feet, so – lithe. He wasn't fifty but nonetheless there was something definitely adult about the way he moved, dignified. Could it be Adam?

Oh, really? said a sardonic voice. *Trespassing in his own garden after bumping off his sister? Having installed you here to make it a bit more of a challenge?*

Well, who then? she asked it. *Who?*

182

Twenty

When Rowan got the call to say she'd been given a place at the university – it was a so-called unconditional offer: two E grades at A-level – her father was in Chile. She tried three times to call him then gave up, relieved. The news was a golden, precious thing: she didn't want to tarnish it by telling him. It was a week or so before Christmas and when she hung up the phone for the final time, she put on her coat and set off for Fyfield Road. She could still remember how she'd felt, the way in which the world seemed subtly to have remodelled itself. As she'd come over Folly Bridge, the old university part of the city had loomed on the hill, the ogee dome of Tom Tower rising above the leafless winter chestnuts, and she'd felt as if she were walking towards her future.

Jacqueline had opened the door, her green-rimmed reading glasses perched on top of her head whence the springs of her hair threatened imminently to catapult them.

'I got in,' were the first words Rowan said.

It took Jacqueline a second to work out what she was talking about but then a huge smile spread across her face. Really, a beam was the word: it was all light and shine and warmth. With a jangle of bracelets and a flurry of red silk shirt – Rowan thought of a Chinese dragon – she had given her a sudden hard hug. 'Brilliant, Ro! Fantastic! God, I'm so happy for you. Not that I ever had any doubt – I'd have gone round there to protest myself if you hadn't got an offer.' Another squeeze then she'd stepped away and yelled up the stairs. 'Marianne!

'What did your dad say?' she said, coming back. 'He must be so thrilled.'

'He's in South America. He'll probably ring when he sees the missed calls.'

'He doesn't know?'

'I couldn't get through.'

'Oh.' A pause. It always bothered Jacqueline, the amount of time Rowan's father spent away, particularly if he was uncontactable. 'Well, Seb's in London tonight, it's just Mazz and me, so why don't we go out, the three of us? To celebrate. You two can go on afterwards,' she nodded to Marianne, who'd just reached the foot of the stairs, 'but let me buy you supper first.'

She'd got on the phone straight away and booked a table here, at Gee's. Another opening door, this one literal. For years, especially since she'd been spending so much time in Park Town, Rowan had wanted to come to this restaurant in the beautiful old glasshouse on Banbury Road. It looked Parisian – the awnings and decorative ironwork; the round-topped wrought-iron archway at the pavement like an entrance to the Métro – but at the same time she imagined it as the greenhouse or orangery of a great English estate, the sort to which Victorians might have brought back exotic plants from the Grand Tour, citrus fruits and succulents. Above a low base-wall, everything was white-painted wood and glass, all light and air. If she walked by at night, when it twinkled with candlelight, it seemed like a carousel, the diners inside bright and happy, turning to silent music.

Adam, two years older, had been away at university then but tonight it was he who held the door open for her. He'd called at lunchtime to say that the reservation was made for eight o'clock but why didn't they have a drink first? He was going to stay at the house and drive back to Cambridge in the morning. She'd been in her room when she'd heard his key in the door and then 'Hello' called up the stairs. As she'd come down, fastening the back of her earring, there had been an odd moment. He'd turned from the basket of Marianne's post on the hall table and for a second or two he'd watched her. She grinned and said hello rather too loudly but it hadn't dispersed the sudden strange tension.

It persisted now, as they handed their coats to the man at the door and took the two free stools at the little bar in the back room, Adam's exaggerated courtesy a sign, she thought, that he was as self-conscious as she was, as careful not to bump arms or knees. They ordered gin and tonic and watched the barman make them as if the process were performance art. Adam tipped the rim of his glass gently against hers. 'Cheers,' he said, 'and thank you again.'

She shook her head. 'You really don't have to.' She nodded at a table tucked into the corner. 'Your mother brought us here – Marianne and me – the night I got into the university. We sat there and had a glass of champagne before dinner. She was the first person I told – my dad was away – and she insisted on taking us out to celebrate.'

He smiled. 'Sounds like Mum.'

'It meant a lot to me, her support.'

'She was a big fan of yours. Still is.'

Rowan frowned, embarrassed. 'She felt sorry for me then, I should think.'

'The opposite. I think she was very impressed by you, how self-sufficient you were. And driven. You probably reminded her of herself at that age.'

'No, Marianne was the driven one. And look at me now. Jacqueline had published two books by my age – *Mirror, Mirror* and *Bed, No Breakfast*.'

Adam shrugged, smiling again. 'You're the same age as Mazz, thirty-two? I think you've got a bit of time.'

'I hope so.' She pulled a face.

He took another sip and the ice rattled as he put the glass down. Behind them, the restaurant was filling up, the hubbub of voices and silverware becoming a hum under the giant glass cloche. Rather than easing the tension, it seemed only to emphasise the silence whenever there was a break in their conversation. 'Tell me about California,' she said. 'What were you doing out there?'

He described living in Berkeley, his teaching work and the research he'd done for his book while he'd been in the US. 'I'm looking at how religious extremists – terrorists – structure their networks, fund themselves. What they've learned from organised crime. Gangs and cartels.'

'Cartels? Really?'

He'd spent weeks in Colombia and Miami, he said, and she remembered how he'd taught himself Spanish in Sixth Form, the battered yellow dictionary that went everywhere in his back pocket. 'But I wasn't properly fluent until much later,' he said. 'I travelled in South America for a year after my doctorate; that's when it really clicked.'

She pictured him in Medellín and the maximum-security prisons where he'd visited the gangsters. Someone who didn't know him would surely predict disaster, this middle-class, hyper-educated Englishman amongst dangerous criminals, but he'd managed to persuade three members of a cartel to talk to him, he said. She wasn't surprised: he shared Jacqueline's same air of non-judgemental interest, integrity.

As they got down from the stools to go through to their table, they bumped elbows and Adam sprang away as if he'd been burned. They apologised at the same time.

After they'd ordered, he went to the bathroom and she watched him cross the restaurant. His teenage lankiness had become elegance; there was grace in his movements, the way he stood aside for a waitress, dipped his head to avoid the branches of the potted olive tree. The place had been refurbished, the terracotta cushions on the banquettes, pale wooden tables and Moroccan tiles chosen to echo the Mediterranean and North African menu. When she'd come with Jacqueline and Marianne, the atmosphere had been formal, crisp white tablecloths, pre-laid glasses for water and red and white wines, roast lamb and beef in traditional French sauces. To save going home again, she'd borrowed one of Marianne's dresses that night, a pale green silk shift so short that Marianne had to wear it with leggings though on Rowan it had reached a semi-decent mid-thigh. They'd sat next to each other, facing Jacqueline across the table. She'd ordered a bottle of Chablis to go with the salmon they all had to start, the idea that they were seventeen and not legally allowed to drink either not crossing her mind or dismissed without mention as irrelevant.

Tonight they had red wine. Rowan knew she was drinking quickly but her hand seemed to be reaching for the glass of its own accord. She wanted to be slightly drunk, to let the edges blur for a few hours and numb the constant throb of anxiety, but she knew she had to stay in control, even if Adam's glass was emptying just as fast. They talked about her work, and moved on from Catholic safe houses to Julian Assange, Guantanamo. Marianne hovered at their shoulders, the unseen third person at the table, mentioned but not discussed until Adam, soliciting Rowan's say-so with his eyebrows, ordered a second bottle.

He was quiet while the waiter went through the whole production, showing the label, cutting the foil, twisting in the corkscrew, but when their glasses were full again and the man retreated, Adam swallowed hard and said savagely, 'I hate the new pictures.'

Taken aback by the sudden change of direction, Rowan hesitated to speak.

'I know,' he said. 'And I know they're good but it doesn't matter. I just can't bear to look at them.'

'I think I understand,' she said cautiously.

'The mental pain – the anguish. To see it like that, all beautifully painted – I mean, we knew, we had an idea anyway, but to see it from her perspective, to see what it felt like, being inside it . . .'

Through the alcoholic haze, Rowan struggled to think. Usually her thoughts were crisp, like decisive steps on a hardwood floor, but someone seemed to have put down carpet between her temples. 'At the time, do you mean?' she said. 'When it all happened – your dad?'

He looked at her and she was momentarily transfixed. Adam's irises were green, an aqueous colour pale enough to be mistaken for blue in bright light but rimmed with a darker grey-green. They were Marianne's eyes, and for a dizzying couple of seconds, Rowan felt as if she'd slipped down a wormhole and here she was, her seventeen-year-old self again, looking at the best friend she would ever have. But it was more than that: they were her own eyes, too, because although their colouring had been so different, Marianne's hair so dark, hers *tawny*, their eyes, bar the flecks of yellow that circled Rowan's pupils, had been very similar. 'Like sisters' eyes,' Jacqueline said once.

'Do you think you could ever completely get over it?' Adam said, pulling her back. 'When you've been so bad?' He broke eye contact and looked down. Pressing up a small piece of bread crust, he turned it between his fingertips. 'It has to stay with you, doesn't it, in some form? Memories – a shadow? You couldn't forget, not completely. I don't know – she wouldn't ever talk to me about it. We were open with each other about so much else, relationships, money, everything, but never that. I think she was ashamed of it, even with me.'

'Ashamed?'

He glanced up again then dropped his voice. 'You know she had a breakdown – well, everyone does now. But it was more serious than anyone really knows. She was hospitalised.'

'Was she?'

'At the Warneford. Not that she could ever say the name – if she had to mention it at all, it was "the nut house" or the "loony bin", even with the doctors. They thought she was a danger to herself.'

'I didn't know.'

'It pains me – it actually physically hurts – to think that she's gone but those pictures are still here. Like a hideous Cheshire Cat smile. I wanted to cancel the New York show – I still do – but Mum won't have it. She said Marianne painted them and she wanted them shown. I don't want people to think of her like that – I don't want them to associate her with those feelings. That wasn't her – that wasn't my sister.'

'I don't think people will see it like that, Ad. Honestly. It's embarrassing to admit but even I didn't, not straight away.'

'Really?'

She shook her head, remembering how humiliated Cory had made her feel. Did Adam know about him, she thought suddenly, his portrait? She battled the haze in her frontal lobe: had Cory said he'd told Jacqueline about it? She couldn't remember. If Adam didn't know, she should tell him, she had to, but the conviction was superseded by the equally rapid recognition that this wasn't the time. She needed to be sober, clear-headed.

Adam took a swig of wine. 'What a waste,' he said. 'What a fucking waste. My lovely, lovely sister.'

Rowan was ambushed by a memory so vivid she saw the exact position of her hands on the damask cloth. The hum of the restaurant around them, the carousel-whirl of candlelight and jazz, glinting silverware, the cascading laughter of a woman on the other side of the room. Jacqueline's armful of bangles had made a musical sound as she'd fallen back against the banquette and looked at them. 'Lovely, lovely girls,' she'd said, shaking her head a little. 'I'm so bloody proud of you both.'

Without warning, Rowan's eyes filled with tears. Mortified, she fumbled for the napkin on her lap only to discover it had fallen to the floor. As she moved to reach for it, however, Adam leaned across, took her hand and squeezed it gently. She expected him to let go, take his own hand back, but he left it where it was, on top of hers on the table. She looked at him, face flushing, and saw that he was crying, too. 'Don't be embarrassed,' he said.

They were almost the last to leave the restaurant and Rowan wondered if Adam had wanted to put it off, too, the moment of standing up and walking outside, forgoing the protection of the glasshouse and its circle of light. As she put on her coat and scarf, she had the idea that she was putting back on the distance between them.

Outside, the Banbury Road had gone quiet enough that they heard the whirr of an approaching bicycle for some seconds before it overtook them, and when the lights at the crossing turned red – so bright to Rowan in her wine bedazzlement – there were no cars to stop. Frost held the garden of the hotel on the corner in icy paralysis. Apart from an exclamation at the cold as they came outside and a brief remark about how much he'd always liked the violin-maker's shop two doors down, where the curvaceous wooden shapes of instruments-to-be hung pale and unvarnished in the window, Adam said nothing. They walked eighteen inches apart. She'd been right about the distance being reinstated, Rowan thought: the hand-holding at the restaurant had been about comfort, that was all. But of course: how could it be anything else? And the reason for the dinner had been made plain from the outset, he'd even told her explicitly: *a thank you from us both, Mum and me.*

As they passed the Maison Française, however, he reached for her hand again. She remembered the night of the party, the feel of his fingers on hers as they picked their way round the people on the stairs, and she told herself to stop. Even if he was attracted to her – and there was no evidence: he hadn't flirted or asked if she was seeing anyone – it wasn't fair. He was grieving, vulnerable. And drunk.

Still hand in hand, they reached the corner of Fyfield Road and Adam stopped in a pool of streetlight. He turned to look at her. 'Okay?' he asked. Rowan hesitated. What was the question? Was she okay now, not still upset? Or is *this* okay, whatever 'this' was? He watched her, waiting for her answer.

'Yes,' she said.

He nodded, *Good*, then moved on, pulling her with him beyond the spot of amber light. No need to look before crossing the road here, nothing stirred, and their footsteps were the only thing that broke the silence as they crunched across the drive. At the top of the steps, Adam let go of her hand to find the keys in his pocket and while he unlocked the door, she watched a ragged moth dance a deadly *pas de deux* with the carriage lamp. The bottom of the shade, she noticed for the first time, was filled with the bodies of earlier suitors.

He motioned for her to go in. As she reached for the switch on the inside wall, however, he stopped her hand. She turned, surprised, and the door shut quietly behind them. The faint glow of the lamp through the glass panels cast muted colours on one side of his face; the other side, except for the shine of his eye and teeth, was lost in the darkness.

He moved closer and along with the wine on his breath, she caught the scent of subtle aftershave, fresh and green, like newly cut wood or the floor of a pine forest. He found her hand again, intertwined his fingers with hers and lifted them into the faint light.

Rowan felt a surge in her chest, an expansion, and – had he seen it on her face? – Adam stepped forward and kissed her. At the touch of his lips, a shiver went through her, almost a shudder, and he pulled away, startled. 'God, I'm sorry. I—'

'No, don't be,' she said. 'I mean, nothing's wrong. The opposite – it's tension. I . . .'

He wrapped his arms around her, her cheek against his chest. She could feel the pulse at the base of his throat. He pressed his lips against the top of her head and, when she looked up at him, he kissed her again. The sensation travelled over her skin, ripples spreading from a stone thrown into water. Fleetingly she thought of the other time, years ago, up in the room that no longer existed, the rush of desire that had taken her by surprise. She hadn't known then if he'd felt it, too – there'd hardly been a chance before Marianne and Turk came crashing in – but there was no doubt now. The kiss escalated in seconds, a dissolution of boundaries.

He pushed her coat off her shoulders and it fell to the ground behind her with a soft thud. Seconds later, his fell, too, and he pulled her upstairs. 'Which room are you in?' he said on the landing, his hands in her hair. Strange, she thought dimly, leading him down the dark corridor, to be taking *him* to *her* room here. She started to say so but he shook his head, *Shhh*, and backed her on to the bed. Kneeling at her feet, he unzipped her boot, cupped her heel with his hand then pulled the boot off.

Encircled by his arm, Rowan had an unpleasant memory of being in the same position with Theo only ten days earlier – not even that. But this wasn't just a drunken thing, she told herself: she liked Adam, she always had.

Despite the coldness of the room, there was a light film of sweat on his skin. Turning on to her side, she propped herself on her elbow. She'd seen him in shorts and swimming trunks many times in the garden but his body had changed since then, become stronger and more defined. He'd mentioned over dinner that he'd rowed in California as a way to meet people outside the university, and now he was back at Cambridge, he'd rejoined his old coxless four. He was fit, flat-stomached, his arms and shoulders padded with muscle. The hair on his chest had thickened to become a soft triangle that spanned his pectorals and tapered to a point at his sternum.

She expected a smile but when he turned to look at her, his face was solemn. 'It's bad timing,' he said.

Rowan's stomach plunged. He was seeing someone. 'Are you . . . going back overseas?'

'No. I just mean, that this is happening now, that we'll always associate it with Marianne dying.'

'Yes. I know.'

'But it is what it is. And I'm very glad about it.' He pushed himself up and kissed her. 'And thirsty. I'll get some water – don't move.' He pulled back the sheets and swung his legs over the side of the bed. His back was tanned above a stark white line where his shorts must have begun and she imagined him running along a white American beach in dazzling sunshine. He showed no signs of self-consciousness as he walked naked to the door.

Rowan lay back against the pillow. She'd slept with Adam – she turned the idea over, feeling the strangeness of it. After the party, she'd thought about him, hoped, for months, but though there had been several gigs and other drunken parties that summer, they hadn't ever got together again. At Christmas, he'd told Mazz he was in love with a girl called Saira at Cambridge and she'd had to accept that that was it. But now, years later . . . what did he think this was?

He returned with the bottle of Evian from the fridge door, sat down on her side of the bed and poured her a glass. When she'd finished, he filled it for himself, drained it and then got back in. His fingers found her hip under the sheet, doodled softly on her skin.

'Do you remember,' she said, 'we kissed years ago, at that party? Mazz and Turk found us, we . . .'

'I remember.'

'Why didn't we ever track each other down again that night?' *Or any other.*

'I wanted to – I was going to. And the next day, there you were in the kitchen and we'd had that one kiss and I just wanted to grab you and do it again.'

'You should have. I wanted you to.'

'Mazz asked me not to.'

'What?'

'She asked me not to get together with you – she knew I liked you, that it wasn't just going to be a drunken thing. Well, maybe from your point of view,' he raised his eyebrows, self-deprecatory, 'but not from mine.'

'I . . .'

'She said it would be too weird, you and me getting together, her best friend and her brother.'

Despite all the time that had passed, the fact that Marianne was dead, for God's sake, Rowan felt a rush of anger. The next day, while they were clearing up, filling one black bag after another with the bottles and plastic cups that littered the house and garden, Rowan had waited until she and Marianne were on their own then broached the subject of the kiss so that it didn't become an issue between them. Marianne was the one who championed total honesty, transparency, but she hadn't even hinted that the idea of Adam and Rowan together made her uncomfortable. She'd apologised again for bursting in on them and sympathised – yes, Rowan remembered quite distinctly – she'd *sympathised* that it seemed to have messed things up. And all the time, she'd secretly warned him off.

Rowan played it off as nothing, saying she was sure she'd have felt the same if she had a brother, but when they turned off the light, she lay awake. How could Marianne have done that, scotched things and then lied to her – kept *on* lying? When the heat went out of the anger, a deep sense of hurt took its place.

She listened to the change in Adam's breathing as he fell asleep and abandoned her to the silence of the house. The wardrobe loomed at the end of the bed, a black behemoth in the darkness. Marianne's drawing was in there, stowed right at the bottom of the box, its decade-old Sellotape undisturbed, but nevertheless fewer than ten feet away. What would he think if he saw it? However this worked out, whatever happened, she must make sure that he never, ever did.

The clock's luminous hands glowed in the dark: three. She'd seen the same time last night, lying here with the echo of running feet in her ears, knowing that as soon as she fell asleep, she would be deaf to the sound of footsteps on the patio, the turn of a door handle, breaking glass. In normal circumstances, she could never sleep in a man's arms but she pulled Adam's more tightly around her waist, grateful that tonight, instead of being across the landing, he was here in her bed, his skin sticky and too hot where it touched hers, his chest hair tickling her back.

She didn't remember falling asleep but as the first weak light began to edge the curtains, she woke suddenly, soaked in sweat, with Marianne's voice in her ear.

'*Dad's got a new dolly bird.*'

Twenty-one

The next time she woke up, it was much later and the doorbell was ringing. For a second or two – she must still have been drunk, she thought afterwards – she took it for a dream or a particularly vivid bit of déjà vu but then Adam stirred and the night came flooding back. He opened his eyes and smiled. 'Who's that? Are you expecting someone?'

The image of Michael Cory, coffee in hand, flashed into her head. *Shit.* She hadn't worked out last night if Adam knew about the portrait: by the time she'd thought of it, she'd drunk too much. As she stumbled into her jeans and picked her top off the floor, she tried to think straight. Obviously Adam knew Marianne had known Cory, he'd been at the funeral, but he would have mentioned a portrait, surely, if he'd been aware of it, given how strongly he felt about Marianne's anorexics. Given Cory's reputation. And either way, said the dry voice, whether he knew or not, wouldn't he find it a little odd that she hadn't mentioned Cory coming here, to their house?

'It's probably Jehovah's Witnesses,' she said. 'Nice and early on a Saturday morning.'

'Not so early – it's eleven.'

'Is it?' She glanced at the clock. 'I'll go and get it, anyway, then bring some coffee up. Stay in bed.'

The size of the silhouette on the step did nothing to quell her alarm but when she opened the door, it wasn't Cory leaning against the porch wall but Peter Turk. His eyes went straight to her silky top. 'Big night? I like the bed-head look on you.'

In her relief, she resisted the urge to tell him that she liked the ageing-rock-star look on him. Today's outfit – black leather jacket, black skinny jeans and a torn grey T-shirt with a peeling transfer of a naked woman – was so perfect, it could go on tour on its own. The only thing that detracted from the impression of classic rock debauch was the rucksack at his feet, a new-looking blue JanSport, standard geek issue.

'Come on then, spill the beans: who was the lucky sod this time?' he said, coming in and closing the door behind him.

'No sod at all, I'm afraid – sorry to disappoint – but I'll admit to a hangover.'

'I'd worked that out for myself. Got any coffee?'

'If you'll make it.'

She sat on Jacqueline's sofa and drank a pint of water while Turk moved around the kitchen with easy familiarity, opening the cupboard and reaching for the bag of beans without think-ing. She thought of Adam in bed upstairs and hoped he hadn't heard the exchange. Was there any chance she could keep him up there until Turk left? Turk had a world-class nose for gossip. But Adam's being here wasn't incriminating, was it? It was his house, for God's sake, of course he would stay here, and they were old friends so why wouldn't they go out for a drink? She'd just made up her mind to tell Turk that when she was pre-empted by the sound of movement overhead. He turned to look at her, eyebrows halfway to his hairline.

'Adam,' she said.

'No way.' His eyes widened. 'You didn't?'

'No, I didn't. Stop it – just behave yourself.' She gave him a warning frown as footsteps started down the kitchen stairs.

'Pete. I thought I heard your voice. How are you?'

Adam looked substantially brighter than she felt. He'd left yesterday's shirt in its wrinkled pile on the carpet and just put his jumper on, which, with the jeans, was a plausible Saturday-morning outfit. He and Turk gave each other a brief man-hug, a quick squeeze of the shoulders followed by a reassuringly distant clap on the back.

'Doing okay,' Turk said. 'But I think on a deep level I still don't really believe it.'

'I know. Especially here.'

Turk nodded, bleak. 'Rowan says you're putting the place on the market.'

Adam, taking his mother's chair at the end of the table, looked at her, surprised.

'I mentioned the agent from Savills was coming,' she said.

'We're thinking about it,' he said. 'Mum can't bring herself even to come here now. What are you doing up in Oxford?'

'I've just come for the day to visit *my* mum – she's got a few things that need mending and I said I'd do them, save her hiring anyone.' Rowan had forgotten that side of Turk, the surprisingly handy fixer of things. When Dan Whyte had pulled the downstairs sink off the wall during that party, it had been Turk who'd mended the tap and redone the grouting before Jacqueline and Seb got back from Barcelona.

He brought the coffee pot over to the table. At the sight of the three mugs, Rowan, under-slept and still full of alcohol, felt laughter bubbling inside her. It was too much, too strange, to be expected to sit here in last night's outfit making polite conversation when, only hours ago, Adam's hips had pressed her down into the bed. Her nostrils flared with the effort of keeping a straight face and she saw Turk's eyes narrow infinitesimally: *What are you up to?*

Adam, thankfully, seemed not to notice. He poured the coffee and took what had to be a scalding sip. 'What have you been doing lately, Pete? Work-wise.'

'Actually, I've been working on a film script. I met this guy who's a producer and he's really keen on the story so . . .' He tipped his head from side to side.

'Good for you. What kind of thing is it?'

'A thriller. It's about a guy who's approached by someone who insists he's his brother even though his mother died years before this guy could have been born. It's pretty dark – gothic, really.'

'Would we have heard of him, the producer?' Rowan asked. 'What else has he done?'

'Well, nothing yet – he's just started his own company. But I like him and he's got a friend who's a hedge-fund guy and wants to get into film production so, you know, we're sort of working it out as we go along . . .' He tailed off.

'Are you still writing music?' Adam took a sip of coffee.

'Sometimes. Kind of. I did a couple of jingles for radio adverts last year.' Turk looked down and turned the mug between his hands as if he'd never seen such a thing before. 'I don't know,' he said. 'I've been feeling a bit . . . I suppose burned out is the best way to describe it. What's it like for you being back, though? You must be missing the Californian weather. Cambridge is bloody freezing in winter, isn't it, wind straight from the Urals?'

Adam gave Turk a potted version of what he'd told Rowan over dinner then abruptly put his mug down. 'Right,' he said, standing. 'I'm sorry to have to run off but I've got to be in London by two, I'm meeting an old friend. No, don't get up, Pete.' He ushered him back into his chair. 'I'll just go and grab my stuff then let myself out. Good to see you.' He put a hand on Turk's shoulder and then came round the table. Rowan stood, expecting to walk him out, but he shook his head.

'Don't let your coffee get cold. I'll let myself out. Thanks again for everything . . . looking after the house.' He touched her shoulder but his eyes met hers for only a second before he looked away. 'I'll ring you,' he said.

Turk busied himself with pouring another half-mug of coffee and waited until Adam's feet crossed the hallway above their heads before leaning across the table. 'Sure there's nothing on your conscience? You're hungover as dogs, the pair of you. Come on, don't be shy – you can tell your uncle Pete.'

It was clear by the way he was looking at her that he saw the heat in her face. It was shock, though, not embarrassment. How could Adam do that after last night, just get up and go without a word?

'We went out for dinner,' she said, 'and ended up drinking two bottles of wine after a couple of gin and tonics each. Nothing more salacious than that, I'm afraid, unless you count falling asleep in your clothes.'

'Hmm.'

The front door closed and they heard the scuff of Adam's feet on the steps then the fading crunch of gravel. Rowan thought suddenly of the night before last, the sound of running feet.

'Does he know?' Turk said.

'What?'

'Adam, about Cory – the portrait.'

'No. At least I don't think so – he didn't mention it.'

'Did you?'

She shook her head, making the room lurch queasily. 'I was going to today, before he went. It didn't feel like the right time, last night. Too much booze involved.'

'What did Cory say, when he came here? You didn't tell me on the phone.'

Rowan hoped her eyes wouldn't give away the frantic mental calculation going on behind them. How much should she say? 'He didn't give a lot away,' she said. 'He told me that he'd been spending quite a bit of time here, getting to know Mazz, sketching.'

'Do you think they were having a thing? An affair?'

'No, Pete, I don't. Honestly. Stop tormenting yourself – please.' She wondered why the idea bothered him so much. It wasn't as if he'd ever stood a chance with Marianne; she'd been straight with him about it years ago. 'And you told me yourself you thought she was happy with Greenwood.'

'I know. I know. It just sticks in my craw, the idea of that ... slippery, opportunist *creep* coming here, trying to expose her.'

'What was there to expose?' She looked at him sharply.

He shrugged. 'Nothing. I mean, nothing extraordinary, nothing we don't all already know, her friends and family. Just ... she was fragile, wasn't she, the breakdown, what Seb did, and Cory's ... predatory. You only have to look at his record. He'd use all that, her past – he wouldn't hesitate.'

'Pete, did Mazz ever talk to you about dying?'

'What?'

'Exactly that – did she ever talk about dying? Death.'

His eyes didn't leave her face for a moment. 'What are you saying? That she spoke to him about it? Cory?' His voice was rising quickly. 'For fuck's sake, Rowan – did she talk to him about suicide? Did he know she was going to ... ?'

'No. *No.* That's not what he said. He just said it was a subject she came back to a lot. I think it was because of the anorexics, that it made her think about ...'

'If he knew – if he was pushing her, mining her for ...' Turk stood up from the table, the legs of his chair screeching against the floor.

'Stop it!' Rowan's voice came out louder than she'd planned. 'Just stop it, Pete,' she said more quietly. He was radiating anger; it came off him like a heat haze over tarmac. 'Come on – sit down.'

His breathing was high and shallow, and he glared at her for several seconds before capitulating and reaching for the chair.

'I asked him specifically,' she said when Turk was sitting. 'I called him on it. He knew about the breakdown, obviously: it was in the newspapers, even if she hadn't told him herself – which, for the record, she had. I asked him if she'd ever seemed suicidal and he said no.'

Turk considered that. 'And was he telling the truth? You believed him?'

'Yes.'

'Because if . . .'

Rowan put up a hand. 'He told me about Greta Mulraine,' she said. 'Straight up, unprompted.' She saw surprise cross Turk's face. 'He said he knew what suicidal looked like. Actually, he asked me if I thought he was the kind of person who would do that, know someone was desperate and stand by. He asked if I thought he was a monster.'

'And do you?'

She paused. 'No,' she said. 'Not like that.'

'What was Marianne's costume?'

'Her what?'

'For the party, when she borrowed the cufflinks.'

'Oh, right.' Turk nodded. 'Al Capone. It was gangsters and molls.'

Rowan remembered Marianne standing in front of the long mirror in her parents' room forcing a safety pin through the back of a cardboard dog collar.

'I'm not dressing like a stripper just because Martin decided it was fancy dress. Tarts and vicars? What is he, a middle-aged swinger?'

'That's my girl,' said Rowan. She picked up the mugs and carried them to the sink. 'I had a look for them yesterday. I don't know if she had a jewellery box – she never used to – but there weren't any cufflinks in the tray on her dresser, which seemed like the obvious place. Or her bedside table – there are some bits and pieces in the top drawer. Maybe they got mixed up with Seb's – his things are still there, in their old room.'

'All right. Thanks for trying, anyway. Okay if I run up and have a quick look?'

'Of course.' She turned the tap on then glanced over her shoulder. 'You've got the advantage of knowing what you're looking for.'

She washed the coffee pot and put it on the rack to dry, trying to think. In that momentary glance, she'd seen something odd though she hadn't quite registered what it was. When the last of the water gurgled away, she stood still, hands on the edge of the sink, and listened for movement in the house overhead. Nothing – silence.

She crossed the kitchen quietly and made her way up to the hallway. At the bottom of the stairs, making sure she was invisible from the landing, she stopped and listened again but there were no sounds of opening drawers or feet on creaky boards.

He'd taken his rucksack up with him; that was what had struck her. When he arrived, she'd noticed, he hadn't dropped it under the coat pegs as they always used to do with their schoolbags. He'd brought it with him down to the kitchen and kept it by his feet, and in the few seconds she'd had her back to him, clearing the coffee things, he'd picked it up and slung it over his shoulder.

As quietly as possible, she went upstairs. From the hallway, she'd seen that the door to Seb and Jacqueline's room was closed. Going along the corridor to Marianne's, she composed her face into a benign expression just in case but when she put her head around the door, her suspicions were confirmed: the room was empty. As she turned to go, there was a squeak overhead.

The pieces dropped into place one by one but when she reached the top landing, what she saw through the open doorway still shocked her.

Turk was on his knees in front of the worktable, one of Marianne's square boxes pulled out, its lid off, five or six A4 sketches ranged on the boards around him. The rucksack's soft canvas mouth was open and next to it, also open, was what it had contained: a rigid artist's carrying case. A sheaf of papers rested on it now, a charcoal sketch of a pair of cupped hands on the top.

'Explains why the police couldn't find any signs of a break-in.'

Turk hadn't heard her coming. He spun around, eyes wide with shock.

'But it's not burglary if the owner asks you in, is it?'

He scrambled to his feet. Under the studio's relatively low ceiling, he seemed even taller and as he stepped towards her, Rowan felt a moment of physical fear. He was strong – much stronger than she was.

'She would have given them to me if I'd asked. Don't act like I'm *stealing.*'

She considered that. Marianne *did* give her friends sketches – her own were downstairs in the wardrobe as they spoke. 'Why *didn't* you ask then?' she said. 'Why didn't you ask Adam just now? And why the hell did you let Mazz go on thinking someone was breaking in?'

But then, clicking like domino tiles, another run of connections: the nerdy 'friend of a friend' with his chickpea curry; the unrenovated kitchen; the radio jingles; the film script that was clearly going nowhere. And the high prices that Marianne's work commanded. 'Oh,' she said. 'You've been selling them.'

Turk laughed as if it were the most ridiculous thing he'd ever heard but it didn't work. The hollowness was patent and, out of the blue, Rowan felt a bolt of pity for him.

'Where did all the money go, Pete?' she said, gentler. 'From *Liars in Love*? You made a fortune, didn't you? The deal, royalties . . .'

'It was years ago,' he spat. 'Years and years ago. Divide it up, calculate the annual salary, and I'd have made more tossing the fries in McDonald's.'

'Wouldn't that have been better than stealing from a friend?'

204

A different laugh now, bitter. '*You're* going to lecture *me* about taking from Mazz? Really?' He laughed again and this time he actually sounded amused.

'What are you talking about?' she said.

'Come on, Ro, was there ever a bigger leech than you? Coming here like something out of *Oliver Twist*, the poor little latch-key kid whose daddy didn't love her, grateful for any pathetic crumb of attention that fell from the Glasses' table.'

She felt it like a punch in the gut. Unkind – so unkind – but not untrue. She'd tried not to be or at least not to show it but, yes, at times she *had* been grateful.

'Mazz was happy when you finally got the message and buggered off,' he said. 'She was *relieved*.'

Another punch. 'Did she tell you that?'

'She didn't need to. Remember that afternoon? She couldn't wait to be shot of you.'

To her horror, Rowan felt a lump in her throat. *Don't cry. Don't you dare bloody cry, Rowan.* It wasn't true – she knew it wasn't. He didn't know the whole story: Marianne had clearly never told him. The thought was fortifying, a shot of energy.

'What's the plan now?' Turk was saying. 'Get your claws into Adam? Sorry if I messed things up this morning but I wouldn't worry – I'm sure you'll use your wiles to find a way back in, wind him round your little finger. Poor sod – I should warn him.'

Don't rise to it, she cautioned herself. *Don't show him he's getting to you*.

'Perhaps I should put him in touch with Josh.'

'What?'

'Remember him? He really liked you, Rowan, I think he *loved* you, but you dropped him without a word, moved on as if the whole thing had been a one-night stand. He told me you tried to talk to him at the funeral like nothing ever happened.'

'That was years ago, for God's sake – we were teenagers.' *Stay calm – don't get distracted.* 'Who do you sell them to?' she said. 'Obviously Greenwood doesn't know anything about it.'

Turk rolled his eyes as if she were the one beneath contempt. Turning, he went down on his haunches and picked up the sketches that were spread on the floor. Rowan saw an arm, the nape of a neck beneath a low bun, the charcoal silhouette of one of the earlier girls, who had just enough meat on the bone still to appeal to a buyer appreciative of a nubile female body. She watched as he dropped them into the carrying case and clipped it shut.

'Were you threatening her, Peter?' she said.

'What?' He looked up from stuffing the case into his rucksack.

'Were you threatening Marianne? Frightening her.'

He zipped the bag shut with a furious flourish and slung it over his shoulder. She felt the air stir as he pushed past her towards the stairs. 'You know what I think?' he said. 'I think you're fucking insane.'

Rowan sat in the dark. She'd been here for hours – she'd watched the last of the light slip away across the floor like the hem of a wedding dress. On the arm of the sofa, her phone started ringing, startling in the silence, but the number on the screen was Cory's again. She let it ring out.

This was how she'd felt years ago, when she'd left Fyfield Road for the last time. Vulnerable as a hermit crab yanked from its borrowed shell, soft flesh exposed to the predators that moved like clouds through the water overhead. She felt like she'd been kicked in the heart.

The bells of St Giles struck ten and the boiler clicked off. Why had Adam left so abruptly? Why hadn't he called? If they were strangers, people who'd met in a bar, she'd understand but with their history, the way things were, it didn't make sense.

I'll ring you. When? Had he meant later, when Turk had gone? Or had it just been a formula, a way to make an easy exit? She felt a wave of self-disgust. Who was behaving like a teenager now, picking over his every word for indications that he really did like her? Every word she could remember, anyway, through the fug of booze. Was that what it had been for him, a drunken hook-up? Perhaps – the kinder interpretation – he'd just been looking for comfort with someone who'd loved Marianne like he had. But no: hadn't he said that Mazz knew the kiss years ago would mean something to him? Hadn't he said they would *always* associate getting together with her death? *Oh, for God's sake, Rowan, just stop.*

A darker thought: what if Turk had done what he'd threatened and called him? Maybe he *had* warned Adam off. But what could he have said? That she'd always loved the Glasses and been grateful for their affection? Adam knew that. And he knew who made the running last night. She hadn't set out to 'get her claws into' him.

She couldn't wait to be shot of you. The look on Turk's face as he'd spat it at her. A leech – was that really how he'd seen her, a disgusting formless creature that latched on to others and sucked? No, it wasn't true; it just wasn't. Turk was on the defensive, lashing out. The Glasses had been fond of her – they'd told her, they'd *shown* her. They'd given her a lot, it was indisputable, but it hadn't always been one-way traffic.

At quarter to eleven, the landline rang. Adam had called on the house number when he'd asked her out to dinner; she stood quickly and ran upstairs.

'Where have you been? I've been calling your cell all day.'

Cory.

'I left it at a friend's house last night.'

'I couldn't get hold of you. It was just luck I remembered Marianne called me from this number once when she dropped her phone in a taxi. I've had to go back through my call history and . . .'

'What is it?' she said. 'It's late. I was on my way to bed.'

'I have an idea. I'm not sure, at this stage, it's really just a . . .'

'What?' She cut him off.

'Marianne told me her father had affairs. You knew that, right?'

A cold hand reached between Rowan's ribs and took hold of her heart.

'What if it *wasn't* an accident?' he said. 'The death she was talking about. I've been over everything again and again and I keep coming back to her breakdown when Seb died. I read a rumour online that there was a woman involved – that Seb was drunk out of his mind over losing a woman. What if that had something to do with it? What if this woman he loved didn't break up with him but *died*?'

When she spoke again, Rowan's voice seemed to come from a long way away. 'Are you saying what I think you're saying?'

Twenty-two

'Bryony?'

The slender girl in the middle of the trio stopped, seemed to pause, then turned around. Rowan saw James Greenwood's eyes, his high forehead, and felt a stab of panic: this was a mistake; she shouldn't have come. Bryony would tell her father and he'd know for sure that something was going on, that Rowan was still poking around days later, that she'd lied when she'd gone to the gallery. As quickly as it came, though, the doubt was replaced by the conviction that, risk though it was, she was doing the right thing. She'd allowed Adam and Turk to sidetrack her but Cory's call had pulled her back, reminded her of what was at stake.

'I'm Rowan Winter,' she said, stepping away from the wall. 'An old friend of Marianne's. We met briefly at the wake – I don't know if you'll remember.'

Bryony's face registered a fleeting expression – was it surprise?

'I'm sorry to accost you like this. I'm staying at the house at the moment, looking after it for Jacqueline. I wondered if we could talk.'

The dark-haired girl on Bryony's left raised her eyebrows a degree or two, as if to say, minder-like, 'Is this woman bothering you, Bry?'

'Talk?' Bryony shook her head. 'No. I mean, I don't know – I'm not sure.'

'A couple of minutes,' Rowan said.

'I don't . . . I'm not supposed to talk to anyone about it.'

'Why?'

'The media – journalists – the whole thing's just out of . . .'

'I'm not a journalist. Please.'

Bryony looked at her then seemed to give way. 'Okay, but only if it's really quick. I have to finish an essay for a class this afternoon and this is the only time I've got. I was just going to quickly buy some lunch and . . .'

'Do you want us to wait?' asked the other girl, a petite strawberry blonde, but Bryony shook her head. Her purse was in her hand and she opened it and took out a folded note. 'Will you get me a chicken sandwich? And some orange juice.'

Rowan waited until they moved off. As they crossed the road, the dark girl turned her head and gave her a monitory look: *She's grieving, all right, so don't mess with her*.

It was a better day than the last time Rowan had come, no snow at least, but the breeze had a sharp edge and Bryony pulled her blazer tighter and crossed her arms. Her friends had both been wearing the giant knitted Mobius strips that nine out of ten of the Sixth Form seemed to have but Bryony's scarf was made of fine cotton, perhaps Indian, shot through with silver thread. There were flicks of pewter liner at the corners of her eyes, against school rules if they were still the same.

'I'm so sorry,' said Rowan. 'I know you two were close.'

'I loved her,' Bryony said simply.

'Me, too.'

Bryony only nodded and Rowan saw that her eyes had filled with tears. She cautioned herself to be careful, tread gently. 'It's my biggest regret,' she said, 'that we didn't get a chance to straighten things out before . . .'

Not yet trusting herself to speak, Bryony gave another upward nod.

'I'm sorry, I know this seems insensitive – it *is* – but I wanted to ask you if you thought anything was bothering Marianne before it happened. Had she talked to you about anything? Peter Turk told me the two of you used to talk a lot so I wondered . . .'

'Wasn't it an accident?' Bryony looked at her, startled. 'Why are you asking? You went to see Dad, too, didn't you, in London?'

Shit.

'Do you think something happened to her?'

'No – no. That's not . . .' Panicking, Rowan tried to think. 'I mean, the police are sure it was an accident, aren't they?' Behind them, the gate opened and another pair of girls came out, the sound of their laughter almost eerily incongruous. It occurred to Rowan now that if one of the staff saw her with Bryony, she would be the one answering questions. 'She didn't ever talk to you about dying?' she said quickly.

Bryony stepped backwards as if Rowan had revealed herself to be dangerously unhinged. 'No. Why would she?'

She felt as if she were scrambling up a bank of scree that fell away beneath her as fast as she tried to get purchase. 'No reason,' she said, trying to sound reassuring. 'I suppose I just wanted to make sure. Get some closure. It was so . . . abrupt. When someone goes like that, without warning . . .'

'Yeah.' At last, Bryony's tone seemed to say, something borderline sane.

'Anyway, apologies again for coming to find you like this. I didn't mean to upset you.'

'It's all right.' Bryony's tolerant look suggested that she was the adult here. She frowned, making a crease down the centre of her pale forehead, and Rowan saw James Greenwood again, as if Bryony's face was a body of water, a river, and his had risen momentarily to the surface before sinking out of sight.

'I'll leave you to get on with your essay.' Rowan gestured back at the school. 'I went here, too, St Helena's – it was where Mazz and I met.'

'Really?'

She nodded, surprised: hadn't Marianne told her? 'You know Michael Cory was painting her portrait – still is? We were in the Upper Sixth when he painted Hanna Ferrara and there was that huge media furore.' As she said it, however, she realised that Bryony would only have been three or four. 'I said to your father, it feels so strange that we'd talked about him so much then, Marianne and I, and now here he is.'

Bryony said nothing. *Oh, come on*, thought Rowan, desperate; *throw me a bone here*. 'Do you know him?' she said, cringing inwardly at the transparency. 'Through your father – or Marianne?'

Bryony shrugged. 'I've met him, obviously, through Dad, and two or three times at Marianne's, when I went over.'

'What was he like?'

'You've met him?'

Rowan calculated. 'Yes.'

'Then you know. He's all right, a bit intense but not as much as the hype would have you believe.'

'What kind of relationship did they have?'

Bryony's stare was hard. 'What are you saying? She was with my dad.'

'No, no, no – sorry. All I meant was, did they get on? Were they on the same wavelength? Were they friends?'

The hostility level dropped but marginally. 'I never heard them talk about anything that personal, it was mostly art – what they'd seen, what they'd liked. Styles, techniques, that kind of thing. A lot of it was over my head, to be honest. But yeah, they liked each other. They got on.'

Keeping off the Banbury Road for as long as possible to minimise the likelihood of bumping into Bryony's friends, Rowan walked into Summertown and found a seat in the gloomy recesses at the back of Costa Coffee. When he'd called this morning, Cory had announced that he would come to the house at three but she didn't trust him not to turn up whenever he felt like it and she needed to regroup first. Everything was spinning out of control. Seeking Bryony out had been a big gamble and she'd gleaned nothing she hadn't already known. Without a doubt, the encounter would be related to Greenwood word for word.

But what choice had she had? In her efforts to stay a step ahead of Cory, she was running out of lines of inquiry. He was making one connection after another, sure-footedly picking his way towards the truth of what happened back then, while she was struggling to discover anything at all about what happened a month ago. Dead end after dead end, and the few times she'd felt as if she were homing in on something, getting closer, there had been a seismic shift and she'd been thrown sideways. When she stood up again, bruised, the landscape had been transfigured, leaving her not only without an answer but faced with a different question. A different *set* of questions.

When she was younger, she'd loved puzzles. She'd been a jigsaw fanatic as a child and, later on, one of her favourite Glass family traditions had been the pre-Christmas purchase of an enormous one – 3,000 pieces, 5,000 – which they set up in the dining room on Boxing Day and worked away at in the grey days before New Year's Eve. They'd sat, talking or in companionable silence, coffee cups or wine glasses at their elbows, and slowly covered the table, all of them making self-deprecatory jokes about how uncool they were, all of them loving it. They'd loved cryptic crosswords, too, and whoever got to *The Times* first in the morning had to make photocopies for the others on the little Xerox machine in Seb's office. When Rowan was there, they'd made her a copy, too, and she'd joined in the daily race to finish it. Adam was very good but Seb won most days; the one time she'd beaten him might still go down as her proudest intellectual achievement.

Now, though, she felt as if she were doing a giant logic puzzle for which there weren't enough clues. The few there were told her what hadn't happened and who hadn't done it but didn't give her anywhere near enough information to deduce what or who *had*. So Turk stole the sketches but he hadn't broken in. Had there ever been a break-in? Possibly not, if the police hadn't found any evidence. But if the man in the garden wasn't casing the house, what *was* he doing? And was he the same man who watched from the window in Benson Place? Drawing her bedroom curtains after midnight on Saturday, she'd seen him standing there again, an unmoving silhouette against the light, and she'd had a disturbing thought: had he seen her with Adam? Watched? She couldn't remember drawing the curtains but she knew the light had been on.

Adam. She'd woken up yesterday, the paranoid fog of the hangover almost lifted, and she'd been ashamed of herself. How had she managed to get into such a stew about him not calling? He'd only left precipitately because Turk had been there and he probably thought ringing the same day would make him look a bit keen. He'd call today, most likely, after a decent interval. The thought had cheered her up as she'd walked to North Parade to buy milk and a Sunday paper but as the day had gone on and the phone stayed silent, the negative feelings had started to creep back. Why wasn't he ringing? Had Turk called him? Or was there something else entirely going on here?

She'd barely opened the door before Cory pushed past her into the hallway. He was vibrating with impatience so Rowan took her time, closing the door gently, bending to pick up a wet leaf he'd brought in on his boots. She straightened again and gave him a calm smile.

If he sensed she was doing it on purpose, he chose to ignore it. 'I think I've found something.'

Her heart gave an exaggerated beat. 'What?'

'I've been in the library for hours, on Saturday and again this morning – God, I hate microfiche. It was just long enough ago that not everything was on the Net.' He pinched the bridge of his nose and pressed his eyes shut. 'The nationals were, obviously, but the archives of the local papers don't go back that far online so I had to talk to the librarian, tell her what I wanted, get her to show me how to use the machine . . . It was like the seventies in there.'

'Where were you?'

'The big public library in the centre of town. Hideous, over that shopping mall – what's it called, the Watergate Centre?'

'Westgate. Please,' she said, 'tell me you didn't mention Marianne or Seb.'

He gave her a withering look. 'It was real needle-in-a-haystack stuff, to start. I was trying to find a woman with a connection to Seb who died just before him, within a period of time that meant he would still have been grieving when he got loaded and crashed the car.'

Rowan shook her head to convey incredulity that he was still gnawing away at this crazy theory.

'I took it week by week, working backwards, nationals first, just in case, then the microfiche – news and obituaries. I didn't know if she would be here or in London. He travelled a lot, didn't he, lecturing, book tours, so there was also the possibility that . . .'

'Like I said on Saturday – *again* – you're barking up the wrong tree. There's no way Marianne killed anyone, accidentally or otherwise, full stop, and that includes any woman her dad may or may not have been seeing. She just . . .'

'She was a grad student.'

'Who was?'

'The woman I found.'

Rowan stared.

'Lorna Morris. She died six weeks before him, almost to the day. The *Oxford Times* had a picture of her and as soon as I saw it, I got a feeling. She was twenty-six, beautiful. I focused on her, cross-referenced, and I found out that a) she was an experimental psychologist, and b) she'd been working at the labs where Seb did most of his research.'

Stay calm, Rowan ordered herself. 'There are a lot of psychologists at Oxford and I don't know how many of them worked at those labs. Everyone who was doing experimental work, I should think – definitely the vast majority. I'm not sure how many other labs there even were for that.'

'She died in a fire,' Cory said as if Rowan hadn't spoken. 'Actually, an explosion. She lived on a houseboat on the river and there was a gas leak and . . .'

'I know.' She cut him off. 'I remember. It was a big story here – in Oxford. Horrific. But it was an accident. There was a police investigation, obviously. An inquest.'

'I read the reports. It said that it looked like she'd left the gas stove on, unlit. She went out, came back after dark, hit the light . . .'

'It was horrendous. A terrible way to die.'

'What if it wasn't an accident, Rowan?' He eyeballed her, demanding that she take him seriously. 'What if Marianne did it? Messed with the stove, made it *look* like an accident.'

She shook her head and moved towards the top of the kitchen stairs. 'I can't listen to any more of this.'

Whip-fast, Cory reached out and grabbed her forearm. 'She jumped for a reason.'

'*If* she jumped at all,' Rowan shot back, yanking her arm away. 'Seb had lots of affairs, okay? Lots. He was a tart, a butterfly collector: he couldn't help himself. It's *possible* he slept with Lorna, I suppose, not that there were ever any rumours about it – and there usually were, I have to tell you, because he wasn't the best keeper of secrets on

216

that front. But if he did, *if*, she would have been one of three or four that *year*.'

'Who would know?'

'How the hell could I tell you that? I hadn't seen the Glasses for years – I *never* knew Lorna.'

'Have you spoken to Peter Turk about this?'

'Of course not. You think I'm going to plough in and start spouting all these mad theories to her grieving friends?'

'I'm going to.' He took a step in the direction of the door, as if he were leaving to go and do it right away.

'Stop,' she said, too loudly. 'Please – just stop.'

'Why?' He turned back, face alight with new interest.

'He was here,' she said slowly. 'Turk was. On Saturday. He told me this story about wanting to find a pair of cufflinks he'd lent Marianne for a party but really he'd come to steal sketches.' Despite all the unkind things he'd said, Rowan felt a pang of regret at betraying him to Cory. 'He's been selling them,' she said. 'He's broke.'

Cory strode to the bottom of the stairs and sat down. Elbow planted on his knee, he put his fist to his mouth, *The Thinker* in jeans and a top coat. Several seconds passed. 'Were you going to tell me this?' he said.

'Haven't I just done that?'

'Under duress.'

She rolled her eyes. 'If you hadn't shoved your way in here all guns blazing, I might have got round to it earlier.'

They faced each other off. Cory, to her satisfaction, looked away first. 'Do you think he was blackmailing her? If he was broke, and if he knows something, maybe he was extorting money from Marianne, too.'

'I thought about that,' Rowan said. 'I went through her financial paperwork yesterday, her bank statements, but there are no strange payments, no transfers or big cash withdrawals. I think we can discount the possibility that he was blackmailing her fifty pounds at a time.'

'I still want to talk to him.'

'Do it then but just wait a day or two. He's . . . humiliated. He was so angry when I caught him – I've never seen that side of him before. Let him calm down and then talk to him. You'll get more out of him.'

Cory put his fist back to his mouth and considered her. 'Okay,' he said eventually. 'But I will talk to him – I'm not going to let it go. I'm starting to get close here, Rowan, I can feel it.'

Twenty-three

Rowan hadn't known Lorna but she had met her. It had been mid-June, a week after she'd put down her pen for the last time and stepped blinking from the Exam Schools into the heat of the midday sun, her scholar's gown billowing behind her like a final puff of infernal smoke. As she'd crossed Radcliffe Square the day of the party, the cobbles had sparkled with the glitter that people threw like confetti as their friends made their exhausted way to the pub. The sky was high and cloudless, the kind that arced over pine-covered hillsides on scorched Aegean islands, a harbinger, as it turned out, of the heat that late July and August would bring.

It was Seb's fiftieth birthday. Demob happy after her graduation show and still in a state of ecstatic incredulity about the sales to Dorotea Perling, Marianne had driven up from London for the weekend. She'd phoned at nine that morning to ask if Rowan could come early to help. 'It was supposed to be a sit-down lunch for sixteen,' she said, 'but Mum's done her usual thing and invited everyone who's crossed her path in the past fortnight. We managed to pin her down last night and it sounds like there might be ninety.'

'Bloody hell.'

'Maybe more, she says, if everyone brings partners. Pete's asked his dad if we can borrow the Rotary Club barbecue and we've called the butcher with an emergency order.'

'Emergency,' Jacqueline scoffed in the background. 'It'll be fine. So dramatic, Marianne.'

The van from the off-licence pulled up just as Rowan arrived and she showed the driver the side gate so the wine could go directly to the garden. In the kitchen, Marianne was stirring pesto through a huge bowl of pasta, hair stuck to her neck with perspiration, while Jacqueline sat at the table sipping a cup of coffee and writing a letter. An old claw-footed bathtub with copper stains under the taps lurked in the shade on the patio. 'The Dawsons have lent it to us for the drinks,' Mazz said. 'Ad's taken the car to buy ice.' She pointed at a sack of muddy new potatoes and grimaced. 'Sorry. Online shopping – of course it had to be today they arrived filthy.'

The phone rang again and again with people asking what time to come until Seb, who was writing a piece for the following day's *Observer*, thundered down the stairs, yanked it out of the wall and carried it away to his study. 'You can have it back when I'm finished. It's like trying to work in bloody Bedlam.' The door slammed shut.

When Rowan looked at Marianne, she'd shrugged. 'He's been like that since I got home.'

With planks from the shed, they constructed an ersatz buffet table and covered it with the Greek lace tablecloths Jacqueline had inherited from an aunt. They made bowl after bowl of salad and ran around putting out glasses and silverware, boards for nuts and cheese. Rowan sawed French bread until she felt as if she was developing tennis elbow. 'Major health issue among the middle classes,' said Adam, washing the barbecue tools. 'Along with carpal-tunnel from lobster-crackers and choking on the olive in one's third martini.'

At two o'clock, Seb came downstairs, plugged the phone back in and went outside to the bath. Fishing out a beer, he knocked off the cap against the patio wall and took a long pull. As he lowered the bottle, he caught sight of the pair of undergraduates corralled at Marianne's insistence to man the grill.

'Jesus, Jacks,' he said, 'is someone getting married?'

The first guests arrived as Rowan came down from getting changed. Standing at the sink to wash lettuce for a final salad, she watched Seb through the window. His editor at the *Observer* had already emailed an enthusiastic thumbs-up but Seb hadn't relaxed like he usually did after a deadline. Here was his party avatar, voluble and charismatic, but there was an energy about him today that she couldn't isolate, a potential, a glinting edge.

The patio doors were wide open and his frequent laughter carried into the kitchen. He wore jeans and a blue shirt with the sleeves rolled up, its cotton softened and faded as if by countless summers on yachts off Capri. If you didn't know otherwise, she thought, you'd have guessed he was thirty. Jacqueline had chosen a green sundress she'd bought on their honeymoon in Istanbul twenty-five years ago, she said, and a pair of cork-heeled wedges that her old Sussex crony Miriam Jacobs had talked her into buying after a boozy lunch in Spitalfields the previous week. She was trying not to look as if she cared too much but twice Rowan caught her surreptitiously turning her ankle to admire them.

'Miriam is a good influence,' Seb had said a couple of years earlier, when Jacqueline returned from London with a pair of black cigarette pants and a biker jacket. 'Without her periodic interventions, you'd still be wearing the things you had at college.'

'I *am* still wearing some of them,' Jacqueline replied. 'If I could get into them, I'd wear more.'

The lawn quickly filled with people. By half-past three, the barbecue was running at capacity, Jacqueline's first-years red-faced with heat and the pressure of maintaining a constant supply of lamb and grilled chicken. As they carried out the

221

last two trays of raw meat, Rowan felt like a lion-tamer or a city steward tasked with keeping a ravening monster at bay, outside the gates. 'Mum deliberately downplayed it,' said Marianne in a low voice. 'Again. Just counting the families, I've got seventy-four.'

They were sick of food and too hot so they ate nothing themselves and plunged straight in to the middle of the crowd. Over the past seven years, Rowan had come to know a lot of the Glasses' friends, and they asked about her exams and what she was planning to do next. Seb, she was touched to discover, had told several people about her job with Robin Poretta at the BBC. 'Of course,' he said, when she mentioned it. 'I'm boasting – I want to bask in your glory.' He'd glanced over her shoulder as he spoke, as if he were looking for someone.

Afterwards, she remembered that hour as euphoric, hyper-real: the heat, the wine, the sense of belonging, being part of the team that had somehow pulled the party together, while the promise of the future unfurled like a banner against the exhilarating blue of the sky. She'd felt it in her chest, the expansion: a joyful growing pressure.

She should have known.

It was pure chance that it was she who opened the door. She'd been talking to Nina Dowling, a former protégée of Jacqueline's who was tutoring at Trinity, and she had only gone inside to go to the loo. The bell rang as she jogged up the stairs from the kitchen. Hearing the din from the garden, those who knew the Glasses well were letting themselves in through the side gate so whoever this was, she thought, wasn't part of the inner circle.

Light was Rowan's first impression – light shining on long straight hair, flashing off a silver bracelet. The sun was behind her, outlining the shape of her head and a crown of tiny new hairs round her temples. She wore a simple shirtdress in blue and white cotton with a woven tan belt and a pair of gold

Grecian sandals that Rowan knew were from Accessorize because she'd seen them herself during one of her aimless post-exam afternoons. They'd been cheap, Accessorize was, but this woman made them look as if she'd bought them on Bond Street. Was it her posture, the way she seemed naturally to stand straight, her shoulders back, chin up?

She'd adjusted the bottle of wine and the straw clutch bag tucked under her arm and smiled. 'Hello,' she said. 'Am I in the right place for Seb's party? I'm Lorna.'

Rowan's brain, so recently afloat on a sea of endorphins, had lit up like an old-fashioned switchboard. The last time she'd seen Seb for lunch had been at the end of April – '*Before you disappear down the Finals rabbit hole,*' as he'd written in the note she'd found in her pigeonhole. They'd met in the University Parks and walked for half an hour or so by the river and under the cherry trees, then frothy with blossom. 'Like frilly pink knickers at the *Folies Bergères*,' he'd said, making her laugh. They'd had lunch at the Rose and Crown in North Parade, where the beer garden had been warm enough for them to sit outside comfortably for the first time that year, the vines on the trellises offering their tender green leaves to the sun.

She'd known almost immediately that day that there was a new woman on the scene. He'd had the exaggerated lightness of movement and touch that he always had, the extra quickness of wit. She'd thought before – by then, she'd come to know the signs as well as Marianne did – that there was something puppyish about Seb in the first weeks of a new affair as if, waking up, he was raising his head and seeing the world afresh again, all his faculties rendered hypersensitive. Perhaps it was the knowledge that he was behaving badly that made him channel so much of that energy towards other people and their well-being or maybe he'd just wanted everyone to feel as good, as alive, as he did. He'd been particularly great that day, distracting her with an outrageous bit of gossip about a writer whom she'd met over supper at Fyfield Road, reassuring her that no one – it wasn't possible – could read everything on the exhaustive reading lists that her tutor handed out twice a week. 'I know you,' he said, 'so I know that when you say you haven't done enough work, you'll have done twice as much as anyone else. You'll do well – very well. We're all rooting for you so in moments of doubt, just think of us at Fyfield Road cheering you on.'

He'd never been able to refrain from talking about or at least alluding to whomever it was he was seeing. 'Mentionitis,' Marianne had said a couple of years previously when he'd had an enthusiasm for an English grad from Somerville he'd met at a coffee concert at the Sheldonian. 'Acute. Pathetic.'

As she led Lorna down the stairs, Rowan remembered how Seb had told her about an incredible woman he'd met at the lab, the experiments she'd been running as part of her doctoral work on language development. She hadn't yet finished writing the thesis itself, he said, but she'd already published articles in several august publications and she'd been invited to lecture at a conference in Sydney the following month at which Seb was the keynote speaker. The previous Christmas, quite independently, Rowan had heard him talking to a colleague about a groundbreaking research project at UCL. It turned out, he said, excited, that the woman at the lab – her name was Lorna – had been headhunted for a job there. She'd start when she finished her PhD.

'The one saving grace about Dad's inability to keep it in his trousers,' Marianne had told her the first afternoon they'd talked about Seb's affairs, 'is that he doesn't get involved with bimbos. All his women have brains, at least.'

'How do you know?'

'I do my research,' Marianne had said, trying to play it off as nothing. 'I Google.'

Rowan had never looked up one of Seb's women before – she didn't want the pictures in her head, these girls with the man who'd become her surrogate father – but the way Seb talked about this one was different. Usually, he was fond, smiling, but that afternoon at the Rose, she'd heard respect in his voice, an admiration that went beyond physical attraction. She'd felt almost as if he were trying to convince her of this woman's excellence, sell her the idea. Back at college, she'd gone online. What she'd read had done nothing to soothe the prickling of alarm but then she'd had an essay to prepare, and revision, and gradually, Seb's new affair had slipped off her radar.

She didn't know if Marianne had researched this woman, they hadn't discussed her. Perhaps she'd been so preoccupied with painting for her degree show that she hadn't paid enough attention. Or perhaps, after so many years of Seb's messing around, she'd finally become inured to it, suppressing the anger and disgust and telling herself that he would get over it in a month or two, move on.

But she would pay attention now, she would have to, because by inviting Lorna here, Seb had made an announcement. Blatant as his infidelities were, they had still, as long as Rowan had known the Glasses, been conducted according to certain inviolable rules, the most important of which was that he should never bring his women to the house. Also sacrosanct was the understanding that he would never knowingly let Jacqueline encounter one of them in public. Having affairs was one thing, humiliating her was another. And he loved her – rule or not, he would never have wanted that, the damage it would cause to their marriage.

When they reached the kitchen door, Rowan hung back and let Lorna go into the garden alone. She wanted nothing to do with her; refused to be seen as endorsing her in the slightest way.

But if she was aware that she was on her own as she went up the steps, Lorna gave no sign. Self-possessed, she stood and scanned the garden until she spotted Seb's dark head. At the moment her eyes landed on him he turned, seeming to sense her presence, and Rowan watched a change come over his face. In a second, the sharp, anxious energy commuted into a look of pure happiness. Love. It shone from him like a beacon, so private and yet now horribly, obscenely public. She wanted to cover him, throw a blanket over the light before everyone saw it.

With a single touch on the shoulder, he excused himself from Roger Stevas and forged his way through the crowd towards Lorna. Rowan darted up the steps behind her and skirted the knot of people at the food table. Where was Jacqueline? The last time she'd seen her, just before going inside, she'd been talking to Andrew Farrell, a psychology don from St John's, glass in one hand, untouched plate of food in the other. Yes, there she was – *thank God, thank God* – still with Farrell, angled across the garden in the direction of the Dawsons' side of the house, her back almost turned.

Where were Marianne and Adam? Desperate, Rowan searched the lawn. If one of them could collar Seb, demand that he get Lorna off the premises, perhaps the day – *their marriage*, said a small voice – could still be saved.

Over the shoulder of a couple she didn't recognise, Rowan caught sight of Marianne but as she started towards her, Vita Singh, an old family friend, put her hand on Jacqueline's shoulder. Jacqueline swung around to greet her and as she turned, her eyes snagged on Seb and Lorna at the edge of the crowd.

Even a couple of mouthfuls of wine gave her a high colour but under the two red stripes across her cheeks, Rowan watched her turn pale. Jacqueline knew who Lorna was – she recognised her. She'd always projected utter disinterest in Seb's women, diminishing their power by the sheer force of her apparent obliviousness, but even if she'd never looked up another one of them, it was plain that she'd done her research this time. Seeming to feel the weight of her stare, Seb turned and met her eye, and Rowan saw them look at each other in mute acknowledgement. Jacqueline let go of her plate and it fell to the grass, surrounding her new shoes with a spray of pasta salad.

Marianne got drunk. Stupidly, dangerously drunk. Adam took his father inside for what seemed like a long time and when he returned, expressionless, Seb found Lorna again, excused her from the conversation she'd been having with Ben Milford, the philosopher, and ushered her away. He was gone from the party for an hour. Jacqueline disappeared upstairs for twenty minutes and returned with the pained pallor of someone who'd recently undergone surgery. She'd borrowed the pair of huge vintage sunglasses that Marianne had bought the previous summer at Portobello Market and she kept them on for the rest of the afternoon.

It wasn't easy to judge how many people were aware that something had happened. Among those who were, there seemed to be an unspoken decision to pretend everything was normal, born either from an English impulse to sweep things under the carpet and carry on or, Rowan thought with a rush of tenderness towards them all, a collective urge to reassure and support the plainly stricken Jacqueline. Booze no doubt played a part but the conversations got louder and so, too, a few minutes after she reappeared, did the laughter, as if by putting on a good enough show, they could make it the truth.

Rowan kept a close eye on Marianne who at no point in the afternoon, as far as she saw, was separated from her glass. Twice she begged her to slow down, have some water, but Marianne just rolled her eyes and walked away. In the early evening, as the light began to mellow, Rowan was caught in conversation with Angela Dawson – their daughter had just finished at Durham; she had a place on the management training programme at BP – when she realised that Marianne had disappeared.

Excusing herself, she ran through the house flinging open doors until she discovered her lying on the floor in the top bathroom, her sweating white forehead pressed against the cold tile. The bath was splattered with vomit, the smell of ethanol in the windowless room almost overwhelming. Every few seconds, Marianne retched so physically it shook her whole body, as if she was trying to bring up not liquid but something bulky, enormous. She was too weak to stand or even to kneel so Rowan propped her against the wall with the cleaner's mop bucket between her knees.

After a particularly vicious bout of sickness, she started crying, silent tears rolling down her cheeks. There were footsteps on the stairs and, looking up, Rowan saw Adam standing in the doorway. He dropped to his knees and put his arms around Marianne and she wept against the side of his neck. Despite herself, Rowan had felt a pang of envy at the unthinking way Marianne could wrap herself around him, that physical closeness.

'I hate him, Ad,' she said. 'I hate him.'

'No, you don't.'

'I do.' A burst of ferocity. 'How could he do that?' Sobbing became retching again and she pulled away and threw up another gust of white wine. Pulling a tissue from the box, she swiped ineffectually at her mouth. 'He can't do anything without Mum. He can't even fucking *leave* her without getting her approval of the tart. That was why he brought her here, wasn't it? Wasn't it?'

Twenty-four

The call itself had come as no surprise. She'd expected Greenwood to ring the moment Bryony got home from school yesterday, if not before, and last night while she'd been trying to read, she'd been primed for his name to appear on her phone at any moment. When he'd finally called this morning, however, he hadn't mentioned her visit to St Helena's but asked instead if he could come and look at the new paintings.

'Apologies again for the short notice,' he said when she opened the door. 'As I said on the phone, I thought I was going to Birmingham for a studio visit this morning but the artist's had a family emergency and called to put me off.'

'It's no problem. Really.'

'It felt like a sign that I should stop prevaricating. Get it over with.'

For all his social skills and familiarity with the house, he seemed ill at ease. She'd expected him to sit on Jacqueline's sofa or pull out a chair at the table while she made the coffee but he paced around, going to the window to look out at the garden and then turning quickly away as if he'd just remembered what had happened there. He'd arrived with a burgundy leather portfolio and held on to it as if it were anchoring him in reality. Rowan remembered Cory's self-assurance the first time he'd come here, how casually he'd picked up her book, slung his jacket over the back of a chair.

'Are you managing to get any work done?' Greenwood asked, glancing at her laptop, but that was it, none of the usual follow-up questions about her thesis or when she expected to finish. To spare them both the awkwardness of another exchange, she busied around decanting milk into a jug and filling the sugar bowl the Glasses had never used. Was it possible Bryony hadn't told him she'd been to the school, that the timing of his visit was a coincidence? She glanced round to see what he was doing and was startled to find him staring at her. In the unguarded moment before he composed his face, his expression was hard. She turned away, feeling unsettled.

The kettle boiled at last. Before the coffee had a chance to brew properly, she plunged the filter and poured him a cup. He'd returned to absent mode and seemed only to come back to full awareness as she handed it to him. His smile did little more than lift the corners of his mouth. 'Thank you. Do you mind if I go straight up?'

'No, of course not.' *Please*.

He'd said he needed to see the paintings again to write catalogue copy but she wondered how well he already knew the work. Had he seen the paintings as they developed and discussed them with Marianne, or had she waited, shown him only when they were finished? When it came to her work, was he her boyfriend first or her dealer? Rowan thought of the remittance advices among her paperwork, the six-figure sums.

He had to hand over a kidney on a golden platter. She looked around for the leather portfolio and saw that, yes, it had gone upstairs with him. Was he broke, too, after his divorce? Given the gallery's hefty commissions, it seemed unlikely but the running costs must be hefty as well, that Mayfair location, and who knew what went on in people's lives. Maybe Sophie Lawrence was extracting punitive maintenance payments; maybe he was paying for elderly parents in care; maybe he had unmanageable debts, a gambling problem. She wondered again who would benefit financially from Marianne's death. People would know by now; the will must have been read.

She waited half an hour before going up and took the final flight of stairs quietly, just in case, but when she reached the studio, Greenwood was sitting on the old wheel-backed chair at the mouth of Adam's space, the paintings surrounding him on three sides. The portfolio was open on his knees, a pad of lined yellow legal paper attached by leather corners inside. A ballpoint dangled between his fingers, unused. He seemed not to be aware of her and as she got closer, she saw that his cheeks were wet.

'James?'

He whipped around, eyes wide.

'I'm sorry, I didn't mean to startle you.'

'No, no, you didn't.' He put his hands to his face as if to say, *God, look at me*, then brushed his cheeks with his fingers. 'I knew it would be hard, that was why I was putting it off but . . .' He shook his head. 'These girls, getting thinner and thinner – it's like watching her disappear in front of me.' He frowned, making a vertical crease between his eyebrows, and Rowan saw a glimpse of Bryony, the straight genetic line between them.

'You know Michael Cory's been here?' she said.

He looked at her. 'Yes.'

Rowan turned to the painting on her right, the last, most ravaged woman. 'He said he thought they were a self-portrait, the pictures.'

'What?'

'Not individually, obviously – taken all together, as one.'

'Did Marianne tell him that?'

Rowan shook her head. 'No, he said not.'

'Well, I don't know where he got that idea,' Greenwood snapped the portfolio shut and zipped it, 'but he's way off-beam. They're a statement about the pressure on young women to conform to an approved body image, to be good enough. Her mother's work's in there, she's a huge influence, of course; Susie Orbach and Naomi Wolf as well.' He stood, thrust the portfolio under his arm and picked up the chair.

'How much do you think she drew on her own . . .'

'They're portraits of the individual girls, too – that must be apparent.' *Even to you.* He looked at her, eyes hard again, the chair between them a barrier or, she thought suddenly, a potential weapon. 'Marianne spent months – months and months – going to the clinic, getting to know the girls, talking to them about their illness. Before she could even broach the subject of allowing her to paint them, she had to win their trust – they thought they were so ugly, so . . . despicable. It was a huge achievement, and to suggest anything else is very hurtful. Hurtful and insulting.'

'I'm sorry, I really didn't mean . . .'

'What *did* you mean?' He dropped the chair back into its corner and spun round. 'Do you have any idea how damaging it is to go around broadcasting that kind of rubbish? What are you trying to *do*? Turn her into Sylvia Plath? Let her talent be eclipsed by some utter *bollocks*,' he spat the word, 'about the poor tragic woman plagued by mental illness just because she was depressed when her father died?'

'No, of course not. Again, I'm sorry, I didn't . . .'

'Do you think that's what her family want? Jacqueline? Adam?'

'I know it isn't.'

'Well then, perhaps you should just keep your . . . bloody mouth shut.'

She followed him down the stairs, pulse beating in her ears. She'd heard the tremor in his voice, as if he was barely keeping the lid on a bubbling vat of rage. The contrast with his usual gentility, the sophistication and manners, made it so much worse, as if an elegant curtain had been pulled aside to reveal something malevolent. He'd wanted to swear at her, really let her have it, she could tell; even now, as they made their way down in silence, the air seemed to vibrate with the force of what he was holding inside.

At the front door, he took a deep breath and turned to face her. 'I'm sorry,' he said. 'I apologise. That was . . . uncalled for. I'm afraid you caught the brunt of my anxiety. Even though she's gone, it's still my job to protect her – her reputation. I can't let her become some sort of tragic footnote. I won't.'

'I shouldn't have said what I did.'

'No, I'm glad you did. I needed to know. I have to talk to Michael before he bandies that idea around any more. It'll be taken as gospel immediately, of course, if it comes from him.'

'Well, if I've helped – in however round-about a way – then I'm glad, too.'

He nodded quickly, as if to say, *Well, good, so let's leave it at that*. He looked down, checked the zip on the portfolio and reached for the door handle. Then, just as Rowan had allowed her shoulders to drop a half-centimetre, he turned around again.

'Bryony said you went to find her at school yesterday.'

Fuck.

'Please don't do that again.'

Greenwood's anger had soured the air in the house and she was glad to pull the door closed behind her. The relief was short-lived, however, and as she crossed the road to the car, the uneasiness returned as a sort of hyper-awareness, a prickling at the back of her neck as if she were being watched. She even turned to look but of course no one was there.

She started the engine without a destination in mind, wanting just to put some distance between herself and the house, but she found herself heading down through the centre of town, past the Randolph Hotel and Worcester College. At the bottom of Hythe Bridge Street, she surprised herself by turning left.

For years now, she'd avoided this part of town if she ever had to come to Oxford. There were some happy memories – a few good evenings with Marianne and Turk at the Head of the River and, at university, she'd gone out for a month or so with a guy from Pembroke who'd lived just over the bridge – but for the most part, she associated it with loneliness and abandonment and, later, overwhelming claustrophobia. Today, however, as she passed the end of Vicarage Road, she made herself look. There was the Crooked Pot on the corner, an ugly mean-windowed building never meant to be a pub, and beyond it, in two diminishing terraces, the jumble of houses, some still brick-fronted, others plastered and painted, that had included her father's. Hers. Theirs, she supposed.

She accelerated away, waiting until she'd passed the end of Norreys Avenue before she inhaled again, as if even breathing the air of Vicarage Road was enough to carry her back there. University College sports ground on her left, the allotments, and then the untidy snaggle of shops and low houses that lined the unlovely way out of town.

At the junction with Weirs Lane, she averted her eyes.

Boar's Hill was another world: detached houses set back from the road behind huge established trees and security gates, a Jaguar on this drive, a Range Rover on the next. She'd never really known who lived here. The Oxford houses she understood were low-key and book-filled, slightly shabby even if they sold for millions, but these were ostentatious, many of them modern, the sort of houses she imagined Premier League footballers buying.

The top of the hill was different again, however. Here, the trees ended and the vista opened up: rolling fields of drab winter grass, scrubby hedgerows. English countryside

234

unchanged for a hundred years. There was a single car at the side of the road, a red Nissan Micra, its owner nowhere to be seen. She parked behind it, locked up and went over the stile into the field.

A couple of hundred yards from the road, she climbed to the top of the hill and perched on the wooden fence. The ends of her scarf flapped behind her, twin flags in the wind that drove the cloud across the sky, a tumble of white and grey so low Rowan felt she could reach up and touch it.

The view was a green patchwork quilt, the fields ancient and irregular, stitched roughly together, darned here and there with copses and knots of tiny houses. Four or five miles away, in the shallow dish carved by its rivers, the rooftops and spires of the postcard Oxford floated above a foam of distant trees like the vision of a place, a mirage. Such a small patch of land, a few square miles, and yet how much it contained, so much struggle and striving, Sturm and Drang.

She took deep breaths, pulling cold air into her chest. The conversation with Greenwood had disturbed her – she still felt shaken. The suddenness and strength of his anger, so barely contained, had been frightening. Had Marianne known that side of him, had he unleashed it on her? Could that have been why she jumped, or part of it? Rowan examined the idea, turning it round in her mind, but it didn't feel right. She didn't believe that Marianne, with her upbringing, her deeply engrained belief in a woman's right to security and self-governance, would stay with a man who intimidated her. She wasn't alone or without resources; she didn't have children to consider: if she'd been in a bad relationship, she would have left.

Of course, the person who would know was Bryony but even if she ignored Greenwood's request, if that was the right word for it, and went to the school again, Rowan doubted Bryony would talk to her. She'd made it clear she was loyal to her father.

Another avenue of investigation closed, another person – two people – pissed off. Rowan focused her eyes on the glimmering view of the city. The other person who might know about Marianne's relationship was Adam but it had been three days now without a word. Lying in bed last night, the silence in the house thickening, she'd wondered if something had happened to him. Had there been an accident? Exhausted and hungover, had he crashed the car? No – she'd stopped herself. She would have heard about it, someone would have called. Nothing had happened; he just didn't want to talk to her.

Twenty-five

A light drizzle had started to fall at Boar's Hill and when Rowan arrived back, the house looked damp and sullen, as if the atmosphere inside had seeped through the walls to infect the façade. When she closed the front door, the light coming through the glass panels was barely enough to see by so she walked to the table and switched on the elephant lamp.

Turning back past the bottom of the stairs to hang up her coat, she saw movement at the corner of her eye and gave a cry of alarm.

Four or five steps up, beyond the reach of the lamp, a man was sitting. Weak light from the landing window behind him outlined broad shoulders, a strong neck. His face was hidden in shadow. *Run*, her instincts urged, *run*, but fear rooted her to the spot. She couldn't move her feet.

'So here you are.'

A voice out of the gloom. An American voice. Cory – it was Michael Cory. She put her hand over her mouth as he stood up, extending himself to full height. Rowan's heart beat against her ribcage like a panicked bird. He came towards her, down the steps, and as he moved into the light, she saw that he was dressed entirely in black: black jeans, a black sweater. Black leather gloves. No hat or coat, just gloves.

'What . . .' Her throat was dry; she choked. 'How did you get in here? What are you doing?' She couldn't take her eyes off his hands. Why was he wearing gloves?

'What am *I* doing?' When he reached the bottom of the stairs, he loomed over her, nearly a foot taller and several stones heavier. 'No, Rowan,' he shook his head. 'What the fuck are *you* doing?'

She stared at him. Cory stared back, eyes glinting in the half-light. Then, spinning round, he went to the stairs and reached back into the darkness.

When Rowan saw what he was holding, her skin went cold. The cardboard box from the wardrobe in her room. Marianne's sketches.

'Clearly you know what this is.'

She said nothing. Heart beating wildly, she watched as he carried the box to the hall table and took off the lid. Setting it aside, he lifted out the wad of tissue that held the contents in place then the batch of sketches that Marianne had given her over the years, the hands and the windfalls, Seb's vinaigrette and the nude. As he put them down and reached into the box again, her stomach turned over so sharply she thought she was going to vomit.

He brought it out, careful to hold it only by the edges despite his gloves. Her eyes were accustomed to the low light now and she saw that the Sellotape had already been undone. He folded the edges back with the tips of his fingers, minimal pressure.

As if it were an offering, he carried it on open palms. When he reached her, she turned her head away, kept her eyes trained on the floor, which seemed to be tipping under her feet.

'Look at it, Rowan.'

'No.'

'Look at it!' he roared, his mouth inches from her ear, his voice so loud it was all she could do not to shriek in fright. He thrust it at her.

She kept her hands by her sides, she refused to touch it, but she looked.

238

She hadn't seen it since the night a decade ago when she'd wrapped it up, taped it tightly and laid it to rest at the bottom of the box but ten years had done nothing to diminish its power. The impact was almost as great as the first time she'd seen it, upstairs on the worktable in Marianne's studio. It was so skilful, so gorgeously done, and so appalling.

The houseboat had been moored near Donnington Bridge, where the river was distracted from its course for a few hundred yards by a handful of islets overgrown with willow trees and silky rushes. The day she and Marianne had gone to find it, a breeze had stirred among the leaves, making the whole scene scintillate with light, a million Impressionist brushstrokes. The boat was beautiful, too, not a narrow-boat built to negotiate locks and canals, but one of the wooden barges commissioned by colleges at the end of the nineteenth century to entertain guests for the racing at Summer Eights. Twenty feet wide and high-ceilinged, it had an elegant pillared porch and huge oval windows along the sides to allow maximum views of the rowers in inclement weather.

But if the scene that day had been a play of light, Marianne had reimagined it in darkness. The innocent green was gone, replaced by flickering shards of orange and black. In all but one of the windows, the glass had shattered, and the cabin behind was filled with fire. She'd drawn the scene then painstakingly coloured it: flames in yellow and orange and gold licked with a sort of voluptuous pleasure around the hands and face pressed against the one window that remained intact, the smallest one nearest the prow. The face of a woman whose agony made Rowan think of Hieronymus Bosch's hideous tortured souls. A woman who knew she was dying.

There could be no doubt who'd drawn it. Marianne's style was inscribed in every line, every serpentine branch and tongue of flame.

Cory's stare had a near-physical weight and when Rowan raised her head to look at him, his eyes were dark, all pupil. Lit from below by the lamp, the broad planes of his face were hobgoblin-like, a Halloween mask. Over the roar of emotional turmoil came a wash of physical fear.

'Get out,' she said. 'Just . . . get out.'

Half a laugh: *Come on.*

'I can't believe you.' Her voice was shaking with a mix of fear and fury. 'I can't believe you did this. How dare you break in here and go through my stuff?'

'When did she draw it?' he said.

'This was . . . You must have gone through everything; you must have . . .'

'When?' Surging forward, he grabbed her by the top of the arms.

Rowan gave a cry of alarm and tried to shake herself free but his grip was too powerful, he was too strong. 'Get off me! Get . . . You're hurting me.'

'Tell me.'

The sketch was still in his hand, clamped between her upper arm and his fingers. She heard it crunch as he tightened his grip again. 'It's none of your business,' she yelled, her face inches from his. 'It's nothing to do with you – nothing!'

She thought he'd shake her, shout back, but instead he let go of her and stepped away. He took a moment but when he spoke again, his voice was calm and deadly serious. 'If you don't tell me what the *fuck* this means – the truth – I'm going to the police.'

She made herself look him in the eye. Nothing said he was bluffing.

'I mean it, Rowan. You know I do.'

Behind her ribs, panic rose, bubbling. She was almost in tears. She tried to speak but she couldn't do it.

'Come on.'

'Before,' she said, finally.

'Before what?'

'Before it happened. Before Lorna was killed.'

She expected him to light up, to be filled with the glory of discovery, his triumph, but instead, at the moment he heard her, the glow in Cory's eyes went out. It was as if a wire had snapped: the energy that hummed through him was gone; he slumped. Moving as if underwater, he let the picture drop on the table, went back to the stairs and sat down heavily, head in his hands.

For some seconds, there was silence. The air was thick, it bore down on Rowan, making it hard for her to breathe. She thought of the day Seb died, the unnatural quiet as she'd passed the police car on the drive, walked through the open front door.

'So I was right.' He spoke through his fingers. 'She was Seb's girlfriend.'

The word was a stone on Rowan's tongue. At last she managed to get it out. 'Yes.'

He made a sound in the back of his throat. 'Why? If he had so many affairs, why her?'

'He was going to leave Jacqueline.'

Cory lifted his head.

'None of the other relationships mattered. They were just dalliances . . . crushes. He never loved them. Those women – they weren't in the same league as Jacqueline, they were, I don't know, like a . . . different species. Mazz used to say Seb relied on Jacqueline but it was more than that – much more. She inspired him – she made him see what he could be. They were really young when they met, only nineteen or twenty, and he always knew she'd helped make him the person he became.'

'So why the hell would he . . . ?'

'Seb thought Lorna was the same, as clever and original and generous – maybe she was, how would I know? – but she was younger and . . .' Rowan closed her eyes, struggling. 'Both his children had graduated – Marianne had just finished at the Slade. He wasn't a family man any more, day to day, and he was turning fifty, getting older. He was looking for the next stage of his life.'

To her shame, tears came now, hot and insistent; she dashed them away with her cuff. If Cory noticed, he didn't care.

'It wasn't just about sex for him,' she said, voice thick. 'Not in the long run: it had to be about brains, too. Lorna was both and she came along just when he was vulnerable.'

She remembered the evening they'd understood that it was really going to happen, that Marianne's family as she'd known it was about to implode.

They'd been in the kitchen when Jacqueline arrived home to find Seb getting ready to go out. He was showered and newly shaved, exuding scents of soap and fresh laundry on one of the hottest evenings of the year. The atmosphere had been almost unbearable. Marianne hadn't spoken a word to him since the party but after recovering from the initial shock, Jacqueline seemed to have decided to do what she always did: pretend nothing was happening and wait for it to blow itself out. The act had been tissue-thin, however, the strain visible in the hunch in her upper back, the false brightness of her voice and laugh. 'Like a nursery school teacher in extremis,' Mazz said.

The day after the party, Jacqueline had told Marianne that if it didn't stop, if Seb didn't tell Lorna it was over, she would go to the lab and confront her in person – turn the desks over, if she had to. They'd never known for sure if she'd actually done it, gone there that afternoon, but when she'd walked into the kitchen at Fyfield Road, it was clear that she'd reached breaking point. Her hands were shaking – her hair seemed to crackle with electricity. One look at Seb in his clean white shirt had been all it took. 'Do it,' she told him, tossing her shoulder bag on to the sofa. 'Pack your case and get out. Go on – right now. Out. Here it is.' She bowed, flourishing her hand in front of her like a medieval nobleman. 'My *permission*.'

'Jacq—' He'd moved towards her but she'd put up her arms, barring him.

'Don't you *dare* try and touch me.'

'Please, I never wanted this – I can't bear the idea that . . .'

'*You* can't bear it?' She'd jumped on his words, savage. '*You*? You're tearing us all apart and *you* can't bear it? Fuck you, Seb. Get out – just get out. Go and screw your bimbo to your heart's content.'

A change had come over Seb then, they'd all seen it. Gone were apology and regret, the look that implored them not to hate him, and in their place was anger. 'Don't *you* dare,' he said in a voice that had dropped an octave. 'Don't you *dare* talk about her like that.'

Jacqueline seemed to shrink. She stared at him as if she were looking at a stranger and then, in a whirl of hair and emerald silk, she ran out into the garden. Seb, face crimson, took several deep breaths, picked up his keys and phone and stalked out. Quick footsteps on the kitchen stairs then, seconds later, the bang of the front door.

When Rowan turned to her, Marianne looked as if she'd been slapped in the face. 'It's dying,' she said. 'My family's dying and I'm just sitting here watching.'

'You're telling me she loved her father so much she killed his girlfriend to try and keep him.'

'I'm not *telling* you – you're *forcing* me to tell you.'

Rowan thought of the ten years she'd said nothing, kept the secret so that Marianne – all the remaining Glasses – could live their lives in peace. And here – today, now – she was

243

saying the words. Marianne might be gone, beyond harm, but what about the others? 'It wasn't just to keep her father,' she said. 'It was to keep her family. Without Seb, it was broken.'

'She thought killing someone would fix it?' The look on Cory's face was incredulity mixed with horror.

'She wasn't *thinking* at all.'

'Then what?'

'She was – not crazy but . . . She changed. We didn't know at the time but it was the start of her breakdown.'

'Did you know she was going to do it?'

Rowan recoiled. 'No. Of course not. You think I would have let her? For Christ's sake. I thought it was a fantasy, the picture: a way of getting some of her anger out. A vent, not a . . . plan.'

'You want me to believe that? You think the police would?'

Icy fingers on the back of her neck. 'When we went there,' she said, 'Mazz told me she just wanted to see it. *Know your enemy* – those were her words. It was only when it happened that I realised she'd been working it all out that day.'

Cory looked sick.

'Lorna was away for the weekend, Seb had taken her to Devon, so Marianne knew she wouldn't be there. She went aboard.'

She remembered her own heart pounding as she urged Mazz to get off, come away. Marianne on the foredeck, peering through the windows, lifting the lid of the locker under the bench, examining the cylinder of Calor Gas. Rowan hadn't realised the significance of that until later.

For some seconds, Cory said nothing.

'But if she did all this, how come *you* have the picture?' he said finally. 'It was in your room.'

'I took it. Stole it, Marianne said.'

'When?'

'Afterwards – after she . . . After Lorna died. Mazz was acting so erratically, her behaviour was so irrational, I was scared she was going to give herself away. The police came here – obviously they found out about the affair. I had visions of them going up to the studio and finding it lying on her worktable like I did. I should have burned it. Why didn't I just bloody burn it?'

Cory took the gloves off and dropped them on the step next to him. 'I need a drink,' he said.

As soon as she walked into the kitchen, Rowan saw how he'd got into the house. The door was closed or pushed to, at least, but even so, her eyes went at once to the damage to the jamb. The wood around the lock was splintered – shattered; the mechanism had been knocked right out.

'You kicked the door in?' She stared at him.

Going to it, she tried to press the handle but couldn't: the catch was jammed. Not that there was anywhere for it to go now, anyway. The door swung open and she stepped out on to the patio. At hip-height, there was half a boot print on the paintwork, treads precisely defined. She fixed her eyes on it until she could barely see it any more. Behind her, the rain fizzed like static on the flagstones.

'I'm supposed to be looking after the place.'

'I'll get it fixed,' he said. 'I'll pay for it, obviously. Come in, you're getting wet.'

He'd seen the brandy on the worktop and she left him to pour it while she went to the utility room and turned on the boiler. The old Fair Isle sweater was on the arm of the sofa so she put it on, guessing by the way Cory looked at it that he'd seen Marianne wear it, too.

Going to his usual seat at the table, he sat down heavily. His expression was one she hadn't seen before: he looked sad. He laid his hands on the tabletop, one either side of his glass. 'I suspected. No, I knew – she told me, pretty much. But I just ... Even an hour ago, when I found the drawing, I still hoped there would be an explanation, that you'd tell me she'd done it afterwards, I was making a mistake. I wanted you to tell me it was an accident. Even manslaughter.'

'I'm sorry.'

He took a long sip of brandy. 'All that stuff about you not giving her space after Seb died . . .'

'A lie.' Rowan made herself look him in the eyes. 'It's what I've always said when anyone asked me because I couldn't tell the truth.'

'Couldn't?' He raised an eyebrow.

'Wouldn't,' she said finally. 'I couldn't go on being friends with her afterwards. What happened – it was . . . sickening. Actually sickening – I was ill. I couldn't sleep – it was days before I could eat anything or keep food down. The idea that she could do something like that; that she had it in her, that degree of . . .'

'Evil?'

The word glinted in the air between them.

Rowan shivered, as if it had come to settle on her shoulders. 'I was going to say hatred. But I told her I wouldn't tell anyone. I promised. Not because I was scared of her, she didn't threaten me, but because I'd loved her – I loved all of them. I didn't *want* to tell anyone. The idea of what it would do to the rest of the Glasses if it came out – if the police found out. If there was a trial.'

'She *killed* someone, Rowan.'

'I'm not saying I *liked* it. I didn't *approve*,' she said, with a burst of frustration. She lowered her voice again. 'It wasn't . . . It was hard. It . . .' She shook her head, struggling to find the words. 'Knowing something like this, being party to it – it changes you. It warps you. Look at my life, for someone of my age. You think it hasn't messed me up?'

'Then why do it – why keep doing it? Ten years later, you haven't spoken to her in a decade, and you're still keeping her secret? Risking jail if anyone finds out. Why?'

'Because I understand.'

'What?'

'I understand why she did it. It terrified me, it scared me to death, but it made sense to me.'

Cory was staring.

'I didn't have a family,' she said. 'Not really. When Mazz and I became friends, I became part of hers.'

'But still, you were . . .'

'I loved them,' she said. 'The whole family. I hated what Marianne did, despised it, but I understood. For the same reason she did it, I kept it secret.'

Cory stood at the door to the garden, his back to the room. It had been a minute or more since either of them had spoken and in the quiet, she could hear rain dripping from the gutter beneath the bathroom window.

'It makes sense to me now,' he said suddenly.

'What does?'

'Why you're here.' He turned around. 'You needed to make sure no one had found out. You knew she jumped, and you wanted to make sure that wasn't why.'

'Yes.'

'To protect her, still – and her mother and brother. It's why you're so hostile to me.'

'You wouldn't leave it alone!'

'And to protect yourself.' He looked at her. 'Let's not pretend it's entirely selfless. You have something to hide, too. If the police find out you've known all this time, you'll be in serious shit – aiding and abetting, an accessory. Jail, surely.'

She nodded. 'Probably. Yes.'

'What a God-awful mess. You were twenty-one, -two? Just kids.'

'And after all of it, the irony is, Marianne still lost her father. Completely. What's a divorce, really, once you've grown up?

She could have seen him, talked to him – she hadn't lived at home since she'd started at the Slade anyway. But doing what she did to Lorna and then his drink-driving – from what Peter Turk's told me, I think she felt like she'd killed *him*.'

'Jesus.'

'And the woman Seb killed in the crash, who was driving the other car. A chain of deaths, one after another. Mazz thought she'd set it all in motion.'

She stopped talking. Cory looked back at the window and watched a sparrow in the raised bed pull at a worm. The rain must have brought it to the surface.

'All this,' Rowan said, 'it doesn't make it right, your breaking in. Obviously I'm not going to go to the police but you went through my room – my things. How dare you?'

'I knew you weren't telling me the whole story. When you tried to put me off talking to Turk, that's when I was sure.'

She took a sip of brandy then moved the glass away. She couldn't afford anything other than a clear head. 'Why did you need to know so badly?' she asked. 'What's it all for?'

He came back to the table and sat down. He looked at the bottle and Rowan pushed it towards him. 'Marianne wanted me to know,' he said. 'She wanted to tell me.'

'But she *didn't* tell you.'

'She was trying. Every time we talked, she told me another detail, a hint. Is it surprising that she had to do it gradually, something like this?' He took the top off and poured himself another half-inch before pointing the bottle in her direction. She shook her head.

'I think she was trying to tell you, too, wasn't she?' he said.

'What?'

'That card in your box of sketches – *I need to talk to you*. Her handwriting.'

'Oh.' Shit, she'd forgotten about that but of course, Cory must have seen it. 'I don't know,' she said. 'It arrived the day after Jacqueline called to tell me she'd died. I never got a chance to find out why she . . .'

'How do you do it?' he said. 'Tell someone you've killed someone?'

'*Why* do you do it? That's a bigger question for me. Why, after ten years, would she feel a sudden urge to confess?'

Cory looked at her over the rim of his glass. 'I know you don't trust me.'

'I don't.'

'That's fair. My reputation – Greta, Hanna. But I promise you – I promise you with my hand on my heart,' he laid it on his chest, palm down, 'that it was never my intention to expose or hurt Marianne in any way.'

'What made her different?'

'I didn't mean to hurt the others, whatever it looked like – and I do see how that might be hard to believe – but Marianne . . . Never. We were friends, Rowan.'

'Who needs enemies?'

'We were.'

'What does that mean, in your world?'

He frowned, narrowing his eyes. 'What are you asking?'

'I'm asking what you're going to do with all this now you know. I'm asking if she can trust you now.' She hesitated. 'If I can.'

He took another sip and Rowan suppressed an urge to reach over and knock the glass out of his hand. 'What good would it do?' she said, and the look on Cory's face told her he heard every bit of her fear and anger. Well, she thought, let him. 'What would it achieve, bringing all this out into the open now? Marianne's dead – she can't be tried, brought to justice. Do you think it would help Lorna's family to know that their daughter was killed?' *Murdered*: still, after all these years, she couldn't bring herself to say the word. 'And the Glasses – Jacqueline and Adam – can you imagine how much it would hurt them?'

'I'm not planning to tell anyone.'

'Planning?'

'I'm not *going* to tell anyone. Okay?'

'And your portrait?'

'Is just a portrait. Of a woman I liked very much.' He looked down at his hands and it occurred to her that he was crying. When he looked up again, however, seconds later, his eyes were bright but dry. 'I'm not your problem, Rowan.'

This time the cold fingers took hold of her heart.

'She knew she could trust me, whatever she told me. *Whatever* – I told her that. I've asked myself over and over – Did *I* make it happen? Did she misinterpret me in some way? Did she think she'd told me too much?' He shook his head. 'No. She jumped, I'm sure of it, but . . .'

'How?' Rowan demanded. 'How are you sure?'

'I knew her.'

'For God's sake.'

'I did, Rowan. I knew her and I cared about her. She jumped but I wasn't the reason.'

Twenty-six

Cory had torn a piece of paper from her pad of A4 and, with a pencil from his jacket pocket, he sketched the pile of books next to her computer while they talked. His moments of absorption were a relief, respite: she felt hollow, as if having kept the secret inside for so many years, her body had grown around it and now couldn't spring back.

For the most part, Cory told her, he'd focused on trying to work out what had happened in the past, so Rowan found herself telling him what little she'd managed to discover about Marianne's final weeks. 'I've been going round and round,' she said. 'I've tried everything I can think of, pretty much, but I know as little now as I did when I got here. Less, probably. But something *did* happen to her, I'm sure of it.'

'How about the guy in the garden – the one you thought was me?'

'I haven't seen him again. Maybe I scared him off. Now there's just the creepy guy in the flats. Though they might be the same person – I haven't ruled that out.'

'Who?' Cory pulled back, frowning. 'What are you talking about?'

Rowan told him about the man at the window. 'He's there all the time, just standing, looking – I've seen him at three o'clock in the morning.'

251

'So who is he?'

'I've no idea. I thought *he* might be you, too – I went round there to look for your car.'

'You haven't confronted him? Knocked on the door?'

'No. In case it *was* you – I wanted to know what you were doing first. But then, if it wasn't you ... I'll admit, I was frightened.'

'We should go see him.'

'I don't know. What if he's dangerous?'

'There's two of us now. You went there on your own.'

'When I thought it was you. And I was only ...'

'Me, the voyeur?' he said, looking up. 'The man who drives women to suicide?'

'I'm just saying, we don't know what we're walking into.' She breathed all the way out, trying to ease the tightness in her chest. 'What if it's the police?'

He shook his head, dismissive. 'There to do what? Blow their budget on twenty-four-hour surveillance of the house of a woman who had an accident?'

'I know but ...'

'He was sure about that, wasn't he, your police friend? Marianne was alone – no other footprints.'

Rowan quashed a childish impulse to deny that Theo was her friend.

Her phone was in her lap and while he sketched in the lettering on the guidebook from Harvington Hall, she tapped in her code and checked her messages. Nothing. She thought for a moment. 'Michael.' He looked up at her in surprise. 'What?' she said.

'That's the first time you've ever used my name.'

'Oh. Look, I wondered, have you spoken to Adam?'

'No, but I want to, obviously. Why? Do you think *he* knows something?'

'No. No, I don't think so.'

'Then ... ?'

Rowan felt herself redden. 'He's a friend. I haven't spoken to him for a few days and I just wondered if you had. He's grieving, so . . .'

But Cory was no longer listening. Above the wall at the end of the garden, the light in the flat had come on.

He waited while Rowan locked the front door and they went down the steps in tandem. As they rounded the corner and came on to the section of Norham Road that edged the Dragon's playing field, there was a stretch of a hundred yards or so without houses or streetlamps, and though it was still only early evening, not yet six o'clock, beneath the trees, the road was dark.

Cory walked quickly, though not, thank God, as quickly as the day she'd had to chase after him to the meadow. Were they working together now, as far as he was concerned? Could he possibly trust her, after what she'd told him? And could she trust *him*? Going through her room like that – when she'd gone upstairs, she'd found chaos, her clothes in a great pile, books lying open, clearly shaken out by their spines. And the door. It looked as if the whole upright would have to be replaced. Before coming out, they'd improvised a barrier by putting a plank through the back of a chair and bracing it against the kitchen units, but until the jamb was mended, she'd have to sleep with it like that.

Cory had backed her into a corner and she had very little option now but to go along with him and pray he meant what he said about keeping his mouth shut.

But perhaps teaming up with him – properly – was what she needed to do now anyway. She couldn't have risked going to the flats like this on her own, making herself so physically vulnerable. She tried to ignore the small voice warning her that perhaps, by going with Cory, she was making herself more vulnerable still.

They turned on to Benson Place. Empty parking spaces at the kerb; most of the windows in the flats dark, the residents still at work. Streetlight lay in puddles on the carefully tended patches of lawn. She pointed at the second door along.

Cory pressed the buzzer and they waited. Rowan felt the knot of tension in her stomach pull tight. He was in there, the light was on in the window that overlooked the road here, too, so why didn't he answer? They were under cover of the porch, hidden from view, but had he seen them coming? She wondered suddenly if he'd seen Cory break in. If he had, she realised, he would know that the door was broken, no longer secure.

Cory buzzed again. Seconds later, the intercom crackled, and a voice said 'Hello?' They looked at each other. It was a woman's voice, cautious but not unfriendly. Had he hit the wrong buzzer? No, she'd seen him press number three.

'You speak,' Cory murmured. They changed places and she leaned towards the microphone. 'Hi,' she said, holding the button. 'My name's Rowan. I wonder if I could talk to you for a moment.'

Another crackle. 'Can I ask what it's regarding?'

She looked at Cory then pressed the button again. 'I'm not selling anything,' she said. 'I promise.' Trying to sound human. 'I wanted to ask you about an old friend of mine.'

'Who?' Warier now, unsurprisingly.

When she looked at Cory, he nodded. 'Marianne Glass.'

'Marianne? Oh.' A pause. 'Okay, yes, come up.' With a buzz, the lock on the outside door clicked open.

On the communal stairs, the building's less well-to-do past was closer to the surface, evident in the grey lino with its raised tuppenny spots and the push-button timed lights that reminded Rowan of her hallway back in London. The doors of the flats were ugly, plain expanses of wood veneer whose only detail was the cheap brass number screwed on to each one above the suspicious glass bubble of a spy-hole.

Cory stood to one side while Rowan knocked. The spy-hole darkened then cleared and a bolt was drawn. The sound of a second one caused her a fresh twinge of unease: who would need two bolts in this secluded middle-class enclave? She composed her face as the door began to open then was stopped by a chain. Through the gap, she saw large brown eyes in the anxious face of a woman of sixty or so.

Seeing Rowan, the woman released the chain and it fell against the doorframe with a rattle. As she opened the door, however, Cory stepped into view and there was an audible intake of breath. Rowan realised what he might look like to someone who didn't know about him, tall and broad as he was, shaven-headed.

'I'm sorry,' she said. 'I should have told you I had a friend with me – I didn't want to come alone. This is Michael. He's an artist – a painter. He was a friend of Marianne's, too.'

'Oh.'

'Good to meet you,' he said. 'We appreciate you talking to us. We'll try not to take too much of your time.'

The woman registered his accent. 'You're not police then?'

'No.' Cory's answer contained a question.

'They came to all the flats, of course, when she died. To ask if any of us had seen anything suspicious. Not that they thought there was anything like that . . .' she said quickly.

'No, of course not.' Rowan tried to sound reassuring.

The hallway was narrow, the only furniture an arrangement of dried flowers in a vase on a pine chest of drawers and a small tasselled rug patterned with pink roses.

'Who told you we knew her?' asked the woman, with a glance over her shoulder at Cory.

'No one.' Rowan looked at him too – *we?* – but his expression was carefully neutral. 'May we come in?'

255

The woman hesitated a second then stood aside. The archway behind her led directly into the sitting room, which, as Rowan already knew, ran most of the width of the flat. On the right-hand side, a slice had been carved off for a skinny galley kitchen but the table, which sat four, was at the rear of the main space. At the front, arranged to make the most of the light through the large metal-framed windows, were the sofa and two matching armchairs. The room was immaculate – the tang of Windolene in the air, unmistakable, told Rowan that the glass coffee table and a small display cabinet had been recently polished – but despite the busy floral print of the upholstery and a handful of tapestry cushions, there was a sparseness to the furnishings that spoke of scant money carefully stretched. There were just two small pictures on the wall – a pair of autumn landscapes – and the television in the corner wasn't much bigger than a computer monitor.

'Please – sit down,' the woman said.

It was thoroughly dark outside now but the curtains – terrible shiny faux-taffeta with basic crenellations along the top – were still open and, as she sat, Rowan glanced across the gardens to the back of the house. They'd turned on the studio light before leaving and she could see in as far as the wall of the old bathroom, about a third of the total area.

The woman perched on the edge of the sofa as if she might make a run for it at any moment.

'I'm sorry, we don't know your name,' Rowan said.

'Sarah – Johnson.'

'Rowan Winter and Michael Cory.' She smiled. If Cory's name meant anything to this woman, it hadn't registered on her face. 'Apologies again for coming round like this. I'm staying at Marianne's house at the moment, looking after it – house-sitting – while . . .'

'Oh.' The woman's face suddenly brightened. 'Then it's you he's been seeing.'

'Sorry?'

'My son. Martin. He said he'd seen a woman there – young, brown hair. For a while I thought . . .' She closed her eyes and bit her lower lip, giving her head a shake. 'O ye, of little faith.'

'Apologies,' said Rowan. 'I don't understand.'

Sarah Johnson's manner had changed remarkably; the trepidation replaced by what looked like relief. 'Martin told me he'd seen a woman in Marianne's house. I thought he was trying to tell me he was seeing her ghost. Either that or he'd forgotten she'd died.'

Rowan caught Cory's eye.

'I should explain.' A little of the light faded from Sarah's face. 'He had an accident on his bike four years ago. Motorbike. No one else was involved but his helmet came off. He's still making progress – the OTs and the speech therapist at the hospital are very good with him – but he's . . . different from how he used to be.' She stood up. 'Let me call him – he'd like to meet you, I know, Marianne's friends.'

At the end of a short passageway at the back of the room, she tapped gently on a door. 'Martin? Have you finished playing your computer game, sweetheart? Can you hear me? There are some people here – a lady and a man – who were friends with Marianne. Would you like to come and meet them?'

Cory was jabbing his finger at the wall behind her. 'Go?' mouthed Rowan. 'Now?'

He shook his head. 'Look.'

Turning, she followed his direction. On a shelf of the display cabinet behind her, in a wooden frame that was larger than but otherwise very similar to the one that held Rowan's favourite photo of Jacqueline and Marianne, there was one of Mazz's drawings. It was pen and ink, a portrait of a young man, just his head and shoulders but detailed to an extent that told them Marianne had had time to study him. She hadn't done it on the fly: he'd sat for her.

'Here he is,' Sarah said, as if introducing a child, and turning back, Rowan saw the face in the flesh. Marianne had caught him very well, was her first thought, the fine nose and wide eyes, the light brown hair so straight it didn't shape itself even to the line of his temples. It was a delicate face, mild, made arresting by its contrast with his body. The heating in the flat was turned up high and he was wearing tracksuit trousers and a plain white T-shirt under which his muscles – bulky and individually developed – were clearly visible. He walked awkwardly, however, and as he came closer, she saw that one of his feet pointed inward.

'Hello.' She stood and, before she could think, held out her hand to him. He hesitated then took it and gave her a strange sort of handshake. She had the idea that he had been taught how to do it: his grip was gentle – almost tender – but she could feel the power that he was holding in check. She introduced herself and Cory then turned to the drawing on the shelf. 'Marianne drew you,' she said. 'It's a very good likeness.'

The same momentary pause and Rowan had the horrible thought that maybe he wasn't able to talk. Then, though, he said, 'Yes. She got me – that's what she said. She got me.'

'She did.' Rowan smiled. 'How long ago did you sit for her?'

A trace of panic in his eyes, Martin looked at his mother.

'About eighteen months,' she said.

'I went to her house, we had some chocolate cake and then she did my picture. She said I could keep it so I brought it home and we put it in a frame.'

'You were friends?'

'Yes, she was my friend. We always waved to each other.' He said the last phrase slowly, as if the concept were tricky to negotiate. 'I stood here and when she came up to her studio, she waved and I waved back.'

'I've seen you in your window,' Rowan said. 'Here.' She gestured at the expanse of glass. 'At night. You must be almost as bad a sleeper as I am.'

'Insomnia,' he said, pronouncing each syllable carefully. 'I don't like the dark. I have tablets to go to sleep but I don't like them. I don't want to get . . .' He looked at his mother again.

'Addicted,' she said.

At the door, Sarah Johnson moved closer to Rowan and lowered her voice. It seemed an unnecessary precaution: with the air of a teenager who had done his social duty, Martin had sloped off back to his room. Watching him go, Rowan thought suddenly that if Marianne had asked her to describe him, she'd have said he was like a child in the body of a Russian gymnast: the power and the simplicity together, the muscles and the pallor of his colouring, the light blue eyes.

'Is he bothering you?' his mother asked. 'Looking over like that.'

'No. I . . .'

'It's all right – you can say.'

'Honestly, no. Now that I understand. I didn't know about the . . . waving. I didn't know they were friends. I've lived in London for a long time; I was out of touch with Marianne's life, day to day. At night, sometimes, when I saw him . . .' Rowan tried a laugh and shook her head to convey embarrassment. 'Over-active imagination.'

Her eyes came to rest on the pair of bolts and, as if she'd seen and followed the chain of thought, Sarah said, 'He's not dangerous.'

'No, of course not. I didn't think . . . Now I know they were friends, it makes total sense.' She glanced back towards the sitting room, making sure he hadn't returned. She spoke quietly anyway. 'Did he see Marianne's body?' she asked. 'From the window, I mean. I didn't like to ask him but . . .'

'Yes,' Sarah said. 'Not that night, he didn't see the accident, thank God, but in the morning, when it got light enough to see the garden. He was . . . very upset.'

'It must have been traumatic for him. For you both.'

'Horrible. It was . . . horrible.'

'We're sorry to have bothered you,' Cory said smoothly. 'I hope we haven't caused you any more distress. Because Marianne died there, I think you've been a little jumpier than usual, haven't you, Rowan?'

She nodded. 'A bit. It's a big house if you're there on your own.'

'It was strange to me, that,' said Sarah. 'I never understood why she wanted to live on her own.' She looked at Cory. 'But I'm not an artist, so . . . Marianne was a lovely girl, wasn't she? So generous. Not with money, I don't mean,' she said hurriedly, as if they might suspect her of freeloading. 'But her time. When she wasn't working all the hours that God sent, she used to take Martin out – mostly the cinema, lunch sometimes, or a gig – he likes his music. She never said it but I think she knew it was almost as nice for me as it was for him. A break, if you know what I'm saying.'

Twenty-seven

As soundlessly as possible, Rowan slid the little bolt across. If Cory should take it into his head to kick down a second door today, this one on the bathroom would put up no resistance at all but she needed the symbolism of it anyway, just a few minutes in a locked room, alone.

She went to the basin and leaned forward until her forehead touched the mirror. The cold glass felt good and she tried to concentrate on the sensation, let it calm her whirling thoughts. Downstairs in the kitchen, Cory would be putting a neat cross next to Martin Johnson's name, moving on to a new line of inquiry, but she had no idea what to do next. Unnerved as she had been by him, at least the man who watched at night had represented a potential way inside the puzzle. Now he'd become yet another dead-end.

Her breath clouded the mirror. How had she let herself get so very vulnerable? She gripped the edge of the basin until her hands hurt. She should have burned the drawing of the fire – why the hell hadn't she? It would have been so easy. Here, in the basin: put it in, drop a match on top and watch it burn, flame eating flame. Run the tap and wash away the cinders.

Standing straight, she looked herself in the eye. She'd made a big mistake.

—

Cory had left the main light off, and the kitchen was lit instead by the series of lamps that Jacqueline had dotted around the room. Like her daughter, she'd disliked overhead lighting, and it was true that the room looked better like this, the corners softened, units half-hidden in shadow, the focus centred on the long table where Cory sat with his glass and the bottle of brandy. Seeing Rowan in the doorway, he looked up. 'I was beginning to wonder if something had happened to you.'

She came to the table and sat down. 'That was excruciating,' she said, tipping her head in the direction of the flats. Despite the emptiness of the street, they'd walked back from Benson Place in silence.

'Poor woman,' he said.

'Getting in there like that, saying we wanted to talk about Marianne, you standing out of the way until she'd opened the door . . .'

'I know.' He nodded. 'But we had to; she wouldn't have opened it otherwise.' He reached for the pad of A4 again. 'Can I?'

She shrugged. 'Go ahead.'

'You, I mean.'

'What, draw me?'

'Why not? Just while we talk.'

He took the pencil from his pocket again and she watched as he began to sketch out the first framing lines of her brow. There was something soothing about the motion of his hand over the paper, the apparent ease of it; she started to feel calmer almost immediately. He held the pencil loosely between his fingers, as if it decided where it needed to go and he merely provided the support, a medium at the Ouija board. Every few seconds he glanced up and looked at her face, appraising, before looking down again. The soft scratch of pencil on paper was lulling, almost hypnotic.

'Can I talk?' she said abruptly, puncturing the silence.

'Of course. I'm just doodling, nothing serious.'

'Do you think there's a possibility we're imagining all this? That it really *was* an accident.'

'After what you told me earlier?'

'But it all leads to nothing. Everything that seemed wrong or suspicious. He,' she tipped her head at the window again, 'was just her friend; Turk was stealing the sketches, and it looks like the only person who's broken in here is you.'

He smiled at that but shook his head. 'No. I'm more certain than ever that something happened. I – we – just have to keep going.'

Under the lip of the table, Rowan clenched her fists and she heard Marianne's voice, low and urgent, as if she were whispering just behind her: *I need to talk to you.*

When Cory spoke again, his words seemed to come from a distance. 'Are you all right, Rowan?'

'How do I know it's safe, what I told you?' she said, pulse drumming. 'That *I'm* safe? How do I know that you won't drag it all out into the open? If Marianne died because of Lorna, you won't be able to help exposing the truth about what happened back then, even if you don't mean to.'

'I won't do that. I promise.'

'How can you? And why would I trust you, anyway? You kicked the door down, for fuck's sake – you went through my things.'

Hands still, Cory kept his eyes fixed on the drawing for several seconds. She had the sense that he was making a decision. 'I won't tell anyone,' he said finally, 'for the same reason you never have.'

'What?'

'Because I loved her,' he said. 'No, that's still not the whole story. I was *in love* with her.'

The words echoed. There was no question that he was telling anything other than the truth: it was written on his face. As if he knew it and was embarrassed, he looked down abruptly and went back to the sketch. Rowan was beginning to take shape on the paper before him. He'd drawn her almost in profile, one eye visible, the other nearly hidden. Now the soft pencil was shaping a corner of her mouth.

'Did she know?' Rowan asked.

'I don't know. Yes, I think so.'

'Was there ever . . . ?'

'Nothing happened,' he said, fierce again. 'Ever. All right? Not that it's anyone's business.'

Except perhaps James Greenwood's, she thought, but she kept her mouth shut.

'I didn't plan it,' he said. 'She was in a relationship and I wasn't looking for anything like that. I had a girlfriend in New York and it ended very badly. She left me – crushed me, actually, if you want to know. I thought we'd get married, have kids, but as it turned out, she didn't. It was one of the reasons I decided to come here. The trigger, anyway – I couldn't be in that apartment any more. Even the city. I needed to be somewhere I wasn't reminded of her every time I turned a corner.'

'So why choose Marianne for a subject? Forgive me for saying so but you seem to have form when it comes to getting involved with the women you paint.'

'No. The other way round. I've painted the women I've been involved with.'

'Subtle distinction.'

'Not really.' He gave her a hard look and she struggled not to snap at him. Why did he talk to her as if she were an idiot? Why did she *feel* like an idiot around him?

He went back to the sketch and, with a series of tiny strokes, hatched in an area of shadow below her lower lip. A pout.

'Marianne,' he said, '*she* was subtle. She was a will-o'-the-wisp – I couldn't get a hold on her. She fascinated me – the more she told me, the less I seemed to know, and I wanted all of it. I wanted to know everything.'

For all her annoyance, Rowan felt a pang of envy. How would it feel to be described like that by a man like Cory? To be able to captivate someone like him?

'Don't you feel differently now?' she asked. 'Now that you *do* know.'

He held the pencil at both ends and turned it slowly between his fingers, watching it as if it, too, suddenly fascinated him. 'I'm not sure yet,' he said.

'Here.' He took a final look at the sketch then planted his fingertips on it, hand spider-like, and spun it across the table so that it reached her the right way up. It had taken him ten minutes, less even, but he'd caught her. There she was, not the version of herself she liked, the best-angle, soft-focus Rowan, but her knowing, thinking, hard-eyed avatar, Rowan the survivor, the one who had to do everything on her own. The version of herself that, in the privacy of her mind, she knew was the real one.

'What do you think?'

'You got me,' she said.

'Will you be okay?' he asked on the doorstep. 'I feel bad leaving you with the door like that overnight. I'll find a carpenter first thing tomorrow, pay whatever it takes to get it fixed right away.'

'I'll be fine. Two break-ins in a day would be unlucky even by my standards.'

He rolled his eyes. 'At least you know Martin only wants to wave to you now. I'll call tomorrow morning when I've got a carpenter.'

She stood inside the doorway and listened to his footsteps. Once he reached the pavement, they faded quickly and silence engulfed the house again. *Did* she feel comforted, knowing the truth about Martin? No. It wasn't just the way they'd got in there that had left a bad taste in her mouth. It was unkind, she knew she should feel sympathy for him and she did, but at the same time, she admitted to herself, he'd made her uncomfortable. The juxtaposition of the childish mind with his ultra-adult body, the developed muscles – perhaps he'd started weight training as part of his physiotherapy and got hooked on it. She thought about his broad chest and ham-hock arms. With the damage to his leg, of course, that inward-turned foot, he wouldn't be able to run easily.

The hairs on the back of her neck stood on end. Martin was the man in the window, yes, but he couldn't be the one in the garden. *That* man had been slight and nimble: there had been nothing awkward about the way *he'd* moved.

Waves of cold ran down her back. Shit: the door. In daylight, with Cory here, the arrangement with the chair had felt secure enough, but not at night, alone in the house. She needed to make a real barricade, pile furniture in the doorway so that even if someone did try their luck – even if they got in – there'd be noise, advance warning . . .

But just as she reached the kitchen, the phone rang in the hallway overhead, startlingly loud. She turned then stopped. Was it a trick? Was someone watching the house? Had they seen Cory leave and now they were calling her away so that they could force the door, get in on the ground floor before she blocked it properly? She wavered, paralysed by indecision, then pulled herself together: was he a mind-reader, this guy? Had he known about the barricade the moment she'd had the idea? For God's sake.

Before the phone could ring out, she ran upstairs and picked up the receiver. 'Hello?' She tried to sound calm but the anxiety in her voice was unmistakable.

'Rowan?' said a man's voice.

'Yes?'

'It's Adam.'

Twenty-eight

At the northern point of the narrow island made by the two prongs of Magdalen Street stood the Martyrs' Memorial. It was a monstrosity, spitefully Gothic, an intensely carved spike blackened with soot that, whenever she saw it, put Rowan in mind of the charred, skyward-pointing finger-bone of one of the men it commemorated, burned at the stake around the corner on Broad Street.

A flight of shallow steps, incongruously plain, had been built around the base. She crossed the road and climbed them. She was four or five feet above the pavement, if that, but it was enough to give her a view across Magdalen Street and in through the lit windows of the Randolph Hotel's formal dining room.

At the end of her first year at university, when she called to tell him she'd got a First in the Mods exams, her father, just back from an extended stint in South America, said he wanted to take her out to lunch. To celebrate, he'd said.

Punctuality had always been a big deal with him and when she'd arrived, stepping in out of the dazzling sunshine from a pavement already starting to radiate the day's heat, he was waiting for her at the desk in the lamp-lit reception area, the heavy staircases climbing away Escher-style over his head, illuminated – as much as they ever were – by pointed Gothic windows. The carpet was blood red, enhancing her impression of finding herself suddenly, Jonah-like, on the inside of an enormous beast.

'You look well.' He'd pressed his cheek briefly against hers. 'I expected you to be white as a sheet after all that studying.'

'I finished three weeks ago,' she said and, hearing how he might infer criticism or resentment, quickly added, 'The weather's been great so I've spent a lot of time outside since.'

'That's good. Nothing worse than being cooped up in libraries.'

She'd refrained from saying that actually, that was how she planned to spend the rest of her life, if possible, and instead smiled and let him usher her down the hall to the dining room. It was at the corner of the building with windows on both sides, those on Beaumont Street looking out towards the grandeur of the Ashmolean Museum, the others this way, towards the Memorial and Balliol College beyond. By contrast with reception, it was filled with light, and the glass and silverware glinted on stiff white linen. Wood panelling, oil paintings. From the window table that her father requested, she had a view of the room and the three other parties of early eaters already ensconced, a trio of businessmen all wearing grey suits, and two couples in their seventies, the nearest pair sipping sherry while they perused the menu. The weekday lunch, she thought, preserve of those on pensions or expenses, and those consciously or otherwise avoiding the intimacy of dinner with its candlelight and greater likelihood of drinking too much truth serum.

To her surprise, however, her father immediately ordered two glasses of champagne. 'To you,' he said, chiming his glass gently against hers, 'and your double first.'

'God, no pressure.'

'No,' he said, 'no pressure. But you'll do it.' He took a sip. 'Your mother would have been proud of you today, Rowan.'

She had been startled: he never talked about her mother. When she was younger, she'd resented it, wanting – needing –

information, but as she'd grown older, she'd understood and even come to appreciate his silence. It was too painful, she'd thought; for him, the memories; for her, the lack of them. Blood aside, loss was what they had in common. She'd felt an intense pang of longing for her mother then, a void yawning at her centre like a hole burned all the way through. In recognition of what it must have cost him to say it, she stifled the questions that came afterwards: *Are* you *proud, Dad? Could you tell me?*

Their elderly neighbours had taken delivery of salmon mousses and, glancing over, Rowan caught the woman's eye. She wondered if they shared the habit of analysing fellow diners, working out their relationships and situations, and if so, what this woman made of the girl and the man entertaining her. Their colouring said they were family, his genes had dominated her mother's timid ones, but given their formality with one another, she could be excused for guessing they were niece and arm's-length uncle. Her father was making an effort, though, she had to admit, and as they ate, they carried on a polite trade in information. She told him about the papers she'd sat and the ballot for rooms in college in the autumn; he talked about Rio and Santiago and a new cancer drug in which Stern Rizer was investing a huge amount of research funding.

Halfway through his main course, however, he gestured to the waiter for more champagne and she knew that something was going on. She'd attributed his animation to the first glass, the effect of lunchtime drinking on someone who wasn't used to it, but with the second glass she realised that, in fact, her father was nervous. He was fortifying himself. *Girding his loins.*

He'd waited until she'd finished her risotto, at least. Then, downing a full inch from his glass in a single swig, he'd looked across, almost bashful. 'We're celebrating two things today,' he said. 'Three, actually.'

'Are we?' Her heart started pumping harder.

He smiled. 'I know this will come as a surprise but I didn't want to bother you with it before the exams and . . . Well, no point beating around the bush: I'm getting married.'

Something at the very centre of her collapsed. She felt it behind her ribcage: a house of cards, a shirt slipping off a hanger to fall shapeless to the floor. The room pulled away, and she had the impression that she was looking at it from the end of a tunnel, her father a tiny figure far removed across the white plains of the tablecloth. A rushing sound in her ears, the sea heard in a shell, and the floor tipped dangerously beneath her chair. She grabbed the edge of the table.

Her father didn't notice. '. . . waiting for dates but probably the second week of December,' he was saying. 'Jessica – she's looking forward to meeting you – wants a winter do. The village church is very pretty there and, of course, it's traditional for it to happen on the bride's home turf so . . .'

'What's the third thing?' said Rowan, her voice sounding as if it belonged to someone else.

'What?'

'Three things.'

Her father gave a smile she could only describe as coy. 'Well, I promised Jess I wouldn't say anything because it's early days and you're not supposed to tell anyone until the three-month all-clear, are you, but . . .'

She stood up, dimly aware of dragging the tablecloth with her, and on uncertain legs she made her way back across the room. 'Rowan,' he hissed, but the restaurant had been almost full by then and he hated scenes. Down the passageway into the gloom of reception and then out, gathering speed as she came down the steps to the pavement and emerged into the full glare of the sun.

She hadn't had to think about where to go. On legs like heat-softened plastic, she took St Giles' at full tilt, the lump of risotto a painful pendulum in her stomach. People looked at her – a couple at the crossing near the church turned to stare as she passed, her breath coming hard by then, her back damp with sweat. The soles of her summer shoes had been so thin that she bruised the balls of her feet. It had hurt to walk for days afterwards.

She'd rung the doorbell and while she'd waited, she'd begged: *Let them be in. Please, let them be in.* The seconds stretched and the door took on symbolic significance: would it open or was she always going to be left outside, belonging to no one, loved by no one?

She'd started to shake by the time she saw the dark silhouette swim up behind the glass. When Seb opened the door, he understood at once that something had happened. He'd put his arms around her and held her tightly. 'It's all right,' he'd said. 'We've got you. We've got you.' When her breathing began to normalise a little, he'd pulled back to look at her face. 'Bad?'

'Quite bad.'

He'd frowned, real concern in his eyes. 'Everyone's here,' he said. 'All four of us. We're in the garden, doing the crossword. Come with me – come and tell us what's going on. We'll get you straightened out.'

When the bells chimed the hour, she stood up and started to make her way along Broad Street. It had worked: just looking through the window and remembering had been enough. Since she'd been back in Oxford, especially since the night with Adam, the old feeling had been pushing at the lid of its box, the insidious idea that she was not just unloved but fundamentally unlovable, that her life before she met the Glasses hadn't been bad luck, the result of a mother who died too young and a father who couldn't handle his situation, but her fault, the consequence of some deep essential flaw in her. Tonight, before going to meet Adam, she'd needed to be reminded that she *had* been loved; that even though her own family had been a disaster, she'd been welcomed into someone else's. Wasn't that better, in a way, a stronger confirmation? The Glasses hadn't needed to envelop her as they had, there had been no biological imperative. They'd chosen to.

On the phone, Adam had given very little away. He'd apologised for the radio silence, saying that he'd needed to think, and then he'd asked if he could drive over and see her. She'd said yes, of course, but she'd suggested they meet at The Turf, a good fifteen-minute walk from the house. Even if it was what he was hoping, which she doubted now, she'd wanted to make the point that after letting four days pass before ringing, he couldn't just take up where they'd left off at the weekend. As well as a symbolic retrenchment, the distance was practical: he wouldn't be able to drink much if he had the car, and if they did go back to the house, she'd have a sobering walk in which to ask herself some stern questions.

A stranger to Oxford was unlikely to stumble on The Turf by accident. It was entirely enclosed by other buildings, invisible from the road and accessed only by two obscure alleyways. There was something of the faerie about the building itself, too: timber-framed with crooked windows in an assortment of styles, it was covered by a roof as steeply pitched as the lid of a toadstool.

Inside, the ceiling was ribbed with beams and barely cleared Rowan's head by a foot. She made her way down the little passage to the back bar and found Adam waiting at the table by the window. He saw her as she came in and stood up immediately.

'Hello,' he said, kissing her cheek. 'Thank you for coming.'

It struck her as a strange, formal thing to say and there was an awkward second or two in which she searched for the right response and failed. After insisting that she take the better seat on the old church pew, he went to the bar and she had a chance to look at him. He was wearing almost exactly the same as he had on Friday: jeans and a round-necked navy jumper though, this time, the shirt just visible at the neck was faded denim. His hair had been cut since then, however, exposing a new quarter-inch of pale skin at the nape of his neck and, when he'd kissed her, his cheek had been smooth, shaved more recently than this morning.

He returned with two glasses of red wine. 'How's your week been?' he asked and she imagined what would happen if she told him the truth.

'Okay. Yours?'

He shrugged. 'Busy – the writing and . . . Ro, I'm so sorry I wasn't in touch earlier.'

At college, even in her twenties, she might have said it didn't matter, waved it away as nothing, but now, wiser, she kept quiet.

'As I said last night, I needed to get my head straight before I talked to you. I needed to work out what I was doing, whether I was . . .' He rubbed his thumb over a watermark on the base of his glass. 'But I'm sorry. I can see it was selfish. I didn't mean to leave you hanging.'

'Did you?' she said. 'Get your head straight?'

'I think so. Yes. It's . . .' He looked at her. 'I felt guilty. I felt happy on Friday and it felt wrong. Disloyal – to Marianne.'

'Disloyal?'

'It didn't feel right, being happy about something so soon after her death, and for us to be together there, at the house . . .' He shook his head. 'I don't think I would have done it if we hadn't drunk so much.'

Rowan felt as if she'd been slapped. Blood rushed to her face, and even in the low light, Adam saw it. 'God, no, no, that's not what I meant! I meant, it shouldn't have been *there*, at the house, not that I wouldn't have . . . Aaargh.' He put his elbows on the table and buried his face in his hands. When he looked up again, his expression was composed. 'Let me do this the other way around. I like you a lot, Rowan, and I always have. On Friday I was happy, I felt like I'd finally got the opportunity to do something I wanted to do – should have done – a long time ago, but then I thought: am

I some kind of monster, thinking about myself, a new relationship, when my sister has been dead less than a month? When the woman I like was my sister's best friend.'

'I know.'

'And what I told you about Mazz asking me not to pursue things with you back then . . .'

Rowan thought of her father, the relationship he'd carried on with Jessica for four years, it turned out, before that lunch at the Randolph; the weeks when he'd been not in Lima or Buenos Aires, as he'd claimed, but a small village in Kent. 'Adam, it's all right,' she said. 'You don't have to explain.'

'No, I do.'

'It was bad timing – you said on Friday. It's one of those things; you don't have to . . .'

'What I'm trying to say,' he cut her off, 'is that I don't think Marianne would mind. Now. Back then, when you two were so close, when we were younger, I can see why she wouldn't have liked it, her brother and her best friend, but now – especially now – there's no clash.'

'I . . .'

'I think she'd be pleased. If we can find something good in all this . . . I mean, if you want to, of course; I don't know how you feel at all . . .' He made another strangled sound. 'I'm bad at this.'

She laughed, a soaring feeling in her chest. Steady, she cautioned herself, at least try to play it cool, but when he reached across and squeezed her hand, she felt herself grin like a fool.

'With everything else that happened on Friday,' he said, 'I didn't tell you but a couple of weeks before it happened, just after Christmas, Mazz and I had a drink and she mentioned – only briefly: she said it and then the conversation changed direction or her phone rang, I don't remember – but she said she wanted to get in touch with you again. To sort out what happened back then.'

Rowan stiffened. 'Did she?'

'I don't know whether you know or not but she'd become good friends with Michael Cory, the artist. They met through James, at the gallery.'

'Yes,' she said. 'That was what I wanted to say to you on Friday before we . . . got distracted. He's been in touch with me – he's been to the house, wanting to talk about her. He's painting her portrait, Adam.'

She waited for the look of horror or else a gradual realisation as he worked through the implications but instead he nodded. 'I know. She talked to me about it.'

'You weren't worried?'

'About his reputation? No. You've met him?'

'Yes.'

'So you know it's all a load of crap, then, the stuff about him setting out to destroy people. Undoing them – I love that idea, it sounds so Victorian, doesn't it? All corsets and repression, like he's some devil with a waxed moustache going round loosening stays. I haven't met him yet – actually, he left a message on my phone earlier, while I was driving . . .'

'Did he?'

'Mazz said he was a good man. Sound was her word – she said she trusted him.'

'I don't know, Adam. I mean . . .'

'Apparently the stuff about him and psychology is true, though. She said she shouldn't have bothered seeing the shrinks back then, when she had her breakdown; she should just have called him.'

Adam had found a parking spot in Broad Street where, he told Rowan, developing a sudden interest in the empty picnic tables outside the window, the car could stay overnight.

'So . . . ?' She raised an eyebrow.

'So,' he said, 'we could have another glass of wine if you'd like one.' She laughed.

They left when they finished their third, just after ten o'clock. A handful of hardy smokers huddled around one of the patio heaters but otherwise the courtyard was deserted, and in the unlit passage that led out to Bath Place, Adam reached for her hand, pulled her back to him and kissed her. 'I've wanted to do that since you walked through the door,' he said quietly, his mouth still close enough that she felt his breath on her cheek. 'The soul-searching this week – please don't let it give you the wrong impression.' Rowan felt the joyful soaring in her chest again, a rush of desire as strong as the one all those years ago, up in his room.

Parks Road was quiet, and on the stretch before the turn to the science area, he drew her off the pavement. It was like being back at college, these drunken walks home punctuated by shameless public kissing. Ivy covered this part of Wadham's long perimeter wall, a huge sheepskin rug thrown over the top. Perhaps he'd thought it would be more comfortable than the stone but its leaves were cold as he pressed her into them, enveloping them both with an odd scent, dusty and chemical at the same time, that made her think of the graveyard at St Sepulchre's, the smell of the dry earth path beneath the avenue of yews with the bench where she and Marianne used to sit and talk. Adam kissed her harder, pressing the full weight of his body against her.

Male voices approaching, young and drunk, and as he cupped her head between his hands, one of them called, 'Get a room.' Adam pulled away as if he'd been burned and she looked at him in the darkness, expecting embarrassment, the return of his reserve, but instead she saw he was grinning. 'It's not a terrible idea.'

With the coldness of the air and the speed at which they walked, she was breathing fast by the time they reached Fyfield Road, and as she turned to him on the top step, her breath made clouds in the pool of light under the carriage lamp. For the past five minutes, her mind had been whirring. She couldn't tell him the truth, there was no way, but she had to say something. It pained her to lie to him, especially now, when they were just starting out, but the truth would ruin his life.

'Adam,' she said, 'I've got a confession to make.' She watched his face turn serious. 'No, it's nothing major. Just – yesterday, when I went out, I forgot my keys and locked myself out. The Dawsons are still away – I know you used to leave a spare set with them – so in the end I had to break in through the kitchen.'

'You broke in?'

'I didn't want to smash the glass so I kicked the door, hoping it would force the lock, but it broke the jamb – the whole lock came out, the wood just shattered.'

'Wow, Karate Kid.'

'I'm really sorry.'

'Don't worry about it, we can get it mended.'

'It's already done. A carpenter came this morning.' True to his word, Cory had called her at ten o'clock and the carpenter had been there at half-past. 'He replaced the whole jamb – he said it was rotten, anyway. Damp – probably why it always used to stick.'

'You paid him?'

Rowan hesitated momentarily. 'Yes.'

'I'll pay you back.'

'No. No way. It was my fault – if I hadn't forgotten my keys, it wouldn't have happened.'

'You're a student, Ro. You're doing us a favour, anyway.'

'I had a job for years; I'm not a complete down and out.'

'We can argue about it later. Have you got your keys now? It's cold – let me in.'

She'd left the elephant lamp on so that she wouldn't have to walk into a dark house; she remembered thinking she'd almost certainly be coming back alone.

'So the back door's safe again?' Adam hung up his coat. 'Secure, I mean?'

'Yes. Come and see it.'

He followed her downstairs. 'I haven't painted it yet,' she said, as they came into the kitchen. 'I've bought the paint but I hoped I'd get away without telling you until it was done.'

He ran his thumb up and down the new upright and unlocked the door, letting in a blast of cold air. 'It looks like a very good job,' he said, shutting it.

'I'm glad.' She had no idea how much Cory had had to pay the guy to do the work so quickly but she'd been more grateful than she'd wanted him to know. Last night the house had felt like a birdcage, she the canary inside while an unseen cat prowled the shadows. She'd lain awake past three o'clock, tensing at every creak and tick. Thinking she heard something in the garden, she'd got up twice to peer out from behind the curtain but there had been nothing to see except the large lit rectangle of Martin Johnson's window.

Adam locked the door but as he turned and came towards her again, he caught sight of the drawing on the table. 'Is that . . . ? It looks like Michael Cory's style.'

'It is. He did it while we were talking. It's not much – just a sketch.'

'May I?'

'Of course.'

Adam slid it very gently to the edge then picked it up with the tips of his fingers. Rowan thought of the three million dollars Hanna Ferrara had paid for her painting and wondered suddenly how much this was worth. Something, surely, even if she was nobody. Adam looked at it in silence for several seconds.

'Does he like you?' he said finally.

'What?'

'It's you, obviously, but it's not how I'd draw you. You look . . . tough.' He frowned. 'Not to be messed with.'

'That's not how you see me?'

She was teasing but Adam took the question seriously. 'No, not tough. Self-sufficient – wasn't that what I said on Friday? It's one of the things I've always admired about you.' He put the sketch down and turned to her, putting his hands around her waist. They kissed and she pulled him closer, wanting to breathe him in. She was surprised when, a minute later, he pulled away.

'*You* could have called *me*,' he said.

She looked at his face, his serious eyes, and wondered if she would ever be able to tell him that, no, after what Turk had said about her getting her claws into him, she couldn't. If they had a relationship, she had to know that he'd chosen it. If Turk ever said it to his face, she wanted Adam to be able to dismiss without a thought the idea that she'd pursued him.

She shook her head. 'I needed to know you were sure. And that it wasn't too soon.'

'It's not too soon.'

He fell asleep before she did and after she'd reached gingerly over him to turn off the light, she lay awake again. *Was* she tough? Yes, when she had to be. If she had to fight, she could do it.

Twenty-nine

When she woke, the other side of the bed was empty. She sat up quickly. A thin grey light came around the edge of the curtains, enough for her to see that his clothes were gone from the chair. His shoes were gone, too. She slid her hand across the fitted sheet and, discovering it was still slightly warm, she threw back the blankets and stood up, the sudden change in posture giving her a head rush. When it passed, she threw on her clothes and went out to the landing. Silence at first and then, like music, the sound of crockery being taken out of the dishwasher. The relief was so intense that when she turned on the bathroom light and saw herself in the mirror, she was grinning. She brushed her hair quickly, rubbed the mascara from under her eyes and cleaned her teeth. The room was warm and slightly humid; he'd taken a shower.

As she came in to the kitchen, the kettle was boiling. 'I thought you'd gone.'

'Really?' He was surprised. 'No, I wouldn't leave without saying goodbye.' He came over and kissed her.

'What time is it?' She peered at the clock on the cooker.

'Half-seven. I wish I could stay – not that I want to distract you,' he tipped his head in the direction of her untouched books, 'but I've got to give a lecture at two and God knows how long it'll take me to get back. I should have come on the train – it's a hassle having to go into London and out again but the drive's so boring, all those crappy little roundabouts. There used to be a direct line, apparently, years ago.'

He filled the coffee pot then took the milk from the fridge. She watched him from the corner of her eye. Even under-slept and mildly hungover, he had the elegance she'd noticed at Gee's: his hands moved lightly over the cups and spoons, as if he were conducting the process of coffee-making rather than actually doing it. She wondered which distant ancestor had bequeathed him that gene; it wasn't his mother.

'You've got to stop poisoning me with all this booze,' he said, bringing her a cup.

'*I'm* poisoning *you*?'

He smiled. 'Shall we do it again tomorrow? I've got a meeting in college in the early afternoon but I could come back tomorrow night?'

The tentative note at the end of the question surprised her but it made her happy, too. This mattered to him; he wasn't taking it for granted. A sensation of warmth, as if the sun had broken through and come streaming through the window. 'I'll buy some Alka-Seltzer,' she said.

Before getting out of the shower, she turned the water to cold and stood under it until her back and shoulders started to go numb. She needed a clear head today, perhaps more than ever.

Adam's pillow still held the shape of his head, and when she came back downstairs, her eyes went straight to his coffee cup on the table. It had an elegiac poignancy, as if it already belonged to a past she would never recover. She gave herself a sharp mental shake, telling herself to stop being mawkish. As long as she didn't mess it up, he was the future, not the past.

Cory's sketch was on the table, too, where Adam had left it last night. She picked it up and looked herself in the eye. When he'd called yesterday, Cory had said he'd pick her up at two-thirty. She tapped her phone to check the time. Nine o'clock.

Thirty

'Will you take me there?' he'd asked her on the telephone. 'I've read the reports, you've told me, but I need to see it.'

'Why?'

'I can't picture it – in my mind. I'm trying to understand how the person I knew could actually have done what she did and I can't.'

With a glance down the street now, Rowan opened the door of his car and lowered herself into the passenger seat.

Cory leaned forward to turn off the radio. 'Hello. How are you doing?'

'All right.' She paused. 'Michael, are you sure you want to do this? I don't know if it's going to help. I mean, I don't think we'll ever be able to understand it. Maybe we should just forget about it.'

He frowned. 'Forget?'

'Not *forget* . . . Just, it was years ago – there won't be anything left there and . . .' She trailed off. 'I suppose I'm just trying to ask if you're sure you still want to go.'

He turned to look at her properly. 'Of course,' he said. 'Why would I change my mind?'

It was quiet inside the car, even the engine barely audible, and as it passed by on the other side of the tinted glass, the city had a foreign, filmic quality, as if she were looking at old footage. She gave directions and he drove the way she'd taken on

Tuesday, his callused hands whispering against the leather steering wheel. As they passed the Head of the River pub, she remembered how she'd had to pick her way through the undergrowth to get out of the meadow. A week ago today. She put her fingers to her cheek but the scratch was almost gone. Cory glanced across.

'That looked sore,' he said. 'When you got it.'

She ignored the implied question. 'Not really.'

'Didn't you tell me you grew up in this neighbourhood – south Oxford?'

'Yes. Just . . . there, in fact. Vicarage Road. Quick: keep driving.'

He laughed.

The houses and shops were set further back from the road here, making the sky seem wider. At eleven or so, a breeze had come up, riffling the evergreens in the front garden, but a stronger wind was at work among the clouds now, blowing them across the sky like soap-scum, shades of cream and grey against a torn and dirty backcloth.

As they waited for the light at Weirs Lane, Cory looked over again. 'Have you seen Martin since we went round there?'

'Yes, just now – I was up in my bedroom before I came out.'

'Did he wave?'

'He did, and I waved back.' In fact, it had been the other way round. She'd turned on the light – it had been so gloomy in there – and as she'd gone towards the window, she'd seen him appear at his. She'd raised her arm in salute and after a moment, he'd done the same. She'd stood there for a few seconds, self-conscious, then given him another quick wave and walked away.

Over the years, she'd trained herself to shut down any memory of that day the moment it started, but when they made the turn and came along between the facing rows of terraced houses, some of them redbrick, some pebbledashed and sprouting satellite dishes like fungus, their images in her mind were as crisp and well-kept as Marianne's sketches in their box.

The lights were flashing at the zebra crossing a few hundred yards along, a woman waiting with two little boys, and as they stopped, Rowan leaned forward and retied her shoelace.

'Did you come this way?'

'What?' She sat up again as they moved off.

'When you came here with Marianne.'

'Yes.'

'You didn't walk all the way from Park Town? Or did you come from Vicarage Road?'

'No, we never used to stay there. We were at Fyfield that morning. We took a bus down Abingdon Road then walked this part. It was hot – it was hot most of that summer.'

She remembered the sun beating down on her hair and the back of her neck, her forearms turning pink. She'd forgotten to bring any water and she'd been so thirsty by the time she'd reached the bank that the river had felt like a taunt. *Water, water everywhere*, murmured Marianne's voice in her ear. Rowan thought of Adam's breath on her cheek last night as they'd left the pub, the way he'd kissed her.

They passed a cyclist and then, at the foot of the bridge, a woman in jogging gear. As they came over the water, Rowan made herself look. It had sparkled that day, dappled with sun and shimmering leaves. This afternoon it was dull pewter, the reflected branches like stress fractures around its edges, the clouds formless creatures moving under the surface.

'That's it?' said Cory. 'A lot of bridge for so little water.'

'It's strange. That's the main body of the river but there're lots of small inlets and creeks, too. Here – this turn.'

Meadow Lane, so innocuous-sounding. Cory slowed down and they cruised past the entrance to the rowing club. She'd brought the baseball cap and she put it on, tucked her hair behind her ears. The car park had been busy that day but now, in the middle of the afternoon in the first week of February, there wasn't a single vehicle on the muddy patch by the boatsheds, and only a handful of cars were parked outside the houses across the road. The pavement was empty: too early for the school run.

She pointed to the second, smaller car park among the trees, overflow parking for the club or perhaps the scout hut further down. 'We can go in there,' she said. 'I'm sure no one will mind – we'll only be a few minutes. If you go up on the grassy bit, we won't get too muddy.'

When he turned off the engine, the world went quiet. She closed her eyes as a sudden intense wave of nausea swept over her and she heard the creak of leather as he shifted in his seat.

'Are you sure you can do this, Rowan?'

'I have to.'

'You don't. If it makes you feel . . .'

'It's fine,' she said, and opened her door. A *thunk* as he closed his and then the double beep of the electronic fob. The sidelights flashed brightly. She peered ahead into the trees. 'We can get through this way, it looks like; we don't have to go back to the road.'

She'd borrowed Seb's old wool overcoat and she was grateful for its weight, the protection both from the brambles and the wind, which seemed harder and colder now. As they came out on to the unmade track, she took her gloves out of her pocket. On their right was the open meadow for which the road was named, the wind blowing runnels in the unkempt winter grass. Rowan's mind served her a sudden snapshot of that afternoon: two girls in bikinis stretched on their fronts reading magazines; an older woman talking on the phone while she watched a baby kicking in the shade of a parasol. The sky had been high and blue, cloudless. She'd kept her head down.

The meadow was deserted today and the cars passing on Donnington Bridge were hidden by the trees. The river was ahead of them, marked by a line of willows, and when the track came to an end, Cory followed her across the grass towards the gentle slope to the water's edge.

'It's isolated,' he said. 'Much more isolated than I imagined. It's like being out in the country.'

'It must have helped, when she did it. It took us a long time to find the place, when we came. Marianne knew it was near the bridge somewhere, on the river, but we went down on the other side first, walked through scrub for what felt like miles.' She could remember it so clearly, the heat, the long grass tickling her hands, covering her with dust and seed. There had been an electrical substation and, just beyond it, a homeless man, old and toothless, had reared up out of the undergrowth and scared them half to death.

Cory looked back along the track and with a flare of alarm, Rowan looked, too. No one – it was deserted. 'Lorna really lived down here on her own?' he said. 'Why would she do that?'

'Look.'

At the top of the bank, Rowan stopped walking. That afternoon, the view had made her catch her breath. They were two hundred yards at most from the bridge but this world had nothing to do with tarmac and streetlights and pedestrian crossings. What she'd seen was a private creek, almost a lagoon, hidden from view from the main part of the river by a narrow island overgrown with willows. Even now, leafless, the branches were dense enough to screen the inlet from anyone who might motor downstream, but that day, the place had been a riotous pixellating spill of green in every shade, the surface of the water mirroring the sky and the trees so precisely that after she'd stared for a minute, the lines had blurred and she'd no longer been sure where one ended and the other began. And there, nestled into the creek, had been the houseboat, white as a wedding cake, its long low sides lined with windows, the base of the flagpole on the foredeck surrounded by pots planted with herbs and tomatoes, hot-pink geraniums.

'It was moored there,' she said, pointing. 'Totally secluded, hidden in a sort of green private world. It's hard to explain how beautiful it was.'

'I've seen photographs of it. And the drawing.'

Rowan shook her head. 'Not just the boat. The whole thing . . . the river, the trees, the sky. And the peace – it was like going back in time. It could have been nineteen twenty. *Eighteen* twenty. The isolation was the point.'

The wind whispered across the meadow behind them, stirred the willows' whip-like branches.

Cory walked a little way down the bank. 'What happened to it?' he asked. 'Afterwards.'

'After the investigation? It was destroyed, I think. Broken up, what was left of it. It must have been so badly damaged – the explosion as well as the fire. No one would have wanted to live on it after that, anyway. Even if it had been rebuilt, it would still have had that history.'

In the mud just in front of her there was a flat grey stone about eight inches long, five wide. Its edges were rough, as if it had been quarried once upon a time, used for a wall or a path, perhaps. Why was it here? Had it been part of the barge set-up? Her mind slipped a memory across the table like a card: Marianne on stepping-stones to the gangplank, Rowan herself standing under the willows begging her to come away.

'She must have been insane,' Cory said. 'Temporary insanity caused by psychological stress. Maybe the pressure of finishing her degree combined with grief at the idea of losing her father. It's the only way I can explain it.'

'Have you been in touch with Adam yet, Michael? Have you called him?'

A momentary pause, imperceptible unless you were listening for it. 'No,' he said, without turning around.

'Have you got his number?'

'No.' Still he faced away, hiding his lying eyes. 'Could you give it to me?'

Now. Do it now. Keeping her feet clear of the mud, Rowan crouched and, as silently as possible, picked up the stone. It was heavy – heavy enough. With a final look around, she raised her arm and, summoning the full force of her anger, she brought the stone down on the back of his head.

A sickening crunch. For a moment, the world seemed to stop – the birdsong went silent, the lapping of the river, even the stir of the breeze among the leaves. They were on the point of time, a fulcrum.

But then – a warning flag – the blood. It welled up in a second; nothing and then, all of a sudden, a torrent. There was so much of it, blood running down his head, the back of his neck – he had no hair to absorb it or even interrupt the flow. She panicked: she couldn't risk him falling with his head on the bank. If it were going to look like he'd slipped, hit his head, fallen in the water – an accident – there couldn't be blood spattered on the mud.

Staggering, knees buckling beneath him, Cory turned. His eyes were wide – stunned, disbelieving – but then, even as he started to lose focus, she saw realisation. 'You . . .' he said.

She gathered her strength again and shoved him. For all his heft, it didn't take much: he was already reeling. He fell straight backwards, feet on the bank, head and shoulders in the water. *Thank God.* The splash set the birds chattering, excited, and the leaves seemed to carry the sound: *Did you see? Did you see?*

Stepping on areas of stones, she waded in after him. His eyes were open, unseeing, but when she took off her glove and put her hand close to his mouth, she felt his breath, warm in the cold air. Glove on again, she plunged her hands into the water, grabbed the back of his coat and pulled. Now his weight *was* a problem, and the water in his clothes made him heavier still – she felt her back strain. Another moment of alarm – what if she couldn't turn him? Then, though, planting her feet firmly, she took hold again and with every ounce of her strength, she managed to roll him on to his side and then his front.

Hand at the base of his skull, careful not to touch the wound, she held his face under the water. The resistance was physical only, his body's unconscious fight for survival, but she held him firm until the bucking slowed then stopped and the bubbles came to an end.

Thirty-one

The miniature woman huddled in foetal position, downy forearms hugging her skeletal knees, scalp gleaming white through her lifeless hair. From her spot beneath the window, Rowan could see the three who preceded her, each smaller than the one before, and for the first time, she had the idea that the women were shrinking not just from the world, the anonymous viewers who would stand in front of them in galleries and museums, no doubt, in years to come, but specifically from her. She looked at the way the last one curled in on herself, turning her face towards the pitiless varnished boards, and the posture struck her suddenly as defensive, fearful. Cowering. *'Why?'* wailed the ruined O of her mouth. *'Why, Rowan?'*

She'd waited for Marianne at Vicarage Road all that day, listening to the busybody tick of her father's fussy carriage clock and the bulletins on Fox FM. She'd watched the local news on TV, too, but she hadn't needed it to tell her what had happened. Just after eleven o'clock the previous night, down in the dark in the scrubland beyond the allotments, she'd heard the explosion for herself. Minutes later, as she'd let herself back into the house, the sirens had come screaming down Abingdon Road followed by the dull beat of the helicopter overhead. From her father's bedroom window, she'd seen the spotlight angling down over Donnington Bridge.

Rowan had expected her sooner but it was five o'clock by the time Marianne came. She'd beaten on the front door as if she were going out of her mind, pounding with her fists, leaning on the bell. In the few seconds it took Rowan to get there, Marianne started shouting her name. She'd opened it and pulled her inside as quickly as possible. 'For God's sake, are you mad? What are you *doing*?'

Marianne's face had stopped the words in her mouth. She'd never seen her look like that before, not when she'd had a bout of real flu in the Lower Sixth, not even the afternoon of Seb's party. She'd been feverish, wild-eyed. White.

'What have you done, Rowan?' she said. 'What have you done?' She was trembling. Shaking.

'Mazz, come and sit down. You're going to give yourself a heart attack.'

'Get your hands off me!'

A shadow shivered across the patterned glass behind her: someone on the pavement, only feet away. They must have seen her frenzied knocking – what had they heard?

'Tell me it wasn't you, Rowan. Please,' she begged. 'Tell me it was an accident – that it's all just an outlandish coincidence. Say it wasn't you.'

Rowan looked at her, confused. She seemed really to be asking. 'I don't understand,' she said slowly.

'Tell me,' her voice was rising, 'that you didn't go to that boat and . . .'

'Quiet! The neighbours.' She glanced to left and right as if they might even then be listening. 'I thought it was what you wanted.'

Marianne's eyes widened and she shrank away, pressing back against the wall. 'No.' She shook her head. 'No.'

'But it *was*. I was with you – we went there together, remember? You made me go with you.' She lowered her voice again. 'The gas tank, the stove. Your drawing – I . . .'

'It was a *fantasy*, Rowan. A way of . . . expressing the anger, getting some of it out. A vent, not a . . . a plan.'

'But it *was* a plan. A good one: it worked. It's early days, obviously, we're not out of the woods, but everything they've said on the radio makes it sound like they think it was an accident, just like you thought.'

Marianne stared.

'Mazz, look: all I did was go there and turn on the gas on the cooker. One knob. It was so simple – that's why it worked. She came home, turned the light on . . . I did it for you because it was better like that, safer: I don't have a motive. Who would suspect me? It's perfect.'

Marianne started to cry and Rowan felt the stirrings of impatience. 'Come on, I know it feels bad at the moment but it'll pass. Lorna's gone and it's all going to get easier. Your dad will get over it and forget about her like he always does and everything will be fine again. He and your mother will be happy and . . .'

'You're insane.'

'What?'

'You've gone mad,' Marianne said. 'You've lost your mind.'

'Oh, just stop it. Pull yourself together.' Her voice was stern and decisive, calm in the face of Mazz's unexpected inability to deal with the situation. Rowan had thought she was tougher than that. 'You can't pretend this was nothing to do with you.'

'But it wasn't. It wasn't,' she sobbed.

For the first time ever, Rowan felt a stab of contempt. Contempt, for Marianne – even in the moment, it was shocking. 'Don't be a coward,' she said. 'She was going to destroy your family so you made a plan to get rid of her and it worked. You should be pleased.'

When Mazz spoke again, her voice had changed. The panic and disbelief were gone and in their place – ridiculous – was fear. 'You're a monster,' she said.

'I only did it for you.'

Marianne shook her head. 'This is *nothing* to do with me – nothing. It's about *you*. What would you do without my family, Rowan? Without my mum and dad pandering to you, saving articles for you out of the paper, taking you out, *feeding* you? Is that why you stayed in Oxford to do your degree? I can't think of any other reason – there was nothing else to keep you here.'

The words had cut her. 'I love them.'

'No, you don't, you're not capable of it,' Marianne had thrown at her. 'You're . . . damaged. Fucked up. You're a *murderer*, Rowan.' Her voice was rising again. 'Do you even understand what you've done? You've killed someone – *killed*.'

'For fuck's sake, keep your voice down,' she'd hissed. She took a breath, tried to think. One of them had to keep a clear head if they were going to make this work.

'Do you think my family would want anything to do with you if they knew what you'd done? Do you? Do you?'

Rowan had felt the first breath of cold air, the gust of wind before the door slammed shut. She saw suddenly that there was another way this could all go wrong.

'What you have to ask, Mazz,' she said carefully, 'is how the police would see it. A jury, come to that. Would anyone – apart from you, it seems – think I had a reason to want Lorna out of the way? I really doubt it. You, though – watching your parents' marriage break up, your mum going to pieces . . . And the drawing is so obviously yours. No one else draws – could draw – like that.'

Marianne looked as if she were about to vomit. 'Where is it? The drawing – where is it?'

'I've taken it. I'm going to look after it until I'm sure I can trust you to keep your mouth shut. I'm going to keep it safe.'

—

Except in the end, after a decade, she hadn't. Of all the stupid, stupid mistakes to have made. If everything fell to pieces now, she had no one to blame but herself.

What if Adam hadn't been driving yesterday when Cory called him? What if Cory had told him about the drawing, Marianne's plan for Lorna's death? It would have changed his view of his sister forever, torn his world apart.

And what if Cory had told him more than that? Her heart made a strange double beat, two punches against her chest wall. Cory's lie about the call had confirmed it: he was still digging. Compromising as her story had been, as much damage as it could have done her, he still hadn't believed it. He'd still thought there was more. How much had he discovered?

She'd been right to do what she'd done; the proof had come almost immediately. Before pushing his body away from the bank, she'd searched his pockets. His phone was locked and of course she had no idea of his code but as she'd held it, it had vibrated in her hand like a frightened mouse. A text message appeared on the blank outer screen:

J Spelman

Hey Mikey. Looking 4wd to Tues. Usual spot? Btw, asked re yr friend Rowan but Jon P didn't know her. Sure it's Queen Mary? Maybe diff college within uni? xJ

When she turned off the studio lights, Rowan had the fleeting impression of herself as a mother; Marianne the child she was leaving curled up in bed. *Good night, sleep well.*

No more mistakes. Everything depended on meticulous attention to detail now. The moment she'd picked up the stone, she'd felt her brain shift gears. She remembered what Marianne had said about the times she knew she was doing her best work, how the world became brighter; everything was relevant. It was as if her senses had sharpened. The temptation had been to take the phone with her, destroy it, but no, she'd calculated at once that it would look suspicious if it were found elsewhere. The water would ruin the handset, buying her time, but whether they found it or not, the police would be able to get Cory's data. She'd tossed it into the river. The stone was much heavier, it travelled only ten or twelve feet, but she'd thrown that in, too.

As she'd made her way through the undergrowth along the bank at the meadow's edge, staying below the eye-line of anyone walking a dog or looking out of a window in the houses across the field, she'd felt like a fox, keen-eyed and pricked of ear, nose alive to every new scent in the air.

She'd come out on Bedford Street, headed up to Iffley Road and then into town. The walk back to the house was several miles but it had been safer than taking a taxi with a driver who might remember her or a bus with a CCTV camera and a timed ticket. She'd had to leave Cory's car where it was. It would attract attention, a Mercedes like that abandoned in an empty car park, but that was still preferable to the risk of being seen driving it. And where would she have taken it? Plus, if his death was going to look like an accident, his keys were better in his pocket. When the body was found, the police would use someone with knowledge of the river to work out where he'd most likely gone in and the location of the car would help confirm it. Everything had to add up.

Down in the kitchen, the washing machine was still churning away with her jeans and shirt and socks. The trainers, drying on top of the radiator, emitted a smell part pond-water, part hot rubber. They were dark so their wetness hadn't drawn attention on the way back but when she'd taken them off, her feet had been clammy and deathly pale, rubbed sore at the heel. She hadn't felt a thing while she'd been walking.

As she turned them over, her own phone vibrated with a text from Adam: *Wish I could teleport myself to North Oxford this evening. Tomorrow . . .* The familiar buzz was tempered this time by a new awareness of how much she had to lose.

She made a cup of tea, lingering in the window for Martin's sake while she waited for the kettle, then went upstairs to Seb's study. After Cory had gone that day he'd broken in, she'd taped up Marianne's drawing carefully and brought the box here. She couldn't risk putting it back in the wardrobe where he could have gone straight for it again, but here in the study, on the stack of other boxes and packs of printer paper at the side of the desk, it was hidden in plain sight. She should have kept it here all along. She slid it out again now and put it on the desk. Then, finding the drawing and Marianne's card, she carried them to the bathroom.

She dropped the card into the basin and took the matches from her pocket. Marianne's heartbeat handwriting pulsated up at her from the basin. *I need to talk to you.* Rowan felt a flare of anger. This was all her fault. If she hadn't felt the need to talk, to start unburdening herself to Cory and digging into a past that had lain peacefully for ten years, none of this would have been necessary. Marianne had made her do what she'd done today – she'd left her no choice. With another burst of fury, she remembered how she'd prevented her going out with Adam years ago. Well, not this time, not twice. Opening the box, she struck a match and, in the mirror, she watched it burn. When it was almost at her fingertips, she dropped it onto the card. A dark circle ate Marianne's words, then burst into flames. They flared and died in seconds; Rowan turned on the tap and washed the embers away.

She picked up the drawing and dropped it in. She paused to look at it one last time. Thousands of people – hundreds of thousands, probably – would look at Marianne's paintings and drawings in years to come but only she and Michael Cory would ever see this one: the barge, the fire licking out through the shattered glass, the prow window filled with the tiny agonised face.

The crunch as the stone hit his skull ... As Rowan had gone through his pockets, she'd been struck by the enormity of it. Two minutes earlier, he'd been alive, talking to her – *lying* to her – and then he was dead, face down in that icy water. It had been easier last time, less personal: there'd been no physical contact, she hadn't even had to *see* Lorna, just check the windows were closed and turn on the gas. And this time, she'd had to do the whole thing on her own; whatever Marianne claimed afterwards, really, last time, they'd done it together.

Looking up, she caught her own eye in the mirror and felt a burst of painful longing. I need to talk to *you*, Mazz, she thought. Despite all this, Cory, the trouble, I really wish I could talk to you.

She'd missed her so much over the years; every time anything had happened – whenever she'd met someone or been promoted; when she'd had to leave the BBC – it had been Marianne she'd wanted to tell. She'd made do with talking to her in her head, imagining what she'd say. And of course, once a year at Christmas as she had posted her card, she'd let herself hope that this would be the year she'd get one in return.

She'd tried very hard to keep the lines of communication open. Despite the state Marianne worked herself into that afternoon at Vicarage Road, she'd finally managed to make her see a degree of sense. 'What would people think?' She had asked her. 'How would it look if suddenly, after all these years, you and I stopped being friends the very same day your dad's girlfriend died? Think, Marianne – try to be logical. The police are going to find out they were having an affair, there's no way it's going to stay a secret. Everything's got to look as normal – as *uneventful* – as possible.'

She'd seen the reason in that, at least, but the burden of carrying it out had fallen almost entirely on Rowan. In the fortnight that followed, during those horrendous days when the police seemed to circle Fyfield Road like vultures, Marianne had sequestered herself in her bedroom and left Rowan to keep up appearances, drinking tea and talking to a shell-shocked Jacqueline in the kitchen or sitting upstairs watching black and white films while Seb worked his way through a bottle. Jacqueline's reaction had taken Rowan by surprise; she should have been relieved, at least.

At first, Rowan had had sympathy for Seb. He'd loved Lorna, after all; it would take a while to come to terms with her being gone. But if anything, as the days passed, he'd got worse, not better. In those first two weeks, she'd been to the house five times and, though Jacqueline had tried, surreptitiously removing the bottle or clearing his glass away to the dishwasher, he'd only ever really been without a drink when the police were there.

And then, a month after Lorna died, Rowan had bumped into him in town. It had been a Saturday afternoon, she remembered, she'd texted Marianne to see if she could go over but, when no reply came, she'd decided to walk up to Waterstones. She'd needed to get out of the house: there were viewings lined up. Her father had made a big song and dance about how he wouldn't sell Vicarage Road until she'd finished her degree – her 'home base' in Oxford, he'd managed to say with a straight face – but a fortnight to the day after she'd sat her final paper, he'd called to say he was putting it on the market.

Books bought, she was thinking about heading up to Fyfield Road anyway when she'd seen Seb coming round the corner of St Michael's Street. He was one of those people who appeared sober long after anyone else would have been on their knees but even so, she'd seen straight away that he was drunk out of his mind. He was weaving along the pavement, lurching left and right in his exaggerated efforts to avoid people coming in the other direction. As he got closer, she heard him talking to himself, not words that she could make out but a sort of highly inflected mutter punctuated with emphatic stops. His hair was dirty and one side of his denim shirt was soaked. As she'd stepped into his way, she smelled the booze at once.

'Seb.' She put a hand out, touched his arm.

It had taken him a moment to recognise her but then he'd thrown his arms around her. 'Rowan!' The hug turned into a lean and she'd staggered a little with the effort of supporting him. 'I was just at the pub. Come and have a drink with me.' He'd turned and scanned around. 'This way. The Three Goats' Heads – just round the corner.'

'Why don't I take you home?' she'd said. 'You look a bit . . .'

'No, no, no, don't *you* have a go at me, too. I just want company. That's all. Company and a drink. Is that too much to ask?' Taking her arm, he'd started pulling her in the direction of the pub and, trying to think, she'd gone with him. What should she do? Call a cab and take him home herself? Or call the house and tell Jacqueline? There was no point calling Marianne's mobile; she wouldn't pick up.

As they'd approached the pub, however, a large man standing on the pavement outside to smoke a cigarette had seen them and started shaking his head. 'Sorry,' he'd said to her, 'I've told him already: he can't come in. He's wasted, isn't he? We can't serve people in that state.'

'Fascist,' Seb had muttered.

'What was that, mate?' The barman had taken a long pull on his cigarette and looked at him, stony-faced.

'You're a fascist. Why do *you* have power to decide if . . .'

Over his head, she'd mouthed an apology. 'I'll take you home, Seb. Come on, we'll get a cab.'

But with a sudden burst of energy, he'd pulled his arm away. 'No. I don't want to go home. I want Lorna. I want Lorna.' Like a petulant child crying for its mother, he'd burst into tears. She'd watched, stunned, as he'd stumbled back in the direction of Cornmarket. Weeping audibly, he'd fallen against the wall of Austin Reed and slid slowly to the pavement.

The barman had been watching, too. 'Do you need a hand?' he said. 'I can phone you a cab, help you get him in?'

'Thanks,' she said, 'but don't worry. I'll take care of it.'

She'd waited until he'd gone back down the stairs into the pub then walked to where Seb had by then been sitting, legs straight out in front of him like a ragdoll. She'd gone down on her haunches. 'Come on, Seb,' she said. 'Pull yourself together. For Jacqueline. For Adam and Mazz.'

He'd looked at her, bleary-eyed. 'I can't,' he said. 'I can't.'

'Pathetic,' said Rowan, and the look in his eyes said he agreed with her. She'd left him there.

When he'd had his accident, Marianne had blamed her. She'd never explicitly said it – she hadn't talked to Rowan for a month by that point other than to tell her to get lost whenever she went to Fyfield Road to try and sort things out – but she hadn't needed to. The afternoon that Rowan had gone to the house and found the police car on the drive, the door open, she'd felt it in the air before she'd even seen Marianne's face. It wasn't my fault, she'd wanted to say to her, *I* didn't make him drink, *I* didn't force him to get in the car, he was weak, he didn't deserve all this – you – he brought it on himself. But she knew it would have been pointless. By then, Marianne had stopped listening. She'd tried that one final time, the day Mazz had made Turk choose between them, when she'd shrunk from Rowan as if she were a monster, and that was it, the last time they'd seen each other.

The nostalgia, the painful yearning, was gone now, replaced by frustration and anger again: it had all been so unnecessary – such a waste. Carefully, Rowan reached into the basin and lifted the drawing out by its edges. It was damp in places and the water had caused the orange and yellow of the flames to run here and there but to destroy it would have been a mistake. If the nightmare happened and the whole thing came out, Cory reaching back through Marianne to Lorna, she would need this. Whatever Mazz said, killing her father's lover had been her idea; here was the proof.

She took the last one of Marianne's Ambien tablets but as she'd feared, she lay awake for a long time. She could almost feel it, the hypnotic drift of the pill battling the frantic activity of her brain. Up and dressed, doing what she could to make everything water-tight, she'd managed to control the anxiety but lying in the dark, she thought of all the things she was powerless to influence, any one of which might be the thread that brought the police to her door. Down by the river, with so much else to think about, she'd managed to contain her alarm at J Spelman's text but now the thought of it made her almost sick with fear. She hadn't been able to look him or her up – if the police ever suspected her, they would almost certainly take her computer – but she'd remembered the American friend at Imperial whom Cory had mentioned. Was *she* J Spelman, and if so, what else had he told her? When the police got hold of Cory's phone records, that text would be sure to raise eyebrows.

But J Spelman was just one person – whom else had he spoken to? With another access of alarm, Rowan remembered his research at the library, the woman who'd shown him how to use the microfiche. She would remember him, the sophisticated American, the hours he'd spent there. What if he'd made notes? When the police searched his room at the Old Parsonage, would they find a notebook with his ideas and suspicions? He hadn't had one on him; when she'd gone through his pockets, she'd found just his phone, his wallet and the car key.

Eyes wide in the darkness, she remembered the sketch he'd made of her books. He hadn't given her that one but it wasn't here – while she'd been getting ready to go round to Benson Place, he must have folded it up and slipped it into his pocket.

Where was it? Had he had suspicions about her studies? Was that why he'd asked J Spelman about her? It wasn't really a lie, her doctorate: she was applying – she'd even applied to Queen Mary. Anyway, she didn't need to worry about that: if and when Jacqueline or Adam found out, she'd just tell them the truth: that she'd been too embarrassed to admit she was between jobs.

So many little threads but there were bigger ones, too. Was it credible that Cory could have given himself that head wound by slipping and falling? It seemed unlikely that frogmen would find the stone but then, she had no idea what the riverbed there was like. If it was just mud, a single large sharp-edged stone would be immediately apparent. Perhaps she should have left it on the bank – perhaps by throwing it away, she'd made it look suspicious when it needn't have been.

Lorna's accident had been neat, self-contained, but this felt sprawling, messy. Rowan pushed away the idea that she'd worked better with Marianne; that without her – like Seb without Jacqueline – she just wasn't as good. And the police hadn't given up easily last time; they'd had their suspicions. As Turk had said that day in his kitchen, they weren't idiots.

And on top of it all, she thought, the sheets tightening round her chest as she turned in the bed again, the question of how and why Marianne had died was still unanswered. With Cory's death, the immediate urgency had gone, but without him, her chances of finding out what had happened had withered almost to nothing. Her own ideas were exhausted. As the clock by the bed ticked on, she clung to the idea that Mazz had jumped because, having thought better of telling Cory about Lorna, she'd realised she'd told him too much to be able to backtrack. Much as she wanted that to be true, however, Rowan knew it was a fragile straw at which to clutch. Time and again as she writhed beneath the blankets, she had to shut down the voice that whispered in her ear that nothing Cory ever said had given her reason to believe it, either.

Thirty-two

Adam had barely stepped through the door before things escalated. He'd kissed Rowan hello and she'd pressed against him without thinking, wanting the reassurance of his solidity, his weight and warmth.

They were still getting dressed when the taxi driver texted to say he was outside. Earlier she'd had the idea that she should cook – it would take concentration, she'd be forced to focus on something other than the constantly looping anxiety – but when she'd suggested it to Adam, he'd texted back to say he'd booked a table at Chiang Mai. 'It was a nice idea, cooking dinner,' he said now as he bent to pick up the wallet that had fallen from his jacket pocket in their rush to bed, 'but to be honest, I don't want to spend any more time here than I have to – at the house, I mean. Every time I'm here, I imagine her lying out in the garden and . . .' He shook his head. Rowan crossed the room and pulled him into a tight hug. 'While the pictures are still here,' he said, his words warm in her hair, 'it makes sense for me to come to you but as soon as they're moved, I can stop.'

She felt a jolt of alarm. 'Do you know when that'll be?'

'I wanted to ask you. I spoke to James today and he's been able to free up space for them in storage until they need to be shipped to New York. When we give him the word, he'll come and pack them.'

She jumped as his phone rang but it was the driver again, calling to make sure they'd got his text. She ran her hand over the bed until she found the earring she'd mislaid and they went downstairs but as they came on to Banbury Road, the cab taking the turn so sharply they slid against each other on the shiny back seat, Adam returned to the subject.

'How have you been getting on with your work?' he asked. 'How much longer do you think you'll need with the archives?'

'I'm not sure,' she hedged. 'There's one more collection of papers I want to see but until I get a proper look at them, it'll be hard to say.'

He reached over and rested his hand on her thigh. 'It'll be much better when you're back in London,' he said. 'Easier. It means I'll be able to see you without having to face this place. And the journey – people commute from Cambridge to London every day.'

Every day. Rowan smiled then remembered her shoddy, down-at-heel flat. She would have to move, find a way to afford something better. She couldn't let him see her there.

'You could come and see me in Cambridge,' he said, as if he'd read her mind.

Chiang Mai Kitchen was located in three little wood-panelled rooms in a centuries-old building in Wheatsheaf Passage, a narrow, overhung cut between the High and Blue Boar Street that had always reminded Rowan of Pudding Lane before the Great Fire. Once, in her first year at college, she remembered, she'd been brought here for dinner by a man she hadn't liked at all and she'd spent the evening imagining it was Adam across the table instead. As they climbed the sloping spiral staircase, she wondered if Cory had ever eaten here. He would have liked it, too: the old wood and odd angles, the lingering shades of other lives.

Cory. By the time she'd fallen asleep last night, it had been four o'clock and she'd woken at ten-thirty to find incongruous sunlight cutting into the room. For a few seconds, her mind had been gloriously empty but then it had all come streaming back. She'd got up at once, gone down to the kitchen and turned on Jacqueline's radio. If a body had been found in the river, it would certainly be reported on the local news. Then, with a nauseating twist in her gut, she'd remembered that while a body in the river would be local news, Michael Cory's body in the river would be national news. International.

The waitress took their menus and Rowan ran the chain of her necklace between thumb and forefinger. 'Did you manage to catch up with Michael Cory?'

Adam frowned and shook his head. 'I've called him twice, left a message, but he hasn't called me back.'

'Hmm.' Relief flooded her. Among her nocturnal terrors had been the possibility that Cory might have reached him yesterday morning, before they'd gone down to the river. 'I called him as well,' she said, 'we were supposed to have a cup of coffee this afternoon, but I got voicemail, too. He hasn't rung me back, either.'

'Is that unusual?'

'Yes. I mean, as far as I know. I've only met him a few times but he's never stood me up before.' Her heart was beating so hard she was afraid Adam would hear it in her voice but as far as she could tell, she sounded steady enough, and if he noticed the flush in her face, she hoped he'd put it down to the room's over-zealous heating.

'Artists,' he said. 'Mazz used to go AWOL for days on end – weeks, sometimes – when she was in the thick of something.'

Rowan took a small sip of wine and cautioned herself: under no circumstances could she afford to get drunk tonight. 'Ad, I've been meaning to ask,' she said. 'Is the house on the market now? Will people be coming to see it?'

'No. We can't put it on the market until her estate's settled; we needed a valuation for probate as well. Marianne left me her share – but I don't know. Even though I find it so hard being there, when we got the valuation, I just felt . . .' He shook his head again. 'I can't live there, not now, maybe not ever, but the idea of selling it, letting it go out of the family . . . Even though we'd decided that Mazz would live there and I only had a third, I somehow always thought I'd bring up my kids there.'

The night air was sharp as they left the restaurant, the sky over the High Street cloudless. The city lights put paid to any stars but a huge moon hung overhead, the grey lacework of craters like a veil over its face.

At Fyfield Road, the front garden was full of silver light, the steps clearly visible without help from the carriage lamp, and even in the hallway, the glow of the moon through the panels in the front door was enough to show the edge of the telephone table and the lamp, the shapes of the coats on the pegs. They kissed in the semi-darkness then went downstairs to get some water to take up to bed.

Adam went ahead of her but three steps into the kitchen, he stopped so abruptly Rowan almost trod on his heel. When she reached out to switch on the light, he grabbed her wrist.

'What's . . . ?'

In the dim light, she saw him hold a finger against his lips then point towards the window. 'There's someone in the garden,' he murmured.

Rowan went cold.

He put up his hand, indicating that she should stay still, then stepped into the shadow of the units. Out of direct sight of the window, he began to move towards the back of the room.

Sweat broke out across her body; she felt it on her forehead and under her arms, between her breasts. No thoughts at first, just fear, but then they came spilling, one after another: this was it; Cory had been right that someone else knew, and now, in front of Adam, it was all going to come out. Everything was ruined, and all of it – trying to discover what happened to Marianne; dealing with Cory – had been for nothing. She hadn't even been given a chance.

Adam reached the back of the kitchen and, stooping to stay hidden, manoeuvred his way to the door. He held up his hand again, *Stay there*, and for a second she considered running forward, creating a diversion so that whoever it was could get away. But before she could move, Adam reached for the key in the dish, shoved it into the lock and yanked the door open.

In the same second he sprang out on to the patio, Rowan saw a figure start up from behind the rhododendron at the end of the raised bed but, moving too fast, he slipped on the frosty grass and in the moment it took him to get both feet planted again, Adam was up the steps to the lawn. 'You – get back here!'

He was fast but the other man was smaller and nimble, and he managed to get far enough ahead of Adam to be out of arm's reach until, with a sharp cry, he tripped on the edge of the flagstone path and went sprawling.

With a guttural sound, Adam threw himself down on top of the man but then, across the freezing garden, she heard him say, 'Oh, Christ.'

Between the navy beanie and the black Puffa jacket, Bryony's face was milk-white. Despite the cold, her hands were bare and as she came into the kitchen, Rowan saw that her palms were bleeding. The knees of her jeans were muddy, too, and the left one was ripped.

'I'm so sorry, Bryony,' Adam said. 'If I'd had any idea it was you . . .'

'It's fine,' she said. 'I'll just have some bruises.' She gave him a pale smile. 'I'm sure there are plenty of people who'd *like* to be rugby-tackled by you.'

Had she looked in her direction as she'd said it? Rowan wasn't sure. 'Come and sit down,' she said.

'Here, let me see.' Adam took the chair next to Bryony and gestured that she should hold out her hands. He grimaced. 'There's a lot of mud in there. You should probably have a tetanus jab tomorrow.'

'I'll be all right.'

'No, it's not worth risking. I'll take you to Casualty myself if you don't want your dad to know.'

'Thanks but I can do it on my own. Easy to explain to Dad, anyway. I'll just say I fell over.'

Adam stood and went to the cabinet that housed the fuse box and the family's first-aid supplies. At the bottom of the old ice-cream container where Jacqueline had kept them, he found three antiseptic wipes and a pair of tweezers. 'Come and run them under the tap, get the worst off, then I'll see what I can do.'

He directed a gentle stream of water over Bryony's palms then brought her back to the table where he put a clean towel on his knees and bent over her left hand.

'So what's with the night manoeuvres?' he asked, eyes trained on the tweezers. Bryony winced as he pulled out a piece of grit.

'I've seen you out there before,' said Rowan, 'haven't I?'

'Yeah.' Bryony's expression was a mixture of sheepishness and irritation.

'So . . . ?' coaxed Adam.

'I just miss her, that's all.' Her voice was belligerent, as if she resented being put on the spot. 'I feel close to her here.'

'You can knock on the door any time,' said Rowan.

Bryony shot her a look that said she couldn't possibly understand. 'It's not like that. It's . . . private. I don't want to *talk*.' She bit her lower lip as Adam extracted another chip of gravel. 'Marianne was my friend,' she said, fixing her eyes on the floor.

Adam nodded but said nothing, leaving a vacuum for her to fill. Rowan remembered what Turk had told her about Marianne and Bryony, how close they were. Best buds, he'd called them; they'd shared clothes and shopped together, gone to gigs and shows.

'Marianne knew what it was like,' Bryony said after a while, 'when your parents split up. Everything turning upside down.'

Rowan frowned. 'But wasn't she . . .' Adam glanced up and she gave him a look of apology, '. . . sort of . . . involved?'

Bryony shook her head. 'Not really. Not so it made a difference. The papers loved all that, didn't they, the scandal?' She pronounced the word with heavy irony, and for a second, Rowan had the impression she was hearing not Bryony's voice but Marianne's.

'Mum and Dad were on the rocks anyway,' she said. 'They'd been talking about divorce for months before Mazz came on the scene, whatever Grandpa likes to think.'

It was nearly midnight by the time the first aid was finished and, standing up from the table, Adam told Bryony they would take her home. 'I can walk,' she said. 'It's ten minutes.'

'No way, José.'

'I've only had a glass, Ad,' Rowan said. 'I can drive.'

The Greenwoods lived in Southmoor Road, it turned out. As they crossed north Oxford, Bryony, simultaneously irritated at being treated like a child and patently glad that she hadn't had to walk, answered Adam's questions about what she was going to do when she left school. She wasn't going to take a gap year, apparently; she was going straight to Edinburgh in the autumn to do English. 'I'm ready to get away from Oxford,' she said. 'I don't love it. Especially now.'

The houses in Walton Manor were significantly smaller than those in Park Town, though still large by most standards. Years ago, when they'd been growing up, the area had had the lovely academic shabbiness of so much of Oxford then but even in the dark, it was obvious from the up-lights and potted trees that money and interior designers had landed here, too.

They waited while Bryony found her keys and let herself into the house. Outlined by the light in the hall, she gave them a brief wave then shut the door.

As they cruised carefully away between the cars parked nose to tail along both kerbs, Adam reached over the gearstick and let his hand rest on Rowan's knee.

'Apart from nearly having crushed her,' he said, 'I'm relieved.'

She glanced at him. 'How so?'

A pause. 'I promised Mazz I wouldn't say anything to anyone but a few days before she died, she told me she'd been thinking about her relationship with James.'

Rowan's antennae went up. 'Really?'

'She loved Bryony, too, and that complicated things even more, but she was beginning to feel like the age gap was just too big. She wanted to have children and James' daughter was about to leave home – Mazz worried that he was finished with that stage of his life while she hadn't even started. That was part of it.'

He turned to look out of the window, deliberately, Rowan thought. The seconds stretched. 'Part?' she said.

He hesitated. 'She didn't say anything but knowing her so well . . . She'd started to talk a lot about Michael Cory. I think she liked him. No, more than liked: she was falling in love with him.'

Rowan's mind started to whirr, the potential implications running like lines of code. 'Why are you relieved?' she asked.

'Because the only microscopically small good thing in all this – apart from *this*, you and me – is that the Greenwoods never had to know.'

Lowering the blankets gently back over him, Rowan eased herself out of bed. Adam stirred. 'Are you all right? Can't you sleep?'

'I'm okay, just a bit of a headache. I've got some aspirin downstairs – I'll be back in a minute.'

In the kitchen, she navigated her way to the sofa by moonlight. She'd had to get up: she couldn't take lying there any longer. Listening to his soft breathing, feeling his warmth radiating across the bed, her brain skipped from one anxiety to the next and all she'd been able to think about was losing him. How long would it take before she could fall asleep easily, secure in the knowledge that the morning wouldn't see her life as she knew it torn out like a page from one of Marianne's sketchbooks?

From over by the window came a sudden drilling sound. She jumped but then she saw a spot of greenish light on the work-surface near the back door. A phone, the vibration as a message arrived. But her own mobile was in her bag and Adam's was upstairs; he'd brought a charger and plugged it in next to the bed.

By the time she reached it, the light had faded but when she pressed the button, the home-screen brightened again. The text was from a magazine she'd never heard of – the new issue was available to download – but the photograph behind it showed Bryony and the dark-haired girl who'd been with her that day at St Helena's. Bryony's phone – of course, Rowan remembered now: Adam had picked it up when she fell, put it on the work-surface here as they'd come into the kitchen.

Back on the sofa, she pulled Jacqueline's old tartan blanket around her shoulders. When she'd realised it was Bryony outside, she hadn't known whether to laugh with relief or be frightened. No armed attacker or housebreaker, then, just a teenage girl – but a teenage girl who'd been close to Marianne.

Could Bryony have been involved in her death? What if Adam was wrong and the Greenwoods *had* got wind of Marianne's doubts about the relationship? Could Bryony have lured her to the roof, pushed her off? But no, of course not: Marianne had been alone, hers the sole set of footprints in the snow.

Thirty-three

Rowan heard the doorbell above the static fizz of water into the shower tray and tensed immediately. 'I'll get it,' Adam called on the landing and his feet drummed down the stairs. She still had shampoo in her hair but she turned off the water and opened the cubicle door. Bryony, she hoped, come to collect her phone, but when she made out the burr of voices, it was deep. Male. Wrapping herself in a towel, she walked carefully across the room and turned the door handle, letting in a blast of cold air that made the hairs on her arms stand on end.

'Would you mind if we came in?'

The voice reached up the stairs and Rowan closed her eyes. She knew it, that amiable middle-class tone with its hint of Ironbridge. Theo. A wave of pure panic washed over her, hot then cold, as a hand took hold of her heart and squeezed.

The door closed and the voices receded as Adam took Theo into the sitting room. Rowan's heart was racing now, the beats falling over one another in their haste. She thought of her mother, the coronary she'd had at twenty-eight. Momentarily, she was paralysed by fear but then she stuffed the towel onto the rail and turned the water back on. She rinsed her hair roughly then, as quickly as she'd ever done it, she dried off and dressed.

At the top of the stairs she listened but coming from the sitting room now, the words were muffled beyond audibility.

She went down slowly, heart still galloping. As if he'd been waiting for her, Adam called her almost at once and Rowan barely stopped herself giving a shriek of alarm.

Theo was in the same spot on the sofa that Jacqueline had had the day Seb died, and as she came into the room, Rowan saw the emotions play across his sunny expressive face like the shadow of clouds on a whitewashed wall: surprise, amusement, interest. 'Hello,' he said. 'Good to see you again.'

Next to him sat a skinny man still wearing a black outdoor jacket. He seemed younger than Theo, late twenties probably, but perhaps that was only the comparative smoothness of his skin, the lack of laughter lines around eyes that were looking at Rowan now as if they wanted to absorb every detail.

'This is DS Grange,' said Theo. 'Rowan Winter.'

Adam looked between them. 'You know each other?'

'We were at college together,' Rowan said.

'Yes,' said Theo, 'we were,' and, eyes sparkling with innuendo, he glanced at Adam in his crumpled T-shirt and then her wet hair. Oh, fuck off, she wanted to say, you're the one who's bloody married.

'Ro, come and have a seat.' Adam touched the cushion next to him and the gentleness of the gesture, the care it implied, was an arrow in her chest. 'Chief Inspector . . .'

'Please, call me Theo. Rowan and I are old friends.'

Adam gave a sort of half-nod, evidently uncertain. 'There's some bad news, Ro.'

'A body was found earlier this morning, Rowan.' Theo seemed to train his eyes directly on her face. 'It hasn't been confirmed yet – the formal identification is later today – but we're confident it's Michael Cory.'

Blood boomed in her ears. 'Cory?' she heard herself say. Was she imagining it, the focus with which both he and the other man were looking at her? Her face felt suddenly alien, as if it were beyond her control and might betray her at any moment.

'It was a dog-walker who found him – isn't it always? – up early along the river.'

'Where?'

'Down near Iffley.' The slightest lift in Theo's eyebrow told her he'd found that an interesting question, was making a mental note.

The floor banked like the deck of a ship in high seas. 'What happened?' she said, from a distance.

'We can't say at the moment.'

Can't or won't? Were they holding back information, laying a trap?

'He has a serious head wound,' said Grange. 'Whether it was an accident or not, we don't know yet. We'll have to wait for the post mortem to be clear about the actual cause of death. Whether he was alive when he went into the water or . . .'

'As Mr Cory's agent in the UK,' said Theo, 'James Greenwood is going to identify the body for us.'

'Gallerist,' Adam said.

'Gallerist, sorry, yes.' Theo nodded. 'He was the only British contact we could find online.'

'James said they should talk to us.' Adam reached out and took Rowan's hand. 'He told them that Marianne and Michael were friends and he was going to paint her.'

'Actually,' said Theo, 'it was you that Mr Greenwood mentioned specifically, Rowan. Both he *and* Mr Glass tell me you've been spending time with Mr Cory lately.' *Forgive me if I'd forgotten how morally upstanding you are.*

Putting her hand over her mouth, she looked at Adam. His eyes were wide and serious but he seemed not to have picked up on Theo's subtext.

'We met three or four times,' she said. 'Four. We were supposed to have coffee yesterday . . .' She looked at Adam again as if to say, *This is why we couldn't get hold of him. We were trying to call him and all the time . . .* 'He was asking me

315

about Marianne,' she told Theo. 'About what she was like as a teenager and in her early twenties.'

'You were talking?'

'Yes,' she said, looking him in the eye, 'we were.'

DS Grange turned sharply to Adam. 'But *you* hadn't talked to him yet, Mr Glass? As Marianne's brother.'

'Not yet.' Again, Adam seemed not to hear the real question. 'Perhaps he was being sensitive, giving me some time. He called me on Wednesday, late afternoon. I've still got the message on my phone, I think, if you need it.'

'Thanks. Yes.'

'Do you happen to know by any chance, Rowan,' said Theo, 'where Mr Cory was staying?'

She hoped her look conveyed the full weight of her disdain. 'He had a room at the Old Parsonage.'

Grange made a note in his book.

'The thing is,' said Theo, looking first at her, then at Adam, 'I'm sorry but I'm sure it will have occurred to you already – the fact that Mr Cory has died so soon after your sister, Mr Glass,' a small nod of respect, 'raises obvious questions. Two artists of their stature – and friends. That Mr Cory appears to have died here in Oxford, too – though that has yet to be confirmed, of course. He was living in London, Mr Greenwood told us, so . . .'

'They're going to look into Marianne's death again,' Adam said, squeezing her fingers. Rowan watched Theo watch him.

'I'm afraid so,' he said. 'There are coincidences, even big ones, but this . . .' He shook his head. 'We have to proceed on the basis that there's a connection.'

'Do you have any idea what that might be?' Adam asked.

'No, not yet. It's too early. The body was found at seven this morning so we're still right at the beginning of things.'

Glancing at the mantelpiece, Rowan saw it was eleven. From first becoming aware of Cory's death, it had taken the police less than four hours to make it to her door.

'Do you – either of you – have any thoughts? Observations,' he said. 'Rowan, if you'd been talking to him . . . ?'

She shook her head, vague. 'No.'

'Anything strike you as off, anything bothering him, that you could tell, the last time you saw him?'

A mental image of the bare back of his head bisected with blood, the look in his eyes as he'd turned. *You.*

'No. No, I don't think so.'

'When was that?'

'Um . . .' She tried to think. The day they'd driven to the river was the day before yesterday; when had it been before that? *Think, Rowan, for Christ's sake. Quick.* 'Tuesday,' she said, and her voice sounded firm, she thought, reliable. They'd gone round to the Johnsons', hadn't they? Met Martin. She remembered Sarah Johnson telling them that the police had gone to the flats after Marianne died and realised she had to mention it now if it wasn't going to look suspicious later on. 'Actually,' she said, 'he did something for me that day. A favour.'

'Really?'

She glanced at Adam. 'I'd been a bit worried,' she said. 'I'd noticed a guy looking over here at night from the flats in Benson Place.'

'You didn't tell me that.' Adam frowned.

'I know. I didn't want to worry you. I thought you had enough on your plate. Michael came round that afternoon and I asked him to come with me to find out who he was, what was going on.'

'And?'

'It wasn't anything to worry about at all. It was Martin Johnson – do you know him?'

'Martin?' said Theo. 'Yes, I know him. He's a nice enough guy.' He turned to DS Grange. 'We spoke to him at the time. He had a bike accident a few years back, head injury, but he's not dangerous. He saw Marianne's body in the garden that morning.' He gave Adam a brief look of apology.

317

'He was her number one fan.'

'I didn't know they were friends,' said Rowan.

'He was one of the people my sister took under her wing,' he explained to the police. 'She was good like that, looking out for other people. We always worried that she'd pick up someone dangerous one day but she never did, thank God.' He stopped. 'Unless . . .'

'Let's not jump to any conclusions,' Theo said. 'We'll talk to Martin, obviously. But Marianne's death may still turn out to be an accident – Mr Cory's, too, even. Let's try and keep those possibilities in mind until we find out otherwise.'

Adam nodded, looking bleak.

'But Ms Winter,' said DS Grange, 'just to go back to Martin for a moment – you said he was looking over here?'

'From his window, at night. A couple of times during the day, too, but it was easier to see him at night, I suppose, with the lights on.'

'What did you think he was doing?'

'I don't know,' she said, scrambling. 'At night, I wondered if he was a Peeping Tom.'

'Forgive me – business and pleasure,' Theo glanced in Adam's direction, 'but when you and I had a drink the other day, Rowan, you seemed to express some . . . uncertainty about the idea that Marianne might have fallen. Unless I got the wrong end of the stick.'

Adam shifted next to her and she felt his eyes move to her face. Could he see the crimson spreading up her cheeks? 'It just felt . . . odd,' she said, more to him than to Theo. 'With her vertigo. We hadn't spoken for so long, as you know, and that could have changed, I wasn't sure. I didn't have any other reason for asking.'

Adam looked at her for a moment then back at the police. 'But she'd been worried – Marianne, I mean – that someone might have been getting in here.'

'I remember.' Theo nodded. 'We'll go over our information on that again.' A faint buzz came from his pocket and he took out his phone and glanced at it. 'Right,' he said, looking at DS Grange, who stood up immediately. 'We'll have to leave it at that for now, I'm afraid.'

Adam stood to walk them out.

'I'm so sorry you're being put through this,' Theo told him. 'The only thing I can promise is that if there is anything untoward going on, we'll do our very best to find out what it is.'

'Thank you.'

Perhaps she was being paranoid, Rowan thought, or perhaps he just hadn't been able to resist a final cheap shot but as he rounded the door, Theo looked back at her and said, 'We'll be in touch.'

When she heard their shoes on the tiles in the porch, Rowan let her head drop briefly into her hands. She was screwed. Panic swamped her, increasing the pressure on her heart until she could barely breathe.

She'd had no choice. If she hadn't done it, it would all have come out anyway. But here in Oxford – should she have gone to London, done it there? That would have taken planning and time – time she hadn't had. There was no way of knowing how long Cory had intended to stay here but she guessed he wouldn't have left until he was satisfied he knew the truth about Marianne. Given what Adam had said last night in the car, his commitment made sense now: he'd been in love with her, he'd said so himself, and Marianne had been falling in love with him, too; Rowan didn't doubt Adam was right about that. Of course Cory hadn't believed she'd jumped, if they'd just been starting something.

The light through the window outlined her fingers in blood. At the click of the door and Adam's feet across the carpet, Rowan put her hands in her lap and composed her face. 'Oh

319

God, Adam.' She stood up and went to him. His heart thumped through the cotton of his T-shirt and when she looked up, he was crying.

'How am I going to tell Mum?' he said.

Rowan closed her eyes against a mental image of Jacqueline at the funeral.

Adam swiped his cheeks with the heel of his hand. 'Ro, what you said to the police about the vertigo just now – you meant it? That really was the only reason you had any doubt that Mazz's death was an accident?'

'Yes.'

'You promise me?'

'Yes.'

'And Martin?'

'I should have told you about that. I'm sorry.'

'If anything else happens, if there's anything remotely suspicious or you're worried or frightened, you've got to tell me. Straight away. This is serious, Rowan – don't even think about trying to be a hero. People are dying.'

She felt a shudder, a frisson in the air like a premonition.

'All right?' he asked, and she nodded.

'Okay.'

He let her go and turned towards the window as if to follow Theo with his eyes. 'That policeman,' he said. 'Was he a good friend of yours?'

'Not *good* – not really. He was kind of on the edge of our group at college.'

'Did anything ever happen between you two? Did you ever go out or . . . ?'

'With Theo? God, no. And he's married now. He's got a son.'

'I didn't like the way he looked at you,' Adam said. 'It was . . . predatory.'

Thirty-four

Before going back to bed last night, Rowan had turned off Bryony's phone and put it on the kitchen table so they'd see it in the morning. Now, as she let herself out of the house, she put her hand in her pocket and touched its cold metal back.

Rain was forecast, and the bellies of the clouds had a bruised grey hue. A woman cycled past, bat-like in a plastic poncho. Gee's was busy, lunch evidently having struck a lot of people as a good way to deal with an overcast February afternoon, and she glanced through the window at the table she'd shared with Adam.

Waiting to cross Woodstock Road, she watched a couple come out of the chemist on the corner of Observatory Street, a little girl aged three or four holding their hands. Outside the hairdresser, the woman kissed them both and the man unlocked one of the cars at the kerb and lifted his daughter into the back seat. So normal, so ordinary and so completely alien – the old longing echoed behind her ribs. And yet – and yet ... In Rowan's mind, something was taking shape. She couldn't see it, it wasn't fully formed, but it was starting to glimmer, to pull at the corner of her eye like a twitching muscle.

She'd reached the old Eagle Ironworks when her mobile started ringing. On the empty street, the tone sounded especially shrill and she took it out quickly, hoping to see

Adam's name on the screen. *Number Withheld*. She hesitated then answered.

'Rowan? Hello, it's me again. Theo.'

His charming, summer's-day voice, as if he hadn't just tried to slut-shame her in front of Adam. Anger supplanted the alarm. If he'd been there, she'd have struggled not to hit him. She held herself in check: she couldn't afford to lose control.

'Sorry to bother you again so soon,' he was saying. 'It's just a quick one. I'm trying to get a few things straight – work out a rough chronology. When we were talking about the vertigo this morning, you told Adam that you hadn't spoken to Marianne for years, and I remember you said the same thing to me at the pub, more or less. I just wondered, how long was it exactly?'

Could she fudge it, obfuscate? No, there were too many people who knew the truth – Turk, Jacqueline. Adam himself. 'Ten years,' she said. 'The summer we graduated, actually.'

'Oh, as long ago as that.' Was the surprise in his voice genuine, Rowan wondered, or a move in whatever game he was playing? There was a pause, a rustle of paper. 'Sorry,' he said, 'I'm just going back over some notes. That was the same summer her father died, wasn't it? Seb Glass?'

Fuck. She was on the point of launching into the old story – her insensitivity; Marianne's irrationality in grief; the bust-up that ensued – but at the last second she stopped. With every word that came out of her mouth, she laid herself wider open. 'Yes,' she said.

'Right.' Another pause, as if he were jotting something down. 'Okay,' he said, thoughtful. 'That's it. For now.'

He hung up without signing off and she stood on the pavement and felt fear crawling up her back, down her arms. Should she try to make a run for it, throw her things in the car and go? She could get on a ferry – there was probably still time. She could lose herself in Europe somewhere; go to ground. If it came to it, she'd thought last night as she'd lain awake, she didn't know if she would be able to stand life in prison. Day in, day out, grinding towards a date in the distant future when she would be let out – to what?

But perhaps she was being premature: perhaps, like the flurry of police activity after Lorna's death, this would all come to nothing. Let Theo think she was a tart: it wasn't a criminal offence. And there was no surer admission of guilt than running, no more certain way of pulling all police attention in her direction. And if she stayed, she thought, chest aching, even if it all went wrong later, she could have a little longer with Adam, a few more hours or days. Leaving meant leaving him.

At the door an hour ago, she'd struggled not to give herself away. Please don't go, she'd wanted to beg. Just ring Jacqueline: you don't have to see her in person. She'd wanted to put her arms round him and hold on forever but she'd limited herself to one quick hug. 'Drive safely.'

He'd kissed her. 'Always. I'll see you tonight.'

Putting the phone back in her pocket, she felt Bryony's again and remembered why she'd come here: Greenwood.

The velocity with which he'd sent Theo in her direction had piqued her interest at once. Why had he been so keen to do that? Directing the police to Jacqueline or Adam made sense – it was their daughter and sister whom Cory had been friends with – but to Rowan, specifically? Was he trying to deflect attention from himself? And if so, why?

What if he'd got wind of the situation between Marianne and Cory after all? Maybe Marianne had even told him, tried to end their relationship. But then what? Had he driven her to jump? Threatened her? With what? Dumping her from the gallery? No, that wouldn't have mattered very much – the letters in her box of paperwork showed how many other options she had. What if he'd discovered what she'd done to Lorna? Rowan's stomach turned over but then she remembered how upset he'd been in the studio that afternoon, how defensive of her. And anyway, *how* would he have found out?

No, it didn't feel right, none of it added up. But there *was* something. Something . . .

She turned onto Southmoor Road and walked along until she came to the house that Bryony had gone into last night. Opening the little gate from the street, she went up the path to the door. The glass in the bay window on the raised ground floor shone like water, cleaned very recently, and through it she could see exactly the sort of sitting room she'd imagined Greenwood would have: heavy lined curtains, an abstract oil above the original fireplace, books packed tight on the shelves either side. She felt another flush of anger at Marianne: she was so spoiled, she always had been. To have all this and even consider giving it up.

As Rowan pressed the bell, the telephone rang inside. A few seconds later, there were footsteps on a wooden floor and James Greenwood's patrician voice as he answered. Then the deadbolt clunked and the door cracked open. Surprise and annoyance and, she thought, a hint of relief flickered across his face before they disappeared behind a mask of bland good manners. He pointed at the phone by his ear and held up a finger.

'Saul, can I call you back? I've got someone at the door. Yes, on your cell – a minute or two.'

Greenwood put the handset on the stand then came back to the door. He'd barely said her name before the phone started ringing again.

'Please,' Rowan said, 'do get it. I can wait.'

'They'll call back, whoever it is. But how can I help? The media's got hold of the news about Michael and the phone's ringing off the hook, as you can see, so I really haven't got time to . . .'

'No, of course. I won't hold you up: I just came to drop off Bryony's mobile. She left it at Fyfield Road yesterday.'

It was a simple thing, a small and simple thing, and if she'd been anyone else – if she hadn't been her father's daughter – she might have missed it.

At the mention of Bryony and Fyfield Road, a momentary but unmistakable look of alarm crossed James Greenwood's face and Rowan realised that she was right: he *was* afraid. But of what?

Making no attempt at subtlety, she peered behind him into the house. All was good taste and order: a sisal stair carpet and another abstract oil, the hall table with the phone and a glass-based lamp. And then, this side of the table, lined up neatly next to one another on pages of newsprint as if to dry off after a walk together, two pairs of wellies, father's and daughter's: his basic dull green ones of the kind that cost a tenner, hers navy Hunters. Envy was her first response – *not for you, Rowan, a dad like that; closeness like that.* Her second was *navy Hunters*.

Greenwood seemed to see the flare that went up in her mind and he moved closer to the doorway, blocking her view. 'Was there anything else?' he said, voice icy.

She put her hand on the jamb, preventing him from shutting the door. 'Are those Bryony's boots, James?'

A look passed between them, and along with the fear in Greenwood's eyes, Rowan saw pure hatred. 'Are they?' she pressed.

She moved her fingers just before he slammed the door in her face.

The rain started as she stepped out from under the porch, and by the time she reached Walton Well Road again, barely a minute later, it was coming down hard and cold, driven by the pernicious breeze that had sprung up as enforcer. Rowan barely noticed: she was dizzy with revelation, almost ecstatic. If earlier she'd been frightened that her face would give away her guilt, now she was afraid that anyone passing would be struck by her euphoric relief.

Marianne had been wearing wellies when she died. Hunters – navy blue Hunters, though probably the colour made no difference. She'd been wearing them when her body was found and, Theo had told her, the police had CCTV footage of her wearing them a few hours before she died, after it snowed.

The lane towards Port Meadow was deserted, the weather keeping people indoors, and Rowan allowed herself one loud laugh at the idea that having slept with him had paid off after all. She'd thought what he'd told her had ruled out anyone else being at the house the night Marianne died but perhaps – perhaps – it had ruled *in* just one person.

Those three words: *after it snowed*. There had been one set of footprints going into the house, he said, and one coming out, and Marianne had made them both. By which, presumably, he meant that they'd been made by the same boots. *They were shopping together*, Turk had said. *They used to share clothes and shoes.* And shoes. If they'd shared shoes, they must have been the same size. Had they bought their matching Hunters together, Marianne and Bryony?

Greenwood *had* been trying to deflect attention but not from himself: there had been no larger, male footprints in the snow. She remembered his ferocity when he came to the house to look at Marianne's work, the rage he'd barely contained. He wasn't trying to protect Marianne that day, though: he was afraid for his daughter. *Bryony said you went to find her at school yesterday. Please don't do that again.*

Marianne had made the footprints going in, that was certain – at some point between appearing on CCTV in North Parade and falling to her death, she must have entered the house in order to have come off the roof. But if she'd been out of the house *before* the snow started and came back *after it stopped*, perhaps she'd made only the footprints that headed into the house. If Bryony had been at Fyfield Road that day *before* it started snowing, maybe hanging out and reading, waiting for Marianne to come home, she, in her identical boots, could have made the ones that headed out.

Rowan reached the end of the lane and stood at the gate to the meadow. It was as bleak as she'd ever seen it, a pock-marked stretch of drab grass stretching away under a grey sky towards an unremarkable length of river, but to her, now, it was beautiful. Bryony could have been in the house that day after all, and if she'd seen the relationship that was growing between Marianne and Cory, or even, like Adam, only intu-ited it, she'd had a motive.

When she announced herself over the intercom, Sarah Johnson sounded surprised but also a little pleased and Rowan remem-bered what she'd said about Marianne's trips out with Martin being almost as nice for her as they were for him. *A break, if you know what I'm saying.*

Rowan accepted tea in a fussy china cup and saucer and sipped it while she waited for Sarah to prise Martin away from his computer game. 'Hello again.' She smiled as he came into the room with his deliberate, muscular gait, the men's senior champion approaching the springboard.

'You're Marianne's friend,' he said baldly. 'You were here before.'

'That's right. Martin, I'm trying to help Marianne now – well, her family. I wondered if I could ask for *your* help?'

He looked at her, expressionless.

'The day Marianne died.' She glanced quickly at Sarah to check she wasn't going to upset him. 'That afternoon – I don't know if you'll remember but just in case. Was anyone else there, during the day? Did you see anyone?'

'Yes,' he said, as proud as if he knew the answer to a diffi-cult question in class. 'The blonde one. The one who was there all the time. She was there all day. She stayed there the night before.'

Rowan felt another joyful upsurge in her chest. It was a struggle to keep the elation off her face.

'The day that Marianne died, Martin?' said his mother, frowning. 'You're sure?'

'Yes.' He was annoyed at that. 'I remember. Marianne was my friend.'

'Why didn't you say anything to the police when they came?'

'They didn't ask me. They asked if I saw anything susp . . . susp . . .'

'Suspicious,' supplied Sarah.

'Did you?' said Rowan.

'No.' He shook his head, emphatic. 'I went to bed. I waved to them, Marianne and the blonde one, and then I went to bed. I woke up and Marianne was lying in the garden. She was all . . . broken.'

Thirty-five

They waited for Theo and Grange in the sitting room. When Rowan heard their feet coming up the front steps, she felt another rush of adrenaline. It was as if she were walking a tightrope over a dizzying gully, peace on the far side, the promise of a future with Adam, but first the narrow cable underfoot, the knowledge that any misstep now could be ruinous.

Coming in from Benson Place, she'd allowed herself a single nerve-settling brandy. Adam had arrived back just after six so she'd had two and a half hours to work out the best way to make known what she'd discovered while attracting minimum limelight herself. She'd realised at once that going direct to Theo could backfire dangerously. She imagined the puzzled frown above those twinkling eyes: So this morning you knew nothing at all, Rowan, and now, suddenly, you bring us the scalp of Marianne's killer?

Adam had seen Bryony's phone on the table this morning, however, and before he left, she'd told him that to pass some time and keep herself occupied – she couldn't study today, after hearing the news – she would walk over to Southmoor Road and return it. It was a small thing, just an innocent-seeming seed, but what she had to say would seem all the more plausible for having grown from it.

But there was also the question of time. On the one hand, it wasn't good that her discovery had come so close on the heels of the news of Cory's death – Greenwood's haste was what had drawn her attention, after all – but on the other, the sooner focus shifted to Bryony, the better. Theo's phone call had shown her how thoughtfully he was working. She imagined him doing his jigsaw puzzle in the same methodical way as the Glasses at Christmas, separating out the edge pieces, making the frame, then patiently – piece by piece, minute by minute – building the picture. The two and a half hours she'd waited for Adam had seemed an eternity.

As soon as he came through the door, he'd known from her face that something had happened. 'Tell me,' he said. When she'd finished, he sat with his head in his hands for a full minute. 'This is a nightmare,' he said finally.

'I'm so sorry, Adam.'

'There's no way you're making a mistake?'

'It's possible – anything's possible. I mean, we won't know for sure until the police talk to her – but James' response – the way he slammed the door in my face like that . . . I don't think so.'

Her mind had proffered another image of Theo at his jigsaw and she'd felt almost mad with frustration. Come on, Adam, she wanted to shout, call the police, do it, but even after he'd fetched his phone, he'd hesitated. 'I like them, Rowan,' he said. 'Both of them. Greenwood's a good man. And Bryony – she's so young. This—' He made a despairing gesture, raising his hands from his knees then letting them fall limply back. 'Even if it's true, doing this . . . I feel dirty.'

Though he'd made the call, he let her tell the police the story. 'It was you who worked it out, Ro.'

Theo and Grange barely uttered a word while she told them about Bryony's phone, the boots in the hallway,

Greenwood's alarm, Martin Johnson's confirmation. All the time she was talking, her heart fluttered with anxiety, at times seeming to stop altogether and then giving a run of sharp, clutching beats that threatened to take her breath away. And their eyes seemed not to leave her face for a moment, even though DS Grange made note after note in the book balanced on his knee.

She'd expected them to be excited by such a major break – the solution, potentially – but instead Theo in particular was muted, even deflated. She thought of Cory the day he'd broken into the house and found Marianne's drawing, the way the light in him had seemed to go out. She wondered if Theo was embarrassed. She, an amateur, had managed to work out that Bryony had been there the night of Mazz's death while his investigation had concluded it was an accident.

He looked at her, face solemn. 'This is a very serious allegation, Rowan.'

'It's not an allegation,' she said. 'They're observations. Thoughts.'

'No. If you're right, you've given us motive and opportunity.'

'Bryony was eighteen just before Christmas, she had a party,' Adam said suddenly. 'If she did . . . I mean, if she was . . . involved, she'll be tried as an adult, won't she? Not a juvenile.'

Rowan thought she saw sympathy in Theo's eyes. 'Let's not get ahead of ourselves,' he said. 'There could still be a completely different explanation. We need to talk to her.' He stood up from the sofa then looked at DS Grange, who was flipping back through his notes as if he were searching for something. 'Okay, David?'

'Just to double-check I've got everything straight,' he said. 'The footprints in the snow we know about – you told Ms Winter about those when you met for drinks.' *Drinks.* Rowan saw the tangle of sheets on the bed upstairs, Theo's blond head next to hers on the pillow, the fine hair on his chest so unlike Adam's thick dark mat.

He avoided her eye. 'Yes.'

'But the information about the shoe size, or Marianne and Bryony sharing shoes at least – that came from Peter Turk?'

She nodded.

'And when did he tell you that again?'

'It was a Saturday – yes, the Saturday before last. He had biscotti from Borough Market – he'd been to buy them that morning.'

'So you met him in London?'

'Yes.'

'But you were already here by that point – looking after the house, I mean.'

Shit. Rowan made herself look him in the eye. 'Yes.'

'You made a special trip back to London to see him?' asked Theo.

Now she felt Adam's eyes on her and she turned to meet them. 'After Marianne and I fell out, I lost touch with Turk, too. When I saw him again at the funeral, I realised how much I'd missed him over the years – his friendship. I thought, if we could find anything good in all this . . .' She reached out and took Adam's hand.

By the time the police went, it was after ten o'clock. Adam closed the door and, when the car pulled away on to the street, he locked it. Even in the buttery lamplight, his face was drawn. 'I'm exhausted,' he said. 'All this – the shock, the police. And God, having to tell Mum that it might not have been an accident – I can't even begin to explain how terrible it was, Ro.'

Downstairs, they made tea and sat on Jacqueline's sofa for a few minutes to drink it. The Johnsons' window was bright as ever, and Rowan pictured Martin padding around up there, destined for another sleepless night of watching.

'Are you going to tell your mother about Bryony?' she said.

'No, not until I have to. I'm still praying you've got your wires crossed and there's some other explanation, something totally innocent.'

'I know.'

In bed, skin to skin, Rowan wanted him as much as she ever had but she held back. Adam seemed glad just to have her close and she hugged him for a long time in the dark. Eventually his breathing slowed and she thought he was falling asleep when abruptly, sounding wide awake, he asked her, 'How did Theo come to tell you about the footprints?'

She hoped he hadn't felt her jump. 'Like we said: when we had a drink together just after I came back. I rang him.'

'I thought you weren't particularly good friends.'

'No, but we've got friends in common, we know each other well enough to have a drink, especially when I hardly know anyone in Oxford any more.' She tried to put a smile in her voice. 'I couldn't *just* work.'

Thirty-six

When Theo told them Bryony had confessed, Adam dropped his head into his hands. Rowan closed her eyes and let the relief wash over her. *Thank God.*

'As you suspected, Ms Winter,' said DS Grange, 'she guessed that Marianne had feelings for Cory, or rather knew – she'd overheard them talking on the phone in the morning. When she and Marianne went up on the roof later the same day to look at the snow, she confronted Marianne who said she couldn't deny it – apparently she thought it wouldn't be right to.'

On the sofa next to Rowan, Adam made a sound of despair.

'So Bryony pushed her?' Rowan asked.

'It wasn't quite as simple as that – there was the fact of Marianne's vertigo to take into consideration. You were right about that being significant, too.' Theo tipped his head briefly to Rowan.

'Your sister was trying to stop Bryony from jumping, Mr Glass,' said DS Grange.

Adam lifted his head. 'What?'

'Bryony said that when Marianne admitted how she felt about Cory, she – Bryony – was desperate. She loved your sister and knew how badly the news would hurt Mr Greenwood.'

'She said she was trying to make Marianne change her mind.' Theo's voice surprised Rowan with its gentleness. She'd expected triumph, a hunter's delight in the kill, but there was none. 'If Marianne knew how much it mattered, she said, if she could be made to understand . . .'

'So Bryony went to the edge of the roof,' Grange continued, 'and told your sister she'd jump if Marianne left them. Marianne went after her, tried to pull her back . . .'

'She slipped?' Adam said, and Rowan heard a clear note of entreaty.

But Theo shook his head. 'We hoped so, too.' He shot a look at Grange, who gave a slight nod. 'No. Just as Marianne tried to grab her and pull her back from the edge, it sounds like Bryony lost her temper. She was very distressed when we spoke to her, you can imagine, and it's going to take time to get a complete picture, but basically, as we understand it now, there was a struggle, some back-and-forth, and in the middle of it all, it sounds like Bryony saw red and shoved her over.'

The story settled on them like fall-out, and for several seconds there was silence. Adam spoke first. 'Did James know?'

'Yes,' said Theo. 'Bryony told him as soon as she saw him the next day. He'd been in London overnight after a late dinner with a collector from India. That was why she was staying here. She did that if he was away, apparently; she didn't like being alone in their house at night.'

'Will you charge him? Aiding and abetting, would it be, or perverting the course of justice?'

'That's yet to be decided.'

'Our opinion's irrelevant, obviously,' Adam said, 'but if it did have any weight, I know I can speak for my mother when I say we'd never want that, charges against James. We'd never blame him for trying to protect his daughter.'

Keeping her face carefully composed, Rowan asked, 'Theo, how about Cory?'

'Actually,' he said, 'we don't think Bryony was involved there. We're a long way off knowing anything for certain but she told us she doesn't know about it and I'd be really surprised if it turns out she's lying. Obviously, we're going to go over everything extremely carefully, we're not going to take anything at face value, but first off, she's admitted her involvement in your sister's death, Adam, and to be frank, as a detective, you develop an instinct for these things after a while. Nine times out of ten – more than that – I find that if I think someone's telling me the truth, they are.' He looked directly at Rowan. 'And vice versa.'

Making sure Adam couldn't see, Rowan returned the look, stony-eyed.

'You have to be careful with obvious explanations,' Theo said. 'It's the easiest way to make mistakes.'

'Also,' said DS Grange, 'the pathologist's report isn't in yet so we're not even sure in that case whether we're looking at anything unlawful at all.'

'Thank you,' Adam said as they showed the police out again. 'For coming to tell us in person. And for being so . . . gentle about it. I appreciate it.'

To Rowan's surprise, Theo reached out and put his hand on Adam's arm in a gesture that reminded her of Jacqueline, her arm-rub of support and consolation. 'No problem,' he said.

'We'll keep you posted as soon as we know any more,' said Grange, stepping out into the porch.

Theo patted his jacket pockets as if he were looking for his phone or making sure he had his keys. 'Right,' he said, apparently satisfied. 'We'll speak to you soon. Quickly, though, before we go, I've got to ask: how long have you two been together?'

Taken aback, Adam looked at him and then at Rowan. 'Why have you got to ask?'

Theo gave a little shrug, playing it down. 'Pure curiosity. And when we saw each other the other day, you didn't mention you were in a relationship, Rowan.'

'Well, maybe we *weren't* then,' Adam said, frowning. 'We knew each other years ago, obviously, so we've known each other a long time, but actually, this – a romantic thing – can we even use the word relationship yet? – it's brand new. Days.'

Thirty-seven

Adam couldn't eat the soup she heated up so she made him a sandwich for the car instead. 'I know you don't want it now,' she said, 'but have a couple of bites later if you can, just to keep yourself going. Driving on an empty stomach, with all this going round in your head . . .'

'I'll take it slowly,' he said. 'And I'll text you. Keep your phone with you.'

He took his coat down from the peg and Rowan saw a flash of the dark wool one she'd worn to the river. As he was putting on his scarf, however, footsteps crunched across the drive and, seconds later, a silhouette appeared in the glass door panel. When the bell rang, he looked at her. 'Are you expecting anyone?'

She shook her head. 'No.'

A single silhouette and smaller: not the police, then, or any of the big men who'd haunted the doorstep over the past couple of weeks. Instead, when Adam opened the door, Rowan saw a woman in a navy parka, a pair of black skinny jeans and heels. For a moment, madly, she thought it was Bryony but of course it couldn't be: she was in custody.

This woman was blonde, too, but her hair was curly and cut short. The crisp afternoon sun shone behind her, creating a halo effect at her temples that reminded Rowan suddenly, startlingly, of Lorna on the day of the party.

'Mr Glass?'

Her voice was softer than the outfit suggested, with the hint of a Yorkshire accent. With a defensive pang, Rowan recognised that she was pretty, too: navy-framed glasses half-way down a nose with freckles, the remnants of a tan that suggested Christmas skiing.

'Yes,' Adam said, cautious. 'Can I help you?'

'Hello. My name's Georgina Parry, I'm with the *Mail*. I wanted to ask you about Michael Cory.'

Fear hit Rowan broadsides and as if she'd actually been knocked off her feet, tumbled underwater, she had to fight for breath. The hallway swam in front of her eyes.

Half an hour ago, while she'd been in the kitchen, Adam had answered the landline. The call had lasted less than a minute, she hadn't got into a position to hear what he was saying before he'd hung up. He'd come straight downstairs, anyway, his jaw clenched. 'It's started.'

'What has?'

'The papers are on to it. That was the *Telegraph*. A reporter.'

'What?' She'd stared. With everything else that was going on, the police, she'd forgotten about the media. But of course, this was the Glass family. 'What did they want?' she said. 'What did they ask you?'

'He wanted to know about Michael's connection to Marianne. He used the word *relationship* but I don't know if he meant . . .' Adam had shaken his head. 'It's too much. Do we have to go through all this again? Now – so soon? I don't know if Mum's going to be able to handle it – or Fint.' He looked at her. 'You saw all that at the funeral, with the photographer?'

She remembered accosting the man in his car outside the house afterwards, trying to buy the pictures. She'd told him he was a carrion crow.

'I'm sorry,' Adam told the woman now. 'I know he's died, very sadly, but I'm afraid that's all I do know. You should talk to the police, I . . .'

'Are you concerned there's a link between his death and your sister's?'

From her position behind him, Rowan saw Adam stiffen. 'As I said, you should . . .'

'I've seen photos of the funeral so I know they knew each other. There's got to be a connection, hasn't there? The two of them artists, both here – in Oxford, I mean. And dying so close together – a matter of weeks, isn't it?'

'Please,' said Adam, and now Rowan could hear how much it was costing him to keep his cool. 'I know this is your job but Marianne was my sister. We don't know anything about Cory's death at all. Nothing. So please, just . . . let us do our grieving in peace.'

Undeterred, the woman opened her mouth again. 'Can you tell me anything about Cory as a person, then? He was controversial, wasn't he – Hanna Ferrara, *The Woman Who Has Everything*?'

'If you want career information, you should talk to his gallerist.' Adam paused momentarily. 'His American gallerist, I mean. Saul Hander.'

Calmly but firmly, he shut the door on her.

'If anything happens, Ro, ring me straight away.'

'I will.' She breathed in his woody scent then let him go. 'Adam, will you tell your mum how sorry I am? That I'm thinking about her and sending my love?'

'Are you really going to try to work?'

'I don't know. No,' she admitted, 'probably not. I was, but now . . .' She glanced in the direction of the front door. They'd waited ten minutes in the hope that she'd go, but just now, looking out of the window in Seb and Jacqueline's bedroom, they'd seen Georgina Parry on her mobile in a black hatchback parked across the street.

'The idea of just sitting here and her coming to the door again. Or the phone ringing. If you think it's okay – to leave the house unattended, I mean – I could go for a walk or have some coffee, wander around and try to distract myself. Theo's got my number so if anything comes up, I can come back.'

'Are you ready to go now?' he asked.

'Except for shoes and my purse.'

'Come with me, then – I'll drop you somewhere.' He glanced towards the door. 'You don't need to run that gauntlet on your own.'

Thirty-eight

She asked him to drop her on Parks Road and until half-past four, when it closed, she drifted among the amulets and instruments, pots and African masks in the Pitt Rivers Museum. Coming into the vaulted central atrium, she thought, was like stepping inside a vast, eclectic Victorian intelligence, wonderful, but the museum was always marred for her by memories of her father.

One wet afternoon when she was eight or nine, he'd been moved by some unexplained impulse to bring her here. She'd been entranced – by the weirdness then, most likely: she remembered standing for a long time in front of the shrunken heads, fascinated and repulsed – and for years thereafter, if there were even a hint of rain in the forecast and thus a chance they would have to spend the afternoon in the house together, he'd whisked her straight here and encouraged her to get lost among the display cabinets.

Six or seven years ago now, he'd called to ask if she'd meet him for lunch in London. He'd suggested a restaurant in South Kensington and because she'd been giving him excuses for three years by then, she'd capitulated and said yes. Of course, it had been another trap. The table he'd booked was for four: he'd brought Jessica and Harry, who'd just turned six. On the phone, her father had said he'd chosen South Kensington because it would be an easy trip from Putney, where Rowan had been living at the time, but in fact the salient point was its proximity to the Natural History Museum: Harry wanted to see the dinosaurs.

All he was asking, her father spat across the table when Jessica took Harry to the loo, was for Rowan to be civil to her. She'd refused to go to their wedding and since then had only come face to face with her father's wife twice, both times ambushes. Her father had known that Harry would charm her, though – how could he not? He was so guileless with his wide brown eyes beneath the chunky fringe of chestnut hair, so openly curious about his 'big' half-sister, and when he had asked to hold Rowan's hand as they'd crossed Cromwell Road, she'd felt as if she'd been punched in the chest. Then, though, she'd watched her father holding *his* hand as they walked through the museum, crouching to show him how many bones there were in a skeletal foot, pointing out different species of beetle, and she'd felt her heart ice over again. Had her father ever done that for her? Looked at her with soft eyes even once?

St Giles was chiming seven o'clock as she rounded the corner on to Norham Gardens. With no cloud for insulation, the bright day had turned into a sharp evening and her feet scratched along the pavement past front gardens already spiky with frost. Between the streetlights, her breath looked ghostly.

She'd spent the past hour and a half at Caffè Nero on the High Street where, to justify lingering, she'd drunk the two large coffees that now added an extra edge to her anxiety. At four, Adam had sent a text to say he'd reached Highgate but she'd heard nothing since. She'd thought he might send a quick message or call to check in but of course, she told herself decisively, he'd be busy with Jacqueline. When she heard about Bryony, she would be devastated all over again.

'Why don't you stay with her?' Rowan had asked him. 'I can hold the fort here.'

'No, she's got Fint, and it's not fair to leave you alone here while this is going on. *You* could go home.' The idea had seemed suddenly to occur to Adam. 'Do you want to? God, I'm so sorry – I should have thought.'

'I'm all right,' she said. 'Until the dust settles, let me stay and keep you company.'

'You're sure?'

She pulled a face.

'Thank you.' The smile he gave her was genuinely grateful. 'Having you here makes it a lot easier. For me.' He'd taken a long breath. 'God knows what we're going to do about the pictures now.'

As she turned in to Fyfield Road, Rowan's eyes went immediately to the spot where the journalist's little black car had been parked. It was gone, and she felt her shoulders drop a fraction. She'd been bracing herself for another approach, or worse: what if while she'd been out, the rest of the press had sent people and she arrived back to find a gang of them? But the street was empty and she walked the last twenty yards breathing deeply, letting the freezing air crackle in her lungs.

Just as she stepped on to the drive, however, quick footsteps ran up behind her and a hand caught at her elbow.

She gave a yelp of fright; she couldn't help it. When she spun around, however, she saw the journalist.

'Sorry,' she said, soft-voiced and disarming. 'I didn't mean to scare you.'

'For God's sake.' Rowan pressed her hand against her chest. 'You can't do that, sneak up on people in the dark.'

'I wanted to talk to you.'

'Oh, fine then.'

The woman ignored her tone. 'You were with Adam earlier, weren't you?'

'Yes, but he didn't want to talk to you and neither do I.'

'Sometimes people feel differently when they're on their own. They . . .'

'Leave us alone. We don't know anything, all right? Nothing.'

'Are you his girlfriend?' the woman said. 'You were at the funeral, too, weren't you? There was a picture of you out here, in the road . . .'

'Just – piss off.' Clutching her bag against her chest, Rowan turned and ran up the steps. Her hands were shaking so much it took three attempts to get the key in the door.

'Georgina Parry, from the *Mail*,' the woman called from the bottom of the steps. 'If you change your mind, I've put my card through the door.'

Rowan ripped the card into pieces and stuffed them to the bottom of the kitchen bin. Even the thought of the woman made her queasy. To sit out there for hours in the freezing cold, she must think she was on to something.

She sent Adam a text to warn him but at half-past nine there'd been no response. Her anxiety rose another notch. It was one thing not to be in touch to see how things were, but not to reply to a text giving him information – *that* information – was out of character. She went so far as to check that the message had been delivered then told herself he couldn't text, he was driving. But she'd sent the message just after seven and the journey shouldn't take two and a half hours. It was Sunday night, too: most of the traffic would be heading into London, not out.

There'd been a disaster, an accident. He'd been driving under-slept and overwrought, his reactions were dulled . . . Or – the idea came accompanied by a wash of nausea – what if Theo had called him? What if the police had discovered something new about Cory, managed to link her to him that afternoon? She'd been sure no one had seen them but if she was wrong . . . At ten, she called Adam but the phone rang out and went to voicemail, and the same thing happened again twenty minutes later. Nerves frayed, she paced the house, incapable of sitting still for longer than a minute. Should she ring Jacqueline? Could she, even? If something had happened to her son now, too . . . *Stop it, Rowan.*

It was almost quarter-past eleven when she heard a key in the door. Seeing Adam, she nearly ran into his arms with relief. She went to kiss him but he pressed his cheek sideways against hers then, a second later, moved away.

'I was worried,' she said. 'I thought you'd be earlier – I . . .'

'I'm all right.'

'Was it a bad drive?'

'Not great. I'm going to have a glass of wine. Do you want one?'

'I'll get it,' she told him in the kitchen, 'you sit.'

'I've been sitting for the past hour and a half,' he said, brusque.

'Is she still outside – the journalist? Did you get my message? I texted you.'

'Yes, I saw it.'

Did he think he'd replied? Did the message get lost? Confused, Rowan turned to the worktop to open the wine, glad of the excuse to hide her face for a moment. She poured two glasses then carried them to the table. As she handed him one, he met her eyes properly for the first time and, with a jolt of trepidation, she saw something new in his, more than just emotional and physical exhaustion. After hours of waiting, imagining catastrophe, she couldn't take any more. 'Is something wrong, Adam?'

He took a sip of wine, seeming to consider. 'I went to see Peter this evening.'

'Peter Turk?' she said, too quickly. Then, trying to compensate, 'Why? Did you want to tell him in person, too? The news, I mean.'

'That was part of it.'

The knot of tension in her stomach pulled tighter.

'Why did *you* go and see him, Rowan? The week after the funeral. Was it really just to try and build bridges?'

'I don't understand.' She frowned, trying to mask her alarm.

'Pete told me you wanted to talk about Marianne. He said you didn't believe she slipped.'

'You *know* I didn't.'

'You hadn't spoken to either of them for ten years and yet you made a special trip to London to talk to him. He reminded me, by the way, that you vanished just when Dad died, when Mazz really could have done with having you round.'

Rowan looked straight at him. It was a gamble but she had to do it: she couldn't let him pursue this line of thought any further. 'Did Pete tell you I'm a gold-digger, too?' she asked, heart thumping. 'A leech – that was his word. Did he ask if I'd got my claws into you?'

As she'd hoped, Adam was wrong-footed. 'What?'

'That's what he said to me the last time I saw him – which, by the way, was the day he came here, to the house, the morning you saw him, too. He made up a story about having lent Mazz a pair of cufflinks for a party, but it turned out he'd come to steal instead.'

'Steal? What are you talking about?'

'He's furious with me because I caught him stealing her sketches. Lots – ten or fifteen of them. It wasn't a spur-of-the-moment idea, either: he came prepared. He had a sort of press in his rucksack to carry them.'

Adam was looking at her as if she'd started speaking in tongues. 'Pete was stealing sketches from Marianne?'

'Yes. To sell. He's broke.'

'No.' Adam shook his head. 'That doesn't make sense. The royalties from the record . . .'

'*One* record, split between four, years ago? What's he done since? Some radio jingles last year?' She stopped: being a bitch wouldn't cover her in glory. 'Did you meet his lodger?' she asked. 'The friend of a friend, staying for a few days?'

A look of dawning realisation told her he had. 'Why didn't you say anything?'

'Because I felt bad for him. And he said that Mazz used to give sketches to her friends and that was true, too.' She thought rapidly, made another decision. 'Also, I didn't want to leave.'

Adam looked up.

'That morning, when Turk was here – that was the first time you and I . . . got together and then you vanished. I thought that if you knew there hadn't been break-ins after all, you might think it didn't matter so much, my being here.' She felt the flush rising up her neck. 'I wanted to see you again.'

They moved to the sofa, and Adam put his arm around her shoulders. He told her how he'd broken the news to Jacqueline, and Rowan related her brief run-in with Georgina Parry. 'She was gone when I arrived,' he said, 'she didn't come after me, anyway, but if she's back tomorrow, I'll ask Theo if there's anything he can do. Not that there will be.' He drained his glass. 'I still can't believe it was Peter who was taking the sketches.'

'I know.'

'Do you know *where* he was selling them?'

'No. We didn't get that far before he told me I was mad and stormed out.'

Adam smiled. 'Have you still got the sketch Cory made of you? I was looking for it down here this morning, thinking about him, but I couldn't find it.'

A single drumbeat of alarm in her chest. 'I put it away. It made me feel strange, knowing he's gone.'

'Can I see it?'

'Now?'

'Yes, but don't get up – I'll go and get it. Where is it?'

'No.' She put her hand out, keeping him in his seat. 'It's okay. You stay there, I'll fetch it.'

348

Thirty-nine

She fell asleep as it started to get light and it felt like only minutes later that she was woken by the sound of the doorbell. Sitting up, she found Adam's side of the bed empty again but when she stumbled to her feet, she heard him on the kitchen stairs. As she came out on to the landing, pausing briefly to pull her jumper over her head, he was unlocking the front door. Her first thought was of the journalist – bad enough – but as she came down the stairs, she saw Theo and DS Grange on the doorstep. She could tell from their faces that there had been a development.

In the sitting room Theo took a seat but Grange stayed standing. He had the air of someone who'd learned to discipline the energy that kept him so lean. There was a controlled quality to his stillness but his eyes moved constantly, looking at everything with a focus that said they were taking it in, recording.

'We've had the results of the post mortem on Michael Cory this morning,' said Theo without preamble. 'It's a murder inquiry now.'

Rowan turned cold. For a long moment, several seconds, she – her mind – seemed to detach itself from her body. She felt as if she were hovering over the scene, there but separated from everyone else by an infinitesimal screen, the thinnest plate of glass. Theo's voice reached her as if from a distance. '. . . position of the wound too high on the head – near the crown – to be easily seen as an injury sustained by falling backwards. Tiny fragments of slate in the wound, not naturally occurring along the riverbank here.'

Fuck.

'Also telling,' said Grange, pulling her focus in his direction, 'are traces of blood on the collar and back of his coat. It looks like the blood ran *down*, which suggests he was standing when he was injured. If he'd fallen, it likely would have pooled around his head, and if he'd fallen directly into the *water*, there might have been no direct staining at all.'

Adam's face was white. He sat on the edge of the sofa, elbows planted on his knees, fingertips pressed against his mouth.

'What we also have now,' Theo said, 'is an approximate time of death. The pathologist is telling us it was sometime on Friday afternoon.'

'Likely mid-afternoon,' said Grange.

'So we have to ask you both, I'm afraid, where you were at that point.'

'Are we suspects?' said Rowan and her voice floated away from her, a frail thing, disembodied.

'Not suspects, no,' said Theo. 'Not as such.'

'Cambridge,' said Adam. 'I had a supervision for an hour at two o'clock with two of my undergraduates – they can confirm. Also, actually, the college handyman – a sash window in my rooms was jammed open, over-painted, and he came to sort it out just afterwards. That took about ten minutes. Then I left college – there's CCTV in the lodge and the porters saw me. I cycled home then I got in the car to come here. Oh – I filled up with petrol just outside St Neots. The receipt's probably in my wallet but if not, I'll be on their CCTV, too. And I paid on my credit card. It would have been about four, quarter-past – I can tell you which garage.'

'Thanks, we'll check all that out,' said Grange. 'But it's just a formality. Due diligence.'

'Rowan?' Theo fixed his eyes on her and the sentences she'd formulated while Adam had been talking disappeared from her head. The closest thing she had to an alibi was being seen by Martin Johnson before she left and after she returned but now she saw that if she gave those details, she'd only be drawing attention to the large lacuna of time in between. Theo raised his eyebrows, prompting.

'Sorry.' She shook her head as if she were having difficulty refocusing after the shock. Better, she decided, to give an answer that sounded honest even if it didn't get her off the hook. 'I was working,' she said. 'Studying.'

'Where?'

'Here. At the house.'

'Can anyone back that up?'

'No, I don't think so. I was on my own. Oh,' as if she'd just remembered, 'I waved to Martin Johnson in the flats at lunchtime when I went upstairs to put an extra jumper on.'

'No one else? You didn't leave the house at all? Buy a pint of milk or take a walk?'

'No.'

'Did anyone ring you on the landline?' Adam said. 'Phone calls?'

Shit. What if someone *had* called? Would it come up on the records? *Focus, Rowan, worry about that if it comes to it; you'll have to say you were in the bathroom or something*. She narrowed her eyes as if she were thinking. 'No . . . no, I don't think so.' From the corner of her eye she saw Grange make a note in his little book and sweat bloomed under her arms. 'God, I just don't know – I'm sorry. I'll check my email, my mobile, see if that helps me remember anything. But I was here, all afternoon, I know I was.'

'If you do think of anything,' Grange asked, 'ring us, will you?'

'How about Bryony?' Adam said.

'Cast-iron alibi.' Theo gave a dry smile.

351

'Really?'

'She was at school.'

When the police were gone, Adam walked to the bottom of the stairs and sat down. She looked at him, uncertain what to do. He'd withdrawn, pulled away into himself: his eyes were open but unfocused. She wondered if he even saw her: when she sat down next to him and put her arm around his back, he jumped. For a long time – a minute, maybe two – neither of them spoke.

'Ad, what can I do?'

A delay, as if her voice had reached him via satellite. 'Nothing,' he said. His face was blank. 'I just need some space. To think. Do you mind?'

It made sense, it was completely reasonable, and yet the request turned her stomach. 'Of course not,' she said. 'I'll have a shower and then I'll go out. To the library. Perhaps work is what I need – distraction.'

She waited but he only nodded. As she stood to go upstairs, the landline rang, too loud in the fraught silence. Adam seemed to hesitate, it rang and rang, but then, just when she thought it would ring out, he stood and grabbed the handset.

She was too far away to hear what the tiny voice at the other end asked him but she saw how Adam gripped the phone, the way the tendons stood up on the back of his hand. 'I've no comment now,' he said, 'nor will I have at any point. Don't call this number again.'

He stood across the kitchen and watched as she packed her laptop and books. She hoped he couldn't see how much her hands were shaking.

Cory's drawing was on the table where he'd left it last night. When she'd come back downstairs with it, he'd looked at it carefully. Her heart had flailed then, too, and into her head had come his response the first time he'd seen it. *Does he like you?* 'I was thinking about what Mazz said when we had a drink after Christmas,' he'd said after a minute, maybe even longer, 'about getting in touch with you again, sorting out what happened back then. She said Michael was helping her get her head straight.'

Into the silence now, Adam spoke again. 'Why did you and Mazz fall out?'

'What?'

'Back then. What did you argue about?'

She shook her head. 'Ad, you know all this. You've got enough to worry about without going back through all . . .'

'I'm not sure I do know. Not really.' He looked at her, waiting.

The old story; there was no time to come up with anything better. 'Because I pushed her too hard after your dad died,' she said. 'Marianne wanted space, time alone, but I was afraid of losing her.' She paused, sweat prickling in her hairline.

'Why would you have lost her?'

'I don't know. It just felt like everything was changing. She'd made those big sales to Dorotea Perling and I was afraid she was going to be so successful, such a supernova, I'd lose her that way. And then things fell apart here. Your dad . . .'

Georgina Parry's black hatchback was parked frankly at the kerb outside. As Rowan opened the front door, she saw her look up at once. When she turned to say goodbye to Adam, she could feel the woman's eyes on her back.

'Speak to you later on,' she said. 'If you need me at all, just call. I won't be doing anything that can't be interrupted.'

He nodded but by the time she reached the foot of the steps, he'd closed the door behind her. As she crossed the gravel, however, Parry's car door came open.

'Morning. How are you?' Her quick footsteps followed Rowan down the pavement. 'The police were here earlier, weren't they? You know that Michael Cory's death is definitely being treated as murder now.'

Shaking with fury, Rowan spun around. 'I said no. *No*. What about that do you not understand? What the *fuck* is wrong with you?'

Afterwards, in the relative sanctuary of the café in the vaults of St Mary's Church, Rowan was angry with herself. Why had she lost control? Why had she let herself? The very last thing she needed now was a journalist who thought she had something to hide. Since seeing her with Adam yesterday, the woman had clearly gone back and looked at all the paparazzo's pictures from the funeral, not just the ones that had made it into the paper. She'd seen the one he'd snapped from his car window. What if she talked to him, found out that Rowan had tried to buy the pictures, stop them being published?

But in the scheme of things now, that was a minor problem.

A murder inquiry. *Too high on the head; not naturally occurring along the riverbank; it looks like the blood ran down* – the phrases landed on her again like blows, every one of them evidence of how badly she'd messed things up, how vulnerable she'd left herself.

Was there any way it could be all right now? The pieces were gathered: between them – Adam and the police – they had them all. Rowan imagined them as a reflection on water, like the leaves and the sky on the river the day she had gone to the houseboat alone, a swimming, shimmering, fragmented image. All it needed was for the light to catch it a certain way.

And if they had everything, she had nothing left. Just like in those final days with Cory, she'd used her resources.

The newspaper she'd bought was open on the table but she couldn't read. She'd chosen the café because it was close to the library – it was plausible she'd take a break here – but after the waitress cleared away two cups of cold coffee almost untouched, she started to feel conspicuous. She put her coat back on, stuffed the paper into her bag and left.

As she climbed the stairs out of the vaults to street level, she felt her phone vibrate in her pocket again and again. Outside in Radcliffe Square, she looked at it: six missed calls, all from Adam's mobile.

Light-headed, hot then cold, she rounded the corner into Brasenose Lane and leaned against the railings while she waited for a wave of nausea to pass. Before her heartbeat had regulated itself again, the phone buzzed in her hand. Adam. She took a deep breath and answered.

'Where are you?' he said. 'I've been calling and calling; your phone went straight to voicemail.'

'I'm in Radcliffe Square – I've just come outside.'

'What college are you at?' he said.

'Sorry?' Momentarily, she was confused: here was her college, Brasenose. It was directly behind her.

'I said, what college are you at, in London?'

Rowan felt her gorge rise, cold sweep across her body, and she swallowed down hard. 'Why?' she said.

'Grange rang to ask.'

The afternoon passed in a blur, a series of images and locations that left only the shallowest impressions. Her old haunts: Blackwell's, Waterstones, Queen's Lane Coffee House for a bowl of soup she barely touched. Just before four, cold and exhausted, she went to the Odeon on George Street, bought a ticket for the next film starting and hid in the dark.

Should she run, she asked again; get in the car? But if she disappeared now, the police would alert the ports, have her stopped at the border. And she couldn't even try without going back to the house – her passport was there, up on the top shelf of the wardrobe with her mother's pearls; she'd left them there when she'd moved the box.

And yet perhaps, still, she was jumping the gun. Grange's question might not mean anything more than that he was compiling facts. Due diligence. And the police hadn't called *her* today. In fact, since Adam's calls, her phone hadn't rung once.

The film played out in front of her, animated wallpaper, while she went back and forth, desperate and hopeful, terrified and resolute. At half-past six, however, the credits ended and the lights came up. She made up her mind: one last try.

Forty

Even a week ago, she wouldn't have believed that going back to Fyfield Road – to Adam – could fill her with such dread. As soon as she saw the house, however, the feeling intensified. She knew he was there, he'd told her he would be, and yet the house was dark. If he'd had to leave for any reason, she thought, he would have texted – *Gone to buy wine. Back in ten* – but when she checked her phone, there was no message.

The moon slipped between a gap in the clouds, sending a momentary gleam across the house's blind eyes. It was still early, not even seven, but with the emptiness of the street, the absence of any human-made sound, it felt like the small hours. The only movement came from the wind that shivered the leaves on the evergreens, rattled the thin branches of the willow that bowed its head on the drive.

She glanced over her shoulder then crunched across the gravel and up the steps to the front door. The carriage lamp was off so she located her keys in her bag by touch.

A strange pressure on the door made it harder than usual to open, as if someone was pushing against it from the other side. When she turned to close it behind her, a gust of wind seemed to come from within the house and slammed it shut. In the silence, the sound was violent.

She wasn't imagining it, she thought: the wind *was* coming from inside the house. There had to be a window open but where? Not at the front, she would have noticed. But why would he open a window at all? It was below freezing outside.

Something had happened. As soon as she thought it, she knew she was right.

'Hello?'

She put on the light and the hallway materialised around her. The draught, she realised, was coming down the stairs. She stood at the bottom and called up but again there was no answer. The sitting-room door was open and she slapped the light on, went quickly to the fireplace and picked up the poker.

When she reached the landing, fear formed a fist in her stomach. The cold air was coming from the very top floor. The studio. She climbed the final set of stairs with her pulse thrumming in her temples.

In the glow of the moon she saw the chaos of sketches strewn across the worktable and the floor. When she saw the open skylight, the stepladder underneath, the poker dropped to the floor with a heavy clang. The smell of cigarette smoke – ˙˙˙ Her hands shook as she started to climb the ladder.

He was waiting for her at the top, perspective making him a colossus, his feet planted wide. The wind snatched at the sheet of paper in his hands but she didn't need to see it to know what it was. She'd lost him forever; that was clear – his face was closed. Hard. Vengeful.

The paper buckled and cracked, wind-whipped. There was nothing she wouldn't do, she thought wildly, literally nothing, for it to be torn from his hands and erased from his memory. To go back even one day.

Behind him was the roof-edge. She felt its power, the force field it exerted, the weird push-and-pull. It was so raw, unprotected – a four-storey fall, death almost guaranteed. He saw her looking and stepped to one side.

'Do it,' he said.

'Adam, please, just let me . . .'

'What the *hell* is this?' He thrust the drawing out in front of him as if it were a shield.

You fool, Rowan. You bloody, bloody fool.

'How ... How did you find it?' The wind distorted her words, softening them to nothing, then booming them out.

'How did I *find* it? That's your question?'

His voice cut her. Gentle Adam.

'I put it away. I ...'

'With the sketch Cory made of you. I heard you in my father's study last night, Rowan. Every step across those fucking boards.'

'I ... I wanted to protect you. Marianne's gone – I wanted you to remember the person you knew, *that* Marianne, not the one who ...' She looked at the picture but obliquely, as if she couldn't bear it.

He gave a bitter laugh. 'You're unbelievable – incredible.'

She looked at him, bewildered. 'What do you mean?'

'Your fight, Rowan – your sheer fight. You never stop. You're a cockroach – come Armageddon, you'll be sole survivor.'

'Adam, just let me ...'

'Did you think,' he said, 'for a *second*, that I'd believe my sister did this?' He shook the drawing at her; it crackled like fire in the wind. 'My *sister*.'

'But she did! Look, it's there – you're holding the evidence.'

He lifted it up and then, in one savage move, he tore it in half. Hearing her cry, he tore it again and again, eyes never leaving her face. Then he cupped the pieces, raised his hands above his head and let go. Paper whirled around them, a storm of sick confetti.

'My sister might have painted the picture,' he said, 'she might have fantasized about Lorna's death – *I* did, God knows – but she would never, *ever* have done anything to make it happen. Do you think you can know someone like I knew her – Marianne, my *sister*, my *family* – and not know that?'

'Please Adam . . .'

'It was you, wasn't it? All this time. *You* killed Lorna – *you*, not my sister. And Cory, too – they found his car on Meadow Lane this afternoon, right where Lorna's boat used to be. You're asking me to believe it was a coincidence?'

'No,' she said. 'No, I didn't. It wasn't me who . . .'

'Oh, come on! What have you told me that's true? One thing.'

The pain – Rowan fought to control the burning anguish in her chest, the urge to throw herself at his feet and beg. 'I told you,' she said, 'that I wanted to see you again. Your family, all of you – I love you all, I always have. I'd do anything for you.'

'Oh, I know that now.' The bitterness.

'But you – especially you, Ad. Please believe me – please give me a chance.'

The moon sailed out from behind the cloud and washed him in icy white light. She looked at him, at the eyes that were ~~so, too. She'd loved them both~~ so much.

She took a step towards him and he thought she was going to embrace him. The look of horror on his face – no, not horror: revulsion.

Revulsion.

An explosion of rage more powerful than any she'd felt before. To be rejected again, pushed away a second time by the people she'd loved most – it was too much. She lunged at him. He staggered, almost losing his footing, and behind him, she saw the garden. He caught her arm, twisting it, and she screamed but the pain seemed to make her stronger, and she pushed back against him as hard as she could, heard his feet scrape the asphalt. *Come on.* Summoning all her strength, she pulled free of his grip, stepped back and threw herself against him, head at his chest.

He moved just in time – half a second later would have been too late – but she had too much momentum, she couldn't stop herself. He grabbed after her, tried to catch her – she felt his fingers clutch at the fabric of her sleeve.

For a moment she was floating, weightless. The view of the garden stole her breath. The rhododendrons and the birch trees, the roses, the lawn – all of it outlined in silver, like the promise of another world. She was lying awake with Marianne again, the moonlight streaming through the open curtains, and they were talking.

Acknowledgements

In writing this book, I was privileged to have the guidance of several brilliant women: Helen Garnons-Williams, my agent Kathleen Anderson, Alexa von Hirschberg and Rachel Mannheimer. To the exceptional teams at Bloomsbury, especially Ellen Williams, Lynsey Sutherland and Imogen Denny, an enormous thank you.

On a practical level, this would likely not have been possible – and would certainly have been significantly less enjoyable – without the help and support of Mweemba Nchimunya and Polly and Guy Meacock, invaluable partners in crime on our epic Great North Run of 2014 and too many other occasions to count. Gillian Thomas, thanks for the doughnuts!

And Joe and Bridget – without you, it absolutely wouldn't have been possible or meant half as much.